FOR THE GOOD OF ALL

(DIE GLOCKE)

IAN J ROSS

First published in Great Britain in 2021 by
The Book Guild Ltd
9 Priory Business Park
Wistow Road, Kibworth
Leicestershire, LE8 0RX
Freephone: 0800 999 2982
www.bookguild.co.uk
Email: info@bookguild.co.uk
Twitter: @bookguild

This work is entirely fictitious and bears no resemblance to any persons living or dead.

Typeset in 12pt Adobe Jenson Pro

Printed on FSC accredited paper
Printed and bound in Great Britain by 4edge Limited

ISBN 978 1913551 469

British Library Cataloguing in Publication Data.
A catalogue record for this book is available from the British Library.

For Bobby and Aurora – my raison d'etre

CHAPTER

ONE

Whether it was eyes wide open or eyes shut tight, it was always the same. The low, irritating drone of an air-conditioning system which cried out for the healing hands of an engineer; the metallic movement of trolleys down a polished floor, the weary laughter of young women who would shortly find salvation at the bottom of a wine glass.

Steve Diamond was thirty-three years old and, according to his specialist – a man who declined to follow convention and who never added a veneer of sympathy to bad news – he was "fucked".

It was an interesting diagnosis, and one which had prompted him to smile on many occasions since its initial delivery. That had come on July 4th, 2012; a date he was hardly likely to forget. Nightmares come in various shapes, sizes and densities, but they all boast a starting point.

It was dark in the room. The blinds were always closed, bathing the magnolia walls in an unsettling half-light, as if attempting to shield him and others cast adrift from the real world, the one which had receded into the far-distance with awful speed in the seconds after his diagnosis.

Of course, there was hope. There is always hope. It goes with the territory. There is numbness, despair, tears, fear, regret – and then hope. Hope is embraced even when the cause is all but lost. Even the most cynical of men will clutch at a dangled straw when there is nothing else on offer. Life is awash with choices and human nature decrees that you reach for the most attractive.

One of the plus points of being ill – seriously ill – is that there is time aplenty to think. Like anyone who considered himself young enough to still feel relatively invincible, Diamond had never considered the twin perils of old age and death. Why should he? Life was good. He was happy enough and whilst his personal life had featured more lows than highs, he was confident enough to believe that his parents were right in their dual assertion that "The good will ultimately prosper."

It was a theory based in old-time religion. His mum and dad had never questioned those who forced a suspect doctrine down their throats because in those days – in their formative years of the 1950s and '60s – God was real, the Holy Bible (for all its contradictory statements) was authenticated fact rather than suspect fiction, and it was easier to claim belief than it was to rail against the subordinate, sheep-like masses.

Diamond's illness, and the accompanying black dog of intermittent depression, had, predictably, changed many of his hewed-from-stone views but as the specialist with the blunt edges had told him on the day his glass became somewhat less than half full, "You are where you are. You must accept it and live accordingly."

It was sound and sensible advice but, as Diamond now acknowledged, the desire to sink swiftly into a bout of self-pity was, at times, totally irresistible. He often felt sorry for himself. He often blamed the blameless for where he now found himself.

The specialist had been right – this was now his very own, exclusive world and he must learn to live and prosper within it. That or take the soft option and fast-track the inevitable from the future to the present.

Diamond did two things when he was as miserable as sin – he either read Oscar Wilde or listened to Bruce Springsteen. He suspected that, had the pair ever met, they would have enjoyed each other's company and complimented each other on their respective works. Sitting up in his hospital bed, Diamond started to read, for probably the sixth time, Wilde's sole novel, 'The Picture of Dorian Gray', an eloquent and haunting story of the consequences of debauchery. Diamond, along with millions of others, still found it astonishing that a man who had so much more to offer the world of wit and literature had died so very young of cerebral meningitis brought on by a simple ear infection. His mood already dark, he mused that, actually, most of his heroes were now dead – Wilde, Jimi Hendrix, Joe Strummer, Jim Morrison, John Lennon. Even dear old Amy Winehouse had now gone.

His specialist, Dr Barrie Marshall, was a sort of superhero to Diamond despite having described leukaemia, with almost childlike innocence, as "a fascinating disease". His eyes widening and ever so slowly filling with tears, Diamond had waited for the punchline, the 'Don't panic, my friend' moment. It hadn't come. Dr Marshall was a vibrant and compelling man of huge intellect but one who did not believe in either concealing a truth or dressing it up as something it was not. He delighted in telling anyone who would listen that you could put a silk scarf on a pig but that it would still be a pig. And so, leukaemia was what it was: a deadly cancer. It wasn't a minor ailment or a pin-prick which could be hidden away and then cured by a sticking plaster.

Diamond liked Marshall and enjoyed his company. Their meetings always moved down an identical track. First came the medical bulletin, and then the general conversation which was usually fashioned by the events of the previous twenty-four hours. Both men were unapologetic world-event junkies, unable to pass a television set or multimedia device without tuning into a rolling news channel.

Marshall was due shortly. He had acquired the knack of entering Diamond's room at the precise moment his treatment was finished – as the tube attached to his arm ran dry, Dr Death would arrive with the flourish of a Shakespearean villain, all smiles and guarded optimism.

After several weeks of chemotherapy, Diamond was now hardened to a process which those friends who had called him 'Precious' since junior school had assured him he was bearing "bravely and stoically". He wasn't. He usually cried afterwards, he was invariably enveloped by cloying darkness, and always he stood face to face with his own mortality and blinked first. It wasn't fun. It wasn't anything, actually. It was the simple elongation of life by means of modern science. Often he wanted to give up and abandon himself to his fate, but he couldn't because that prospect was even scarier to him than was the prospect of living a reduced life which was no longer judged upon financial or sexual success but upon the success – or failure – of a chemist's vision.

Six months after his diagnosis, Diamond, seeking out a more substantial straw to grasp, had suggested to Marshall that anything was possible and that the miracles which sustained the religion he had abandoned in his childhood do occur. Like a puppy anticipating a treat, he had gazed longingly at the man he now regarded as a friend.

The treat was denied. "If you believe in miracles then presumably you believe that Herman's Hermits were better than The Kinks and that the Conservative Party knows what it's doing," said Marshall.

"Well, no, I just keep reading that remission is not only possible but can become permanent. It does happen, doesn't it?"

"Complete recoveries are usually the result of initial misdiagnosis. Someone is told they are screwed when they aren't... they are only partially screwed. You, my lovely boy, are almost certainly totally screwed," said Marshall, with a partial, paternal smile.

Diamond had more or less assumed that he was approaching the halfway point in his life. As the thrill chaser in him had begun to move, without any real regret, from the fast lane to an inside track peopled by those undergoing a similar process of slowing down and worldly acceptance, he had actually begun to think seriously about the lauded prizes of late youth and early middle age, namely marriage, children and a garden with a rocking chair. Still, no rush – there was plenty of time.

And then there wasn't.

He had begun to feel unwell almost three years ago, just before his thirty-first birthday. It wasn't the sudden opening of a curtain to reveal an awful truth; more a slow process of realisation that things just didn't feel right any more. The stomach cramps, the dizziness, the weakness, the muscular pain, the shortage of breath could all be attributable to something else on an individual basis but when they rolled in like a morning mist as one entity and threw themselves upon him for week after week, it was a case of live in denial or break the manly code and head for the doctor.

No one is diagnosed with cancer on their first visit. Oh no, that's far too simple. The process of observation, diagnosis and recommended treatment is extended slowly, like the pulling of a rubber band. Eventually – at long last, some would argue – you find that the glint has disappeared from the specialist's eyes and that the rustling of papers on one too many clipboards is nothing more than the precursor to *that* conversation.

Diamond would later tell family members that he had been more upset for Dr Marshall than he had been for himself. Since his early teens he had often found himself placing himself in someone else's shoes in search of a different perspective on a certain event. It was midsummer 2012, and as Dr Marshall lowered his half-moon glasses from his forehead to the bridge of his nose, Diamond was already well ahead of the game; he couldn't see the script but he knew the plot.

"Steve. As you know, we have been running a series of tests on your battered body," he said, making what was probably a traditional stab at lightening the mood. "Some of those tests have provided vague, inconclusive results, but—"

"Dr Marshall, I'm a big boy now – a scared one, but a big boy. End your torment and kick-start mine by way of as few words as possible?"

"OK. I suspect that you're fucked, my friend."

Silence seemed appropriate. Diamond closed his eyes, only reopening them when he felt Dr Marshall's hand curl and tighten around his wrist. It was a brief, symbolic coming together; a moment when two men with something in common improbably bonded.

When the moment had passed, Diamond raised his head from a pillow damp with perspiration. "OK. Splendid effort. You have probably done that dozens of times but I suspect it never gets any easier or any less upsetting. Well, that's the cards tossed onto the table – now we must see how they have fallen and what my future holds. Is that reasonable?"

"It is," said Dr Marshall. "I am not telling you that this evening's sunset will be the last you will see – far from it.

We can help, we can assist, we can contain – but what we cannot do just now is cure. Yes, your goalposts have moved but having spent some time with you I know two things about you: you are a very bright man, and you are addicted to the internet. Tell me I'm wrong... tell me you haven't been Googling 'leukaemia'; its causes, its implications, its treatment, its endgame?"

Precisely two minutes after being told that there would be no real requirement for a rocking chair in a garden, Diamond laughed. He laughed so much he started crying again.

The good doctor was right; Diamond had spent hours running into days staring at his laptop screen, carefully scrutinising and digesting as many articles about cancer of the blood as was possible – until, that was, reality found its harsh, unforgiving voice to remind him that he was no casual observer. He was now a sufferer – a sufferer who was destined to become a victim, a statistic.

The days which followed were nothing but a daze punctuated by the hugs, kind words and tears of the few he drew near to him in times of trouble and uncertainty. His father – the finest man he had ever known by some distance – had died many years ago, which left his mother to strike a note of defiance on behalf of a family which suddenly believed in both God and miracles.

The natural person to gravitate towards was his girlfriend – his partner, she always insisted – and this he did, albeit with some reluctance. Noreen was two years younger, part Irish, a reluctant accountant and as far removed from a caring, compassionate soul as it is possible to be. She loved Diamond, but that love had always been temporarily shelved when he was taken ill. He had once returned home from a friend's stag weekend in Bruges with a fistful of broken fingers – the product of a drunken game which revolved around who could best punch a hole in the wall of the Gruuthusemuseum's famous old gate. She could muster neither sympathy nor dark amusement and simply walked out of their shared flat, which lay in the shadow of the new Wembley Stadium, and refused to return for three days.

They fell in and out of love as often as they fell in and out of bed. She had accompanied him on several of his earlier appointments at London's University College Hospital but on the day that mattered, on the day when everything changed, she was absent.

He was carried home by Tube and by bus; a journey which seemed endless and which, he kept thinking, was a waste of what was now highly valuable time. Once the clock had started to count down, each and every minute not only cried out to be filled with something worthwhile but seemed to be dramatically shorter.

It was only as he made his way from bus stop to front door that he gave consideration to precisely how he was going to handle the official announcement of his impending demise. He considered using just that phrase – "I have news with regard to my impending demise, my sweet" – but, as a man who had a deserved reputation for cynicism and sarcasm, he decided it would, on this occasion at least, be somewhat inappropriate.

The flat was nothing special – very little in London is unless you were willing to hand over all your earnings in rent and then accept that a night out was only a realistic prospect if someone else volunteered to pick up all the bills.

"Noreen" he shouted, as he moved from tiny hallway to tiny living room.

No reply.

Wandering into the kitchen, he banged his left leg on the edge of the farmhouse wooden table he had always detested.

A large and ugly bruise was inevitable – one of the less serious side effects of his disease.

She wasn't home, but she had left a hastily scribbled note:

"Gone to shops and to see my gran. Back around 6pm. Hope all went well with the droll Dr Marshall. xxx"

He checked his watch. It was 5.12pm. Forty-eight minutes in which to compose both himself and a speech which was high on information and low on drama. He needed to be direct and honest without suggesting that he had unfurled and raised the white flag of surrender. As someone who had trained as a journalist before abandoning a career which he deemed to be so liberally strewn with affected clowns that he couldn't cope, Diamond was good at delivering a message.

Sinking into his favoured, rescued-from-a-charity-shop chair, he closed his eyes and vainly attempted to rerun his conversation with Dr Marshall. Maybe he had misheard or misinterpreted? When he had said, "fucked", perhaps he actually meant, "a little bit fucked"? As he searched for wriggle room, he fell asleep.

When he felt his shoulder being shaken, he was lost in a dream. He was in a park with a friend who had been goalkeeper in his school's under-fifteens side – before, that was, he was killed whilst trying to outpace the police in a car he had stolen simply because he liked its colour.

Noreen was doing the shaking, and she was talking. He couldn't actually hear the words but her mouth was moving in a manner which suggested she was, for once, willing to concede that she had a heart.

"You OK, hon? Sorry if I made you jump. I thought you'd be on your laptop so I didn't try to be quiet. You OK?" she asked again as she headed for the kitchen, Aldi bag in hand.

"I got some chicken and stir-fry stuff... and some of that tiger bread you like. It'll be about twenty minutes. Did everything go OK at the hospital?"

Diamond wasn't sure that shouting, "I'm going to die" in the hope that it could be heard over a blaring radio and a sizzling pan of chicken was the thing to do. He could wait until after Noreen's largely tasteless evening meal had been served and eaten before telling her, or he could wade in right now. He had many uncomfortable decisions to negotiate in the weeks ahead, but this one was particularly awkward because the best way to reassess your feelings for someone is to run, headlong, into a major crisis.

Noreen almost waltzed into the room, planting two plates of noodle-adorned fried chicken on the table. She turned, smiled the smile which had so engaged him when they first met, and simply said, "What's wrong?"

If it wasn't a rhetorical question, it sure sounded like one. As she awaited Diamond's response her eyes widened markedly and her arms moved outwards away from her waist as if in supplication.

He had worked out the words he would use. A short and measured statement designed to both inform and reassure. Yes, it was bad; but, yes, he was, if not fine, then dealing with it in a wholly adult manner.

But the words wouldn't come. Instead he could feel his brow furrowing and his eyes narrowing. He was gasping, not speaking. He wasn't sure who started crying first but it seemed that Noreen was actually shrinking – dissolving – before him.

No words were exchanged as she fell forwards into his open arms.

"Tell me," she said, her face buried in his chest.

"I have leukaemia, which is—"

"I know what it is," she said, slowly pulling up her head to meet his eyes. "Stay there."

She rose to her feet and disappeared into the kitchen. She re-emerged with the bottle of cheap brandy they both used to ward off coughs and colds, and two glasses, one chipped and one bearing a faded image of Popeye. Pouring two generous measures, she settled, cross-legged, on the floor in front of him, wiped a tear from a bleary eye and said, "OK – tell me everything. Do not omit a single detail… do not fuck around. I want it all."

He had never loved her more than at that moment, and looking back now he realised he had never loved her as much since. The irony wasn't lost on him – their mutual love had reached its peak in the midst of their greatest tragedy.

Diamond had hoped the brandy would be a panacea; it wasn't. As he stared at Noreen he realised that, even though she was holding tight to her crossed legs, she was shaking. She was also rocking, backwards and forwards, gently beating out a rhythm as she waited patiently for him to tell her what she already knew.

The thought that he was stating the obvious crawled over his skin as he mentally sorted out a running order.

"Dr Marshall says I'm fucked," he said.

There, he'd said it. That wasn't what he had wanted to say or planned to say – but the doctor had done a good job in journalistic terms, insomuch as he had sorted the wheat from the chaff, the relevant from the useless, the facts from the base details, and then delivered the bottom line as a headline.

"Sorry… that wasn't what I had intended to say," he muttered, instinctively lowering his head.

"It's OK, hon. It's me you are talking to. Just tell me everything he said."

"Well, he said he got back eighty per cent of the test results – mostly the bloods and the biopsies. It was as he had feared: I have leukaemia and that's it – there's nothing they can do."

"There has to be something they can do, Steve. There's always something. They can't just send you home…"

She didn't finish the sentence, but she didn't have to. Diamond mentally filled in the missing words for himself: "to die", that's what she was going to say. Had she done so, she would have been the first person since his illness started to mention death.

"No, you're right. It isn't the end of the road; it's just that the road has suddenly become rather shorter. If I opt for the treatment, and if it works, if it slows down the progress of the problem, I may have… well, I don't know. Anyway, we can still go to Whitby."

Only the previous week, Diamond had booked a week away in the North Yorkshire harbour town so beloved of Bram Stoker devotees and young Goths. The black dog of whispering depression was telling him he had to go because it could be his last holiday; the mental battle between optimism and pessimism had already begun and he was finding the opening shots hard to bear.

"So, he sent you home? He didn't insist you stay in the hospital for treatment? They can't just send you home with a blank appointment card and no medication. That can't be right, Steve. Did you actually listen to what he was saying? He must have said more. He must have listed options and given you a plan of action. Did you listen to him?"

She was now both shaking and screaming. Having stood, she was also moving swiftly around the room, waving her hands in a motion universally accepted as one of pleading. And she was crying uncontrollably. They both were. It was inevitable, for, after all, it was the traditional form of cathartic release.

Diamond was recovering his poise with sufficient speed to mentally accept that we cry for a reason, and that the reason is almost always rooted in either pain or love... or both. "I am going back to see him next Monday. It's just the way they do it. There's no point in having an ultra-serious discussion when someone is in shock – and no matter how strong your reserve, you do lose your senses for a while after being told you won't ever be in a position to draw a pension.

"I felt sorry for him. He is a gifted man who saves lives. He probably worked his arse off for twenty years only to find himself having to stand in front of people and tell them that he found a Post-it note from the Grim Reaper stuck above their bed. It can't be easy. In fact, it must be fucking terrible," said Diamond.

After the storm, the silence. They both sat staring intently at nothing in particular. Diamond wanted to turn on Sky News but, safe in the knowledge that he wouldn't feature on the hourly bulletins, it was a temptation he resisted.

His life had changed but everything else was the same. Life went on all around him with scant regard for the calamity which had almost swallowed him whole. It was the awful sense of continuing normality which so hurt him. The woman reading the news didn't have cancer, the man urging you to buy car insurance didn't have cancer, Vladimir Putin didn't have cancer, Donald Trump didn't have cancer and, sadly, neither did the leaders of Islamic State.

The hurdles came thick and fast. Family, good friends, flaky friends, casual associates and then employers and colleagues – he felt the need to inform them with almost indecent haste. Not because he was seeking pity or casting himself in the central role of a modern-day martyr, but because he was seeking the form of partial closure which only honesty can provide.

CHAPTER

TWO

Diamond had always loved his job; a role which, he readily admitted, he more fell into than achieved through the normal avenues of pursuit. He was a very proud part-time lecturer in 'Science: Fiction and Fact' at a local college; a role which saw him surprisingly well paid simply for talking about what was his one genuine passion in life.

In truth, he had initially adored his first job as a trainee journalist – a wannabe hack, stalking the streets of North London in search of the scoop which would propel him to the big time, Fleet Street and all that. This vision of establishing himself as some sort of modern-day Samuel Pepys was partly based on one of his favourite films, 'Ace in the Hole', which cast Kirk Douglas as a hard-nosed reporter who deliberately ensures that a man trapped in a cave rockfall isn't rescued in order that his exclusive story might run and run. All very unethical, but that was how the young Diamond saw reporters – frank, fearless and willing to stand at Robert Johnson's crossroads to make a pact with the Devil himself in order to land the story which mattered ahead of more seasoned but less ambitious rivals.

However, his first six months on the *Islington Gazette* had crushed most of his dreams as he trudged wearily from dull council meeting to dull arts committee meeting to dull flower show. He realised very quickly that his new role in life involved moving news no one was actually interested in to the pages of a paper no one read.

His sole comfort during those days of cheap takeaways and canned lager was his weekly slot in the magistrates' court. The lowest level of the British judiciary system was a constant joy to a man who boasted the cynicism – if not, perhaps, the skill – to move to the very top of his profession. There was a never-ending stream of the great unwashed and the simply stupid for the court to deal with – people who had neither the basic intelligence nor the desire to put up a fight. It was a simple, carousel-like process: the charges were read out, the accused scratched his or her tattooed arms, yawned and pleaded guilty. The court was informed that the defendant had several dozen previous convictions for identical offences and they were duly sent on their way, their pockets £10 lighter than when they arrived.

Occasionally there was meat on the bones. An accusation of rape (usually a trembling student watched by his weeping mother); a remand to the Crown Court for a wounding. Once, memorably, Diamond sat less than twelve feet away from a genuine, twenty-two carat murderer. The elderly man who had brought down the curtain on his wife's life by way of bringing down a vase – ironically, a wedding present – on her head was hardly Premier League in terms of London villains, but he was ultimately told he would spend at least twelve years behind bars for his drunken assault. Diamond had the feeling the old man had been living behind bars for many years – quite possibly since he uttered the fateful words, "I do."

With youth comes impatience, and fourteen months into his three-year apprenticeship – his indentures – Diamond became bored; so bored, in fact, that he began to write things which were designed not to inform and entertain but to irritate and annoy.

He prompted a mini rebellion amongst the borough's am-dram community by describing Gilbert and Sullivan's *The Pirates of Penzance* as "lyrically interesting but musically banal", he likened the Deputy Mayor to a chimpanzee in a flippant report on a ribbon-cutting event, and he deliberately misspelt Councillor Jean Birch's name so she was labelled in a photo caption as "Jean Bitch". The dressing-down for the latter was, he felt, genuinely unfair as he had assumed the subeditor would spot and correct it before inserting it on page twenty-three. He hadn't because, if anything, he was less committed to his role than was Diamond.

Diamond's undoing, his finest hour, came one hot July night when he was down to cover some kids' reworking of *Bugsy Malone* at a rundown theatre where the sky was clearly visible through a gaping hole in the roof. Kids' shows were always covered simply because the editor, a brash but talentless individual called Paul Swarbrick, knew that each and every parent who gathered to watch their very own 'baby' belt out tuneless songs would buy the paper the following week. It was an exercise in crass marketing, but one which actually worked.

Diamond was all set to leave for his night of family entertainment when his closest friend, Toby, rang to invite him for a pint and a curry. Initially at least, he resisted the temptation by insisting that, as a member of Her Majesty's Press, he was, if nothing else, a true professional. Toby, a massive intellect whose full name was Tobias Callaghan, sighed down the phone, gave the details of where he was going just in case, and then gently berated his friend for being over-conscientious.

Diamond had reached the Tube station when a spirit of uncommon recklessness got the better of both his conscience and his common sense. As if to aid his act of self-delusion, he began speaking out loud to himself. "The kids will sing and dance, everyone will clap like seals, they'll all go home, and when they open next week's paper, they'll read a glowing review beneath a cliché-ridden headline. Simple," he said.

That was that sorted. He switched platforms and duly headed for an evening of ribald conversation, strong beer and gum-burning curry. Indeed, as he raised his first headless pint in The King's Arms, he toasted the kids he had chosen to abandon with a cheery, "Good luck to the young gangsters and molls of *Bugsy Malone!*"

As he was due in the magistrates' court at 10am the following morning, Diamond had promised his editor he would type up and deliver his review to the office first thing in the morning. The editor didn't actually require his copy for another twenty-four hours – it was simply his way of drawing a line in the sand between those who command and those who serve. Diamond loathed such pettiness but fell in line, bashing out a glowing four-hundred-word review in the small hours; a task punctuated by several trips to the toilet as his body attempted to place clear blue water between itself and the evening's intake of alcohol and over-spiced food. He dropped his review in the 'New Copy' basket inside the cramped and deserted editorial section before strolling off towards the court.

It was the usual fare – drunks, shoplifters and car thieves. The only case of any interest was that of a former member of the borough's Trades Council, who seemingly had developed a desire to expose his genitals to any woman over sixty who was walking a dog. As the case against him was outlined by the police prosecutor, the soon-to-be-disgraced former grandee repeatedly shouted, "It wasn't me, sir. It was them. They came in the night and took me up to the mother ship. The man who waved his dick about was an alien – one of those grey chaps."

Diamond was amazed that the alien abductee was granted bail rather than being committed to a secure unit whose lead roofing would almost certainly have prevented a repeat night-time flight to infinity and beyond. The man was clearly ill, but, from a parochial perspective, the story was both interesting and amusing.

Diamond left the court, dug out a 10p piece and dialled his editor with the news of a possible front-page lead. "Morning, Paul – I have something good for you," he said with, for once, genuine enthusiasm.

"Morning, Steve. I got your review. Did you enjoy the show last night?" said Swarbrick.

"It was OK; you know what they are like. The kids were cute and the mums and dads clapped in all the right places."

"Good, good. Can I tell you something which you may well find of interest?"

"Yeah – go on."

"The show was cancelled an hour before it was due to start because the theatre caught fire and burned down."

"Ah... right. OK... shall I come and see you?"

"Yes please, that would be nice."

Later, much later, Diamond realised that the one thing you must never do is hand the advantage to a man who wants you out of the building. On his first day in the job, a wizened old hack with sunken eyes and the aroma of a wet dog had told him that journalism's first two golden rules were to never annoy either the editor or the man who signed off the expenses.

Diamond felt like an errant eight-year-old as Swarbrick used his limited vocabulary and his dislike of all things youthful to beat him around the head for a good thirty minutes. The words 'unprofessional', 'disgrace' and 'twat' featured prominently in what was, by his lowly standards, a bravura performance. Of course, he had deliberately left his office door ajar so the entire performance could be heard, if not seen, by Diamond's smirking colleagues.

It was only when Swarbrick rose and closed the door that Diamond knew the end was finally in sight. Twisting the ends of his well-groomed, World War One air-ace-style moustache, Swarbrick simply moved his face to within a few inches of Diamond's and said – so loudly it made closing his door seem utterly ridiculous – "Get your coat and hat and fuck off. You, boy, are fired."

It wasn't the sacking which so hurt Diamond; it was being referred to as "boy". Somewhat confused, he scrambled for a suitably robust riposte. He could launch into an obscene rant but, strangely, he felt that to be inappropriate. Aware that those who now found themselves to be his former colleagues were listening attentively, he needed something smart, something which would be long talked about in the office watering hole down the road. He needed a line which would ensure that his name lived forever inside the offices of the *Islington Gazette*.

He was almost as surprised as Swarbrick when he heard the words, "It wasn't me, sir. It was them. It was one of those greys" slip from his lips.

It was sufficiently beguiling as to reduce his ex-editor to silence. Diamond didn't bother to clear his desk; he simply walked out and never looked back.

Pushing the distinct possibility of financial oblivion to the back of his mind, he actually felt a sense of relief as he wandered home. No more garden fetes, no more kids' shows, no more listing, from left to right, the names of dull, dull people on photo captions.

He had always regarded journalism as something of a maverick career, so by the time he placed his key in the front-door lock, he had all but convinced himself that to include a dismissal on his yet-to-be-penned CV would hint at the sort of rebellious nature which, he felt sure, many an editor would find worthy. Anyway, he was now a man of leisure – broke and without immediate prospects, but a man who could pick and choose his adventures.

He decided against informing all and sundry of what he was going to label a 'career change', and called only Toby.

If Toby felt in any way guilty about the part he had played in his friend's untidy downfall, he didn't show it.

"I have been sacked. That show I was supposed to go to – the one I wrote the review for? It never happened – the fucking theatre burst into flames shortly before the fat kid was due to sing the song about wanting to be a boxer," said Diamond.

Toby, for all his middle-class upbringing and well-honed manners, didn't bother commenting; he just laughed... and laughed.

"Cheers, mate," said Diamond, smiling.

The two agreed to meet later for a beer and a full debriefing. Diamond went home and fell asleep in front of the TV. Sky News played out as he slept without so much as a mention of the night thirty kids in badly made costumes narrowly avoided being burned to a crisp.

Tobias Callaghan was the eldest son of two Irish-born scientists who had relocated to London when they realised that Dublin, great cultural centre that it is, was decidedly stingy when it came to handing out grants to those who wished to pursue projects which were deemed to be both "mad and useless" by those who held the purse strings.

London was a different matter; a city awash with cash, and the seat of a government which had, unbeknown to its taxpaying subjects, put aside large pools of cash to fund the most extraordinary of research projects – all mad, most useless.

Toby had met Diamond at a sci-fi convention on London's South Bank, quite literally bumping into him as the pair queued for a coffee. The collision saw Diamond almost lose his grip on his only purchase of the day: a second-hand, plastic *Doctor Who* TARDIS.

"How much did you pay for that?" asked Toby.

"Too much, I think. £10.50. I wanted it, though."

"Why?"

"I've always loved the programme and always loved sci-fi and anything to do with time travel. Last year I almost bought an original letter by H. G. Wells from an American auction site, but the price rose to about £500 at the last minute and that was well out of my comfort zone."

"Wells wrote *The Time Machine*, didn't he?"

"Yeah – my favourite story. What most people don't realise is that Wells wrote the book back in 1895. He wasn't the greatest writer who ever picked up a quill, but he had the sort of imagination I'd die for. Of the modern-day authors, only Stephen King goes anywhere near him."

"I do like King – well, I like his earlier stuff. I'm not sure that he's quite as good as he was."

"Actually, he is. You need to read the one he wrote about the Kennedy assassination. It is wonderful, and I'm not just saying that because it has someone going back to 1963 through a hole in time and space."

"Does someone go back and stop Lee Harvey Oswald? Great idea for a plot."

"It's not quite as simple as that. The complexities – and the possibilities – of being able to shift backwards and forwards in time are endless."

"You can't go forwards – only backwards."

"You can."

"You can't. It isn't possible to be a part of something which hasn't yet happened. You can, however, go back to what has already been. Well, that's what I'm told, anyway."

"You sound very certain about that. I'm Steve, by the way."

"Toby, or Tobias if my mother is within earshot."

It was a friendship which blossomed so swiftly that those who became mutual friends assumed the pair had been joined at the hip for many, many years.

Despite his boyish good looks and a cutting-edge wardrobe, Toby was, at forty, seven years older than Diamond. Their mutual liking of beer, cinema, literature and science – the more screwball the better – guaranteed that the gap was never an issue; they disagreed only on the interpretation of facts, never on their respective right to hold and defend a differing opinion.

Although both had women in their lives, they spent an increasing amount of time together, Diamond unashamedly leaning on his friend emotionally and intellectually in the months which followed his dismissal by the *Gazette*. Only once was the bond between them threatened with rupture: in 2011 when they both lost their hearts to the same woman. She was Toby's new girl, a feisty blonde from the north-west called Saz.

An unashamed pursuer of life's more obvious pleasures, Saz followed a code of practice laid down by her idol Courtney Love, the one-time partner of the dead rock star Kurt Cobain. Courtney, she would announce to anyone who was willing to listen, was happy to be described as a woman with the morals of an alley cat and an appetite and aptitude to party until the close of play.

Whilst neither Toby nor Diamond was particularly interested in Saz's vision of a life outside of the accepted parameters, both were captivated by her more earthly attributes, namely her pure beauty and her inescapable radiance. Within two weeks of meeting her in a Park Lane coffee bar, Toby confided in Diamond that he had found true love for the first time. Whilst it was, to the best of his knowledge, the third time Toby had made such a declaration, Diamond could understand his reasoning.

Saz swept through both of their lives like a rising tornado. The three became almost inseparable, scouring the limited hotspots of the Wembley area for a partner for Diamond; the gang most definitely needed a fourth member if it was to remain intact. Contenders for the role of beau to Diamond were found, auditioned and then discarded. Diamond found solace in a series of brief relationships, but the hunt for a Saz clone was irritatingly frustrating.

Threesomes rarely have much of a shelf life outside of a teenager's imagination, and the inevitable happened seven months after Saz had entered their previously harmonious lives. Toby disappeared for a weekend – "Important work; secret stuff"– and Diamond agreed to meet up with Saz.

For once lacking Toby's financial input, both found themselves broke and fed up. The simple solution was a Chinese takeaway, a large bottle of very cheap wine from a corner shop where the Asian proprietor had once described Chardonnay as "the king of red wines", and a seat in front of the television at Diamond's flat.

Friendship is a quite wonderful thing until the barriers which are erected by mutual respect are broken down and trampled into the dust by the twin evils of lust and alcohol.

The wine, an unpleasant number from an unknown part of Chile, proved to be much stronger than Diamond's will. There was no doubting that Saz was very fond of Toby – but she loved life and its countless forbidden fruits far more. Long before soap operas had given way to newscasts and late-night analysts, she had taken to devouring Diamond as a child does a melting ice cream. The pair were giggling beneath a less-than-pristine duvet before the street lamps outside flickered into life.

Diamond had never dealt particularly well with guilt. His father, a lifelong civil servant who wore a suit and tie even at weekends, had once warned him that, if he went against what he described as "the laws of basic morality", he would burn in the flames of hell for eternity and a day. He had loved and respected his father dearly, but he never actually liked him.

The following morning, Diamond was silently cursing himself even before he had opened his eyes. He knew that one glance would confirm what the gentle, wheezing rising to his left had already told him – that his best friend's woman was naked in his bed. Unsure whether to ask her to join him in a display of contrition by begging forgiveness, or to simply ooze an air of normality in a 'Hey, I do this all the time' sort of a way, he lay uncomfortably still on his side of the bed.

The one thing he definitely didn't want was for the she-beast alongside him to awaken and promptly discover that her lust and desire had not yet been fully sated. *Having sex with your mate's girlfriend whilst drunk on dreadful red wine is one thing; having sex with her whilst sober quite another,* mused Diamond as he slipped from beneath the covers and headed for the bathroom.

The mirror told a predictable tale. Matted hair, bloodshot eyes, stubble and, more pointedly, the haunted look of a man who had quite possibly effected a sizeable change in his already threadbare life because, yet again, his small head had held sway over his big head.

Diamond made an attempt at washing himself in lukewarm water, but it was half-hearted. He was gripped by panic. Toby was not only his closest friend but, in so many ways, his only true friend. He had other people – many – who fell loosely into the bracket, but with them there was affection and liking rather than a true bond. Toby had become the brother Diamond's mother had promised him but never delivered. The age gap was an irrelevance. They shared many things – time, joy, sadness, excitement, goals, hobbies – but, until now, above all else they had shared trust. Diamond was not naive enough to believe that his overnight treachery could be initially contained and then concealed for good.

He had always believed that pretty high on any woman's list of negative points was a complete inability to accept that sometimes 'secret' does actually mean secret. Could he sit Saz down and explain that his life would implode if she told Toby that she was, in fact, some form of ultra-slapper and that he was, in fact, a brazen and wholly unreliable liar? He had reached his conclusion before all the possible ramifications had filtered through his tired mind – absolutely no chance.

So what to do? Two options – push her out of the front door without delay, or sit her down over tea and toast and talk it through like adults.

Making his way into the bedroom, he found Saz awake, sitting up in bed and reading one of his imported American magazines – a pulp-fiction-style rag which covered, or more likely invented, conspiracy theories.

"Morning, Steve," she said, with a smile and a little-girl wave.

At that moment Diamond wished Toby didn't exist at all and that she was his, not just for one night but for good. It didn't feel like a one-night stand; there was a sense of romance and, yes, possible permanence about the whole messy little episode.

"Morning. Not quite sure what to say now – but I think we need to talk."

"About what?"

"Errrrrrrrr, last night? This. Where we are now."

"What's there to talk about? We had a good night, we went to bed, we had sex, end of story."

"That's ridiculous. How can it be the end of the story? The story ends in one of two ways, Saz: either we tell him or we don't."

"Yes? Cool."

"Cool? That's it? Cool? It's not cool, Saz, it's a fucking mess. I have just slept with my best mate's girlfriend and you think it's cool?"

"He'll understand; he's that sort of man."

"You intend telling him? What planet are you from?"

"You tell me – you're the sci-fi expert."

"Are you serious about telling him? If you do that he will probably do two things – dump you and then dump me. He's my best mate."

"I know – but that didn't seem to be on your mind last night when you were crawling all over me, big boy."

"Stop it, please. Let's be sensible, just for two minutes. What are we going to do, Saz?"

"It's already done."

"What is? What do you mean?"

"I sent him an email just after I woke up. I hate deception and I can't live with uncertainty, so I told him what happened. Confession is never easy but, as any good Catholic worth a Hail Mary will tell you, it is very good for the soul."

"Sweet Jesus."

"Precisely – the good Lord will approve. What's done is done. It cannot be truly hidden or ignored, so we should both accept it and move on – either with or without Toby."

"Has he replied yet?"

"No, he has a load of important meetings – the sort of meetings he never talks about. He will probably read my email during the mid-morning coffee break."

"Fuck, fuck, fuck."

"Too tired, sorry."

"No, I didn't—"

"I was joking, Steve. Calm down."

The almost uncontrollable lust he had felt for Saz less than twelve hours earlier had vanished, to be replaced by something akin to hatred. Whilst he couldn't seriously blame her for what they had done, he was appalled by her flippant attitude, and one of the first questions he asked himself was: *Has she done this sort of thing before?* He drew unexpected strength from the belief that she probably had, and within minutes – such is the perverse nature of male emotions – he decided that Toby deserved better. But as the angel sitting on his right shoulder nodded his approval, the devil perched on his left was pointing out that Toby also deserved far, far more from his closest friend and confidant.

His disgust with Saz's indifference was such that he didn't even bother to hang around the bedroom to watch her dress – an act which, curiously, he had always found far more erotic than watching a woman undress.

"I have lost my senses and maybe my libido in one fell swoop," he muttered under his breath as he planted himself in front of the television and switched on Sky News, then his iPad, then his mobile phone. Diamond mused that mankind had made awesome technological advances over the past few years, and yet no one had yet fashioned a chargeable device which could conquer human failings.

Saz left with the minimum of fuss. Craning her neck towards Diamond's unresponsive lips, she gave him what his first girlfriend, Karen, had always called a fairy kiss – the barest contact combined with the least amount of effort.

"Bye, sweetie," she said. "It was fun. Don't beat yourself up. Keep thinking of that line in Springsteen's 'Rosalita' – *Someday we'll look back on this and it will all seem funny*. Be good."

Diamond realised that he should have asked her if she had heard anything from Toby. That mid-morning coffee break must surely have been and gone by now. Then again, why would Toby want to call him of all people? Sure, he would ring Saz and verbally shred her, but the very last person he would want to talk to would be Diamond.

Diamond had almost convinced himself that he was, for a while anyway, reasonably safe from the wrath of Tobias Callaghan when his mobile began to ring. As the sound of rebellion in the shape of his ringtone, NWA's 'Fuck tha Police', filled the room, he winced before turning the screen of his Nokia mobile towards him and looking at it through the sort of screwed-up eyes girls and kids opt for when watching something they fear may be repellent or upsetting. He expected to see Toby's name, but no, it wasn't him – it was Saz.

"Hello," Diamond said.

"He sent me a text. He told me to go fuck myself and that he was going to kill you. Take care and have a nice day," she said.

He would never see her again.

Diamond hung up, and for a brief moment contemplated crying. Next he thought about ringing, texting or emailing Toby. None of the available options appealed, so he did the next best thing and went back to bed.

His eyes closed without a fight. He was tired. He was mentally exhausted. The only thing keeping him awake was the smell of Saz's perfume which clung to his bedding like orchid dust to a jumper.

He was more tired than he had realised, sleeping for almost two hours and waking just after 2pm. Switching his mobile back on, he waited for the screen pic to appear – a black-and-white image of William Hartnell as the first Dr Who – and readied himself for either a series of text messages or confirmation of several missed calls.

There was nothing. Much as an unpopular teenager who craves any form of contact would have done, Diamond refused to accept 'no' as an answer and switched his phone off and then on again in the ridiculous belief that the reboot fairy would provide him with something previously denied.

The reboot fairy was clearly away on holiday, as the screen remained blank. As his mind began to drag itself clear of the deepest of afternoon sleeps, Diamond realised that this meant Toby had made no attempt to contact him despite the gravity of the situation.

Spotting the battered baseball bat which always lay beside his bed as a last line of defence against knife-wielding burglars, Diamond was drawn into a vision of Toby rushing back from his top-secret assignment to carry out his threat of ending his friend's life. A fantasist and a hardcore romantic, Diamond decided it would be a noble death. He deserved it and he would not fight. If Toby wished to do as he had told Saz he would do, Diamond would behave like a disgraced samurai and simply accept his fate. Then his desire for a death which would be talked about down the ages swiftly left him and he decided to get the hell out of the flat just in case the mild-mannered Toby had somehow managed to transform himself into a Ted Bundy-type slayer of the innocents.

With little money, and with all his other close friends gainfully employed and out earning a decent living, Diamond was stuck as to precisely where he should take and park both his guilt and his growing anger at his own stupidity. It had to be the pub, but he needed to strip the bed and deposit the duvet, fitted sheet and pillows into the washing machine before leaving. Unfortunately, moving the evidence away from the scene of the crime did little to improve his mood. As he poured in the last drops of a vile-smelling washing solution bought from the same dubious storekeeper who had sold him the Chilean red wine, he muttered just the one word: "Bitch."

As he was, in essence, running away to hide, Diamond did not hesitate to duck into the first dodgy-looking pub he passed. It was laughingly labelled The Gay Cavalier, and featured a weather-worn sign with a quite sinister picture of a leering individual in a ruffled collar.

As he took a seat in the corner beneath a window which still looked as if it was blacked out against Nazi air raids, Diamond wondered when a gay cavalier had last crossed the threshold.

He sat quietly for several minutes before the barman, an obese individual with a pimple the size of 10p piece on a nose which had clearly been broken on several occasions, shouted across to him. "Any chance that you could actually buy something, mate? This is a pub, not a registered charity."

Diamond felt he should have shouted abuse, turned on his heel and left – but crouched beside the door, beneath a television which was showing *Teletubbies*, was a man who looked like he was no stranger to ultra-violence. First impressions can often be hopelessly misleading – but if ever Diamond had seen a man who was likely to do untold damage to a complete stranger, he was there, sitting just to the left of Tinky Winky.

Making his way to a bar which was littered with overflowing ashtrays and spilled peanuts, Diamond ordered a pint of Foster's, paid for it and then retreated, not to his previous seat, but to an anteroom which, mercifully, offered no view of either the television set or the dark character beneath it.

Diamond had always subscribed to the theory that beer – particularly lager – only tasted good when a person was in a good mood. Bad moods, he believed, were made for brandy, whisky or, as a last resort, Baileys. The beer slipped down quickly enough but it seemed to be all but tasteless; a rather long-winded and time-consuming route towards the light-headed abandon he was so in need of. He was midway through his third pint and wondering what germs infected the curtains which kept flapping forwards and catching the back of his head when his mobile rang. Almost as if he had placed useful distance between himself and his problems, Diamond answered without first checking who the call was from.

"Hello. Steve Diamond, professional dickhead here," he said.

"Spot on," replied Toby.

"Hi. I thought it would be a cold call from someone trying to sell me insurance."

"Life insurance? You worried? Do you need it? Do you want to get your financial affairs in order before you wave a cheery goodbye to this world, Steve?"

"Look, Toby—"

"No, you listen. I think I have the right to do the talking here – as it seems that I am the grown-up in our relationship. Two things, Steven Diamond. Firstly, you are a complete and utter bastard. Secondly, you are almost certainly stupid."

"Yes, I know. What happened was—"

"Shut up. Did you use a condom last night?"

"What? Why?"

"Did you or didn't you?"

"No. As I was going to say, I was drunk… we were both drunk. It wasn't planned or anything, so, no…"

"She's got herpes."

"Is that AIDS?"

"No – if it was AIDS I would have told you it was AIDS. Herpes is like a cold sore which becomes a lifelong companion."

"A cold sore?"

"Yes, a cold sore – but not on the mouth or the lips. Much further down, in a woman's more interesting regions. You know, the bits of her you were most interested in last night? So if you couldn't be bothered to take precautions she has probably left you a little gift which will always remind you of her. Nice, eh? Hey – she isn't on the pill either so she may also be pregnant – a double whammy, mate. Nice work."

"Fuck me. Are you serious?"

"Yep. It's what you get – what you deserve – for trampling all over someone else's garden… someone else's lady garden."

"I can explain. It was—"

"You don't have to explain, Steve. My best mate and a girlfriend I was genuinely attached to waited until I went away for a couple of days and then jumped into bed. As you journalists would say, those are the facts. There is just the one interpretation of those facts. It is cut and dried."

"I'm sorry."

"Of course you are. History teaches us that everyone who is found out is sorry – but until that point they remain bullish and hopeful that their crime will go undiscovered. If I were to play amateur psychologist, I would say that guilt is some way down your list of emotions at this moment in time. Truth is, I really don't care how you or that whore feel right now. Me? I'm pissed off and disgusted."

"I understand."

"No you don't. No you fucking don't understand. What you did is so far beneath contempt I'd need a shovel to dig it up for inspection. I shouldn't even be talking to you. I am disgusted with myself for picking up my phone and ringing you. I should have just blanked you for good."

"That much I do understand. OK. Take care, Toby. I won't say sorry again because it will, rightly, trigger more invective. I am a fucking clown – that's my considered opinion. Be good."

Diamond felt it right that he should end the conversation. He pushed the button and Toby was gone – presumably for good.

Diamond flicked the dirty curtain out of his face yet again, hoping Toby would ring straight back and wave an olive branch. He didn't, so Diamond returned to the bar and asked the man with the inflamed nose for another pint.

By the time he staggered across the threshold of his flat, Diamond was again a man at odds with sobriety. Checking his watch, he saw it was seven o'clock, but was unsure if this was am or pm. He knew he should eat, but faced with a refrigerator which contained just three items – one egg, a half-drunk bottle of cheap Chardonnay, and a chocolate éclair which looked as though it had already passed through somebody's system – he again opted for bed. There was no duvet and no sheet – but at least it no longer reeked of the scarlet woman who had stripped even barer an already bare life.

When Diamond woke it was gone 10pm and his head was banging from the after-effects of the beer. Propped up on a bare mattress, he surveyed his world; an uninspiring empire which held only the reminders of past events and discarded women.

A mock-ivory elephant which blonde-haired Karen had bought for him on a day out in Brighton, a walking stick which brunette Sue had given him to aid his recovery from torn knee ligaments, and the framed cover of the first Sex Pistols album which purple-haired Josie had given him to celebrate their mutual love of music with an undertone of plastic anarchy.

It wasn't much, and in that one moment Diamond realised that he was now cast in the role of one of life's great underachievers. Almost unemployed after his college work had been cut back to one day per week, broke, no girlfriend, no closest friend after borrowing his woman for a night – nothing to illuminate the path forwards.

Diamond resisted the temptation to slide back into a foetal position and again sleep, because, whilst he had been putting it off ever since Toby's phone call, he had an appointment with Google to keep.

His laptop was old and always initially reluctant to respond, so, having pushed the button to kick-start it, he headed to the kitchen – or the kitchenette, as the rental company had insisted on calling it – to turn hot water and powder into the strongest mug of coffee ever known to mankind. A side order of three paracetamol was swallowed whole.

Through bleary eyes which simply refused to clear, Diamond called up Google and typed in just one word – "Herpes". He was presented with two options: herpes (cold sores), or genital herpes (*Herpes simplex*). After calling out the words, "Oh fuck" rather too loudly, he opted for the latter and read on.

He scrolled down and digested the message, which suggested that genital herpes was indeed for life and not just some minor inconvenience which could be banished by the application of an ointment. He stopped scrolling when the first HD colour photograph began to appear at the foot of his screen.

"Oh, my good God," he said. There it was in all its glory, all its ugliness. A penis with a series of running, open sores, and bits of a lady's undercarriage with identical wounds.

He felt like a rubbernecker who slows down on the motorway to look for the dead and injured after a bad car smash. He couldn't take his eyes off what he now accepted was a glimpse into his future; he was mesmerised.

His next action was, he knew, wholly predictable. He typed in, "Genital herpes cures." All the results – and there were 42,786 of them – appeared to give the same answer: that genital herpes, that lovable little disease which really good friends pass on to each other at the height of alcohol-fuelled passion, was simply incurable. It often went away, sometimes for many months, but it lurked around in your system and reactivated itself whenever the mood took it – probably around the time you found the woman of your dreams and were preparing to seal your love with a first bout of robust sex.

Diamond sat back and drank his coffee, wincing at its bitterness and strength but determined to drain it. Panicked by what he had read, he sought to apply logic by telling himself that he might not have been infected by Saz after all; it wasn't certain. At that moment he would have happily taken odds of fifty-fifty.

Only then did he seriously consider the absolute recklessness of Saz's act. She had gone to bed with him knowing she had a very nasty and very contagious disease. Not only had she not bothered to tell him, which he partially understood, she had not insisted that he wear protection. Had she done that, even claiming it was on the grounds of birth control, she wouldn't have had to tell him about the herpes. She was either very forgetful, which he deemed highly unlikely, or she was an inconsiderate bitch who not only took chances with her own health, but who insisted that her friends also engaged in a game of bedroom Russian roulette.

With no one to direct his anger at, Diamond tried to calm himself down by mentally taking a stroll down the bright side of his life's road to nowhere.

Toby had told him on so many occasions that he needed to focus, to reinvent himself. Failure to so do would, he insisted, see Diamond waste his many talents. He knew Toby was right but he had always shied away from taking on board what he considered to be parental-style advice.

His father had been one for face-to-face lectures on future planning, forward planning and what he described as "life plans". His father suffered OCD long before it became a fashionable excuse for bizarre and inconsiderate behaviour. He would arrange biscuits on a plate with geometric precision, wash his car in precisely the same way at precisely the same time every Sunday morning, shine his shoes with Cherry Blossom polish at 9.30 every night. He had even urged Diamond to open a pension account when he was just fourteen years old.

"Get a paper round and invest the money for your future. You'll be grateful for this advice when you're approaching retirement. Let others waste their earnings on girls and fast cars. You need to be sensible, boy," he would say.

Diamond smiled as he considered the one and only car he had ever owned: a reliable but battered Renault Clio with an engine so small he was once overtaken by a tractor.

But, beneath the nonsense, both his dad and Toby did have a point. He was drifting – hopelessly so. He had considered giving journalism another go, but decided that the fourth estate was doing rather well without him. He considered teaching, before realising that would mean low wages and having to deal with unkempt brats he would rather assault than educate. There was always charitable work, but having looked into that possibility last year he had learned that, if you seriously wished to do good and give of your time for free, you would first be required to fill in dozens of forms and applications and then be vetted by people who had probably never been anywhere near the favelas of Brazil or the shanty towns of South Africa.

Perhaps, he mused, he was the proverbial lost soul; a man destined to tread a lonely path before dying in a dark and filthy alley, the herpes having moved from his genitals to the rest of his body, turning him into a seething mass of sores and open wounds.

Having missed the opening shots of *News at Ten*, he considered calling time on what he felt would be a landmark day by going back to bed, again.

Then his mobile rang for only the third time that day. It was Tobias Callaghan, former friend and a man with an axe to grind.

"Don't tell me – she's also suffering from contagious, never-ending diarrhoea?" said Diamond, surprised that he could find any humour in the situation.

"I wish," said Toby. "Where are you?"

"Getting ready to go to bed for the fourth or fifth time in twenty-four hours."

"Meet me at The King's Arms."

"When?"

"Now – well, in fifteen minutes."

The line went dead and Diamond was left wondering if he should pick up a kitchen knife on his way to the front door.

The King's was full of students, which meant that every available table was surrounded by spotty folk clutching half-pint glasses with exactly a quarter-inch of beer inside. It was the first rule of student life – find a pub which will permit you to spend all night talking for the least possible expenditure.

Diamond couldn't see Toby, but the crush at the bar for last orders was such that it didn't mean he hadn't arrived. Pushing his way through a mass of freshers, who had obviously been told it was very cool to be seen out and about wearing their college scarves even though it was June, Diamond headed for the beer garden, a poor excuse for an outside drinking area which featured three low tables covered in pigeon faeces, and two dustbins which seemingly hadn't been emptied since the Silver Jubilee celebrations.

Toby was seated as far away from the bins as was possible; otherwise the garden of no delights was empty. Anyone with an intact sense of smell had wisely opted to remain indoors, preferring the scent of patchouli oil to that of rotting food.

Toby didn't even look up as Diamond approached and sat opposite him. Neither had bothered to buy a drink – Toby because he drank only wine and the patron of The King's was hardly a connoisseur, and Diamond because his head was still banging from the previous night's intake.

They sat in silence for an uncomfortably long period before Toby finally met Diamond's gaze and smiled.

"What's funny, Toby? I can't find anything funny at the moment. Groucho Marx could sidle up to us and deliver a twenty-minute show and I wouldn't find it funny. Tommy Cooper doesn't seem funny right now; neither does Billy Connolly, or—"

"That'll do. I've got the point, Steve."

"Sorry. I am just tired, unwell, fed up and, yes, even regretful."

"Good. Splendid. Serves you right."

"Why did you want to meet me?"

"Just to tell you that I'll let it go this once."

"What?"

"I'll let you off with banging my woman – but if you should ever go near my mother…" Toby was smiling, almost laughing.

"I don't understand," said Diamond, now wishing he did have a drink in front of him.

"I am a kind and generous man, so I forgive you."

"You do? Why? I mean, that's really cool. I don't quite know what to say."

"Why? Because I already knew she was a loose cannon who was sleeping around. Remember Carl, the biker with the tattoo on his face and the leather jacket which doesn't fit? Well, she stayed with him last Wednesday night. I had already decided to dump her before she had the damned nerve to email me and tell me she had slept with you. Good riddance."

"Are you upset?"

"About her? No, no way. I'm still a little bit disappointed in you, though."

"I need a drink now, but the bar's closed."

"Me too. Come back to mine and we will open a bottle or two. I have the car with me. Oh yes… more good news for you – she doesn't have herpes."

"She doesn't?"

"No, I just said that to piss you off."

"Fuck me, Toby, I thought I was going to die. Bastard! I wasn't sure she and I would have forged a meaningful partnership, but she does have a great body. Why is she called Saz?," said Diamond.

" Haven't a clue, mate. I think her real name is Sara; all very odd, " said Toby.

Diamond, a self-confessed boy racer, could never quite understand why Toby had bought a massively powerful car, a big black Audi, only to drive along inside the speed limit. No one drove inside the speed limit, no one.

They arrived at Toby's well-appointed and expensively furbished apartment down by the Thames just before midnight. Toby was very much an amateur drinker, the sort who got drunk maybe twice a year – three times if his annual bonus was larger than expected. But he knew his wine and never attempted to palm off visitors with cheap plonk. The South African Pinotage – Clos Malverne from the Stellenbosch region – was sumptuous, the pair demolishing a bottle between them inside fifteen minutes.

"How much does this stuff cost?" asked Diamond.

"Depends on the year, really. This one is about £25 a bottle," said Toby.

"Jesus. I don't spend that on alcohol in a month."

"You would if you had the money," countered Toby.

They sat and they talked. They sat and they drank. No television, no distractions save the latest Coldplay album in the background. Diamond had always disliked Coldplay but Chris Martin's perpetual girly whine suited the occasion; it was, very much, mood music.

By 2am Diamond had lifted himself out of his downward spiral. Toby, urged on by the sense of freedom which a forthcoming day off so often engenders, was very, very drunk. The conversation swung and moved at many different angles. They covered the fortunes of Chelsea and Arsenal, the various wars across a globe they both agreed was destined to end up a barren wasteland peopled only by students with long scarves, the state of modern British politics, the antics of various '60s and '70s celebrities who boasted wandering hands but precious little talent, and, of course, Saz.

The consensus, reached an hour into what became a quite epic session of wine consumption and soul-searching, was that she was a very bad woman; and – as Diamond remarked in a terrible mock-Jamaican accent – that was bad as in bad and not bad as in good. Saz was denounced as a vile creature of ill repute who could go to hell or, if the "House Full" sign was up, find shelter in one of that state's neighbouring territories. Just over twenty-four hours after seemingly driving a wedge between the two, she proved to be the catalytic force which drove them even closer together.

THREE

Noreen had finally left him and gone to work. He had to be
at his persuasive best to convince her that whilst he was
ill – very ill – he wouldn't be spending his day scouring eBay
for cheap funeral deals.

Neither had slept well that night. Diamond had woken
on countless occasions, almost as if his brain was making him
check he was still alive. For once he was grateful that he was
one of those who instantly relinquished a hold on his dreams
the moment he opened his eyes. For years he had been deeply
envious of colleagues who could seemingly recall every last
detail of the previous night's entertainment, and who would,
no doubt with some slight embellishment, recount tales of
sex, violence and sheer nonsense over lunch.

For no good reason other than that he was lying beneath a
duvet which was somewhat more than damp from the increased
perspiration of two people who had seen their lives change so
unexpectedly in such a short space of time, he thought of Saz.

It was three years since that night of dumb, predatory sex;
three years since he and Toby had moved to the very cusp of a

big falling-out. Diamond remembered quite vividly the wine consumed and the secrets shared in the hours that followed what he and Toby now simply referred to as "the night".

And what secrets they were. In truth, he had had little to offer Toby when, at around 3am, he had demanded that Diamond tell him something that no one else knew.

"Tell me something, Steve... something special." It was classic drunk talk.

Possibly a little more sober than his agitated friend, Diamond played amateur psychologist for thirty seconds or so and duly convinced himself that, whilst Toby wasn't actually attempting to squeeze stories of intrigue out of him, he possibly had something he wished to share. More and more, it resembled a soul-baring session.

The best Diamond could come up with was that he had, as a seventeen-year-old, visited a brothel in Canning Town with a couple of his old schoolmates. Even then he couldn't bring himself to be totally honest. Had he done so, it would have been a harrowing tale of sexual failure and the callous waste of £35.

"Sorry, mate, that's the best I can do. My life has been so dull and predictable. What about you?" he said.

What followed was the most extraordinary of tales; so fanciful that Diamond initially dismissed Toby's claims as the rantings of a man who had used red wine merely as a gateway to the absurd.

Sensibly, Toby prefaced his story, his revelations, with the traditional, "You aren't going to believe much of this." He was right. My God, he was right.

Diamond remembered slouching back into his armchair, clutching yet another glass of wine, as Toby began what was to be a monologue. Not once did Diamond feel inclined to interrupt or to seek answers to the many questions which his friend's curious story posed. He sat back and listened, fully aware that had the words been coming from the lips of anyone else, he would not have hesitated to scream, "Bollocks" and take his leave.

By his own confession, Toby's childhood had been sheltered. He played a largely passive role throughout his early years, simply happy to please parents who demanded much but gave back very little. His mother and father delivered the mantra of "learn and prosper" like an intravenous drip, constantly pointing out that a young man's life should be filled with education and not fun. Toby fell in line, unable to find the courage to argue or fight back. As his young friends and relatives devoured sweets and ice creams, he himself was force-fed a diet of facts, figures and theories.

By the time he was eleven years old he was astute, intelligent, could list the atmospheric make-up of all the planets in the solar system, could quote Shakespeare and Dickens – but he was a child alone, a child whose best friend was a thesaurus.

Having moved effortlessly through public school (he still wouldn't say which one it was), Toby had a simple choice: Oxford or Cambridge. Life is full of choices, but only rarely is a teenager expected to choose between the sublime and the sublime. He was to select Cambridge simply because he remembered seeing, a few years earlier, a TV interview with an Oxford don who arrogantly made fun of those who had to accept the traditional state-school education; brilliant, but with a conscience.

On such seemingly ridiculous reasoning are major decisions taken and futures shaped.

He studied physics and mathematics at the famed Jesus College and, predictably, emerged blinking into the real world three years later with a first, an intact virginity and a loathing of rowing and rugby union.

Diamond remembered, with a certain amount of admiration, that Toby spoke very fondly of his days at Oxford, and that he was immensely proud of having turned down the advances of a variety of young women whom he labelled "revision fucks" – girls who were so bored with working towards their next exam that they temporarily took leave of their senses as they toured the campus in search of pleasurable forms of distraction. He had worked hard and he had earned his wisdom.

Toby was enjoying one of the many end-of-course parties when, he said, he was approached by what he described as a "man in black".

Diamond, his body saturated with alcohol, laughed out loud, asking – all too predictably – if the guy was wearing Ray-Bans and resembled the Hollywood nice guy Will Smith. The rebuke came in the form of a withering glance of almost total disbelief from Toby; the sort of look which told Diamond to listen but not to interrupt.

The very polite man in the smart, dark suit asked Toby to step outside the room to escape the noise of a Madness tribute band going by the name of Bonkers. Toby, drunk and floating on the sort of cloud which academic success provides, was only too happy to oblige.

The man, fortyish and balding, led him out onto a balcony which overlooked the main green, proffered his right hand and congratulated him on his exam results.

Later, Toby admitted he should immediately have asked the stranger how he knew what grades he had attained – and how he knew who he was. At the time, of course, it didn't matter because success is the most potent drug of all, particularly when supplemented by alcohol which had ranged from lager to Babycham.

The man introduced himself as Mr Bramley from the current government's Home Office. Anyone would have been impressed, and Toby most definitely was. Mr Bramley outlined a proposal and agreed to meet him the following day in one of Oxford's finer eateries, The Trout in Wolvercote; the sort of place you go only if rich or invited.

Toby was late for his lunch date but, nonetheless, Mr Bramley welcomed him warmly, ushering him to a prize table inside a huge bay window overlooking the Thames. Mr Bramley's description of himself proved to be somewhat misleading. He did work under the umbrella of the Home Office, but he had spent the last five years assigned to what he described as "a very special unit". It was the inclusion of the word 'very' which ensured Toby's attention.

They spoke for two hours, only occasionally bothering to pick at the expensive meals which sat before them. They drank only water, both men anxious to portray an image of solemn sobriety.

Mr Bramley in fact worked at Porton Down, a government establishment which was invariably described by conspiracy theorists and ufologists as a "profoundly" secret site. In fact, it WAS just that – profoundly secret.

Porton Down covers a considerable area slightly to the north-east of Porton, a nondescript outpost of a town within striking distance of Salisbury. On most available maps, the words "Danger Area" surround the entire complex. It is home to the Defence Science and Technology Laboratory, an executive agency of the Ministry of Defence, and is regarded as one of the UK's most sensitive and secretive facilities for the planning and pursuit of military research.

Porton Down holds much more, though, including the Health Protection Agency's Centre for Emergency Preparedness and Response, as well as a science park. The facility had been prompting public debate – and, it must be said, confusion – since its opening back in 1916 as the Royal

Engineers' Experimental Station. The laboratory within the station, self-evidently primitive by today's standards, was built to conduct research into and improve the development of chemical weapons such as chlorine, phosgene and mustard gas for use in the First World War. By 1918, the original two huts had grown into an established camp for more than 1,100 men and officers.

There were, quite naturally, the usual rumours which surround any building which is deemed to be off limits to the lumpenproletariat; namely that the bodies of dead aliens were taken to Porton Down in 2008 after a UFO had crashed into a hillside in the North Wales Berwyn Mountains. Predictably, Toby was fascinated to a degree that, had Mr Bramley pushed a contract across the table at that moment, he would have added his signature without delay or regret.

Mr Bramley's role within the Home Office was, he said, the recruitment of "the most brilliant available minds".

Toby was flattered but still unclear as to precisely what it was he was being offered.

Mr Bramley explained that, with a first in science and maths from one of the world's pre-eminent universities, he would find himself much in demand by research organisations, drug companies and governments the world over. If he accepted the proposal on offer, Toby would work at Porton Down, be handsomely rewarded in terms of salary, enjoy double the amount of holidays available to most civil servants, and ultimately collect a pension which would mean that – at the age of just fifty-five – he could sit back in some ivy-covered cottage in the Home Counties and drink expensive red wine until his liver gave out.

Toby told Diamond, in a voice set on edge by far too much alcohol, that he had asked Mr Bramley on three separate occasions what it was he would be doing inside the very private world of Porton Down. Understandably, he wanted to know what his actual role would be, but his demand for a specific job description was met with the vaguest of outlines which always featured the word 'special'.

Mr Bramley didn't ask him for a definitive answer at that first meeting, but met Toby for a second time a week later. This time it was at London's Savoy Hotel, and Mr Bramley was accompanied by a man in a cheaper suit: Mr Peterson.

Mr Peterson was a man of very few words. He nodded occasionally, as if required to back up one of his colleague's statements, and he coughed at regular intervals in a manner which suggested he would, at that moment, kill his own grandmother for an untipped cigarette.

Mr Bramley explained that Mr Peterson was involved in security matters, and that it was accepted practice for him to meet any potential new recruits.

After small talk which centred around the previous night's football results, Mr Bramley placed a heavy, tanned briefcase on the table and, after some fumbling, produced a file of papers held neatly in place by a blue cover which bore the words, "Home Office". He pushed one piece of A4 paper towards Toby, pointing out a box at the foot which was reserved for a signature. Toby accepted both the proffered pen and the invitation to embark on a journey into the unknown.

Mr Bramley and Mr Peterson departed almost immediately, the former telling Toby that he would receive a recorded-delivery letter inside forty-eight hours which would fill in at least some of the gaps.

That evening, Toby celebrated with a small group of friends and several bottles of Veuve Clicquot at his favourite wine bar. Annoyingly for those invited along to raise a glass, he was unable to answer even the most basic of questions – what? When? Where?

He slept well that night, but his excitement at having found a role which he was assured would be both challenging and exhilarating was tempered by the sense of mystery and uncertainty which hung over his near future.

Two days later, as promised, a letter arrived, delivered by hand by a curious-looking man whose eyes jumped crazily in his head. There was no stamp, just Toby's name and address on the sort of brown envelope which suggested authority.

Despite being alone, Toby decided to play it cool, placing the letter on a table and then making his way into the kitchen to make a coffee. For no good reason other than that he was incredibly apprehensive about the contents, he waited fifteen minutes before tearing open the envelope and unfolding the letter inside.

Having skim-read the usual opening formalities, Toby learned that he was now Deputy Special Advisor (Scientific Research and Future Development) inside Porton Down's Advanced Technology Department.

He was to be paid a small fortune for a four-day week, and Mr Bramley had been correct – he could retire at fifty-five with a handsome pension and, no doubt, the thanks of a grateful nation. He reread the letter three times and was privately pleased that half of his job title was sectioned away inside brackets; it made him feel very important. He was to start in two weeks' time. He was to attach the enclosed pass to his windscreen to guarantee safe passage through the various checkpoints. He was to bring with him enough clothing for an initial two-week stay which would cover his induction and basic training. He was to complete and bring with him the separate form included with his letter of confirmation.

This was a copy of the Official Secrets Act which, if he read the small print correctly, meant he would be jailed or killed if he told anyone what his day job was. He signed without hesitation. Momentarily he felt like James Bond; a man working for his people against the evils of the world. He felt very special – and rather smug.

On July 2nd, 1998, at the age of twenty-four – many, many years before he bumped into Diamond in a queue for coffee – Toby stepped inside Porton Down for the first time, and in so doing made the quantum leap from child to grown-up.

He was astounded by the sheer scale of the place. Getting to the camp's nerve centre was like moving across a war zone – ring after ring of fences and security men; men who had clearly been told to abandon all pretence of manners and decorum once their daily shift opened.

Eventually – and it took fifteen minutes of pass-checking and card-stamping – Toby found himself at what he assumed to be the front door. There to greet him was a squat, rotund man with a cheery face, 1970s glasses and sweaty palms. He introduced himself as Professor Charles Spenithorne, meeter, greeter and head of one of the camp's many units.

The reception area itself was functional and almost antiseptic. No paintings on the walls, no plants – virtually no decoration at all. Clearly, this was a place of work, not play.

As Professor Spenithorne busied himself with the preparation of yet more forms which required the new boy's consideration and then signature, Toby wandered towards a brass railing which surrounded a sunken area he had been unable to gauge the depth or scale of from the main desk. The view which unfurled beneath almost sucked the breath of out of him. He counted at least eight levels of steel, glass, balconies and workstations – and there were people; hundreds of them milling around like ants at the bottom of a bucket. The place was vast. It was immediately clear to Toby that at least ninety per cent of Porton Down was underground, hidden away from those with prying eyes and suspicious minds.

Professor Spenithorne ushered him into a lift and began a brief tour of the facility. It was a wholly pointless exercise as Toby had stopped listening to his host the very second he had leaned forwards and gazed over the brass railing. The population was a mix of those in white coats carrying clipboards, and soldiers carrying weapons. Once again, Toby felt rather like James Bond.

Toby admitted that his first week – or first four days – had come and gone in a fuzzy mist of disbelief and absolute wonder. The checklist of departments and sections Professor Spenithorne had armed him with suggested he had visited as many as thirty separate units. He had been introduced to chemists, physicists, astronomers, biologists, microbiologists, engineers, architects, doctors, nurses, military officials, security chiefs, mathematicians, experts in space travel, experts in the treatment of terminal illness, the man who bred the mice for the lab experiments… even the head chef, a gloriously loud export from Merseyside who could see the humour in everything and who could find fault in no one.

On day four, Toby was introduced to the man under whose tutelage he would spend the next sixteen years; a well-built man called Dr Clive Stockwell who spoke in a barely audible whisper but who, as Toby was to swiftly discover, delivered common sense each and every time his lips moved.

Dr Stockwell took Toby into his office, a neat and tidy room where reference books rose from floor to ceiling against three walls. In measured tones, he provided a brief verbal CV of a career which would have many peaks but no apparent troughs, before slowly outlining what his 'unit' was involved with, deep beneath the Wiltshire countryside.

Toby was joining a team of just six; a small group which Dr Stockwell wished to see expanded, but, he insisted, a hugely gifted collection of individuals who got on well together and who regarded work as a passion rather than a necessary chore.

Toby yawned and looked at Diamond in a manner which suggested he had merely served up the hors d'oeuvres and was readying himself to wheel in a main course of some substance and style.

"There's more, isn't there?" asked Diamond.

"Yes, there's so much more. But I'm tired, and if I go into any more detail I will breach the Official Secrets Act and will become – believe it or not – an official enemy of the state. Trust me when I say these people don't exactly fuck around. At the slightest suggestion that someone, somewhere has breached protocol or is about to breach protocol, they move very quickly – and they take decisive action."

"What – they just kill people? That can't be right, mate."

"I don't know what they do exactly, but let's put it this way: people who have crossed the line have a habit of disappearing. One minute they are working away at their desk, laughing and joking; the next they have gone and the desk has either been cleared or there's someone else sitting there. I think they must have some sort of waiting list for jobs at Porton Down – a bit like the one for Manchester United season tickets."

"Has anyone you worked alongside disappeared?"

"Not from our team, no… but there was a bloke in the next office who went. When we asked what had happened to him we were told not to ask. So we didn't pursue it. Maybe he just got bored and quit."

"Or maybe he was taken out into a field and beaten to death with a big piece of wood."

"Do you seriously think they would do that? Of course they wouldn't – they'd use a gun, or a speeding car, or an 'accidental' overdose. Anyway, he went, and within a few days most of us couldn't even remember his name," added Toby.

Both men agreed that the night was no longer young and that their bodies were crying out for sleep. Diamond headed for a spare room which was bigger, more stylish and a damned sight cooler than his own bedroom, and was asleep within minutes.

His last waking thought was: would Toby wish to continue his story, his revelations, when stone-cold sober?

The morning was almost over by the time the pair rose to sit opposite each other across a table of untouched toast and hot, steaming coffee.

"Wow – that was some night. That wine was rather powerful. It was like rocket fuel, which probably means it was produced at Porton Down, right?" said Diamond.

"I wish. It is good stuff. If you treat it with the respect which all good wines deserve, it is wonderful. Unfortunately, we treated it like some cheap house red in an Indian restaurant. You're supposed to sip and savour, not drink like cold beer on a warm day. Anyway, glad you enjoyed," said Toby.

"I did – and I also enjoyed the conversation. Hand on heart, I'd no idea what you were involved in up at that place."

"You still don't, Steve. You still don't."

"Are you going to tell me more, elaborate?"

"I shouldn't, but I have always loathed the secrecy and the deception which is such a key component of what we do there. I could die tomorrow and no one – not even my family and closest friends – would have any idea what I have been doing for the past decade-and-a-half. When they ask, as they do often, I simply say it is scientific research which is all very dull and not worth talking about."

"Is it? Dull and not worth talking about, I mean."

"You must be joking," said Toby, with his first smile of the day.

Diamond left shortly afterwards, making a vague agreement that they would meet either later that day or the following evening. It was Monday, and the Indian summer had vanished to be replaced by a blustery, unpleasant day. As the wind blew and the rain fell, Diamond mentally totted up the full extent of what now appeared to be full and proper unemployment. No money, no colleagues, restricted mental activity, far too much free time.

He decided to place reality before natural instinct and headed to the nearest job centre, which stood on St John's Road close to Wembley Arena. He had been before on countless occasions and always found the staff – if not his fellow clients – to be pleasingly polite. It didn't matter how you were dressed, how you spoke or your general demeanour – you were treated with respect and civility. It may have been a rather shallow attempt to make the unwanted feel wanted again but, in Diamond's opinion, it did work.

They had nothing at all to excite Diamond. He could apply to be a shelf stacker in a supermarket, a call centre 'operative' or a trainee plumber. There just didn't seem to be any demand for campaigning journalists, beer tasters or test pilots.

His day having reached an anticlimax much sooner than expected, Diamond headed home. Before immersing himself in wall-to-wall news bulletins, he booted up his laptop and typed, "Porton Down" into a search engine.

There was much to read, but very little which differed from Toby's basic description of a hole in the ground which held many a secret. The photos were, however, interesting, as it didn't appear to be quite as austere as his friend had described; it looked like a cheap hotel attached to the side of an Eastern European airport.

Diamond's desperation for money prompted him to ferret around in his small attic space in search of the one thing he owned which held value – his collection of *Doctor Who* memorabilia. He laid the various pieces – twenty-seven in all – out on the table and then scanned eBay and various other sites where nerds gather in their masses in an attempt to place a rough value on prized possessions. He reckoned that, if he could prise top dollar out of a fellow enthusiast, he might, just, reach £500 – hardly enough to start a new life in the colonies, but sufficient to pay his electric and gas bills and also to enjoy several heavy nights out.

Depressed that, having arrived as a mature adult, he had virtually nothing to show for his journey, Diamond called Toby and left a message saying he was going to end it all but did he fancy one last night out before the curtain fell?

He was asleep when Toby returned his call an hour later, the television showing the exact same news bulletin he had been watching when his eyelids had succumbed to gravity.

"If you intend hanging yourself, make sure you place several towels beneath your feet before you do," said Toby. "It is really messy and it wouldn't be fair on the landlord – he'd never get the various stains out of the carpet."

"Thanks, mate," said Diamond.

"So, you want one last supper, eh? OK, sounds good. There's something I wanted to tell you anyway, so let's meet around 8pm. Not The King's Arms, I'm sick to death of that place. Meet me at The Rubicon wine bar down by the old arches and we will make merry and celebrate your last day on earth."

"Great. Bring money, mate. I'm broke," said Diamond.

As ever, Diamond was early, Toby late. It didn't matter as there were more waiters than customers in the bar; a stylish tapas-style place which had once been a pet shop.

They got the food out of the way immediately, devouring a variety of dishes of dubious quality.

Having moved to the rear of the bar, an area which was cordoned off to guarantee the privacy of the D-list celebrities who occasionally called in, Toby ordered a bottle of South African red before staring his friend full in the face and announcing, "I'm quitting my job."

When you don't have any money, it matters far more than when you do. Diamond's immediate response was to ask, "But what about the neat pension you're guaranteed?"

"Believe it or not, the old saying is true – there is actually more to life than money. I like money only because it is necessary. Money is a bit like wine and cheese toasties, insomuch as you can't live without it."

"Something happened at work? You fallen out with that Dr Frankenstein chap?"

"Stockwell is his name – and no, I haven't. I have simply reached a dead end, a brick wall. I think Stockwell probably has too. I have been told that what I have been working on for almost twelve years is now an ex-project. In Home Office speak, that means it never existed, it never occurred, it never mattered and all details of its existence will be erased from the records. It's gone – and with it the enthusiasm which kept me interested.

"I love the job. I love the people. I love the work. Problem is, I have always hated the place itself; that and the fact that we are classed as the 'invisible men' of science research.

"The security and the secrecy are stifling. I had grown tired of it all long before last week when I sat down with Stockwell and asked him if we were all wasting our time. Astonishingly, he told me that he had spent ninety minutes with the Prime Minister three days earlier discussing the project and its future – or its lack of one."

"That's such a shame, mate," said Diamond. "Have you told them you want to leave yet? Maybe you should have a week off and think it over before doing something rash, something you might regret the next time your car needs a costly repair."

"Nah, I'm leaving, deffo. I have written my resignation letter but not yet handed it over to the powers that be. They will go into meltdown, not so much because I am quitting but because of the security implications. They hate the prospect of someone who knows where the bodies are buried roaming free on what they call 'the outside.'"

Diamond knew better than to try and talk Toby out of something. The last time he had moved down that path they were in a rather classy gents' outfitters in the swankier side of London. Toby had emerged from a changing room sporting the grossest lounge suit Diamond had ever seen.

"Sweet Jesus, man… that's such a bad suit," he'd remarked.

Toby had bought two.

They were halfway through their second bottle when Diamond remembered that Toby had said he had something he wanted to discuss.

"You said you had something you wanted to tell me?" enquired Diamond, as he poured the last dregs of the bottle into his glass.

What followed was another Toby Callaghan monologue, the contents of which were so unbelievable, so utterly bizarre, that Diamond began to wonder if the earnest and erudite man before him was suffering from a stress-related illness.

Toby emptied his glass and ordered yet another bottle before lowering the barriers which had long surrounded the greatest secret of all.

CHAPTER
FOUR

Toby had been working inside Porton Down for just three weeks when Dr Stockwell invited him for lunch. It wasn't quite as grand or exclusive as it sounded as the only catering facility within a fifteen-mile radius was on Floor Four of the complex, where the Scouser with the permanent smile was always holding court.

As they walked, they talked, Dr Stockwell discussing an article in the latest edition of *The Lancet* which suggested that cryogenic freezing had now reached a point in its long evolution where freezer pods were likely to become the next must-have fashion accessory for the rich, the famous and the infamous.

Toby had once read that Walt Disney's head had been removed immediately after his death and plunged into a vat of liquid nitrogen. The plan was to attach it to an available body when a cure had been found for the lung cancer which had killed him back in the mid '60s. Toby, a very poor relater of humour at the best of times, searched in vain for either a smart one-liner or an out-and-out joke relating to Disney and his frozen head, but decided against it at the last minute simply because, during his time working alongside Dr Stockwell, he had never once heard him laugh.

Dr Stockwell ordered the coffees and the sandwiches, both men rejected the dish of the day (a Polish stew featuring an unnamed meat), and the pair sat at a corner table which was overlooked by few and overheard by no one.

"How are you enjoying your new life?" enquired Dr Stockwell, his face cracking with the first genuine smile Toby could recall.

"I am finding it very interesting – strange, but interesting," replied Toby.

"Why strange?"

"Well, I am still not absolutely sure what I am working on. I always feel as though I am working blind, as though all of us on the team are contributing towards a general goal without actually knowing what that goal is. Does that make sense or am I being dumb?"

"It makes a great deal of sense. You are correct in your assertion. We are working on separate issues which will then be drawn together. Some bright spark up in the Human Resources Department – they always have to have a label for things – has decided to call it 'percentage input', insomuch as we all do our little bit. I understand your frustration. I have, in the past, likened it to working on a car production line. You do your bit, you make your part of the car and contribute it, but are then told you will never be permitted to see the finished vehicle," said Dr Stockwell.

"I have been working on inputting streams of data to interact and lie alongside other streams of data. They are then thrown inside what I am assured is one of the most powerful computers in the world – and then yet more data comes out of the other end. I don't know what I am putting in and I haven't a clue what's coming out of the other end. Quite often input and output look identical – well, they do to me, an untrained eye," said Toby.

"I agree that it must be confusing. Like everyone inside Porton Down, you have an extraordinarily high IQ; something which, nine times out of ten, promotes an inquisitive mind.

"My job is multifaceted but my two key roles are to do with observation and timing. That's to say, I watch the new arrivals very, very carefully. I study their mannerisms, their demeanour, their work and, of course, their general progress. That's probably the easy bit, as all I am doing is fulfilling the role of a teacher nurturing a promising student. The tough bit is the timing; and by that I mean I must decide when – or if – you are totally embedded and integrated into our way of doing things. Once I believe that you are, well, then I can tell you much more. I can tell you all, in fact. It is the rabbit-out-of-the-hat moment – thing being, I have to be certain that the rabbit will remain loyal and won't scamper off into the distance," said Dr Stockwell.

Toby threw back his coffee, looked at his mentor and said, "I do loyalty but I don't do scampering, Doctor."

"Good – then take the deepest of breaths and listen very closely. What I will tell you is known only to some of my team, a few members of the hierarchy here, Ministers, Prime Ministers and Presidents. Oh, and the top men in the military in various countries across the globe," said Dr Stockwell. "As you will have noticed, at the far end of our unit, down Corridor B, is a very large metal door which is set behind two preliminary security barriers, or 'spaces' as they are called here. To even get to the metal door, which is twelve inches thick and which would, I'm told, survive a nuclear attack, you need a variety of security codes and voice-recognition accreditation. You haven't been anywhere near it as your security level at present is 'C' and you need a big fat 'A' to get through."

"I did wander down to take a look when no one was looking," confided Toby.

"No problem, that's human nature. I did precisely the same thing within two weeks of my arrival more than twenty years ago. It isn't actually a problem as it would be easier to land a date with Scarlett Johansson than to get through the various checkpoints."

"So what's hiding behind the mystery door, Doctor? The Loch Ness monster? Walt Disney's head?" asked Toby.

"I think we were offered those but turned them down on the grounds that they weren't interesting enough," said Dr Stockwell, smiling. "No, what we have inside the vault is arguably the single most important item produced by the human race – certainly the most astonishing and quite possibly the most dangerous. Have you ever heard of *Die Glocke*, Toby?"

"No. Should I have?" said Toby, his hands shaking ever so slightly as they rested on his knees beneath the table.

"Probably not. *Die Glocke* is German for 'The Bell'. You'll still be none the wiser, Toby, so I will explain as best I can. To some *Die Glocke* is one of history's greatest inventions, a fairy story come true which had its roots deep inside the Second World War; a time when it was almost impossible for even the most learned of men to slide a cigarette paper between fact and fiction.

"Towards the end of 1944 it was apparent to anyone with a basic understanding of warfare that Adolf Hitler's German Reich was not going to rule the world for a thousand years as he had promised, and was in fact perilously close to complete capitulation. The assault on Russia had failed; the Allies, backed by forces from the United States, were reclaiming previously lost ground; and many of Hitler's acolytes were actively talking of either surrender or mutiny.

"In his desperation, Hitler sought to accelerate a project which he had initiated back in the late 1930s; one which was designed to construct a weapon so unique and devastating it would turn logic on its head and win the war within a matter of months, maybe weeks. That weapon was *Die Glocke* – or the *Wunderwaffe*, the so-called 'Wonder Weapon'.

"Rumour spread almost as fast as famine in the very darkest days of World War II and there was genuine concern in London, Washington and Moscow that Hitler's scientists may indeed have somehow produced a top-secret technological device. Certainly Winston Churchill was sufficiently concerned as to call his inner circle together for a 'never happened' meeting at the House of Commons in mid 1944.

"That was just before the Nazis underscored their complete mastery of deadly innovation by unleashing the V2 unmanned rockets on several European cities. The V2, the Vengeance Weapon 2, was a technically brilliant invention; a massively powerful rocket which was both unerringly accurate and totally devastating. It was a single-stage rocket fuelled by alcohol and liquid oxygen. It stood almost fifty feet tall, had a payload capacity of 2,200 pounds and a top speed in excess of 3,500 miles per hour. It was a killing machine, and it worked. The consensus is that, had the Nazis completed its construction twelve months earlier than they did, we could all be speaking German now. Thousands upon thousands died in London, Antwerp and Liege after they first started to fly in early October 1944.

"Many have been given credit for the V2, but the two men who drove the programme – admittedly using many thousands who were forced into slave labour – were Wernher von Braun and Hans Kammler.

"They were totally different men in terms of attitude and outlook. Von Braun was a pure scientist, a genius. Kammler rose to a very high rank inside the feared SS and was interested in science and technological advancement only as a means of producing weapons of mass destruction. In many respects, he was the archetypal Nazi monster; the man who oversaw the installation of the cremation apparatus at Auschwitz-Birkenau, and someone whom even Heinrich Himmler was moved to describe as 'the very personification of ruthlessness' – and that's some recommendation from a madman like Himmler.

"Come the end of the war it was clear that both men were likely guilty of grave war crimes, but while a host of their contemporaries went to the gallows in the aftermath of the Nuremberg trials, von Braun and Kammler actually had the red carpet rolled out for them by the United States. Their expertise was such that the Allies wanted them alive and contributing to a space programme very much in its infancy, and not dangling from executioner Albert Pierrepoint's rope in a converted shed.

"Both were moved to the States as part of Operation Paperclip, which saw a large number – much larger, I suspect, than has ever been admitted to by the authorities – of key Nazi scientists adopted by the USA; a country, in my view, which has never boasted a conscience. In essence they had traded secrets and expertise not only for their freedom, but quite possibly for their lives. It was deal forged in the bowels of hell – but one which, ultimately, was to ensure that it was the Americans and not the Russians who won the great global PR battle and landed the first man on the moon. That's if you believe Neil Armstrong and Co actually went there, of course… but that's another discussion for another day.

"Whilst Kammler didn't seem to contribute very much to anything of note after his arrival in the land of the free, von Braun, now released from the shackles of designing merely to kill, prospered and became the leading light within the USA's post-war rocket programme. In fact he became known as 'the Father of Rocket Science', and it was he who developed the *Saturn V* booster rocket which was to guarantee the success of the 1969 Apollo mission. He was some man, who, after he had moved from the wrong side of the tracks, almost became a national hero in his adopted country," said Dr Stockwell.

"I didn't know any of that," said Toby. "I assumed all Nazis of note were either executed or fled to live in comfortable beach houses in South America. So, what do we have behind the thick door at the end of Corridor B? A V2 rocket?"

"No. Nothing quite that boring. We have *Die Glocke*. We have the Wonder Weapon, Toby. We've had it here since the '70s," said Dr Stockwell.

"We have? I'm confused, because you said earlier that *Die Glocke* was… errrrrrrr… I think you said it was something from a fairy story," said Toby.

"I said that some *believed* it was a fairy story, a myth. In truth, I have to say that most still believe it was nothing more than another piece of very persuasive Nazi propaganda. I believed that – right up until the day in the late '80s when I was ushered into a vast, unlit laboratory in the south of Nevada. I had been invited across to the States by a man who was, you might say, my counterpart there.

"All I had been told was that I was coming to see something very special, and that I should approach the viewing with an open mind. It was all very alien to me – special agents carting me around in very large limousines, security checks every fifteen minutes, underground bunkers.

"It was dark in the room. All I could make out was something large inside that darkness, sat right in the centre of the floor. The importance of the moment became crushingly clear to me when I saw that it was the Vice President of the

United States who touched a button to flood the room with neon light. And there it was, standing in a massive glass box: *Die Glocke*.

"At first, I truly wasn't sure what it was I was looking at. As its name suggested, it looked like a huge bell – a very old one. It was probably about fifteen feet tall and maybe nine feet across at its base. Although I couldn't reach forward and touch it, it seemed to be made of a particularly dense heavy metal. There was some rusting towards the top, where there sat what I would describe as a cap constructed from a different, lighter metal.

"The first thing to attract my attention – although it shouldn't have been – was the writing which ran around that base, all the way round. I say writing, but it wasn't; there were no words, just a series of small illustrations like Egyptian hieroglyphics. I had spent a year, post university, studying the various Egyptian dynasties, but I'd never seen anything like this before. It may have been nothing more than a decorative flourish; I honestly don't know.

"My concentration on the base was such that I had neglected to take in *Die Glocke*'s most striking and obvious feature – the swastika which stood at least two foot high, midway up the main belly of the object. The swastika remains, in my opinion, the one emblem which can reduce virtually all who see it to reflective silence. It has come to represent the badge of ultimate evil; a reminder that when a population is driven to its knees by looming economic oblivion, that population can be led forward by the rhetoric of one madman and convinced that the deeds of the Devil are wholly acceptable.

"I was speechless. I had been stood in front of the object for a good ten minutes before I turned to the Vice President, asking him, as if he was a casual acquaintance, what the damned thing was. He smiled, and simply said, '*Die Glocke*, The Bell… the so-called Wonder Weapon.'

"Of course, like everyone else who was involved in scientific research which may have ultimately benefited the military, I had heard of *Die Glocke* – but, as I said previously, like everyone else I assumed it was a figment of Joseph Goebbels' fertile mind. If a good PR man doesn't have a story to spin he will invent one, especially when the Russian Army is encircling Berlin with daggers drawn," said Dr Stockwell.

Toby was staring at his boss in something akin to disbelief. They had already been talking for more than forty-five minutes but Dr Stockwell wasn't done, hopping to his feet to replenish their empty coffee cups and taking the opportunity to check his mobile for messages. He then returned to the table and gave Toby the sort of paternal smile which is usually reserved for moments when a child simply isn't understanding what his father is saying. Toby was understanding everything – but still it didn't make any real sense to him.

"Any questions so far?" asked Dr Stockwell.

"Hundreds, but I think it might be best if you carry on. Where and when did this happen? You said Nevada?" said Toby.

"I can't remember precisely, but Dan Quayle was the Vice President who turned the lights on so it must have been between 1989 and 1993. Yes, it was in Nevada – the place they now refer to as Area 51, which you will have heard of. The Americans now call it their Porton Down, which always makes me laugh as it was they and not us who started this wholesale subterfuge.

"Area 51 is every bit as odd and secretive as they say. I'm told they have flying saucers and alien bodies in there, but all I saw was a restroom with a CCTV camera trained on the urinals, the executive canteen and, of course, *Die Glocke*.

"Having looked through the glass at what Mr Quayle was moved to describe as 'the eighth wonder of the world', we adjourned for lunch. I had an appetite only for more information. Unfortunately, I was placed in between Quayle and his private secretary; an irritating woman who ate with her mouth open and her eyes closed.

"My inclination was to grill Quayle for more answers, more information, but having read somewhere that he wasn't the brightest pin in the box and often struggled to chew gum and walk at the same time, I opted for the sort of 'how's-your-family' small talk which passes the time but which also irritates both parties.

"My sense of excitement was such that it wasn't until I was flying back to London that I realised I had broken bread with someone who was just a heartbeat or an assassin's bullet away from being the most powerful man on earth. When I got home my son told me off for not getting him to autograph a napkin."

"How long were you inside Area 51 for?" asked Toby.

"A couple of days – or, as I remember writing in my diary, 'a couple of daze'. I spent most of the time there in an office looking at files, photographs and charts, when all I really wanted to do was get inside that glass box and examine The Bell; I just wanted to touch it to make sure it wasn't some sort of hologram or papier-mâché model.

"I did eventually get what I had wished for – just before I was taken back to the airport to return home – but that only came after I had been declared trustworthy and was presented with the facts about *Die Glocke*.

"Even to me, a veteran scientist at the top of my game, the facts were astounding. They say there's nothing quite so unbelievable as the truth. Inside forty-eight hours my own little world order – how I saw, perceived and expected things – was turned upside down and inside out by an ugly piece of metal which, at the time, was more than five decades old.

"I had just about tired of the rather dry presentation of facts when the lead scientist inside Area 51, I forget his name, asked me the most rhetorical question ever: would I care to have a closer look at *Die Glocke* before I departed? I didn't walk back to the laboratory; like a three-year-old child, I skipped.

"Face to face with the object, I was again totally transfixed. It held no beauty at all, but the logical part of my brain was telling me it had never existed in the first place, so I felt rather like Sir Arthur Conan Doyle when he convinced himself that the Cottingley Fairies were real back in 1920.

"Someone, somewhere to my rear, pushed a button and the front section of the glass case – I was later told it was bulletproof glass and three-quarters of an inch thick – moved effortlessly away. Without the prism of its glass shield, *Die Glocke* looked a good deal older and, if anything, even more menacing. There was more rust than I had initially observed, and there was more than a little surface damage to the panels which featured the large swastika.

"First I studied the markings on the base, but still couldn't see anything which formed a pattern or hinted at a code I might understand. I moved around the object. To the rear was its entrance; a sealed hatch. On either side were two rather small windows or ports which held thickened glass and which clearly had not been cleaned for many years.

"As I stared, a voice from within the midst of a growing throng at the back of the room said, 'Feel free to touch it, Dr Stockwell.' I never require a second invitation. It was cold and, whilst this was not possible, felt almost clammy to the touch, which struck me as unusual as the room in which it was kept was almost certainly temperature-controlled.

"I tapped on the main body, just to the side of the swastika. There was a dull echo from within; a sound which seemed to reverberate around the object. I tapped again, this time on the hatch – same sound, same curious echo.

"I turned to the men in white coats and asked what was inside. An unseen hand flicked an unseen switch and the hatch which was directly in front of me began to move as does an aircraft's door: initially outwards and then inwards, before sliding away to its resting position to the left. What struck me was that the movement of heavy metal upon heavy metal was achieved in almost complete silence; the parts didn't move, they slid effortlessly. *Die Glocke* wasn't pretty but it was clearly a precision piece of engineering of the very highest calibre. And it was old, very old.

"Urged to enter the machine by someone I took to be an engineer rather than a scientist, I moved forwards, placed a hand on either side of the hatch and peered inside. There was a smell of damp and semi-corroded metal. The interior space was very limited; the gap between floor and ceiling probably no more than six feet. This meant that the bottom half of the machine was the business section. Whatever drove it, powered it, moved it, gave it life was stored away towards the base behind the indecipherable hieroglyphics.

"I had never been in a diving bell – far too scared of deep water for that – but that is what it resembled. There was just one chair – faux leather, seat belt, armrests and headrest. In front of the chair was a panel of instruments; maybe twenty-five small glass windows with gauges and dials. There were several buttons – some green but predominantly red in colour.

"What was missing was a means of steering, driving, flying or simply moving the thing. There was nothing resembling a hands-on wheel or lever. Whatever it had been designed for, whatever took place when it was switched on and running, occurred with the 'pilot' safely strapped into his seat.

"For such a mythical object, it gave up so few clues. I stepped away from it and walked towards what was now quite a sizeable audience. I had many questions I wanted answered but, realising it would be foolish to start demanding specifics, I used a tried-and-trusted method taught to me by an old school friend who went on to work for the *Daily Mail*. Journalists quite often struggle to settle on the top points of a breaking news story. When there are so many intriguing subplots it can be difficult to find the one true 'line' – the intro, the headline-maker. He always told me you must imagine you are running away from a major incident when a friend across the road shouts to you, asking what has just happened. Your initial response is the story. That one-sentence answer is what you must start your report with.

"And so I simply asked, 'What is it, and does it work?'

"There wasn't exactly a clamour to respond to my double question. After much shuffling of feet and much rustling of papers, a small man on the periphery of the gathering said, 'It works – but as to what it is, we don't really know. That's to say, we believe it to be capable of things we thought impossible. It is a machine from the past, the construction of which really shouldn't have been possible until the far, far future.'

"'So it does work – it can do something?' I asked.

"'Yes, Dr Stockwell, it works – and it can do things which even the great minds of da Vinci, Einstein and Hawking would have struggled to comprehend,' said the nameless man from behind a clipboard which he seemed almost to be using as a screen.

"'OK. So what does it do?' I asked, running the risk of sounding both impatient and repetitive.

"A man in a flannel suit emerged from the pack and led me gently by the elbow into a small office to the rear of the laboratory. Much the same as in Porton Down, there were no adornments – no plants, no pictures on the walls, no framed photos of happy, smiling family members on a desk which had only a red telephone at one end and a pot of pens at the other.

"'My name is Martin Zapruder – and, no, before you ask, I did not shoot the home movie of the JFK assassination! I run one of the many departments here at Groom Lake. We never refer to it as Area 51; we leave that to those on the outside who seem to think we share afternoon tea with otherworldly beings in between working out how to build superior weapons of mass destruction.

"'Your questions – and your obvious sense of unease – are perfectly understandable. I still feel uneasy when I walk into that laboratory and stare at *Die Glocke*, though I have to say that my apprehension is always mixed with great excitement. I am a privileged man, Dr Stockwell. I and a select few – maybe fifty or so – have borne witness to things we thought impossible. We have stood inside that room and witnessed history unfolding before our eyes.

"'I could rattle on for hours about the awe and the glory of that lump of ageing metal, but I won't. You asked, I believe, two questions: what is it, and does it work? Correct?' he asked.

"I nodded, keeping quiet so as not to disrupt his flow.

"'While we believe it was initially conceived as some form of ultimate weapon – the so-called *Wunderwaffe*, a weapon to end the war – we cannot, so far, find a function for it in that particular branch of physics or munitions. It isn't a bomb, it doesn't propel laser beams or launch projectiles, there are no guns, be they standard or hitherto unheard of.

"'We spent the first six months doing little more than X-raying it in case it exploded. It was more than a year before we received the presidential green light to start taking it apart – and that was only after we had agreed to build a concrete blast pit. Those in the White House were, I am reliably informed, more concerned about collateral damage to the base than they were about the possible loss of human life should the thing opt to self-destruct.

'We took it apart very slowly, very carefully, piece by piece – and there were lots of pieces. We logged everything, tested everything, photographed everything – and then we put it all back together again. It was like doing a vast 3D jigsaw puzzle,' Zapruder said.

"At this point my frustration finally got the better of me and, possibly in a raised voice, I asked again, 'What does it do, Professor Zapruder?'

'It moves,' he said.

"How? I have been inside it and it has no means of moving anywhere. No wheels, no jet-engine system, no propulsion system of any description. It doesn't even have a steering mechanism,' I said.

"It moves through time,' responded Professor Zapruder, with a face so straight, so serious he could have been announcing the unexpected death of one of my close relatives."

CHAPTER

FIVE

Toby could no longer remain either quiet or seated. Pushing himself to his feet, he stared at Dr Stockwell before shouting, "What? No way... no way on earth."

As the chef looked on, amused and bemused, Dr Stockwell motioned for Toby to sit down and be quiet.

"Sorry, sorry," he muttered. "But you can't be serious. You just can't be. Time travel?! It's impossible."

"I am serious, Toby. Maybe now you will understand why it is we work underground, beneath soil, rock and layer upon layer of secrecy and bureaucracy. Professor Zapruder's story still has a way to run. Are you bored, or do you want to hear the rest?"

"Bored? You must be joking. This is unbelievable. It's not a *Candid Camera* stunt, is it? I may wake up shortly with a hangover and an old episode of *The Twilight Zone* playing on the television," said Toby.

"OK, but this may take another two hours, so let's move away from here and go to my office. The revealing of what is possibly mankind's greatest ever secret is not what I would consider a spectator sport."

"Yes, of course. And you can trust me, Doctor."

"If I didn't think I could trust you implicitly, your stay at Porton Down would have been somewhat shorter than a week," Dr Stockwell said, before leading the way to his office which stood just off Corridor B. Inside, he handed Toby a bottle of mineral water before rewinding his memory by a quarter of a century and resuming his story.

"My reaction to Professor Zapruder's claim that *Die Glocke* was capable of moving through time was the same as yours. I simply didn't believe him. It couldn't be correct; it had to be nonsense. It took me several minutes to regain my lost composure – although the good professor later told me that the realignment of my senses was very swift compared to some others who had been given the same news. Once I had settled down, Professor Zapruder picked up where he had left off.

"'It's true, Dr Stockwell. *Die Glocke* is a time machine. We feel it may also be several other things, but those better qualified than I suggest it wasn't finished; that the war's end probably left it incomplete. It sounds ridiculous to think that, having built a machine which would defy virtually every known rule in our universe, there may have been more to come. Quite what its additional qualities – its add-ons – would have been, I dare not think, but we must always remember that this thing was not built to further mankind but to ensure that one nation won a war and thus controlled the planet.

"'I should, perhaps, explain where we got The Bell from. We didn't just pick it up in a garage sale. At the end of the war, we, the Americans, with the full agreement of Winston Churchill's UK government, brought over the elite members of the Nazi science pool. The Germans had their shortcomings – a predilection for the annihilation of several races, for example

– but their scientists were the best; streets ahead of anything the Allies could muster.

"The leading light was, as I am sure you will know, von Braun; a brilliant man of innovation and vision who just happened to find himself working on the wrong side of the equation when good locked horns with latent evil back in 1939. Von Braun came up with the idea of *Die Glocke* and it was he who oversaw its development and construction. From von Braun's own written testimonies and from the evidence recovered from the SS Records Office in Berlin, we don't believe that Hitler or any of his ruling elite had any idea at all what was being developed hundreds of miles away in a quiet backwater which was dominated by coal mining, not warmongering.

"The documents seized after Berlin had fallen suggest that Hitler believed von Braun was developing a more advanced and far deadlier version of the V2 rocket – a weapon which almost effected a change in the balance of things as both sides began to run out of munitions and soldiers. That may well have been the case because, as I said, we don't believe that time travel was *Die Glocke*'s primary objective. Personally, I believe that von Braun, a Nazi sympathiser but never a hardcore devotee, realised the game was up probably twelve months before Hitler took his own life, and so stopped working on his invention's capability as a weapon and focused on the many other possibilities.

"'Von Braun was always rather evasive when asked about the purpose of *Die Glocke*. He politely answered all the questions – but always with a wry smile, as though he was playing an elaborate game. Sadly, he died back in 1977 so we won't be getting any additional information from the man who was arguably the greatest mind in history.

"'Having said that, he was sometimes thought to be playing fast and loose with the truth. We didn't even know of the machine's existence until he told us after being offered the chance to relocate to the States after the war. I have studied the transcripts of his original interviews – and they went on for seven weeks – and it was while he was talking about the manufacture of the V2 that he casually made mention of *Die Glocke*. He described it as the ultimate machine one which he said would "change everything". I think the military assumed he was referring to the outcome of the war, but clearly he meant change everything for mankind. He described himself as one of the "fortunate few", explaining that more than 130 people – sixty of them top-class scientists – had been shot dead by a unit of the SS in late 1944 in order to conceal the truth about The Bell.

"When asked where it was, he was only too happy to tell. It was his unique invention, his baby, and he wanted it back. He said it was secreted in a large camouflaged hangar close to the South Pole, where it had been taken by U-boat two months before the fall of Berlin. It sounded implausible until von Braun revealed that Hitler and Himmler had plans to build a large base in Antarctica in the belief that they would be able to establish contact with alien life forms. It was to be a landing site for UFOs. Yes, it all sounds a little crazy, but we are dealing with the Nazis here; a monstrous group who believed anything and everything was possible and who pushed back the accepted parameters of scientific progress.

"We, the Americans, went looking for *Die Glocke* in 1947 – and there it was, exactly where von Braun had said it would be. It was the solitary object in a vast hangar, standing on a wooden plinth, covered by tarpaulin. The base itself was more of a shanty town, a construction site which looked as though it had been abandoned in a hurry. They recovered seventy-eight frozen bodies from the snow, each and every one of them sporting the swastika.

"'That is classified information, as is every word which has fallen out of my mouth since we started our fireside chat. But I suppose you know that. We work on different sides of the Atlantic but we are governed by the same rules, the same red tape.

"'Anyway, *Die Glocke* was transported back to the States under cover of darkness. It was initially taken to a military base in Ohio where it was subjected to a cursory examination by people who had been given no indication at all as to what it was – or what von Braun claimed it was. I saw their report. They described it – correctly – as "a bell-like object with curious markings". They were unable to even make a stab at what its purpose or function was. The best they could come up with was "a sturdy object which may or may not have been designed as the casing for an explosive device". Odd, really, as there's a seat inside and the Germans didn't do kamikaze.

"It stayed in Ohio for years. No one bothered to ask von Braun any more questions about it; no one could be bothered to subject it to exhaustive tests. It was regarded as a Nazi curio. There's even a photograph in the files of the base commander's kids staging a tea party inside *Die Glocke*. If they'd pushed the wrong buttons in the right order they could have gone back and watched their old man getting married – or viewed their own conception.

"By this time von Braun had not merely been dropped into our "race for the stars", as JFK called it; he was damn near running the entire programme. He didn't mention *Die Glocke* and we had stopped asking him about it. Bearing in mind what he had achieved with The Bell, helping to build the rockets for the Apollo programmes must have been absolute child's play for him. He could probably have done it with his eyes closed.

"'*Die Glocke* only ended up here at Groom Lake years after von Braun died at the age of sixty-five. It was moved simply because the Ohio site was "reclassified", as the military say. That means, with this site, they had dug a deeper hole in which to hide away their secrets. Once here, it was again neglected. We had all the files and the records so we knew what it could be – we just didn't have the funding or the inclination to start looking for a solution which may not have existed. It was locked away for a long time. As far as I know, no one requested to see it for at least nine years. It was housed in a wooden crate in a large storage room alongside countless other items which the conspiracy theorists would sell their very souls to see, added Professor Zapruder."

Toby was again restless. He knew it would be wrong to interrupt and he knew that patience inevitably draws its own rich reward – but he was young and he wanted to cut to the chase. "Doctor, forgive me for interrupting but I'm the sort of person who reads the last page of a pulp-fiction thriller when he's only halfway through the book. I don't 'do' suspense very well – so may I ask another question?" he said, almost wincing.

"Of course. I know this must be frustrating for you, Toby. Impatience is one of the joys of youth," said Dr Stockwell.

"I accept everything you have said. It doesn't compute too well but I appreciate that I am dealing with incontrovertible facts here. The impossible has suddenly become possible and the unreal is now reality. Two questions – how did *Die Glocke* work, and how do they know it worked? I am taking a leap of faith here and presuming that they must have got it working: they must have done it, they must have found the 'On' switch, they must have time-travelled?"

"You are correct. They did, to a limited degree. Perhaps understandably, you haven't yet asked what I would regard as the 'pure' physics question. At the moment you are listening and reacting as would a layman. Nothing wrong with that, because the magnitude of the information you have taken on board over the past few hours is simply huge. What you should be asking – what the scientist in you should be asking – is: 'How does it work?' Dr Stockwell said.

"Yes, of course. You're right," said Toby, almost feeling that he had been scolded for an apparent lack of professionalism.

Dr Stockwell promptly started laughing; his initial low-pitched chuckle rising to a belly laugh which must have been audible several corridors away. Heads would have turned, as Porton Down wasn't exactly a variety club. When he had regained control, Dr Stockwell smiled broadly, open his arms wide and said, "We don't know."

"You don't know what, Doctor?" asked Toby.

"We don't know how the fucking thing works," said Dr Stockwell. It was the first and only time Toby heard his boss use a hardcore swear word.

"Well, I guess that makes the explanation a little bit easier, then," said Toby, also smiling, also enjoying a brief moment of banter.

"When I say we don't know how it works, I am taking a few liberties with the facts as we know them. We know the constituent parts as we have taken The Bell to pieces many, many times, but the greatest minds in this country are at a collective loss as to explain how three tonnes of metal, a great deal of wiring, some spinning discs and a combination of everyday chemicals can see an object move around in time like Dr Who's TARDIS.

"All we have to guide us down a road which is hardly littered with useful signposts are von Braun's debriefing tapes. Professor Zapruder believes there are gaps in the records; he thinks some of the tapes have either gone missing or been destroyed. The Americans – as do we, in truth – have a habit of losing important documents when it best suits.

"So what we have are von Braun's basic outlines as to the theory behind the machine's operation. As I have said, he was a decent enough man as well as a genius, but those who attempted to draw information out of him were always left with the feeling that he wasn't willing to go the full mile – and in physics it is the last part of the race which is absolutely crucial.

"Quite why von Braun decided to withhold certain bits of information we will never know. There were fears in the 1950s that he was still in touch with a group of top Nazis who we know fled Germany and washed up in South America – the actual figures are frightening for those who believed the threat of the Third Reich had been eradicated when the white flag of surrender was raised back in 1945. According to a file I saw whilst inside Area 51, more than nine thousand Nazis escaped to South America – mostly to Argentina – using what the Allies referred to as the 'ratline'. So there were understandable concerns that perhaps von Braun was still in touch with some of them. Certainly several members of the Allies' 'Hall of Infamy' had escaped justice by smuggling themselves out of Europe amid the confusion which invariably follows war – Adolf Eichmann, Josef Mengele and Franz Stangl amongst them.

"The other great fear was that von Braun had overseen the production of more than one *Die Glocke*. Once the capabilities of the machine became clear, that suspicion was passed to both the White House and 10 Downing Street. But the passing of time has served to lessen that initial anxiety, the belief being that if the Nazis were going to make a comeback it would have happened by now.

"I can give you a very basic outline of the theory behind the running of *Die Glocke*, but it is dull stuff unless you have a great passion for the theory of antigravity propulsion and the inertial and vortex properties of radioactive materials. Few do these days.

"Anyway, that's enough for today. I feel drained. I have given that little speech maybe a dozen times, and on each and every occasion it leaves me feeling exhausted. Let's reconvene tomorrow. Don't panic – I will try and fill in the gaps. *Die Glocke* isn't going anywhere," Dr Stockwell added.

"It's here, isn't it? *Die Glocke*, I mean. It's here at Porton Down," said Toby, chancing his arm and holding his breath as might a child.

"Smart boy. Yes it is – it's down at the end of Corridor B behind the big door," said Dr Stockwell, rising to his feet and shuffling towards the exit.

CHAPTER

SIX

"Oh my God, are you fucking serious?" asked Diamond.

"Steve, I have a really vivid imagination but it wouldn't stretch to what I have just told you. There's weird, there's very weird – and then there's Porton Down," said Toby.

"So we have a genuine, twenty-two-carat time machine sitting in the middle of the Wiltshire countryside? The most astonishing invention ever is locked in a cupboard in an underground bunker?"

"Not quite a cupboard – but, yes, that's about the top and bottom of it. We are the Time Lords, the masters of the universe, the guardians of events past and those still to come. In fact, we are probably everything Hitler wanted to be."

Both men were tired: Diamond with the sheer excitement of his friend's extraordinary tale; Toby because he felt as if he had lifted from his shoulders – and, perhaps, his conscience – the very heaviest of weights.

As Toby drove home after dropping off Diamond, he knew that the Official Secrets Act lay in shreds at his feet. He had broken the golden rule, he had talked outside of class, and such was his understanding of the dark arts employed by his own country's security forces that he saw impending retribution writ large across the face of everyone he spoke to or passed in the street. He wasn't living in fear because he trusted Diamond to keep his secret, but, as many had discovered before him, attempting to stuff a genie back into its bottle once it has been summoned and released is no simple task. The lid was off and it probably wouldn't go back on even if he twisted and turned it for an eternity.

Toby slept the sleep of a man whose mind had finally found a little peace and contentment. Diamond couldn't sleep at all, his brain running riot with scenarios and possible outcomes. Unable to calm himself, he rummaged around in his bedside drawer and found his last remaining zopiclone tablet; a useful and effective sleep-inducing drug which his doctor had prescribed more than twelve months ago after he was diagnosed as suffering from anxiety. His girlfriend at the time, Angela, had once mistaken them for painkillers and lost almost two days to the deepest of sleeps – waking up some twenty-four hours after a Coldplay concert she was scheduled to attend with her sister. A narrow escape, Diamond was later to remark.

Some twelve hours later, he crawled back through the foggy mists of induced sleep to a state of relative consciousness. No messages on his mobile or on the landline answering machine. On a small piece of paper torn from a Sunday supplement were written the words "*Die Glocke*"; a reminder that fantasy had indeed touched his world of harsh realities the previous day, and that he must trawl the internet for information about the machine.

As he switched on his laptop he spoke out loud – a common occurrence, but one which was more normally associated with late-night drinking and bouts of woman-related self-pity. "This is fucking ridiculous," he said.

He typed, "*Die Glocke*" into his usual search engine and was astonished to see a return of 312,000 items in 0.43 seconds.

"Can 312,000 people plus Toby be wrong?" he asked. No one was listening, but to Diamond it really didn't matter as it was the ultimate in rhetorical questions.

Having spent an hour skimming through a wide variety of articles, Diamond felt quite smug – he knew the truth and they didn't. They were theorising, guessing, taking wild stabs in the dark. They were also filling the void created by a lack of concrete fact with sheer fantasy. It was almost laughable. Several went so far as to suggest that not only had Hitler had very close encounters of the third kind, but he had, in fact, been guided and advised by aliens living inside his bunker beneath Berlin's Reich Chancellery. It took Diamond several hours to erase from his mind the vision of alien greys with swastika armbands directing operations as Hitler busied himself with getting married to Eva Braun and almost immediately writing his Last Will and Testament.

Diamond was so desperate to call Toby, so desperate to devour more information, but he knew that his friend would be, to the last, a particularly quiet man who valued his privacy almost as much as his reputation.

And so he waited. He fell asleep in the middle of the afternoon, despite an unfolding news-channel story about a major plane crash somewhere in the Indian Ocean, and awoke only when his mobile's raucous signature tune cut through the air.

"Hi, Toby," he said, barely able to disguise the fact that he had been awake for only a few seconds.

"You OK, mate?"

"Yeah. Still struggling to take everything in. I spent an hour looking on the web for stuff about The Bell. There's lots on there – including various drawings of what it is supposed to look like. Are they in any way accurate?"

"I don't know – I haven't seen it yet. I say, 'yet', because I am presuming – well, hoping – that I will be granted an audience with von Braun's creation. I can't believe that Dr Stockwell would lead me up the garden path only to deny me entrance at the last minute."

"You still have stuff to tell me? I want to hear it but I understand you're busy – and you're also breaking the law. Just let me know when you are free and in the mood to talk again."

"It's odd. Yes, I know I am breaking the law – far more than that, in fact – but it is as if I need to do this. They always say that unburdening yourself is a very good form of therapy. I have wanted to shout about what I know for a very long time. With denial comes the sort of frustration which can only be ended by a dose of undiluted truth. Sorry – that all sounds very dramatic, very James Joyce," said Toby. "How you feeling, by the way? Any good news – well, any better news?"

"I'm OK. Good news is in rather short supply, but I am doing fine."

They agreed to meet in The Rubicon again; Diamond liked the wine and Toby enjoyed the lack of customers.

Once they were settled in the same seats they had occupied two days earlier, Diamond sat and waited for his friend to pick up where he had left off. Toby seemed distracted, constantly picking up and setting down the wine bottle, picking at a bunch of wilting flowers which stood in the centre of their table. Diamond feared that he had changed his mind about quitting his job and was regretting having opened his heart.

"So, you were saying? It was... whenever – 1998? – and the professor with the odd name was telling your boss, the good doctor, that The Bell had been shifted to Area 51 but no one was interested in it. That right?" asked Diamond.

"Yes, yes. Zapruder told Dr Stockwell that the machine was locked away because, after it was deemed to be safe, it was classified as more of a curio, a relic, than something which demanded further, sustained examination. At that point Zapruder's unit was spending money it didn't actually have and some members inside the Senate were lobbying for its closure. So, cuts were made – three members of staff were made redundant – and The Bell was slipped into the scientific equivalent of a display box, into cold storage," said Toby.

"Where was I up to? Ah, yes. Dr Stockwell is at Area 51 but is acutely aware that his time is very limited. Porton Down wants him back from Nevada to chair his annual budget meeting, so he has, maybe, another twenty-four hours to drain further information from his host, Zapruder.

"They meet again; a typically American breakfast meeting awash with pancakes, syrup and hot coffee. Knowing that he has limited time, Dr Stockwell decides his best option is not to listen but to talk, so he goes straight in with the most obvious of his many questions. He asks if they have tried *Die Glocke* and if it worked. Before Professor Zapruder can even reply, he asks a second question which takes for granted the answer to the first one. How does it work?

"According to Dr Stockwell, Zapruder sat back, lost in thought for at least sixty seconds, before reaching inside his briefcase and pulling out two files; the first one stamped with the famous legend 'Above Top Secret', and the second one a flimsier affair which held what looked like newspaper cuttings. Dr Stockwell was told to take the files, read them and then destroy them. He wasn't to photocopy, scan or share – he was to take on board the information and then, like a true friend of the United States, destroy the evidence.

"There was a lot of trust going on there because Zapruder didn't really know Dr Stockwell. I think it was a sort of we-are-brothers respect thing. I think Zapruder instinctively knew that he could trust his counterpart from across the Atlantic. Dr Stockwell pointed out that he was heading home that afternoon, and that he wasn't even sure the two of them would ever meet again.

"Astonishingly, Zapruder said they would meet again within twelve to eighteen months – because he would be personally supervising the transfer of *Die Glocke* from Nevada to the UK. Predictably, Dr Stockwell was stunned and asked if the British government had sanctioned the move and agreed to meet the related costs. Zapruder assured him that everything was in place and that The Bell was coming home to Europe," said Toby.

"Bloody hell. I bet the doctor's face was a picture when he was told," said Diamond.

"Obviously, he was thrilled. It was the opportunity of a lifetime, even though chances were he would never be able to tell anyone about it. Almost as if to deliberately torture himself, Dr Stockwell decided against reading anything until he was safely tucked up in his business-class seat clutching a large Scotch.

"I won't bore you with the details, but the main file – the 'Above Top Secret' one – explained, or tried to explain, how *Die Glocke* worked; the theory behind it. It also outlined how they had used it in what was a surprisingly limited way. The second file was a sort of backup to underscore that the first one was a version of the truth which could not, and should not, be called into question.

"Listen, Steve, I have copies of those two files. Dr Stockwell is a man of great honesty and integrity, but after reading them he faced the sort of dilemma which envelops all good men of science at some point – should he do as he had been instructed and destroy them, or keep them on the basis that they were major historical documents of great significance?

"As you now know, he kept them. It was only quite recently that he gave them to me; around the time that our wonderful government had gathered together enough mothballs to cover *Die Glocke* and hide it away forever. They've decided to consign it to the pages of history, and have withdrawn all funding. That's why I now wish to quit, and why Dr Stockwell is sufficiently pissed off to start trusting people like me with the most sensitive documents ever to have seen daylight," Toby added.

"They can't just pretend it doesn't exist and hide it away, surely?" said Diamond.

"That's precisely what they want to do. We have experimented with it, but the general consensus on both sides of the Atlantic is that the whole thing is too dangerous and that we are meddling with something we don't truly understand – something which could alter the destiny of our world.

"I do agree with that to a certain degree, but what's invented will stay invented; you cannot un-ring a bell. It's like someone declaring in 1832 that they don't actually care for the electric dynamo Michael Faraday invented the previous year, and then demanding it be airbrushed from history.

"I could spend the next fortnight outlining the case for destroying *Die Glocke*. It would be a very, very persuasive argument. It is like a superhero story – in the wrong hands, mankind's greatest gift becomes a horror which could destroy us all. I accept that. What I don't accept is the government's claim that we have reached the end of the road in terms of (a) understanding what it is von Braun created, and (b) fully exploring what it could be used for – you know, for good as opposed to evil. As far as I know, we don't have Lex Luthor or The Penguin waiting to snatch this thing away from us.

"So, I have those reports – and if you want to see them you can. My offering them to you is, to me at least, final and full confirmation that I have lost all faith in those who have been my masters for the past sixteen years or so. I have given up. When you read about me dying in either a hit-and-run accident or a mysterious skiing tragedy, don't be too surprised, OK?" said Toby.

With that, he reached inside his jacket pocket and handed Diamond a large brown envelope with no exterior markings.

"Read those, and perhaps I will then tell you about how *Die Glocke* fared once it had landed in Blighty. Everything is authentic, exactly as it was; it hasn't been redacted in any way. The only details which have been blacked out are the original list of recipients and the CC list. I know it went to the President and to all Heads of Staff, so anyone who was anyone inside the United States government at the time definitely saw it," said Toby.

Diamond sensed Toby had tears in his eyes, and that he believed that a journey which had taken him to the very outer limits of accepted sense, where fact collides headlong with fiction, was, mercifully, almost at an end.

The pair said their goodbyes and headed to their respective homes, Diamond checking every minute or so to ensure that he still had the envelope tucked away in his inside pocket. He didn't attempt to read the documents on the Tube for fear of being seen. He didn't stop at The Gay Cavalier for a last drink for fear of falling prey to base temptation and having several. He scurried home, and once inside poured himself the last of what was cheap and very nasty brandy, and deposited himself in front of the television. Out of habit he switched on and channel-surfed to find his favourite late-night rolling news programme, before realising that he had something far, far more significant in the envelope which lay on the table before him than the peccadilloes of a serving Tory MP.

Diamond took a large swig of brandy, winced as he swallowed, and opened the envelope, spreading out the contents before him.

CHAPTER

SEVEN

Date: July 2nd, 1997.
From the office of Professor Martin Zapruder.
Memo 67/1.

What is contained in this report is, as we say here at Groom Lake, 'Above Top Secret'. In many respects it actually redefines the parameters of that very phrase.

I have deliberately kept the 'must-see' list as small as possible, for the obvious reasons. To describe the information held within this document as sensitive would be to seriously underplay it. If what is currently known by only a few were to become common knowledge, if the population as a whole were to access the facts, we would wake up tomorrow in a very different world – a world which would, I fear, be a good deal less stable and a good deal less safe.

All I ask is that you read this report (and the contents of the additional, smaller file) and then destroy them. Commit what you will to memory, but regard yourself as one of a very privileged few. Discuss with no one, tell no one. These rules, these suggestions, may seem draconian and you may regard it as improper or impertinent that a mere scientist is demanding so much of our great country's ruling elite, but we are faced with a unique situation, gentlemen.

Rightly or wrongly, I have decided to do away with the traditional form of respectful techno speak in favour of a simple narrative. This is a scenario which needs to be explained in plain, easy-to-understand language. Forgive me if such an official and possibly historic document should come across as laid-back or penned in a matter-of-fact manner. It is a decision I have taken and I will stand by it. As you will see, this is more of a story than a formal document.

As you will all know, in the months after the Second World War ended, we, the United States, took the decision to offer sanctuary to an array of the Nazi regime's finest scientists in exchange for their knowledge and expertise.

At the time the United States and Great Britain could claim some of the finest and sharpest brains in the world but, while it pains me to concede it, we were second best in virtually every aspect to the Germans. In Wernher von Braun – who went on to almost single-handedly develop the space programme which climaxed with the 1969 moon landing – the Nazis boasted the most gifted and brilliant man since Albert Einstein.

Von Braun was the man behind the V2 rocket; a piece of munitions engineering which could conceivably have altered the outcome of the war and given Adolf Hitler victory had it been invented twelve months earlier than it was. By the time the V2s were raining down death on London and other major European cities, both von Braun and Hitler were acutely aware that the tide was turning and that the Allies were finally gaining the upper hand, from Russia down to North Africa.

Von Braun had been working on another project for more than a year. Winston Churchill was utterly convinced that it was, in essence, a V3 rocket – an upgraded version of the V2 with a more comprehensive guidance system and a greater payload.

He was wrong. Von Braun, helped by another German given refuge in the USA, SS General Hans Kammler, was urged on by an increasingly desperate Nazi High Command to develop what he called the *Wunderwaffe* – the Wonder Weapon.

The great irony is that we still don't know what the Wonder Weapon was. I use the word 'irony' because, perhaps, we *should* now know. Why? Well, because we have it.

We were fully aware of the rumours that the Germans were building something which would dramatically alter the outcome of World War II, but it was only after von Braun's transfer to our shores that speculation became fact.

It was von Braun himself who proffered the information – without, it must be said, either coercion or gentle persuasion. He simply told us that the machine he had been working on had been spirited away by the SS in the last days of the war, and that it was secreted in a base on Antarctica. It all sounded hugely improbable – but he was telling the truth.

The machine is called *Die Glocke* – or The Bell. The reason behind the name is simple enough: it does resemble a bell… very much so.

Die Glocke stands about fifteen feet tall and is approximately nine feet in diameter. It is made of a rather ugly base metal, it has a series of Egyptian-style hieroglyphics running around its base – they may well be simple aesthetic adornment, we don't know – and it has room inside for one seated man. Of course, the fact that it is clearly designed to house an individual is curious, as it is, after all, a supposed weapon of mass destruction.

Von Braun told us where it was, and we went and we got it. It was that simple. It *was* in Antarctica, hidden away in a small settlement which, von Braun insisted, was to be the forerunner of a major military base, mostly underground, which would allow the Nazis to meet and greet life forms from other planets. Again, that sounds fanciful in the extreme, but the Nazis – Hitler in particular – were convinced that these life forms from other galaxies would naturally gravitate toward the pure Aryan race on planet earth.

While *Die Glocke* does, at first glance, look very primitive, it is, unquestionably, the greatest invention thus far achieved by mankind – by some considerable distance. The fact that it was designed and built in the 1940s makes it even more remarkable.

I must point out that, while von Braun was happy for us to travel to the South Pole to retrieve his invention, he never fully explained how he had built it, how it worked or what it was for. Many people inside our administration felt we should have applied far more pressure to him as we sought the answers, but he was such a key figure in our space programme – the leading light, in fact – that it was ultimately deemed to be inappropriate.

It was only shortly before his death in 1977 that we again started to demand answers of von Braun, but by that point he was ill and it was, sadly, too late; the knowledge we so desperately sought was to die with him.

We now believe that *Die Glocke* was initially housed in a basement beneath Berlin's Charity Hospital before being moved, in November 1943, to another underground site beneath the northern Sudeten Mountains somewhere near the Silesian coal-mining town of Waldenburg.

At the time there were many reports of what was described as "strange and highly unusual" equipment being taken into a secret test chamber beneath the mountains. The project was code-named Chronos – a Greek god who was likened to Old Father Time by the ancient scholars.

The machine – for want of a better word – contains two counter-rotating cylinders which run on (which use as fuel) a mercury-like substance which is violet in colour. We managed to reproduce that substance but, while I believe it may possibly contain a mixture of thorium and beryllium, I am not privy to the precise chemical make-up as the Chief of the Defence Staff insisted that no one individual should have knowledge of all the component parts of *Die Glocke*. That is a simple and understandable safety measure. If any one of those involved with the machine were to fall into enemy hands, he or she would be unable to divulge all its secrets, and so *Die Glocke* could not be fully replicated.

Von Braun told us that the test chamber was wholly inadequate and that "many" of the scientists and slave workers employed on the project died in explosions or from radiation poisoning at "regular intervals".

The chamber was just forty metres square and lined from ceiling to floor with a combination of heavy-duty ceramic tiles and thick rubber matting. When fired up by enormous amounts of electrical current, *Die Glocke* gave off a very loud droning noise which rose from a whisper to a scream, and also a quite distinct blue glow, particularly around the cone.

The initial tests were, von Braun insisted, somewhat less than exhaustive: the machine would run for sixty to ninety seconds before workers were ushered back into the chamber to "damp down" with salted water.

Above the surface, von Braun spoke of a concrete arch or "Stonehenge-like" construction. *Die Glocke* was often taken there and placed in the centre for testing – possibly to ascertain the worth and efficiency of its propulsion systems.

The rotation of the machine and the use of the radioactive liquid metal (code-named Xerum 525) do suggest that the Germans were looking into the inertial and vortex properties of radioactive material when subjected to high-speed rotation, this rotation being driven by sustained bursts of electricity. These matters are complex, with the chemistry and physics some way beyond the understanding of even the most learned of modern-day scientists, so I have deliberately reduced, to the very bare essentials, the information on this front. Suffice to say, von Braun's work was so far ahead of its time that we still haven't caught up with him – if he had produced *Die Glocke* last week it would still represent a watershed moment in the history of our planet.

The Vice President urged me to try and lay the matters before you in as simplistic a manner as possible in order that the untrained mind might walk away from the debate with at least a basic understanding of context and purpose.

Put very simply, *Die Glocke* is, we believe, a heavy-particle accelerator used as an artificial neutron source to breed Protactinium 233 and Thorium 232. The former naturally degrades after about four weeks into pure bomb-grade Uranium 233.

The process von Braun used in his trials harnessed the fluorescent quality of mercury to invite collisions between electrons and photons which resulted in the release of thermal neutrons. In short, it would seem that the Germans were seeking to build an atomic bomb; one which would have comfortably predated the ones we dropped on Hiroshima and Nagasaki in 1945.

The consequences of the Nazis winning the race for atomic weaponry are, I suggest, obvious: Hitler would have blown the world to pieces rather than see his dream of a thousand-year Reich perish. In that respect we – the world outside of Hitler's kingdom of madness – were very lucky indeed.

Self-evidently, we had absolutely no intention of either priming or testing *Die Glocke*'s capabilities as an atomic bomb. What intrigued our scientists was a tape-recorded interview with von Braun – the last formal one he was ever required to do – from 1950, some three years after *Die Glocke* had been retrieved from the Antarctic wastes. When the subject of his invention was raised and it was suggested to him, correctly as it transpired, that it was nothing more than a bigger and better bomb to drop on the Allies, he said something very curious.

Von Braun said, and I quote from the official transcript: "Yes, it was a bomb – but the key word in that statement relates to the tense. I knew the war would be lost, so I confess I lost interest in building something which would do nothing more than take away so many more innocent lives – I didn't want that to be my legacy. *Die Glocke* you now have is Version 3. It could still be transformed into something which kills, but it is so very much more. It is now yours – and it is for you to uncover and use wisely its many secrets. The answer sits before you, gentlemen. Its time will come and go – as will those who embrace it."

He declined to say anything else on the subject, and, as the interview in question was three hours long, his brief comments about *Die Glocke* were overlooked, ignored and then swiftly forgotten.

The clue, of course, was in the statement, "The answer sits before you." I believe he intended us to take him quite literally, so we did. Those who had been given access to *Die Glocke* worked on the assumption that it was a bomb – so why then did it boast a most complex control panel directly in front of the 'pilot's' seat?

The potential for mass destruction was still there, hidden away in the intricacies of the base unit, but it quickly became clear that this was a modified device – just as von Braun had suggested. He had turned his back on wanton killing and moved on to a purely personal project, no doubt hoping that the ever-present SS officers inside the construction site had neither the intelligence nor the inclination to uncover the truth.

This still presented NASA's finest minds with their first seemingly unsolvable problem in the wake of the Administration's formation in 1958. They had the puzzle, they had been told there was a solution – but they couldn't find it.

Indeed, the harder they looked, the less they found. They took the control panel apart on countless occasions, changed the power supply, changed the levels of that power supply, used the various dials and buttons in a variety of sequences, drained away and replenished the Xerum 525, altered the formula. The net result was nothing. The machine continued to hold on to its supposed secrets.

With the space programme beginning to blossom, initially under Eisenhower and then under Kennedy, *Die Glocke* was all but forgotten; stored away and deemed to be a drain on funds which, even back then, were scarce and becoming scarcer.

The breakthrough came in August 1964, and, like so many breakthroughs, it was by accident and not design.

Die Glocke was to be inspected and examined by the new Head of Biophysics, Eric David, as part of a review of items which were deemed to be cluttering up what little storage space his department laid claim to. It was removed from the casing which had held it for several years, and preparations were made for the inspection. As part of those preparations, a laboratory technician was asked to ensure the base-unit reservoir was refilled with Xerum 525.

The man had no previous knowledge of the machine. Having collected the Xerum from the storage facility which stands adjacent to the base's Chemistry Department, he moved *Die Glocke* out of its casing – it stood on an electric conveyor belt – and duly attempted to locate the fuel-entry point. He had been told it was beneath the main hatch and could be opened by applying limited pressure to a slightly raised surface mounting.

Unfortunately, the man in question was both short-sighted and clumsy.

Unable to locate the surface mounting, he simply began pushing the main body of the machine just above the hieroglyphics in the hope that touch would succeed where sight had failed. To his relief, after two minutes of frantic stabbing, he saw a small hatch spring open. He duly pumped in the hundred litres of Xerum, slammed the hatch shut and left.

What he had accidentally, inadvertently done was to fill a previously undiscovered tank inside *Die Glocke* with Xerum 525.

Eric David was a pedantic, fussy individual who ruled by fear and who was universally unpopular. Twenty-four hours before he was due to inspect *Die Glocke*, two members of his staff opted to ensure all was in order ahead of his visit. They checked the machine inside and out, ensured the power supply was connected and that, when the instruction to kick-start the machine was given, the necessary bulbs would illuminate and von Braun's invention would purr.

The two men were young. Young enough not to have surrendered or had suppressed the sense of adventure which invariably withers and dies on the vine in early middle age. Before leaving the laboratory, they began to fool around as only the immature can. There was laughing, jokes about Hitler, and, finally, a challenge from the taller of the men to the shorter one to sit inside *Die Glocke* while he used, for the first time, his birthday present from the previous week: an eight-millimetre, handheld movie camera (Bell & Howell 414PD). The shorter man duly obliged, sliding into the passenger seat and grinning toward the camera which was being held at eye level by his colleague.

Later the taller one recounted how he had jokingly called out, "Lights, camera, action!" as he prepared to depress the record button. It was actually in jest, but his friend took him literally and began pushing the array of buttons and switches which lay in front of him on *Die Glocke's* control panel.

A few seconds after the camera emitted a whirring sound to confirm that recording was under way, both men froze at precisely the same instant. From deep inside the bowels of *Die Glocke* rose what both described as a "fearsome grinding" noise. Instantaneously, the bank of instruments on the central control panel burst into life, filling the inside of *Die Glocke* with an eerie red shadow. Both men retreated to the back wall – as far away from the machine as they could get without actually leaving the room.

Both confirmed that, as the level of noise rose, the air around the machine began to blur – they likened it to a heat haze which was, perhaps, six inches deep. Both also insisted that as the interior almost pulsed with red, the exterior – particularly near the cap – began to emit a bluish glow.

Understandably scared by what was happening, and fearful that their part in this unplanned event would lead to instant dismissal by a boss they had, ironically, been seeking to please, the men agreed to opt for the most logical solution – they unplugged the mains supply of electricity.

Before it resumed its silent, sedentary position, *Die Glocke* began to slow and wind down, rather as a washing machine does on its final rinse cycle. The air was heavy with a smell of burning rubber – but that was the only evidence that life had briefly pulsed through its various electrical and mechanical systems.

The two men were still staring at *Die Glocke* when a posse of their colleagues raced into the room, two carrying fire extinguishers. They were joined just seconds later by Eric David, who had been alerted to the commotion by his personal assistant.

The details of what ensued are largely irrelevant but, as you might imagine, there was much finger-pointing, a great deal of shouting, and several threats, of both a physical and a professional nature, exchanged. The men were told to report to David's office later that afternoon for what was diplomatically called a "full debriefing" – both attended presuming they would be dismissed in disgrace.

David was indeed a ruthless individual, but he was no fool. The preliminary report on the incident, produced hastily by one of his deputies, pointed out that a new fuel input for *Die Glocke* had been accidentally discovered, and that, as a direct consequence of the childish behaviour of the two junior lab assistants, the machine had been started up – a feat which had eluded greater intellects for many years.

When the men reported to David he was apparently in a conciliatory mood – the bad cop had become good cop simply because he could see an end product which, probably selfishly, he believed would further enhance his standing within an organisation which encouraged naked ambition.

To précis things, the men provided an open and honest account of what had occurred, pointing out that it happened very swiftly and that they meant no harm. They apologised and were asked to provide a detailed, second-by-second account of the incident within seventy-two hours. David insisted that every last detail was to be included – even their exchanges of dialogue as best they could remember them. As they stood to leave his office, David asked for the video camera.

The footage from the camera was studied at great length and in great detail. Excitement grew among David's team when it became apparent that – shaky though it was in parts – the footage had clearly captured the moment when the man seated inside *Die Glocke* had randomly stabbed at the countless buttons and levers.

By slowing the film down to an eighth of normal speed, they were clearly able to see the order in which the man pushed the various instrument panels. It was a sequence, a code. *Die Glocke* did have a function – and they had, by pure chance, discovered the key. Von Braun had been telling the truth; the answer did lie directly in front of them after all.

David spent more than a week seeking confirmation and then reconfirmation that, by inputting the starting sequence again, he would definitely not be priming a bomb which might detonate and so remove Nevada from the face of the earth. He was assured, many times, that, while the original version of *Die Glocke* had almost certainly been designed as a weapon of savage, mass destruction, the one which stood down the corridor was a modified version (as von Braun had claimed), the purpose of which was still a mystery. Reassured, David selected a team of eight whom he invited to join him the following morning. Their objective was to input the starting sequence and to see what, if anything, happened.

At 10am sharp the next day, the group – all wearing protective clothing and goggles – assembled in front of von Braun's creation. The actions observed in the video footage had been translated into a simple sequence: 1) Button A, upper left; 2) Button B, centre top; etc., etc. In all there were seventeen actions to be taken; seventeen buttons or levers to be pushed or flicked.

Once the media team to the rear of the room signalled that they were ready and that their tripod-mounted video camera was rolling, David invited one of his colleagues to step inside *Die Glocke* and begin inputting the sequence. With a notepad in his left hand, the man began working his way down the list, using his right index finger to make contact with buttons and levers, some of which were almost comically large by modern standards. He finished the programming and jumped out of the machine to rejoin David and the remaining members of his team.

Nothing happened. Nothing at all. The silence was broken not by the bursting into life of *Die Glocke*, but by the sneezing of the cameraman. David then asked his colleague to go back inside the machine and repeat the process – but faster. He wanted the various buttons pushing almost simultaneously to replicate the foolhardy behaviour of the lab technician who had been moving randomly when stabbing and poking at the control panel.

Back inside, the man rehearsed his input sequence, moving his finger to within a millimetre of a button before arcing it away toward another. After five minutes of intense preparatory work he was ready, signalling as much by way of a thumbs-up to both David and the cameraman.

David nodded his approval and the man inside *Die Glocke* leaned forward and began his sequence. He made a mistake with the fourteenth button, his finger sliding to the left of its intended target, and duly abandoned his first attempt. A second attempt also failed, but the third was a success.

As he sat back in the pilot's seat, the panels in front of him began to glow, lights flashing and dimming in unison. Beneath him, a grinding sound began to emerge which all present were later to describe as sounding rather like the swooping of helicopter blades.

The man leapt from the machine and rejoined his colleagues, who had instinctively and collectively backed away until their progress was halted by a dividing wall within the room.

Many years later, I spoke to David and he described that moment as the single most extraordinary event of his life, pushing the birth of his only child into a very far distant second place.

As the noise intensified, filling the room, a bluish glow which was said to have distorted the air began to form around the upper half of the machine. Steam – or something similar, maybe light smoke – emerged from underneath the base unit, and the band or ring which held the hieroglyphics gave the impression of rotating.

Unsure quite what he had unleashed, David instructed that the power supply be disconnected after sixty seconds.

He inspected the machine thoroughly afterward, testing its interior and exterior temperature, the fuel and radiation levels (all normal). Inside he ran his fingers across the control panel, noting with delight that there were no visible signs of overheating or blown circuits.

It was during this brief examination that David was drawn to a small window to the extreme left of the control panel. Set behind Perspex or thick glass was something which resembled a digital clock. The window was dirty, covered by a thick film of what looked like soot.

What so perplexed David was that he didn't remember seeing the window on the previous occasions he had sat inside *Die Glocke*. A highly logical man, he had the room locked and secured and then returned to his office to study photographs of the machine taken at various intervals during its residence in the Nevada desert.

He was right – the panel containing the clock-like object did not feature on any of the hundred or so photographs which had been locked away in his filing cabinet. He took one which showed a close-up of the entire control panel back to the machine and climbed inside. Holding up the photograph, he was easily able to compare reality with image. The panel was absent from the photograph... and from what he could see, there wasn't even the merest hint of a concealed window in the crystal-clear black-and-white image.

David deduced that the window had only been revealed after *Die Glocke* had been powered up; it was another part of von Braun's complex jigsaw puzzle.

CHAPTER

EIGHT

Diamond threw down the file before promptly picking it up again and estimating that he was, perhaps, only halfway through it. His eyes were tired and his stomach empty, so he moved into the kitchen in the hope that at least one cupboard would bring good cheer when opened.

He had to settle for soup and bread, contenting himself with the knowledge that the Queen herself had soup most days, albeit as a precursor to some extravagant game bird or other.

Having feasted on his can of tomato soup, Diamond decided to ring Toby, if only to give him an update on his progress with Zapruder's file.

To his surprise, Toby answered after just three rings.

"Do not tell me the ending, Toby," Diamond said. "I am only halfway through it. I'm having a rest."

"It's not a fucking novel, Diamond! How far have you got with it?" asked Toby.

"That bloke David – the nasty one – has just realised that the little window with the dials inside only appeared after the two idiots had set *Die Glocke* in motion."

"OK. There's more goodies to come for you, then. It reads like the script from a sci-fi movie, doesn't it?"

"It sure does – and you know how much I love sci-fi movies, mate. I'm not sure when I will finish it as I have to go down to the job centre to sign on the dotted line, and then I have promised to call and see June. Remember her? Nice girl who used to hang around with that moron from the library who looks perpetually surprised? Anyway, he's dumped her and she's pissed off. She seems to think I talk common sense when discussing matters of the heart. Foolish woman."

"OK, maybe give me a call tomorrow when you have finished reading it. Don't look at the second file until you have finished the first, OK?"

"I promise. Bye."

Diamond headed out on a mission which was only partially successful. He signed on without having to answer any awkward questions about his search for gainful employment but he was unable to stem June's river-like flow of tears. After spending the best part of an hour assuring her that she deserved far better than the funny-looking librarian, Diamond gave up applying sweet logic to a bruised heart, said he had to be somewhere else and left.

Once home he poured his last can of cheap supermarket lager into a dirty glass and opened up Zapruder's file again.

CHAPTER

NINE

Date: July 2nd, 1997.
From the office of Professor Martin Zapruder.
Memo 67/1.

David sent a basic report to various people of some influence before convening a full-scale meeting of everyone who had ever had any contact with *Die Glocke*. He was in charge, but he wished to seek the counsel of men for whom he held a begrudging respect.

The meeting was a curt, humourless affair which offered very little in terms of fresh information. Three times David asked those assembled what the general consensus was with regard to *Die Glocke*'s purpose. All backed von Braun's assertion that it was initially designed as a bomb. All agreed that the version they now held – Version 3, as von Braun put it – was not a bomb. They couldn't come up with anything better than that.

The meeting ended acrimoniously according to the minutes; David standing up behind his desk before telling his colleagues that they were being paid to find out what *Die Glocke* was – not what it wasn't. He asked that the freshly appeared window on the very left of the control panel be removed, cleaned and then replaced. He wanted to know what it was and why it only chose to reveal itself when the starting sequence was correctly applied. While he didn't know its role, he suspected it was integral to the as-yet-unknown function of a machine he was, privately, beginning to wish he had never set eyes on.

His private diaries from the time reveal his enormous frustration at repeatedly having to inform his superiors that little or no progress had been made with *Die Glocke*. At one point he even seemed to be on the verge of arranging an "accident" – presumably a small, contained fire – which would move what he described as "this infernal contraption" out of his life for good.

But his professionalism and his scientific curiosity ensured that he did no such thing, and three months later his protracted search for answers and solutions was finally at an end.

David had taken time off work after fracturing an ankle while rock climbing. To help smooth his period of convalescence he read assiduously – devouring anything he could get his hands on which was based, however loosely, on scientific research. Colleagues across the globe had always sent him magazines of interest, and on that day in 1965, as he sat on his front porch, his shattered leg resting on a footstool, he picked up a copy of *Science Without Limits*, a British publication for those who enjoyed the more adventurous side of scientific advancement.

Its main feature was on von Braun, a man described as a "visionary gone bad" by a writer who was, we should bear in mind, still living in an era when anything German was considered suspicious and not to be trusted. The war had ended twenty years earlier, but the wounds were showing little sign of healing in Europe. The article was lengthy, detailed, and conveyed von Braun almost as a Frankenstein-type genius who could have chosen to make the world a far better place had he not spent his days building weapons designed to destroy it.

There was little in the piece which David hadn't heard about or read before – until, that was, he began to read the final section. Having outlined von Braun's history – the V2 rocket, the work on our space programme – he turned to what he described as "the latest rumours" surrounding von Braun's last acts as a serving Nazi before he was whisked away to our shores.

The writer suggested that the recent examination in Poland of partially burned, classified documents rescued from a furnace in the basement of the main SS headquarters in Berlin's Prinz-Albrecht-Strasse revealed that von Braun was focusing on something far more significant than mere bombs for the final two years of the war – he was working on antigravity processes in the belief that he could build a machine which would move through time. The article concluded with a spot of crystal-ball-gazing, the author suggesting that, had von Braun actually achieved what he called the "impossible dream", Hitler would have sent his finest assassin back through the mists of time to November 1874 and instructed him to shoot dead Winston Churchill just days after his birth.

Ninety-nine per cent of David's fertile mind dismissed the idea that such a project had been undertaken, but it was the one per cent which continued to nag away at him, simply because, to the closed community of scientific research, von Braun was the greatest innovative intellect of them all; the one man who could have sat Einstein down and taught him a thing or two. Even so, David deemed the idea not worthy of serious consideration and made no mention of the article to either colleague or friend.

He returned to work two weeks later, carrying the magazine in his briefcase and with a pronounced limp which would take fully eighteen months to fade away.

He managed to get through two days before asking his assistant what the state of play was with *Die Glocke*. He was told that the machine had remained untouched during his absence and that no one from the military or the Senate had made any enquiries. David asked if the dial beneath the mystery window on the control panel had been cleaned and fully examined, as per his pre-accident instructions. It had, and the report was in his overflowing in tray.

The contents of the report actually scared David. Technicians had carefully removed first the glass (not Perspex) cover, and then the intricate mechanism within. All component parts were cleaned, examined, photographed and then returned to their original housing to the far left of the control panel.

The report was to the point – less than five hundred words, in fact. It stated that the compartment which held the device was "quite brilliantly" concealed, that the glass was high quality and almost a quarter of an inch thick, and that there were in fact two devices, or wheels, held inside. The larger of the two was a circular dial whose diameter was approximately eight inches. The dial was linked to the main body of the control panel by complex electrical wiring, and boasted a small backup power cell, presumably in case of any malfunction in the main exterior power source. The dial itself was nothing more than a list of dates – the years from 1800 to 1944 marked off and divided by the smallest of margins. The report suggested it was possibly "a crude calendar". The second device boasted its own small screen with a largely numeric keyboard to its right.

Sat below the zero on the fascia were the words 'Long' and 'Lat'.

Crude calendar? David suspected it was far, far more. Unsure as to whether he should give a voice to his suspicions or maintain a diplomatic, almost cowardly silence, he gave himself the weekend to consider what his next move should be. It was, he told me, the ultimate dilemma for a man who had selflessly devoted his life to finding – and then breaking down – new barriers. He could ignore the voices inside his head which cried out for him to gamble – or he could risk the ridicule of the entire scientific fraternity by outlining what were both fears or hopes.

He returned to work the following Monday, having come to the conclusion that it would be highly unethical of him to ignore the possibilities which fact, in the shape of von Braun's machine, and fiction, in the form of the article in *Science Without Limits*, had moved into his line of sight. While the logical part of his mind continued to tell him that there was, perhaps, only a million-to-one chance that von Braun's invention could bend space and time, the romantic in him urged him on to at least test the theory.

David's dilemma was that he could not confirm nor definitively rule out the minuscule possibility without confiding in others. He was fully aware that, on countless occasions in the not-too-distant past, carefully fashioned reputations had been reduced to rubble by lesser public claims.

He decided to trim his normal working team by fifty per cent, calling together only those with whom he had enjoyed a long and very professional association stretching back in excess of a decade. Having seen the minutes of that meeting – David insisted that his slavishly loyal PA was in attendance – he handled things in the right way, in possibly the only way;

that's to say, his opening line was, "You're going to think I have gone mad, but…"

But those men and women who trusted and respected him listened attentively, making no comment at all until his monologue was at an end. Much of what he told them they did, of course, already know – *Die Glocke* had initially been a bomb but was now something else, the inventor himself had hinted that it held secrets of great mystery and worth, and the cunningly concealed dial was a list of dates – the one selected for 'use' was to be aligned with a marking to the right of the dial.

David reminded those present that it was von Braun himself who had provided the clues about *Die Glocke*'s possible purpose during his final interview with the US government back in 1950. He recounted the line, "The answer sits before you, gentlemen", and admitted that it was only then that a thorough investigation of the machine's control panel was undertaken.

It was at this point that one of David's scientists, a Dr Kathryn Cherry, raised her arm to suggest that von Braun had left another clue which, while deemed insignificant all those years ago, could now be both relevant and pertinent. Reading von Braun's words from her notebook, Dr Cherry said, "'Its time will come and go – as will those who embrace it.'"

When taken in conjunction with David's new theory, the inference was clear to all, and the sense of incredulity and suspicion which had hung heavy over the gathering began to dissipate, to be replaced by a sense of excitement tinged with absolute wonder. It was more of a nudge than a hint or clue.

David asked his colleagues to do two things – to go home and think about the possibilities overnight, and to keep silent. They were all asked to meet again the following day at 9pm, well outside accepted office hours in order to guarantee at least a measure of privacy.

They reassembled the following night in front of *Die Glocke*, the machine having been fuelled and fully primed earlier in the day under the cover of 'normal maintenance'.

David spoke briefly, believing there was little need for explanations or theories. They were all smart people and fully understood that if nothing happened then their meeting never took place, and that if something did occur they would be bound by a code of silence and honour.

On the previous occasions *Die Glocke* had been started by inputting, with great speed, the correct sequence of button-pushing, the 'calendar dial', as it had become known, wasn't functioning, its intricate inner workings jammed by soot, damp and the first signs of internal rusting. Now cleaned, dried and restored to full health, it was fully operational and in situ.

The honest truth is, they didn't actually understand what they were doing or what they hoped to achieve. It came to represent the ultimate 'lick-it-and-see' moment.

David suggested that they move the calendar dial to an agreed date, insert a map reference, set the machine in motion and wait to see what, if anything, happened. At this stage it was never suggested that anyone should be seated inside *Die Glocke* when the launch sequence was started – but it was agreed that they would place something on the pilot's seat just out of basic curiosity.

There wasn't much to choose from in a base which shunned the conventional trappings of office life. Eventually one of those in attendance left the room, returning two minutes later with a twelve-inch-high teddy bear which his grandson had recently given to him as a birthday gift. David placed the bear on the seat and lifted the glass covering to reveal the calendar dial. He suggested the year 1920; a random selection. Everyone was in agreement.

David moved the circular dial until '1920' was aligned with the marking to the right of the casing. It was then he realised that he needed to input further information – he had to give the machine a direction; a route to follow, in pure geographic terms.

He asked that someone find the map coordinates, in latitude and longitude, for the very centre of London's Hyde Park. The delay seemed to be somewhat longer than eight minutes, but eventually David's breathless PA returned with the data. David inputted 51-30-31 N, 0-09-49 W, swiftly pushed the buttons in a well-rehearsed sequence and, from what the records state, said the words, "God help us all" as he stepped back from *Die Glocke* at the very moment it again groaned into life.

As the level of noise began to rise, David shouted, "It is August 8th, 1964, at 9.45pm. Remember that time and date, people."

Those present had retreated behind a makeshift glass barrier to watch the events. The show was over in precisely eighty-eight seconds. The pattern was a familiar one – screeching and grinding from the lower section (again likened to the sound of helicopter blades), steam or smoke emitted from the base of the machine, a blurring of the air, and a bluish glow. And then silence. No need to switch off the power supply this time; the machine had run its full cycle and had moved back into a position of peaceful neutrality.

Slowly, the group emerged from behind the screen and made their way – almost crouching – toward the machine. The control-panel lights had died, the air was heavy with a cordite-like smell – and the teddy bear was still in the pilot's seat.

David is recorded as saying, "Close, but no cigar", before announcing he would give it one more try. Leaving the teddy bear in situ, he asked for the map coordinates for the Yankee Stadium in New York's South Bronx. He pushed in 40-49-45 N, 73-55-35 W, before selecting the year 1928; the era of Babe Ruth, baseball's legendary 'Sultan of Swat'.

Once again *Die Glocke* ran for exactly eighty-eight seconds before closing down its many systems and circuits. Once again the end product appeared to be nothing more than the shattered hopes of a small group who had believed history of some significance was in the offing.

There was a palpable sense of disappointment, but no great surprise. David was a man who believed that dreams were there to be followed and that chances should be taken; he had given it a go and if his professional reputation emerged intact he would be content – in fact, he would regard that as a bonus.

It was four days later that things began to change. David took a call late one night from one of the colleagues who had been present at the test. The conversation was lengthy but it boiled down to one very simple point; one very simple question. How could they be sure that nothing had happened during those two periods of eighty-eight seconds?

The thrust of the argument was – excuse me for putting this in basic terms – that if a man had invented a way of travelling in time, then surely it was possible he had also discovered a way of elongating time. Could it be that the eighty-eight seconds on 'our' side of the fence was somewhat longer someplace else?

The possibilities with regard to time travel and its paradoxes are almost endless, but the question struck a chord with David, who, while he never told the colleague in question as much, was furious with himself for not alighting upon the possibility first. I am sure all of you will appreciate that science is a most competitive arena in which to work – particularly at the very highest level.

David spent the night considering the possibilities and searching for a viable solution. The one he came up with was sensible enough but, he believed, carried a smaller chance of success than did the prospect of *Die Glocke* having moved anywhere during those 176 seconds of noise, smoke and blue light.

The next day he called the Head of Publicity at the White House – what we would now call the Head of Media and Communications. He asked that someone be sent to Washington's Library of Congress to plough his or her way through two years of old newspapers.

Predictably, he selected *The Times* of London and the *New York Times*. The years he wanted scrutinising were 1920 for the former and 1928 for the latter. The remit of the individual handed the unenviable task was to check each and every edition for any mention of a mystery surrounding a bell-like object.

The White House initially refused his request because he was unable to narrow down the search to a specific month; only relenting after he had thrown some very influential names into the argument.

Fully aware that sifting through many hundreds of newspaper pages would take a significant amount of time, David didn't hold his breath. He carried on with his normal, accepted duties, only occasionally wondering when – or if – Washington's search for something which he wasn't certain existed would be completed. He estimated he would get his answer in about two weeks; maybe less if the one-in-a-million chance came off. He told me that quite often around this time he was giving consideration to what he would recommend to the government if he was forced to abandon his pursuit of the truth about *Die Glocke*.

While David didn't readily admit defeat, there was a part of him which believed that von Braun's invention should be dismantled, placed in a large container unit and then dropped off the side of a liner into the darkest depths of the Atlantic Ocean. He admitted that he would feel safer if it were gone forever, and he felt certain that the world, wholly unstable and volatile place that it was, would also be safer. No matter how many times he attempted to see *Die Glocke* in a positive light, no matter how often he mentally ran through the possible scientific advancements it might provide, he could not remove from his mind the recurring thought that it was the brainchild of Hitler, an evil man – and, more saliently, he always insisted, a selfish man who cared only for himself and his barbaric ideals.

Thirteen days after making his phone call to the White House, David drifted into work as usual on a Wednesday morning. His PA was away in California on holiday and, for once, his diary was relatively empty.

Without secretarial support, David worked his way through his in tray, casually flicking aside memos, circulars and junk mail before finding what he immediately recognised as a government-issue envelope – a large, brown one which bore the postmark of Washington DC.

Carefully, he opened the envelope to find two folded photocopies of newsprint and a letter from a Miss Lynda Roughley, who signed herself off as "Admin Staff, Office for Publicity". That letter read:

Dear Dr David,

First, my sincere apologies for the delay – your task proved to be far more demanding than we ever envisaged. Actually locating the issues to be studied took four days in itself, and then we were further slowed down by a power failure at the library which took more than thirty-six hours to resolve.

However, as you will see from the photocopies I have included with this letter, the hunt did ultimately prove to be successful. We found stories – rather small ones, I concede – in both publications referencing the mysterious bell-like object you mentioned.

The great irony is that the reports appeared in the two newspapers – on opposite sides of the Atlantic – on exactly the same day, the sightings of the object having been made the previous day, almost simultaneously, in New York and London.

I hope that the items I have included are self-explanatory – but if that does not prove to be the case, please feel free to telephone me at any point.

I wish you every success with whatever it is you are currently working on.

Yours…

David was later to admit that he had been stunned by the contents of Miss Roughley's short letter. Unfolding the two photostat sheets, he first scanned page eight of the *New York Times*, dated August 9th, 1928. There it was, all three paragraphs of it:

POLICE AND COUNCILLORS CALLED IN AFTER MYSTERIOUS INCIDENT

The combined forces of the NYPD and the City Council have been asked to investigate a curious incident at the Yankee Stadium yesterday (August 8th, 1928).

According to several eyewitnesses including a member of the Yankees' coaching staff, a large object said to resemble a bell was found in the centre of the playing area.

The object remained in situ for only a few seconds

before, according to a Mr Dan Sterling from the Bronx, "disappearing in a puff of smoke". Mr Sterling said the mystery object had what looked like a large black cross painted on one side.

The second cutting, from page twenty-four of *The Times* of London and dated August 9th, 1920, was equally brief:

INCIDENT IN HYDE PARK
BAFFLES ONLOOKERS

London socialites and afternoon walkers were met with an unexpected and seemingly inexplicable sight yesterday when a giant, metallic bell was said to have been spotted in the capital's Hyde Park.

Onlookers told summoned Police Officers that the object was visible for only a few minutes before disappearing from view.

A spokesman for the Metropolitan Police Force confirmed that they had formally opened a file on the incident and would be talking to eyewitnesses over the coming days.

At this point, gentlemen, I have decided to simply include excerpts from Dr David's own journal. Up until the day when he read of the apparent sightings of *Die Glocke* on the same date, at the same time, in different years, on different continents, he had never even considered committing his thoughts and words to print.

But, concerned and excited by the manifold possibilities which were now opening up before him and his team, he decided a written record would be not only appropriate, but absolutely vital.

The extracts below start on August 23rd, 1964, fifteen days after his two attempts to activate *Die Glocke* and just twenty-four hours after he had seen the two newspaper reports.

Extracts from the Journal of Dr Eric David

August 23rd, 1964: I am now totally and absolutely lost in the mists of confusion, and a small amount of sheer terror. Until yesterday, when I received the two newspaper articles, I had all but resigned myself to admitting failure in my bid to unravel *Die Glocke's* mysteries. Had the search of the *New York Times* and *The Times* of London yielded nothing, I would have had little option but to contact my Senate paymasters and tell them that the machine held future interest only as a curious relic of World War II. I had already decided that I would recommend it be taken to London's famous Imperial War Museum, where it would be listed as Nazi detritus and spend the remainder of its days in a display box.

I concede that, as I sit here at my desk shortly before midnight, I am uncertain as to what course of action I should opt for and down which path I should now travel.

What I do know is that every conceivable route forward from where I now stand is littered with possibilities, dangers, problems and thus-far-unanswered questions. I hope – I believe – that there will also be answers, and if I am blessed there will be benefits for mankind.

If I should make the wrong choices as a result of either stupidity or over ambition it is conceivable that I could cause more damage to our planet and its peoples than even Hitler believed to be possible. I acknowledge here and now that I will require enormous strength of character and intellect if I am to negotiate safe passage through what may well prove to be treacherous times.

Tomorrow I shall call together my team and inform them of developments. I suspect that they will be every bit as amazed (and scared) as I am.

August 24th, 1964: I spent the morning with those I trust and respect. I called them together for an impromptu meeting in what was a mercifully deserted canteen. I believe that many of them suspected I was going to formally announce that the hunt for *Die Glocke*'s secrets was at an end, and that we should all now move on to projects which at least boast an outside chance of success.

So, there was much astonishment when I told them what has happened over the past couple of weeks since the day we gathered to fire up the machine. Having explained the reasoning behind my decision to contact the White House and ask for help with looking through the newspaper archives, I laid the cuttings on the table around which we sat.

There were gasps of absolute astonishment – indeed, one of the female members of the group actually placed her cupped hands in front of her face and burst into tears. They were rendered speechless.

It was left to me to spell out the options as I see them. I concede that I have, in the past, deserved my reputation as a stubborn man who often – too often – ignored the advice of others. It is a failing I have sought to correct over the past few weeks.

Before I said my piece, I asked for the input of those gathered alongside me. I also told them that any contribution would be very warmly welcomed, and that this was not a moment for egos or score-settling. It is crucial, I underscored, that we work together as a collective unit, because the stakes could not be any higher.

It was difficult to keep a true sense of perspective because, clearly, this is a pivotal moment in world history; something which, arguably, dwarfs the inventing of the wheel and the discovery of the power of electricity. It really is difficult to be calm and level-headed when history is not so much beckoning as grabbing you by the throat and dragging you forward. I felt an enormous sense of responsibility as I canvassed opinion in that room.

They urged me to give my opinion first, quite possibly out of politeness. My view is that, while the two newspaper reports are uncorroborated and unconfirmed, there can be no doubt that *Die Glocke* moved through space and time to materialise first in London and then in New York. It is clear that, for whatever reason, the duration of these visits was the same eighty-eight seconds we witnessed in our laboratory. It is also clear to me that the two visits occurred on the same date – that *Die Glocke*, if it does have a fault, can select a year to return to but cannot pick out a specific date. That's to say that, if you go back in time, you will alight on the same date you depart – on the occasion of our test, that date was August 8th. Perhaps this was the flaw von Braun was working on when the SS stepped in between him and his creation toward the end of the war.

They listened attentively and nodded their approval. When the time came for me to fall silent and listen rather than speak, the silence was, at first, deafening. Eventually one of the team proffered the opinion that, for all its marvels, *Die Glocke* is actually all but useless if the duration of any stay in the past cannot be extended beyond eighty-eight seconds. He put it quite beautifully by asking, "What is the point in going back if when you get there you don't even have enough time to boil an egg?"

That, of course, was what we all agreed is *Die Glocke's* second major failing, after the inability to specify a target date. Bearing in mind the genius of the invention, I'm not convinced that it is a failing – I believe it could just be a mistake on our part. After all, we only discovered the second fuel-entry point and the ignition sequence order by pure good fortune.

The discussion centred around two things – what we do next, and who, if anyone, we inform about *Die Glocke's* capabilities.

I have spent long enough working inside top-secret government programmes to know that, if anything of even moderate interest is discovered/learned/gleaned which might – just might – have a military connotation, the men with the big hats and the shiny shoes will step straight in and take over. Sadly, it is their nature; they assume that every advancement in science and physics is purely for the benefit of those who seek to kill the enemy rather than, say, feed the poor or cure disease.

So, we were faced with a huge dilemma today. It wasn't simply a scientific or an ethical one: it was moral. I know that, the very second I call anyone inside the White House and use the words 'time machine' and 'success' in the same sentence, the military will swamp my offices and place everything behind enough yellow (and then red) tape to engulf the Empire State Building.

I am a loyal and respectful servant of my country – I always have been – but there is something inside me which is shouting out to resurrect the rebel spirit which I honestly believed had died inside me more than thirty years ago.

In the end we all agreed that there is no imperative to rush any decision because, ironically, time is on our side. It is Monday night. I asked my team to assemble for another meeting on Wednesday. In the final count, the decision will be mine. I have now accepted this, because with high office comes responsibility and it would be wrong of me to cross the Rubicon and then seek to blame one of those who are standing beside me.

In truth, it is a responsibility which has arrived very late in life – and one I could most definitely live without. Having said that, had someone come to me a couple of years ago and asked me if I would like to have my hands on a machine which can distort the space-time vortex, I suspect my answer might just have been in the affirmative.

August 25th, 1964: We meet again tomorrow. The atmosphere inside the unit was decidedly odd today. We arrived, we got on with our respective jobs – but no one mentioned *Die Glocke* – well, certainly not to me. So, they were either deep in thought ahead of tomorrow's meeting, or they still haven't come up with a suggestion which will meet with the full approval of the whole group. We shall see.

August 26th, 1964 Well, if I am to do what I promised myself I would do – go with the majority – the die is, as they say, well and truly cast. The meeting was everything I hoped it would be, insomuch as it was full, frank and honest. Those who were seemingly rendered speechless yesterday were positively verbose today; at times it was as if several dams had been opened at the same moment.

I was gratified to hear suggestions, proposals, fears, logical solutions, illogical solutions, great ideas, dumb ideas, and – quite rightly – a call for a final proposal and a show of hands. It was democracy in action, and it made me smile.

The main concern was the age-old argument against time travel: that any action carried out in the past, however small, could cause massively significant changes to the future. The most famous example (albeit fictional) is the butterfly tale.

Many years ago, in one of those 'Amazing Stories' types of magazines which all kids seemed to read in those days, there was a story about a man who invented a way of travelling through time. People would turn up at his laboratory, undergo whatever process made this possible, and promptly move back in time, materialising on what was described as a conveyor belt which hung in the air, just a couple of feet above the world below. Traveller and conveyor belt were seemingly invisible to everyone – which was both artistic licence and very convenient.

Before they left on their amazing journey, they were repeatedly told that they must never step off the belt – for to do so would risk making fundamental changes to the time they would be returning to once their fifteen minutes was up.

All was well and good for many weeks. People went back to various points in time, travelled on the mystery conveyor belt and were then returned to the here and now without any problems.

And then it went wrong. A middle-aged man was sent back in time and was happily viewing the world as it was in his home town a hundred or so years earlier when he thought he caught sight of the land upon which his own house now stood. Excited at the prospect of seeing how things looked before bricks and mortar replaced grass and woodland, he leaned forward to try and get a better view. As he did, he overbalanced and his right foot slipped off the conveyor belt and touched the ground beneath. He quickly lifted it, only to discover that his slight tumble had seen him step on a small, white butterfly, which now lay crushed and very dead.

Unconcerned, he continued his adventure until he felt himself being moved forward to his own time. As the haze around him cleared he expected to see his friend, the machine's inventor, smiling and with a hand outstretched to welcome him back.

He didn't. What stood before him was a wasteland of shattered, derelict buildings and burned-out motor vehicles. The few people he saw were dressed in rags and were scurrying around amid the ruins, lifting bricks and metal sheets as if they were hunting for something.

The world had changed – dramatically so. He had stepped on and killed one seemingly insignificant butterfly, but that had been enough to see the whole world change.

I have always regarded the alleged consequences of that particular story as improbable. Clearly, if one were to move back in time and make a fundamental change – for example, killing someone before they have reached the age at which they will make a dramatic contribution to the world's future landscape – there must be a chance of effecting a change in the present. Killing one butterfly? Not enough for me, I'm afraid. In order for the death of one insect to alter everything as we know it (or knew it, for the time traveller), there would have to be the most outrageous sequence of events lying in wait in that butterfly's brief life.

It was good to discuss the many pros and cons, though. It was incumbent upon us to do so because we weren't talking about exploring the consequences of nicotine consumption we were discussing things that are way above top secret and way above simple danger.

The obvious question came up very early in a discussion which spanned more than three hours – would we ever consider swapping the teddy bear for a living, breathing human being? While there was an obvious enthusiasm for doing just that, I had to constantly remind the advocates that it seems we will only have a journey time of eighty-eight seconds – which I referred to as more of an episode of déjà vu than serious time travel.

Some wanted us to repeat the exercise which I have discovered, courtesy of the newspaper entries, was a success. I told them that I can't see the point. All we can do is cower behind a glass wall to watch and listen as *Die Glocke* groans its way through another brief period of activity before we head for the nearest library to seek out reports of an odd-looking, bell-shaped machine which, some claimed, arrived and departed inside ninety seconds.

A meeting which had started with enthusiasm the like of which I have never before witnessed was to end in semi-confusion and near silence. We had mankind's greatest ever invention sitting just down the corridor and yet we don't have a clue how best to utilise it or how to truly harness its power.

The logical thing to agree upon was that we should examine the machine one last time. As one of my colleagues said, it has given up its secrets only with great reluctance, so it would be arrogant and foolhardy to assume that there are no further revelations to come.

Bearing in mind we have stripped down and rebuilt *Die Glocke* on several occasions since von Braun presented it to us on a plate, we all agreed that it's a long shot – but one we should take as it might quite possibly represent a last chance.

As I drove home I confess that I did seriously consider pulling rank and announcing that we would attempt a manned 'flight', and that I would be the one strapped into the pilot's seat. As I sit here now, writing these words, that idea continues to race around a mind which will not slow down and allow my body to sleep.

Is it worth the risk? Would it prove to be dangerous in purely personal, medical terms? Indeed, would I survive at all? The body is amongst the most resilient of organic structures but I remain to be convinced that it is equipped to deal with the obvious rigours of moving through time.

Tonight, I wish I had a far greater mind – a more telling intellect. I also find myself wishing I were braver than I am. It is time to try and rest. I am considering pouring myself what

I would consider to be a purely medicinal glass of brandy – a large one.

August 27th, 1964: It has been a long day, a day of great decisions and a day I fear I may yet come to deeply regret. After a night of fractured sleep and dreams I could not separate from reality, I was up and out of here before 7am, naively assuming that some fresh air and a quiet drive to work would help clear my head.

At times the body can come to represent a comical creation – within five minutes of unlocking my office and sitting behind my desk I was asleep; a crumpled, head-on-folded-arms mess. It was the arrival of my PA which woke me. She asked if I had been there all night, and looked thoroughly unconvinced by my negative reply.

I called the team together and went over what we had agreed in principle yesterday; namely that we would give *Die Glocke* one last thorough going-over with the proverbial microscope, before reaching a final decision as to where its future lies.

The only fresh input I could come up with was that they try and ascertain, as best they could, what function each button, switch or fixture is designed to achieve. I told them that I was looking for something on the front panel fascia which seemed to be redundant during the firing-up sequence. I suspected it was another exercise in straw-clutching but I also asked them to scour the interior of the machine for anything we may have overlooked in previous examinations – simply because the second fuel-input valve had been secreted so brilliantly and found only by pure accident.

They went to work and I returned to my office to field calls from two Senate members, an Air Vice Marshal, and the man with the thankless of task of trying to justify my department's annual budget. Even now, after so many years working inside a rigid system, the only thing I loathe more than budgets is talking about budgets. The good thing about Bobby Marshall, the in-house accountant who has the misfortune to hold my unit's purse strings, is that he is easily handled – which means I fobbed him off with the usual "I'm far too busy for this" line.

Fobbing off Senators and military men is never quite so simple. I simply didn't return the Air Vice Marshal's call. Rude? Yes – but he will only have wanted to ask me about any ongoing developments in the hunt for a weapon which could wipe those "commie bastards" off the face of the earth.

I spoke to both Senators – mercifully, only one was enquiring about where I'm at with the machine. As I lied to him, I knew my position on what we should do in the days ahead was shifting quite dramatically. Had I wished to, I could have consigned *Die Glocke* to being nothing more than a small paragraph at the foot of a lost page on the history of the Second World War.

All I had to say was that von Braun's Wonder Weapon was nothing more than a heap of rusting junk and that would have been it – the museum would have beckoned, life would have returned to normal and the pressure would have been off. I couldn't do it. I just couldn't. After I had told him that we had made some pleasing progress and that I would get back to him within two weeks with a full update, I sat behind my desk feeling as though I had – whether I would admit as much or not – made a decision which I will be unable to go back on.

I was actually smiling to myself when my PA entered my office with shorthand notebook in hand. I said I was remembering a joke someone told me in the canteen yesterday, but that was far removed from the truth. I was thinking that, if the decision I was edging ever closer to proved to have been based on poor judgement, I could always sneak into *Die Glocke* one night and go back in time and change it.

August 30th, 1964: No entries for a couple of days; no need. The team worked hard on *Die Glocke* and I busied myself with interviewing candidates for a vacancy on the 'Experimental Physics Executive'. There were no truly outstanding candidates but that's the norm when you are dealing with the elite in terms of IQ – they are all much of a muchness, they are all technically brilliant, they could all do the job.

I always try to look for someone who can combine intellect and character, but it is all too rare these days to find a graduate who is able to combine a love for life with the demands of modern science. It saddens me to say it, but I do believe we are producing highly qualified but staggeringly dull automatons. That's probably a little unfair as I have never been likened to any stand-up comedian but, even so, I like to work alongside kids who have a real spark burning somewhere inside them.

September 1st, 1964: An interesting and productive day; one which may just turn out to be pivotal. Mid morning, two members of the team who have been carrying out the *Die Glocke* examination came to see me. They were both beaming like kids who had been given free run of their favourite candy store.

They said they had taken apart the control unit and studied the wiring and electrical circuits inside. Nothing they hadn't seen before. Every switch, every button, every light was accounted for – they were either used during the ignition sequence or they were 'standard' features of any machine; fuel levels, etc.

But there was good news… wonderful news, actually. After they had put everything back in its right and proper place, they

– the team of four – sat together drinking coffee and chatted as they stared at a machine which they now assumed would shortly be classified as retro junk. There was much talk of how they might possibly have overlooked something; of how the final piece of a jigsaw is often lost; of how good fortune always plays a part in the solving of great mysteries.

As they were about to leave to begin compiling their collective report – every damned thing has to be in triplicate when you are dealing with the White House – one of them remarked that they could do no more; that they had taken apart everything inside *Die Glocke* except the pilot's seat.

A process of elimination is a key component of any good search, and that was recognised by my colleagues, who placed their cups on the table and returned, en masse, to *Die Glocke*.

Urged on by the other three, one of them – Carl – climbed into the machine and settled into the seat. I am told that he did precisely what he should have done, what I would have expected him to do – he behaved as if the machine were fired up and active. He strapped himself in by fastening a seat belt which I have always believed to be so flimsy as to be utterly worthless. He then began reaching out with his arms to fully understand the extent of his reach. He moved his arms down, which allowed his hands to explore the underside of the seat. He ran his fingers along the seams and then into the space beneath, feeling his way into the dark void. He found nothing, so reached first left and then right, running his fingers across the floor of the compartment; an uncarpeted, sheer metal casing which formed the barrier between *Die Glocke*'s engine section and the control unit.

There appeared to be nothing – and then he felt something. Down to the right of the chair, his fingers roamed around the outline of what felt like a slightly depressed panel, perhaps six inches by four.

Carl unfastened his seat belt and motioned for his colleagues to join him. Someone called for a flashlight. A summoned security guard handed one over. Carl took it, switched it on and pointed it down toward the right of the pilot's chair.

The very faintest of outlines was clearly visible on a surface covered by dust and general grime. Reaching forward, he touched the central point with the index finger of his right hand. There was an almost inaudible click – and a section of the floor pivoted upward and open on a small hinge set to the left of the flap.

What was revealed was a simple, unassuming red button. No graduated dials, no keyboard, no bulbs… just a red button maybe half an inch in diameter.

CHAPTER

TEN

Diamond was in the same room, but only now did he appreciate that something was different. His last treatment, almost six weeks ago, had passed without the requirement for thought or reasoning. Lie down, close your eyes, feel sick, get bored, sleep and go home.

Diamond craned his neck a little to get a fuller sweep of Room 7b, Ward 10, and then realised it was the walls – bloody hell, they'd been painted, the mind-numbingly dull magnolia replaced by a deeply unpleasant turquoise.

Then again, he could be in another room, he supposed. Paying attention is the one thing you most definitely do not do when undergoing chemotherapy. Don't think about the needle in your arm which hurts, don't think about why they are pouring chemicals into you, don't think about the relative futility of it all – and lastly, definitely don't think about the wretched knitted hat your aunt made for you to try and conceal the fact that your hair has long since departed.

Gaunter and thinner, Diamond actually quite liked the bald look. He didn't ask for any form of confirmation but there was definitely a hint of a young Bruce Willis about him these days. Of course, it didn't help that those mates who ignored his predictable 'stay away' pleas, and who still turned up at both the hospital and his home in numbers, had decided to call him either "Telly" after Telly Savalas, or "Baldy Bastard". He often wondered why it is that subtlety is always lost on those who seek to express deep concern. *Probably embarrassment,* he mused as he watched the last few drops of a liquid designed to extend his life drip from bottle to vein.

The admirable Dr Marshall was still in charge of his slow demise and, true to form, he bounded through the door within a couple of minutes of Diamond's arm accepting the last few millilitres of a substance which was disappointingly colourless – he had always wanted it to be a rich green with bubbles and rising smoke.

"Morning, young man," said Dr Marshall, clutching the ubiquitous clipboard and pen.

"Shouldn't that be, 'Morning, young man who will never get old?'" said Diamond, with the sort of self-deprecating mischief which had, down the months, so endeared him to his doctor.

"You're a tart, sir. Shut up and listen. Do you want the good news or the bad news?" Dr Marshall asked.

"Let's start the day on a high and then allow it to slip away without grace, eh?"

"OK, the good news is that the frequency of your visits here to take on board the drugs will be reduced henceforth. No, no – don't complain. I know just how much you love coming here; a splendid place where the conversation is good, the food excellent and the staff engagingly pretty."

"And the bad news?" asked Diamond, smiling at his doctor's predictably sarcastic comments.

"God, where to begin... where to begin. As you know, I have always tried to be disgustingly honest with you, simply because I see in you a man who can probably spot a pile of bullshit at a thousand paces. We started off with being open and level with each other – I said you were fucked, you said you felt like shit – and that's the way we will, hopefully, carry on.

"I would so dearly love to say that, when I have either good or bad news for you, you will get it without embellishment or adornment. Sadly, I never seem to have any good news for you – save the fact that I'm told Nurse Johnson, the pretty one with the ponytail, quite fancies you.

"Of course, as you have cancer, I can always drum up bad news aplenty. If I so chose – if I didn't like you – I could fill your day with miserable updates which would see you reduced to little more than a crumpled mass of misery.

"So, from both our perspectives, this isn't easy or fun. I loathe my inability to walk in here and tell you something good – apart from the Nurse Johnson thing. I am worried about her, actually. She either has a thing for men with a yellow pallor or she's just plain dumb.

"The treatment has gone OK. I can't be more enthusiastic because, as you know, I made it clear from the start that all we can do is prolong your life by fighting the leukaemia; we can't cure it. We have managed to slow it down. The drugs you have been taking have unpleasant side effects – but I don't really have to tell you as much, as you are inside looking out.

"We have quite possibly reached the point where you have to face a big decision. Thus far it has been – in terms of decisions to be made – relatively easy for you because I have made them for you... and because I have a white coat and a stethoscope you have never once raised a hand in opposition. You're the sort of patient I love: you don't ask questions, you place your trust in me and you smile more than most.

"The big question which surrounds chemotherapy when it is being used on a patient who isn't going to get better is when to stop it; when to accept that the time has come to call it a day. Once the treatment is withdrawn the cancer will, of course, have free rein to multiply, spread and basically do what it wants – and it will. It is a simple balancing act in many ways – the treatment won't cure a terminal patient and, whilst it does extend life, sometimes for quite a while, it is unpleasant and reduces the quality of that life. That's to say – breathe deeply, young Steve – if we stop the treatments you will feel better but you will die sooner.

"Sorry, that was very blunt but, try as I have in the past, you cannot dress up that sort of sentence. So, there you have it. I will leave you to have a think. I don't believe they will discharge you until tomorrow so I can call in first thing in the morning to see you. Well, unless Nurse Johnson has whisked you away to a cottage in the Dales for some good, old-fashioned love therapy," Dr Marshall said.

"Here comes the question, Doctor," said Diamond. "If I stop the chemo, how long will I have? Please don't give me the 'how-long-is-a-piece-of-string' response."

"I would love to be definitive in a positive sort of way, so let's just say your piece of string isn't particularly long. Leukaemia is a very hard disease to predict. It can move at a leisurely pace or it can race around a body's system like Lewis Hamilton. Do you want me to make a stab at it? If I do, you must bear in mind that I could be way off… and I mean way off in both a positive and a negative sense."

"Please do."

"All I can do is base any answer on past experiences. I did have a patient similar to you about three years ago. Same age, same problem, same length of chemo treatment. He opted to give up the chemo and lived for nine months, I think it was. I know, I know, that doesn't sound very long at all, does it? I could stand here and lie to you. Indeed, I know for a fact that many of my colleagues do just that. I can understand their reasoning, I truly can. If our relationship was not as it is – open and based on mutual trust – then maybe I would. Maybe I would say that you will live a very happy life with Nurse Johnson for several years. I haven't said that because I don't believe that to be the case – and because the very least you deserve from me is honesty.

"Hey, I could be wrong. I have been many times. The human body is a quite remarkable machine. Often when I have assumed the battle to be lost, a body has fought back and attempted to repel the invading cancerous cells. It can happen," Dr Marshall said.

"Thanks. I would never want you to lie to me or to give me false hope," said Diamond. "I will have a think overnight as I stare at these turquoise walls."

"OK, Steve. See you on the morrow," said Dr Marshall as he headed for the door.

"Doctor?" said Diamond. "Tell Nurse Johnson I am ready for my bed bath."

Both men smiled and waved.

Predictably, Diamond's pursuit of sleep largely ended in failure. As ever when he was in a hospital bed, his dreams were of needles, tubes, and visitors who always seemed to glide in and out as if upon casters. They would deliver flowers – usually an atrocious purple colour – and then tell him how desperately sorry they were that he wouldn't be in a position to attend next weekend's barbecue.

He always woke up with a start, the sweat rolling down into his half-open eyes, his hands shaking and his head aching. On each and every occasion he demanded of himself the answer to one simple question – *What kind of a fucking life is this?*

By the time he had fought his way through the waking fog the next morning, an unusually pleasant dream about a large yacht on an azure ocean quickly fading to grey, he knew that he had reached a decision. He also reckoned that he had reached that decision whilst sleeping, which quite probably said much about both his mental state and the strength of the medication he was receiving.

Almost as if to confirm that what remained of his life would officially start that morning, Nurse Johnson promptly arrived at his bedside holding one of those odd-looking grey cardboard contraptions which bedridden patients use to empty their bladders. "Good morning, Steve," she said in what he took to be a seductive manner. "Can you make it to the bathroom or would you prefer to remain lying down and have me help you take a pee?"

Off to a flyer, he thought. *Off to a flyer.*

Dr Marshall arrived around 8.45am and raised his eyebrows in a manner which almost seemed to pose the question: *Well, have you decided?*

"Morning, Satan," said Diamond. "OK. I don't like being made to feel ill by medicine which is designed to help me feel better. Call me old-fashioned but that just doesn't seem right somehow. So, let's stop the chemo and take it from there. I was going to say let's see what happens, but this is rather like a Sylvester Stallone movie – you don't know the script but you know the ending."

"That's what I thought you would say," said Dr Marshall. "You could spend the next year-and-a-half receiving chemo but you would feel ill throughout that entire process. It is difficult to say what I would do were I in your position because I am not in your position, but... well, let's just say I think you have made the right choice. Fuck the cancer and live a little, son."

"Will I see you again once I have been discharged?" asked Diamond, in a rather sad, almost childlike manner.

"Yep, you'll still be required to come in at regular intervals for check-ups and the like. You won't have any more chemo but there are plenty of other drugs we will be filling you with," said Dr Marshall.

Diamond went home an hour or so later. Noreen wasn't there, which came as something of a relief as their relationship had been listing badly in recent weeks. He was ready for that development, having read online the personal diaries of many cancer sufferers. It seemed so unfair that as your body failed, so too did your relationships. More often than not it did seem to be the fault of the supporting partner, the reluctant carer, rather than the actual victim. Even when both parties are healthy nothing is ever perfect, and the introduction of a serious illness simply serves to widen already existing fault lines.

Noreen had been wonderful, particularly in the weeks that followed his diagnosis. Having moved through the phase of being a surrogate mother with almost indecent haste, she did the wisest thing of all – she simply treated him as if nothing was wrong. Apart from ensuring that he took his daily supply of tablets and mineral supplements, and accompanying him to his chemo appointments, she stood back, giving him the time, space and privacy to come to terms with the bleakest of scenarios.

He was grateful, very grateful, but as his mood swings became more apparent, he found it difficult to show that gratitude. He wished to be seen as a strong man who was handling things with a maturity beyond his years, but the long spells of silence and contemplation told an altogether more miserable story.

Many, many times he had considered ending their relationship, if only to lower the curtain on her suffering. He couldn't decide whether living out his remaining days alone would be a positive or a negative. It did appeal to the roguish poet who he had always believed lurked inside him: days of reading the books he had always promised himself he would read, of listening to old albums by old favourites, of drinking to excess, of a return to smoking dope. When he was down and feeling very sorry for himself, it appealed greatly.

But he realised that, if he was to opt for the Greta Garbo approach, he would also have to sever his ties with everyone else – family, former colleagues and, of course, the redoubtable Toby, who had been a shining beacon of support and a fountain of common sense over the past few months. Whilst he accepted that moving Noreen out of his life would represent a relatively straightforward task, he knew he would never be able to shake off Toby. In truth, he didn't want to. When you are in a hole you need someone with a shovel, even if he doesn't know how to use it to best effect.

The puncture wounds on the inside of his right arm had all but healed when Diamond realised that he was starting to feel better. Without a swirling stream of chemo drugs moving around his veins, the constant feeling of nausea had passed, the headaches were less intense and less frequent and, wonder of wonders, he could actually see his hair returning. It was only a few tufts matted together with the lightest coating of fluff but, hey, it was a start.

He hadn't actually told Noreen that he had decided to stop the chemo as she had been away tending to her sick mother for a few days, and he also needed the moment to be right as he was, in essence, announcing the starting of a stopwatch which would end with those who thought kindly of him gathered in the grim crematorium which, fittingly, stood just behind The King's Arms. The thought of the mourners sitting in The King's lounge and staring across at the crematorium as his earthly remains were belched out of a steel chimney in the form of black smoke really did appeal to him.

"There goes Steve, up to heaven," Aunt Jess would say, pointing to the sky above the pub's backyard.

As time was now most definitely not on his side, Diamond – having dismissed the idea of drawing up a bucket list – decided he would tell Noreen of his decision that night. He put on his awful woolly hat and headed to the nearby supermarket, where he bought the ingredients to throw together some sort of meat-based evening meal, and a very classy bottle of champagne.

He worked away in the kitchen for an hour before succumbing to the fatigue which was the most obvious side effect of his chemical adventure. He was always tired and always falling asleep. He tried to watch the hourly headlines on Sky News but his eyes had closed long before his favourite newscaster, Kay Burley, had finished the first item, which, ironically, was highlighting the plight of cancer patients amid yet more government cutbacks.

He awoke only when Noreen returned from work – she had developed the habit of deliberately slamming shut the front door in order to wake her ailing boyfriend.

"Hello, Sleeping Beauty," she said, kissing him lightly on the top of his head. "Hair's looking good. I may perm it for you later."

She entered the kitchen before popping back into the living room and asking, "Wow, what's going on here? Food? Champagne? Are we celebrating something?"

"Just thought we should treat ourselves – and, yes, I know we can't afford it but sod that. Just my way of saying thanks, hon."

"Thanks for what?" she asked.

"For being you. I really don't know how you put up with me. If the roles were reversed – God forbid – I would have dumped you ages ago," he replied.

"Very romantic, Precious," she said, using, for the first time in years, his childhood nickname.

He again fell asleep, deeply so, as Noreen completed the preparation of their meal. When he was shaken awake, the table was set neatly, steam was rising from hot food and the champagne was waiting to be opened.

He edged the cork out of the bottle and filled the two flutes, carefully so as not to waste any of the contents. "Right, one of us had better propose a toast," he said.

"To us – but more especially to you," said Noreen.

"Why me?" asked Diamond.

"You're still here – and for the moment that's good enough for me; small mercies, grateful thanks and all that."

"Good point. I'm not sure we should be toasting and celebrating, but I am equally uncertain as to precisely what you are supposed to do in these circumstances."

"You do what you feel is right, what you feel to be best. If you wanted to lock yourself away in your bedroom and weep for the next few months, I would still be here to support you. It is just impossible for me to give you any advice. If you had a broken leg or a bladder infection, I could probably help, but when one person has a very serious illness which the other hasn't experienced, advice is absolutely pointless – and probably really irritating to hear. I will be here to answer any calls for help," she said.

"Thanks. That means a lot to me. No, it means everything to me. Life's a bastard, but then again my mother tells me that I have been saying that since I first learned to talk. Let's eat, drink and be merry, Noreen," he said.

Afterwards, after the champagne had gone, they sat together, each clutching a glass of the cheap brandy which was a permanent fixture in their kitchen cupboard.

"I have something to tell you," said Diamond. "I spoke to Dr Marshall and I have decided to stop the chemo. In fact, I stopped it about two weeks ago. I made the decision, not him. We talked things through and we went through the various scenarios."

Noreen kept quiet and still, sensing that Diamond had worked out his speech and knowing he could do without interruptions.

"If I carry on with it I may well extend my life, but that life will be filled with what I have had since I began the treatment; namely sickness and accompanying depression. I don't want that. I don't want to die either, but as I know I am going to do just that, I have decided to make the actual run-up to the event as pain-free and as enjoyable as possible," he added.

"I suspected you'd stopped – the hair starting to grow back was the real clue. I'm glad. You have taken your destiny back into your own hands, Steve, and that's as it should be; that's as it always should be," said Noreen. "And I am glad you told me – not quite as quickly as you perhaps should have done, but you got there in the end. I am not even going to ask the most obvious of questions. I should, but I won't."

"He doesn't know," said Diamond, promptly answering the question which had not been asked. "Could be nine months, could be longer. I suppose it could be less now that the leukaemia has been given the green light to wander about inside my blood. I had often wondered what it must be like for those who know when they are going to die – like prisoners on death row who are told the precise moment their life will be ended."

"You morbid bugger," said Noreen, rising to clear away the dinner plates. Her eyes were filling with tears but she managed to find the sanctuary of the kitchen before her mascara began to drip down onto her flushed cheeks.

CHAPTER

ELEVEN

Extracts from the Journal of Dr Eric David

September 2nd, 1964: Quite often when there is a big prize on offer, the instinct is to rush forward to try and grab it. I decided against doing that today, much to the disappointment of some members of my team.

Having unearthed another of *Die Glocke*'s secrets – quite possibly the final one it has to give up – there was an understandable desire to add fresh knowledge to old and see what we had. I urged caution, as much because I think it is imperative that we all keep a sense of perspective as because I am (again) somewhat frightened by the possible consequences of this new discovery.

My instinct was to fall in line with the others and see what the newly located button is for; it wouldn't be there unless it has a significant function. I canvassed opinion among the team as to what they thought that function might be. Two of them volunteered the same suggestion – that it may well be something to do with the elongation of the trips through time, almost like a pause button which stops the machine moving back to its starting position after eighty-eight seconds.

I was of the same opinion but decided to keep my own counsel – probably for fear of being accused of bandwagon-jumping. I could be wrong, they could be wrong... who knows?

What I do know is that the only way we will provide a definitive answer is to test out the theory. That sounds very simplistic to a man who is sitting here writing as he watches an episode of *Sgt Bilko* over the rim of a full wine glass. It is a decision I know I cannot hide from, because those I represent will be expecting me to show some leadership tomorrow. I have never shied away from major decisions, even when I have been unconvinced about the merits of the choice I have made.

At this moment in time – as Bilko again tries to put one over on Colonel John T. Hall – my inclination is to go with my gut instinct and try another 'flight'. That, of course, will mean someone sitting in the pilot's seat and disappearing back in time – you can't push a button unless you have a finger to do so.

Like the rest of the team, I await my decision with interest. Goodnight.

September 3rd, 1964: We are going to do it. Tomorrow, in fact. So September 4th, 1964 will either be remembered as a watershed moment in science and physics, or it will be just another day; a day when a great gamble didn't pay off and was promptly buried beneath a topsoil of lies and intrigue.

We met early in the morning and it was clear from the outset that the rest of the team had reached a unanimous decision. Whether or not they had gathered for an out-of-hours conversation I'm not sure, but when asked to speak, they spoke as one.

They are younger than me and still boast that special enthusiasm which goes with immaturity. To them, everything is an adventure to be taken on and enjoyed. They couldn't find even one reason why they should opt for safety first; they wanted to roll the dice and damn the consequences. There is a part of me which agrees with them – but, older (and hopefully wiser) that I am, I have a sense of caution which they would possibly never fully understand.

But we live in a democracy and, had it gone to a vote, the motion to push the red button would have been passed with some comfort. So who was I to argue? Actually, there was no argument because, when they asked me for my opinion, I found myself agreeing with them. The best decisions are the unanimous ones – at least then everyone is to blame if things go awry.

I know that I won't sleep tonight. I have that very special feeling in the pit of my stomach which I remember from childhood when Santa was said to be on his way from the North Pole to my house in Virginia.

Hopefully I will be able to add to this journal after the experiment. If that doesn't happen then it may mean that I am marooned in my own past.

If that should happen, I hope my family will forgive me. To that end, I have written letters to those I hold dear trying to explain my decision. They are in a small box behind the wardrobe in my bedroom. Will someone kindly distribute them for me? Thank you.

September 5th, 1964: No need to distribute the letters as I am, self-evidently, back. I say, 'back' as I have returned from arguably the greatest adventure ever known to mankind. I am in a daze – my hands are still shaking with the enormity of today's events. If I wasn't a man whose entire professional life has been based on the virtues of logic, I would be disbelieving of my own words.

While it is very late – almost 3am – I must document this properly and include as much detail as I can recall. I believe it to be important that I do because history was made – and visited – just a few hours ago. Whether or not the world will ever come to know of these events I am, at this point, unsure.

In the same way that no government will ever publicly admit to the existence of life on other planets for fear of sparking panic among a population which will always be fearful of the unknown, I find it highly unlikely that my White House overlords will wish to issue a statement confirming that the space-time continuum has at last been breached, and that trips to visit long-dead parents and grandparents will shortly be available from local travel agents.

I am being flippant because it is difficult to accept what has happened. It is fantasy stuff pulled directly from the pages of H. G. Wells and Isaac Asimov. At the moment it just doesn't make any sense. What was achieved today will either change our world forever or it will become one of its most closely guarded secrets, an enduring conspiracy theory for successive generations.

Let me start at the beginning – as good a place as any, I suppose.

As I said, we had decided that it would represent a dereliction of duty if we did not follow our natural instincts and at least give it a go.

I arrived early at the base and was surprised to find every member of the team already there, gathered in the canteen. I ordered coffee for us all and took my place among them. I asked just one question of the group, and that was, "Are we sure?" There was no hesitation, no second thoughts. The answer was in the affirmative. At that point, I realised that there would be no last-minute rethinks, no going back and, more saliently, irrespective of the outcome, no regrets.

As the buck stops with me, I then outlined what I believed we should do. We would repeat, exactly, the procedures which had prompted the newspaper items in the hope of replicating the same smooth process. The difference this time was that someone would be sitting in the pilot's seat – if we were now in the business of fashioning miracles, we needed a reliable witness to the events.

I knew that each individual member of the team would raise their right arm in genuine enthusiasm were I to ask for a volunteer. I also knew that I wouldn't be seeking a volunteer because I had already made the crucial decision – I was the one who would be inside *Die Glocke* when next it was switched on.

I had expected some form of mini rebellion when I told them, but it wasn't so. I think they had been expecting it. There was actually a murmur of approval and the nodding of several heads. I was pleased. I didn't want it to appear that I was pushing myself forward just because I was in charge. I had hoped they would see the sense in it. Believe it or not, it wasn't a decision based on ego; not at all. It had always seemed wholly sensible to me.

I am the oldest by some distance. I am divorced and my children have disappeared to pursue their own life paths. So, if things went horribly wrong, the world would be losing a mere scientist (in what would be announced as a tragic, in-house accident).

I did have a little speech ready to deliver that revolved around my age, my seniority etc., but, mercifully, it wasn't required. They acquiesced with maturity beyond their years, leaving me to explain the processes we would go through rather than why I was the one who would be strapped into *Die Glocke*'s seat.

Thereafter, it was a case of us moving smoothly into 'operation' mode; something we had done before and which again proved to be a fault-free exercise. My respect for my young team grew by the minute. I asked them to spend the morning running a series of comprehensive tests on the machine – checking fuel levels, electrical connections etc. My distant past was arguably a good deal happier and more rewarding than my last few years have been but, even so, I had no real desire to plant myself in Memory Lane on a permanent basis.

As I let the team busy themselves with their tasks, I thought – in depth for the first time – of the well-documented paradoxes which have always been promoted by those who have argued against time travel. There are so many – and they are usually so very complicated.

The most oft-used one is probably the simplest one – the so-called 'grandfather paradox' – and it is sufficiently straightforward as to baffle or confuse no one. It goes like this: if a man went back in time, sought out his own grandfather as a sixteen-year-old and promptly shot him dead, what would happen? Logic, the lifeblood of my career, suggests it is impossible because if the grandfather died before he could father a child then the man travelling back in time to kill him would never have existed.

Those who have at least one foot in the 'pro' camp argue that it wouldn't happen because the universe wouldn't permit such a broad dilemma to arise. They believe that something would always occur to stop the man with the gun offloading a deadly shot. Of course, when asked to explain what that something is, they cannot; another paradox.

We had agreed that if *Die Glocke* passed all the relevant tests we would have lunch together and then move back to what would be a sealed, off-limits-to-all laboratory. At noon I was informed that *Die Glocke* was all set, so we adjourned to the canteen. I could barely eat. It wasn't so much nerves as excitement. I felt permanently light-headed and was aware of the almost pleasant feeling of vagueness one experiences when slipping out of a general anaesthetic. I was aware the team were peppering me with questions and requests, but I was hardly listening. My focus was on two things – what would happen when I arrived at my destination, and what would I do if something went wrong?

Once they had fallen silent, I outlined my plan. It was obvious that I needed to pick a year and location which would cause as little disruption and upset as possible to those who might see the arrival and the departure of *Die Glocke*. However, it was imperative that I chose a location where I would be able to actually confirm any passage through time. There would be, for example, no point at all in landing in the middle of the Grand Canyon or the Northern Missouri Plains.

To that end, I opted for New York's Central Park – but at a time when the vast majority of locals and tourists would have retired for the night. So it was decided – Central Park at 11pm. I opted for 1910 for no other reason than that it was the year of my birth.

With *Die Glocke* 'arriving' at the same time as it 'departed', it meant that we had an extended wait before we could make our attempt. To fill the time I asked the team to again micro-inspect all aspects of the machine – one last series of checks from top to bottom, from the inside out. By the time that was done it was around 3pm, so I told the team to relax and assemble in the laboratory at 10.30pm (we told security that we were carrying out important maintenance which held a minor threat of human contamination – that would ensure they kept their distance).

Yes, the hours crawled by. I fell asleep at my desk between 6.30 and 7.45pm and awoke feeling both exhausted and nauseous. I read and watched some television, enjoyed a very light snack and then, around 10.20pm, made my way down to the lab.

Mercifully, the security section had fully complied with my instructions and the whole area was neatly cordoned off with yellow-and-black barred tape. If the tape was just fine, the sign hanging from it was, shall we say, a little over the top:

KEEP OUT – DANGER OF DEATH.

By 10.45pm the team was assembled, the barely concealed yawns from two of them suggesting that they too had opted for sleep to help kill the boredom.

We went through the entire procedure again. I would enter the machine at 10.58pm, input the year 1910 on what had become known as the 'time dial', and then enter the coordinates for Central Park. Once that had been done, someone behind the glass shield would turn on the power supply, *Die Glocke* would fire up and I would, hopefully, arrive in 1910.

The closer we moved to the appointed hour, the more I began to consider the dangers posed by what was, I readily concede, an exercise in sheer stupidity and recklessness.

I was working on the basis that the machine would indeed work, and that at some point in the initial eighty-eight-second cycle I would be looking out over a very dark – and hopefully deserted – Central Park.

The moment I arrived I intended to push the red button down to the right of my seat. Having practised this manoeuvre I was aware that I would first have to unbuckle my seat belt in order that I might reach it. The button stayed depressed once pushed and was only released by the appliance of further pressure. Upon this we had built our theory that its purpose was to almost freeze the machine's progress; to pause or suspend it.

Having listened to the various time-travel paradoxes over so many years I was acutely aware that I must, once in Central Park, do as little as possible; I simply could not risk undertaking any action which might cause any form of 'ripple' – a small, seemingly insignificant deed in 1910 which could have horrific ramifications many years down the line. And yet, I knew that I would have to at least step out of the machine in order that I might confirm – one hundred per cent – that I was where I was supposed to be; namely a very long way from home.

Obviously I could not be certain as to *Die Glocke*'s accuracy in terms of meeting the longitude and latitude coordinates. I had selected an area of Central Park between the lake and the Metropolitan Museum of Art. From studying old maps and photographs, the target area was shaded by trees and was away from the main footpaths and thoroughfares.

Curiously, my main fear was arriving in 1910 to discover that I had landed at the top of a very tall tree; the mind can work in strange, unfathomable ways on occasions.

As we ran through a battery of last-minute checks, the air hung very heavy with what I sensed to be a potent mixture of anticipation and fear. By this point I had fully recovered my equilibrium and was calm and focused on what we were about to do. For the first time in twenty-four hours the enormity of the moment was lost on me – we were a team of scientists preparing to do an experiment, and before you could anticipate the outcome you had to apply yourself dutifully to the preparations.

As we approached 10.55pm I wondered if I should make some sort of (hopefully) memorable speech – one which would become my epitaph if things went awry and I didn't return. I decided against it as I feared it would reek of triumphalism – and speeches from the heart have never really been my forte.

Instead I did what I believed to be an acceptable and sensible thing in shaking the hand of each member of the team. It was a nice moment.

I had realised the day before that my choice of clothing may prove to be significant if, once back in 1910, I was either spotted or approached by someone. I wore plain brown shoes, dark trousers, a white shirt and the longest coat I could find. Thankfully, it as it's September, my belief was that the few people I might encounter would be wrapped up against an approaching New York winter.

My inclination was to take with me a camera – perhaps even a small movie camera – but I decided against it at the last minute as I had absolutely no idea whether or not any such action would adversely affect the journey. I didn't think it would, but I wasn't prepared to take any unnecessary risks. If all went well, there would, after all, be further visits back in time from 1964.

So, there I was – all dressed up with somewhere to go. My heart was beating like a piston as I positioned myself in the pilot's seat and secured the seat belt. As I stared out to my right I could see my team taking their place behind the glass partition – a barrier which would offer absolutely no protection at all if *Die Glocke* decided to revert to being a weapon of mass destruction.

I inputted the year – 1910 – followed by the coordinates of the spot in Central Park I had selected: N 40-46-38, W 73-58-05.

Although the base's media team had been neither informed nor invited, the member of my team judged to have the steadiest hand – Dale – had 'borrowed' their cumbersome film camera to capture the moment. He raised his right arm to signal, Hitchcock-style, that he was recording events, and then it was down to me. We had built into our preparations the (distinct) possibility that I might undergo a dramatic change of heart at the very last minute – ironically, the eleventh hour. So, nothing would happen in terms of switching on the power source until I raised a thumb in an 'OK' gesture and shouted – loudly and audibly – the words, "Let's go." My trip into the unknown was being filmed, it was being timed – it was even being drawn, by Sharon, the youngest present who was an amateur illustrator and cartoonist.

I stared at the control panel, looked down to make sure the red button hadn't mysteriously disappeared, and then, I confess, I whispered an almost silent prayer, reminding my kids that I loved them very much.

The large clock on the wall said it was 11pm – so it was time. It was now or never. I input the complex start-up sequence and then raised my arm and gave them the thumbs-up. I then shouted, "Let's do it, team ", and I closed my eyes and hoped.

I knew exactly what would follow. The business part of *Die Glocke* which lay beneath me began to roar as usual – but as I was much, much closer in terms of proximity, the noise was absolutely deafening, so much so that I made a mental note to wear earplugs should I ever opt for a repeat performance.

As the roar built and built I was aware of movement below me, almost as if the machine were seeking to lift itself up and fly. I have only ever been in a helicopter once but it was that sort of sensation; a huge upward thrust accompanied by what sounded like the whirring of giant blades.

I wanted to take in every last detail of the ignition process, so constantly moved my head to scan every inch of the interior surface. I looked out to my left in search of my colleagues but I had lost them – the air was blurred and fuzzy; it looked like the optical illusion of heat haze on a summer's drive down a long road.

The lights on the control panel began to flicker, some seemingly with great reluctance. As the level of noise rose still further it was almost as if I could touch it; it seemed to hold a density, as if it had shape and form. The panel lights were now not just lit but ever brightening in their intensity. I knew that whatever was going to happen would happen within seconds.

The last thing I remember seeing before what I will now always refer to as the great 'whoosh' was the blue tinge which seemed to have infiltrated the air inside *Die Glocke*. Small particles of dirt began to rise from the machine's floor. Several were at eye level when the whoosh came.

I felt myself being pushed down into my seat with enormous force. My eyes closed involuntarily and I remember my mouth opening in readiness to form a good old-fashioned swear word. My entire body was tingling and the hairs on my arms were standing bolt upright.

And then everything stopped. The noise cut out, my body relaxed and almost slumped forward, there was no blue hue, no floating dust particles, no flashing lights on the panel before me.

My instinct was to sit back and relax, to get my breath back. But I was here – wherever that was – to work, not to play. I unlinked the safety belt and reached down to my right, running my fingers across the floor until I found the raised mounting which held the red button. I stabbed it once, very firmly.

I looked up and to my right at the small window through which I had last seen my team. The window was pitch black. I looked to my left at the second window – again, pitch black.

As I readied myself to push down the lever which would open *Die Glocke's* hatch, I cursed myself… in fact, I swore out loud. I had forgotten to start the stopwatch pinned to the outside of my overcoat. Its purpose was absolutely crucial as it would count down toward the magical eighty-eight-second mark. It had been decided that I would remain largely motionless and in situ until after that point. If I was not returned to – or was still inside – the white-walled laboratory after eighty-eight seconds then, self-evidently, I was somewhere else.

All I could do was sit and wait, and try to judge when a minute-and-a-half had passed. They say that a watched kettle never seems to boil. The seconds ticked by so very slowly. I decided to play safe and count out loud up to ninety.

I had reached sixty-eight when I heard a noise to my left. It was a scratching sound, as if someone were dragging their nails across the exterior of *Die Glocke*.

I was frozen, made motionless by a mixture of fear and excitement. As I had by this point moved comfortably beyond the eighty-eight-second barrier, the noise was being made either by a member of my team anxious to check my well-being, or by something else.

I moved out of the seat and attempted to gaze through the left-hand window. I couldn't see anything at all, which was disappointing as the very least I had expected to see were distant street lamps around the periphery of the park.

I sat down again and waited for another minute. Had I still been inside the laboratory, I knew that neon light would have been flooding through both of *Die Glocke*'s windows, tiny though they are. It would also seem logical that one of the team would be pounding on the exterior of the hatch, seeking to gain entry.

But there was nothing. The scratching noise had stopped and everything – inside and outside the machine – was silent.

It was time to open the hatch and see what had happened and precisely where I was. Of course, it did immediately occur to me that if I wasn't in either the lab in 1964 or Central Park in the year 1910, then I was totally screwed. If I was lost in time it could be a permanent move rather than the anticipated day trip.

While a few minutes earlier it hadn't taken me much courage to step inside *Die Glocke* and slam the hatch shut, it took a great deal more to push down on the lever to move me to within seconds and feet of exit from the machine. I pushed down and, with almost a complete absence of noise, the hatch moved inward and then across to the left. I gazed out through the hole and into the darkness.

I could see very little – but I could see enough to confirm that I was no longer inside the lab. They say that a little knowledge can be a dangerous thing, but, strangely, I was no longer apprehensive or concerned. No – I was full of awe and wonder. I felt like a kid.

The first thing that struck me was the smell; a blend of recently cut grass and the faint aroma of what could have been magnolias – kindly remember that I am most definitely not a gardening expert.

I placed my hands on either side of the open hatch, much as you do when attempting to climb through a window, and slowly pushed myself forward so that my head and shoulders were clear of *Die Glocke*. I looked left, I looked right, I stared straight ahead.

Die Glocke was standing, perfectly upright, on a small patch of grass which was surrounded in the main part by trees, many of which still boasted a full complement of leaves. I was pleased with myself because I couldn't have selected a better spot, albeit my success had come about more by good luck than good judgement.

My reluctance to tamper with the fabric of the universe had now all but gone. I had come this far and I simply needed to confirm that the impossible had been made possible and that mankind had crossed a barrier which we had always been told would never be breached.

I edged forward, lifting my right leg out of the hatch and clear of the machine. Mindful of the legion of paradox stories, I was almost tempted to check that I wasn't going to plant my foot on a resting butterfly.

I placed my right foot on the ground; some twigs snapped beneath me. I moved again – and I was out, free of the machine and standing in the chill night air. And it was very chilly. The bushes to my immediate left were coated with a light frost, and I could see that I had left footprints on grass which was glistening and crisp to touch.

I had been asked by two members of the team to take something back with me if the experiment proved to be successful. They were not, of course, looking for a gift or even a memento; their request was a purely scientific one as they wanted to see if items collected from the past could survive a trip to the future. I had told them that I was a little reluctant to do so – but in the event I bent down and picked up a pine cone from the frozen ground. I slipped it into my overcoat pocket and then began to walk toward the one source of light I could see.

As I moved, focusing on the centre of the soft, diffused light, I held my breath, not wishing to betray my presence in the unlikely event that someone was out walking a dog or, God forbid, taking a romantic stroll in the Big Apple's scenic heartland.

A second light came into my line of vision... and then a third... and then a whole line of them. They were street lamps of the classic design; arched metalwork with a drooping, bluebell-like lamp glowing brightly against the darkest of September skies.

I stood and just stared. I wished now that I had brought a camera – stupid mistake, an oversight.

The lamps ran for some distance; I presumed for the length of the park's west side. Ahead of me I could see the Museum of Art, lit only by a handful of dim lights just outside its main entrance.

I didn't want to venture too far away from *Die Glocke*, but I had to see more before I attempted my return journey. Inching my way toward the line of street lamps, I could make out grand Gothic buildings in the foreground and, some distance away in the gloom, the outlines of New Yorkers shuffling homeward in the clinging cold.

And then the moment I had wished for; the signpost to the truth. I heard it before I saw it: a low, mechanical grinding noise punctuated by a clearly audible rattling sound. The car swept around the corner and into my line of sight, forcing a tardy straggler to rush toward the kerb.

It was old – well, old by 1964 standards. No roof, a ridiculously pronounced steering column, and two eye-like front headlights. My late father had a fascination with cars of all eras, and evidently I had gleaned knowledge from him without realising it. As it moved down the road in front of me I knew instantly what it was: a Schacht Roadster – to me a vintage model; to its current owner a state-of-the-art masterpiece of engineering and design.

The odds on that vehicle being driven down that road by a man wearing a cap, scarf and goggles in 1964 were a million to none. While no one had approached me with a "Welcome to 1910" sign, I knew – I just knew – I was there.

My inclination was to sit down somewhere, sigh deeply and spend a few moments reflecting on what had been achieved. In saying that, I had no thoughts at all for my own part in making history; my thoughts were exclusively with Wernher von Braun, a man of incalculable genius who had risen so far in my estimation that he was now very much on a par with history's greatest thinkers and inventors.

I needed no further proof. What we had set out to do we had accomplished – thus far without even the merest hint of a hitch or setback.

I began to retreat into the shadows, creeping more than walking. I was no more than twenty-five yards from *Die Glocke*, concealed from view by a combination of the darkness and the foliage, when a voice rang out, startling me.

"Good evening, sir," said the silhouetted figure standing in front of me. "A damn fine night for a walk, I think."

"Indeed, sir," I replied as I carefully considered my options. To turn and run – or even to simply walk away – would undoubtedly raise suspicion, so I stood my ground.

"What brings you out on a foul night like this? I quite often stroll here at this time of the year as it brings me some relief from my chest ailment – bronchitis, I am told it is."

"It is nothing medical in my case, sir," I said. "Well, save for matters of the heart. I have had what I shall describe as a disagreement with my good wife, so I decided to take the night air to allow a heated situation to cool down a little. She can be a volatile woman, but mercifully she usually acknowledges her mistakes without an undue delay."

"Ah, women. Confusing creatures indeed. Mine passed away two years ago. They said it was some form of liver condition but, as I kept telling her during her last few days as she lay in a sanatorium, I think it was possibly overuse of the vocal cords," he said, before laughing so loudly I feared he would attract the attention of any other late-night strollers in the vicinity.

Before I could either laugh in unison or comment, he spoke again.

"Where do you hail from, sir?" he asked.

"I am originally from Virginia, but now reside in the Manhattan area. The city suits me fine; I enjoy its people and its variety," I replied.

I noticed that my companion – his body swathed in a huge, heavy coat and his head covered by a very large cap – was carrying a newspaper.

"Anything of interest in the news, sir? I haven't seen a newspaper today, such has been my work schedule."

"Not much… same old stuff. Rumours of a war abroad – Europe, I believe. Here, take it; I have finished with it. Take it home and enjoy its pages before seeking reconciliation with your wife," he said, offering me the newspaper.

"Thank you very much indeed. It was good to make your acquaintance but I'd best be on my way. Good evening to you, sir," I said, before bowing my head slightly and moving away into the darkness.

Unable to believe my astonishing good fortune, I almost ran back to *Die Glocke* – which was, mercifully, untouched and, I assumed, unseen. I climbed back in, but simply couldn't resist the temptation to open up the newspaper and take a look at the front page.

CROMWELL DIXON ALMOST PERISHES IN COASTAL ACCIDENT

Mr Dixon was described in the New York Times *as a "dirigible ballooner", and on this particular day he all but met his maker when his engine-powered contraption failed at five hundred feet during the Harvard Aviation Meet in Boston and he almost ended up in the sea.*

There were other stories of even less interest – unions in uproar at changes in work practices, problems with the economy, problems with the President – but my eyes were repeatedly drawn to the dateline just beneath the masthead… September 4th, 1910.

My God, I was actually there. I was there, but the imperative was to get back home swiftly and without problems.

Taking one last look out of the frosted windows at New York in the year of my birth, I removed my coat, dropped the newspaper to the floor of the machine and fastened myself into the seat. I knew that my fate would be decided the very second I applied pressure to the red button, and that, if nothing happened, I would be staying precisely where I was. As my hand dropped down beside the seat it was trembling – not shaking, but twitching just enough to remind me that I had undertaken the most dangerous of adventures with the false bravado of a reckless, naive fool.

As my index finger hovered above the button, I found myself almost shouting out the words, "Move, you bastard, move."

I pushed down and felt the button release itself from its position of neutrality. As I lifted my finger, the button rose up and clicked back into place. My eyes had involuntarily closed, but they burst open as the machine growled back into life. Never has such an awful noise been so warmly welcomed.

The familiar grinding from beneath me began; the lights on the control panel began to glow and then flash before settling into a steady stream of red and yellow beams. I could feel the slightest of movements as the air seemed to close in on me. There was the vague smell of burning rubber, and as I gazed to my right and out of a window now free of frost, the usual blue hue hung in the distorted air.

And then it stopped. The noise drained away; the lights in front of me dimmed and then died away completely. Everything was still. I was fearful of opening my eyes for what I might see. I actually felt the urge to sleep – in fact, I felt compelled to sleep; every muscle in my body felt as though it had been pounded and stretched. My chest was heaving; I was almost gasping for breath. In short, I felt utterly exhausted.

But for the commotion which erupted outside *Die Glocke*, I would have slept, I know I would. It was as if I were in a hotel room and the mother of all late-night parties had erupted in the next room.

As I slowly opened my eyes, I moved my head to the right. There at the window was a pair of eyes covered by large-framed glasses, and a mouth which seemed to be moving at an almost unnatural pace. I could hear nothing at all.

The person outside began pointing downward and imploring me to do something. He was gesturing wildly. He wanted me to push the lever which opened the hatch. I didn't actually want to – I was content where I was and simply wished to be left alone to sleep. But I fought the temptation and dragged the lever down. The hatch lifted, moved across, and the party in the next room promptly moved into my room.

I heard so many things – fragments only, though.

"Give him some air."

"Get the medics!"

"You OK, Dr David?"

"Did it work, sir? Did you get there?"

I raised my right hand in the universal signal for quiet, and the noise duly died down to barely a whisper. I then held out both hands in order that I might be pulled free of *Die Glocke*.

I stood in front of them and instructed them to remain both silent and motionless for the next sixty seconds. They did as they were told, some looking at me as they might a specimen in a jar.

What I wanted to do – what I had to do – was convince myself that nothing had changed, that I was surrounded by the same people I had left behind only minutes earlier; people who had the same features, characteristics and mannerisms. As far as I could make out, the stationary frieze of human flesh and bone in front of me met all the criteria. Only then could I smile and embrace the person closest to me.

The questions started again, an endless stream of queries which I would have readily answered there and then, had I possessed the strength.

I told them that we had accomplished the most astonishing of feats; that we had rewritten history, made history, visited history – all inside the space of fifteen minutes. Yes, I told them, it had worked. Yes, I had gone back to New York's Central Park in the year 1910. Yes, I had met someone back there, and yes, we had chatted. I asked them to forgive the brevity of my report; to blame it on understandable fatigue. I announced that I was going to go straight home to gather my thoughts and to sleep the sleep of a contented and happy man.

Before shaking each one of them by the hand, I walked back to *Die Glocke* and picked up the copy of the *New York Times* from the floor. I handed it to a colleague and asked him to ensure both its preservation and its safekeeping.

As he placed the paper on the table, there were audible gasps of delight. Applause broke out as I left the room and headed for the car park.

September 7th, 1964: Excuse the forty-eight-hour gap. When I got home I gave myself up to the fatigue even before I had made it to the bedroom. Having poured myself a most generous measure of Irish whiskey, I sat in my living room and switched on the television, forgetting the time – it was way past midnight.

I can recall taking one large gulp of my Bushmills Black Bush – then I awoke almost three hours later with a start, a stiff neck, an empty glass in hand and the smell of spilled whiskey rising from my stained trousers.

I wasn't particularly concerned by this quite dramatic bout of tiredness but I did find it rather confusing. I was physically fit and had done nothing at all in terms of exercise save wander around a dark and deserted park for a few minutes.

Needless to say, I slept pretty well that night – so well, in fact, that I didn't wake until after 9am, which was unfortunate as I knew my team would have assembled early for a debriefing session they would have already conducted in their dreams.

I arrived at the base just after 10.30am, making my way through small groupings of workers who smiled courteously as I passed, all oblivious to the fact that the man in their midst had actually gone where no man had ever gone before. Yes, I confess, I did feel special… well, maybe not special; I felt somehow apart from everyone else. I knew this feeling of uniqueness would fade very quickly because there's nothing quite like a group of younger people in interrogation mode to strip away any veneer of grandeur.

Embarrassingly, when I walked into the main office, they applauded again. I had to quickly silence them for fear of 'outsiders' gatecrashing the gathering to enquire what we were all celebrating.

I ushered them into an anteroom, taking a seat at the head of a table which, confusingly and inexplicably, had an unmarked rack of test tubes in its centre. This was the easy bit, the straightforward bit. The previous forty-eight hours had held so very much that could have been pulled from the pages of *Astounding Tales* or *Weird Wonders*.

For a while we all just sat and smiled. It was the collective coming together of a small group which had experienced something unique. There was a bond between us that neither time nor circumstance could ever break; we had all danced with the Devil and emerged unscathed to dance alone. It was a quite lovely moment.

Eventually – almost reluctantly – I broke the spell by shrugging off the mantle of superhero and returning to the role of humble, self-effacing scientist. All I could think to do was give them a run-through of what had happened from my perspective. They listened with the intensity of a senior-school class, occasionally nodding in approval, often smiling with what appeared to be something akin to undiluted adulation. I had never experienced that before and I suspected I would never experience it again.

I am neither hero nor role model, but being feted by people who, just a few days earlier, had quite probably viewed me with suspicion was interesting and enlightening. If I needed proof that what we had achieved was off the proverbial scale then here it was, reflected in the faces of those who had accepted my tutorage in pursuit of education and not recognition.

So we sat and we talked. I went through everything I had witnessed– the moments after the power surge, the arrival, the walk in the park, the sighting of the classic car and the meeting with the man and his newspaper. I told them of my exhilaration and then my fears as I readied myself for the return journey. Finally I relayed the joy which had enveloped me when I looked through the tiny window to see their familiar faces.

Far more interesting for me was their version of what happened. Strangely, the whole event, from the switching on of the power to my return, lasted just nine minutes – for me it had seemed so very much longer. I was told that I still had the film footage to view, but that it showed precious little apart from the familiar transformation *Die Glocke* underwent when in active mode.

They were all anxious to talk and to question, but my mind was still somewhat dulled by events so I asked Dale to be the group's sole spokesman.

He said that, while spectacular in its accomplishment, the actual event had been rather "dull". I laughed out loud at the temerity of youth. I had smashed the laws of physics into very tiny pieces and it was being described as dull. He apologised but I told him there was absolutely no need as I fully understood what he meant.

So, the power was turned on, the lab was filled with noise, the air distorted and turned blue around *Die Glocke's* cone, and, yes, I was gone. After I had jumped through time, *Die Glocke* moved itself into standby mode – in fact, it appeared to switch itself off; another feature we had had no prior knowledge of. They weren't supposed to but, quite naturally, the team approached the machine after the ignition process. One of them stepped forward and peered through the window – the red button was clearly depressed and *Die Glocke* was empty.

I asked what they did in the minutes between my disappearance and reappearance. Two went to the toilet and the rest drank coffee and talked about the World Series.

They admitted that, after five minutes or so, they began to worry. The question was asked – "What if he doesn't get back?" One ventured that he thought I had a dog at home which would need to be first fed and then rehoused. So kind.

It was only after nine minutes that the familiar guttural rumblings of *Die Glocke* began to fill the room again. The team, correctly, returned to their positions behind the glass partition and waited. Ignoring my instructions to stay clear of the machine for at least fifteen minutes after any return, they moved forward en masse to see if I was back inside the cockpit. I was, and they apparently queued up to catch a glimpse of me strapped into the seat.

It felt strange – almost uncomfortable – to have dissected such a momentous occasion in less time than it took me to finish my coffee. I asked where the copy of the *New York Times* was, to be told it was in a secure, temperature-controlled tank normally used to house small rodents. I was impressed; it was a sensible and smart move.

Curiously, after I had answered questions about what New York had looked like and what the man I met was wearing, the conversation tailed off, drifting away into an uncomfortable silence. We had achieved the impossible, but what now? What, if anything, should we do next with *Die Glocke?* There was the obvious attraction of becoming 'time tourists'; moving around inside the time-space continuum to visit specific dates in the past and witness specific events. I ruled that out as far, far too dangerous – too many butterflies.

I wouldn't describe it as an anticlimax but there was a pronounced sense of frustration. We had unearthed the greatest secret of all – and there lay our problem: it was just that; a secret. We couldn't share our joy, we couldn't tell the world, we couldn't anticipate a Nobel Prize. We found ourselves stuck, marooned, in our own little world of wonderment. I suggested that we all spend a couple of days reflecting on what we had done and trying to work out what we should do next.

As the team went about their normal duties – in a daze, I suspect – I asked Dale to show me the film footage he had taken. In truth, there wasn't a great deal to see. Watching myself enter and then, nine minutes later, exit *Die Glocke* made me regret that I hadn't taken some form of camera with me on my journey. Yes, I was so very grateful to have returned with definitive proof of my trip in the form of the newspaper – and the pine cone I had since found in my overcoat pocket – but had I been able to sit my team down and show them either still or moving pictures... well, that would have been all the more impressive.

But I was being both greedy and slightly irrational. Deep down inside, I know that I should simply be grateful for having come back in one piece.

CHAPTER

TWELVE

Date: July 2nd, 1997.
From the office of Professor Martin Zapruder.
Memo 67/1.

That is the last entry I have reproduced for you. There were more – many more – but, so very sadly, they dealt with altogether more serious matters than machines and science.

Dr David never set foot inside *Die Glocke* again. Indeed, his trip back to 1910 to collect a newspaper and a pine cone constituted the first and last time the machine was used for its intended purpose.

In the weeks and months which followed his journey there was, of course, much talk of further use, but each and every time it was mooted David was haunted by the same question: *Why?* If there was no desire to go back and alter something then why do it at all, he repeatedly asked those members of his team who urged him to change his standpoint?

There was never any shortage of volunteers; every member of the team approaching him at some point to offer his or her services. As the level of frustration rose, the first suspicion of a leak from within the camp began to emerge. Fellow workers David barely knew began to ask pointed and awkward questions about *Die Glocke*'s function and capabilities. He began to suspect that someone in whom he had placed his trust had let him down, perhaps in a case of either drunken talk or pillow talk.

The fear of being revealed as the man who was harbouring history's greatest ever invention was enough to convince David that he should, literally, place *Die Glocke* in cold storage. He was sufficiently unnerved by the Chinese whispers which swept around the base that he also took home with him the copy of the *New York Times*, wrapping it in a sturdy protective cover and placing it in his attic.

David was taken ill shortly after Christmas of that year, spending endless hours in a hospital local to his home undergoing a barrage of tests. In mid February 1965 it was confirmed that he was suffering from leukaemia. Indeed, the progress of the disease had been so rapid that he was given – as a maximum – four or five months to live. He died at home, surrounded by family and friends, just seven weeks after being told that he had moved from a position of sound health to death's door in almost record speed.

To David, and to the members of his team inside the base, the obvious conclusion was drawn, reached, discussed and accepted within a matter of days of his initial diagnosis. There was no proof at all, but the fact that a perfectly healthy man had bent the rules of the natural world by moving back in time – albeit for the very briefest of spells – and had promptly fallen victim to great illness was enough for most. Dr David had travelled in *Die Glocke*; Dr David had contracted an almost untreatable form of cancer within months – it was difficult to believe anything other than that the two must be connected.

The news of David's illness not only stopped the flow of false information and rumour to a wider audience; it also served to emphatically draw a line under the *Die Glocke* saga. The machine was, in the view of many, now unusable and was promptly pushed, literally, into the darkest, quietest corner of the base, away from the prying eyes of those who might just have begun to believe it to be something more than just a failed Nazi weapon of war.

Despite being hidden away, *Die Glocke* continued to be a very sad reminder of a tragedy: a good man dying, we believe, doing what all good scientists should do; namely seeking to further our understanding of the world in which we live.

In many quarters, *Die Glocke* came to represent the very personification of undiluted evil. Few people knew the truth surrounding the machine and its suspected role in Dr David's death, but there were rumours, no doubt fuelled by those members of his team who fell prey to guilt. That team was to split up very quickly, three members leaving our employ within a year of their mentor's demise.

As for *Die Glocke* itself, we, the scientific arm of the government, were told to almost airbrush it from history. Even so, no one felt moved to order its destruction. Instead, those who decided its fate were happy to leave it rotting in a locked case which stood inside a locked storage unit within a locked room.

And there it stayed, unwanted and unloved, until the only other country which was aware of its existence and location – the United Kingdom – asked whether they might be permitted to examine it.

The normal diplomatic dialogue ensued, but it was a further eight months before someone on Capitol Hill saw fit to apply a rubber stamp to a formal document, finally clearing the path for *Die Glocke*'s exit from the United States.

It took a while to untangle the red tape and to formulate what was described to me as an "exit strategy", but eventually, in the dead of a Nevada night, *Die Glocke* was placed in a wooden crate and wheeled out onto an airstrip in readiness for a return to Europe.

Those who remembered Dr David with great fondness were hoping it was a one-way ticket.

THIRTEEN

There were various other largely irrelevant notes, prompting Diamond to close the file and pick up the slimmer volume which held just the two photostat copies of the newspaper cuttings. He read both reports, staring at the dateline beneath the masthead on several occasions.

"Fuck me," he said, as if to an imaginary childhood friend.

He knew that Toby would be expecting a call the very second he finished reading Zapruder's report, so he rang him.

"I've finished it," he said.

"And? What do you think?" said Toby.

"It's all true, isn't it – I mean, you're not just taking the piss like you did over that Saz thing?"

"It's all pukka, mate. I know it sounds like total bollocks but on this occasion the truth is actually a great deal stranger than fiction."

"Strange isn't the word, mate. I was going to say it is unbelievable – but I do believe it all."

"I know. It makes you wonder what other things have been hidden away from the general public, doesn't it? Maybe there is a Holy Grail and a Spear of Destiny... and maybe we do have aliens living amongst us. It has made me seriously question virtually everything I have always taken for granted. Fancy meeting up?"

"Yep. Tomorrow OK? I have had this flu bug for days now. I took the medication suggested by that doctor I fancy down at the health centre but all it's done is make me feel as horny as fuck and drowsy."

"You could always give June a call," said Toby.

"Thanks but no thanks. I will give you a call tomorrow. Bye."

Diamond couldn't settle. He watched a little television – another truly appalling reality show called *Manchester Mingers Go Wild in Turkey* – before flicking through Zapruder's report. It seemed even more fanciful the second time around but he knew and accepted now that, if it was ever to be published, it would be allocated a spot in the non-fiction section of his local library.

Diamond had so many questions for Toby that he did what his ageing grandma did most nights – he scribbled down some notes on a pad he had placed on the mock-Georgian cabinet which stood beside his bed. It was a list of predictable questions, plus a reminder that he needed to head down to the shops to buy the very basic essentials of bachelor life – soap, washing powder, toilet rolls and lager.

He slept in again. By the time he found the enthusiasm to get out of bed it was almost 11am. He checked his mobile for messages but, having forgotten to plug it into the charger, it was dead.

He rang Toby from the landline and arranged to meet for what London's executive class like to call "brunch" – to him and to everyone else happy to describe themselves as working class, that meant a late breakfast. Toby suggested The Rubicon but to Diamond that was a place for alcohol, so he overruled his friend and said he'd meet him at Aurora's Cafe, a reliable if grubby place which probably hadn't witnessed a Health and Safety inspection since Egon Ronay was a short-order cook in a downmarket Budapest restaurant.

Aurora's was within walking distance – just – so Diamond set off on foot clutching the notes he had written down late last night before a long night of curious dreams which revolved around a large rabbit which had taken up residence in his wardrobe.

He arrived first and ordered without hesitation Aurora's speciality: a full English breakfast which was unashamedly awash with cholesterol, calories and – its key ingredient – grease.

By the time Toby turned up, Diamond was mopping his plate with a fourth round of toast and beginning to feel rather bilious.

"You greedy bastard," said Toby.

"Correct. That'll probably have to do me for the day as both my fridge and wallet are empty. Well, that's not strictly true as I do have just enough cash to buy either four cans of piss-poor lager or one bottle of piss-poor red wine," said Diamond.

"The life of one of society's outcasts, eh? I'm doing cut-price tickets for a ride in *Die Glocke*. You can go back to last week and win the lottery if you want to."

"Now there's a thought, although I think I would prefer to go back to do serious damage to some of those who did me no favours when I was younger."

"Don't blame others – we mark out our own paths in life. You are now reaping what you sowed years ago."

"A bit philosophical for you, mate. Anyway, you mentioned von Brown's machine, so let's discuss."

"It's von Braun, you clown. There's not a great deal to add, really. What did you make of the Zapruder stuff?"

"It's totally mind-blowing. Incredible. It reads like fiction. The one thing which kept occurring to me is that the secret is very safe – simply because no one would ever believe you or me if we went public with the story. It doesn't sound right, does it? Mad Nazi scientist starts to build large bomb, switches track when Hitler isn't looking, converts into time machine etc. You couldn't sell that story to the *National Enquirer*. I am pleased to have been trusted with the knowledge, but even I feel a sense of great frustration and I'm not even involved. Those in the loop – like yourself – must find it hard to take," said Diamond.

One of the more curious aspects of the learning curve which would end with his own funeral was that he was becoming uncommonly close to people who weren't really friends in the accepted sense of the word. He felt a genuine affection for Dr Marshall; the sort of bond which, perhaps, builds and prospers when two strangers are thrown together and asked to deal with a calamitous situation. He had grown very fond of the head nurse at the hospital where he received his treatment, the pretty nurse with the softest of touches, and the man at the nearby shop who sated his desire for basic food and rough alcohol. He also felt renewed and deepening affection for both Noreen and Toby, which was, he knew, inevitable as they had become his confidants, his sounding boards and the guardians of his secrets.

Oddly, several members of his extended family whom he had assumed would be all over him like a rash had chosen to stay away. Yes, they had sent cards and emails expressing their shock, horror and sympathy, but they stopped short of actually visiting. *The word 'cancer' does have that effect on many people – it is*, Diamond mused, *the most feared word in the*

English language; six simple letters which can make the strongest of people wince and retreat into the shadows.

Diamond was acutely aware that, whilst his death would be greeted with dismay and genuine upset by many people, his life would amount to very little. This didn't bother him unduly as he was also aware that 99.9 per cent of those born on planet earth exist and then depart without making any memorable contribution to anyone outside of a tight circle of family and friends. Even so, he wished that he could be remembered by a wider audience for something – anything, in fact. He'd never play cricket for England, never score a winning goal in an FA Cup Final and never write a classic book or song – both death and anonymity beckoned.

Self-pity was becoming more and more of a problem for him. All he was doing was marking time, wasting time, in much the same way as someone waiting for a bus or a train does. As he had nothing but a short, immediate future in front of him, he had long since left behind all thoughts relating to ambitions and dreams. As he didn't have a clue when the leukaemia would tighten its grip and begin to squeeze the life out of him, he kept thinking that to waste the next week would be utterly foolish as that period of time might very well constitute half of the rest of his life.

He had been wrestling with the question of how to make cheerful a man with no hope for some time without finding an answer which didn't involve either alcohol or sex. He had even considered launching a charitable fund, The Steve Diamond Appeal, but a lifelong fear of failure and subsequent embarrassment ruled that out. He had considered doing voluntary work in the oncology wards at the hospital which had treated him with such generosity of spirit, but concluded that talking to fellow sufferers was likely to prove counterproductive for both parties.

He decided that the next time he was out sharing beer and a laugh with Toby he would ask him if he could come up with anything even remotely worthwhile for a bad-tempered dying man to undertake.

That opportunity presented itself the next day, when Toby called and admitted that he needed a night out to lighten a mood made dark by what he called "a career gone bad".

Diamond was certain that his friend's loss of faith in modern science would not last too long, but he knew that Toby was desperately unhappy with the way things were going inside the labyrinth of Porton Down. Budget cutbacks, redundancies and the mothballing of several key projects had seen morale plummet and there was a genuine fear of an exodus, a brain drain which have pleased only the most unsympathetic inside the Human Resources Department.

Just for old times' sake, they decided to make a rare return to The King's Arms, a pub which both now acknowledged to be almost beneath contempt, but one which was often a source of genuine ribald humour – normally provided by the army of students and vagrants who descended on the place each and every night.

Toby was already there when Diamond arrived, seated in a distant corner which offered a perfect view of the rolling, non-stop pantomime which so amused them. They didn't speak to each other for the first ten minutes because the cabaret had begun early doors.

Two spindly students, both wearing ill-fitting tweed jackets with leather patches on the elbows, were standing almost nose to nose and jabbing each other in the chest. The gist of the argument seemed to be that Student A had attempted to steal Student B's new girlfriend, and he wasn't at all happy.

Diamond knew from his own student days that to gain maximum respect within a group of complete strangers thrown together to study, all you had to do was acquire either a woman or some drugs.

Inevitably, the classic line wasn't too long in coming, Student B shouting across a crowded lounge, "I saw her first."

"Isn't that splendid?" said Toby. "They've been at university for only a relatively short period and already they are talking about the opposite sex as if they were objects to be gathered up and used at their convenience."

"You can bet your life that the one making the claim will end up as an MP and will be on our television screens in about twenty years arguing the case for women's rights," said Diamond. "So, why are you so pissed off?"

Toby proceeded to deliver a monologue of such vitriol that at one point Diamond assumed his friend had been cloned and that the person opposite him was a nasty, Simon Cowell-style version of the one he knew so well.

"What's the point in opening a department, filling it with really top professionals who were actually headhunted, starting a series of very promising projects – and then pulling the plug?" asked Toby.

Appreciating that it was a rhetorical question, Diamond sat back, raised his glass and braced himself for the next instalment.

"I have had enough, and so has Dr Stockwell. If anything, he's angrier and more pissed off than I am. He has invested so much into these projects and now he's been told he has to halt them all and instead study the effects of climate change on plant life.

"He may go before I do. I know I've said this before – that I was going to quit – but this time I think I have actually convinced myself that the time is right for me to move on. I have already grown stale inside that fucking bunker and if I stay, before too long I will wake up one morning and realise that I have also grown old.

"If we were wasting our time, I could half-understand it – but we have produced clear and identifiable results. The worst thing is, you can never actually find out who has decided to make the cuts – they are always the invisible ones who hide behind HR and get them to do their dirty work. I feel sorry for the girls who work in that department as all they are doing is delivering bad news generated by someone else, someone who doesn't have the balls to look people in the eye and tell them they are going to be leaving.

"I appreciate that this isn't an industry-specific problem, that it happens in many different workplaces, but to treat people as wholly disposable is wrong, especially when they were lured to Porton Down in the first place," Toby added.

As Diamond headed for the bar, staring at Student B in an uncharacteristically aggressive manner en route, Toby shouted across, "Get some brandy too."

The order of two pints of lager and two brandies was to be repeated five more times as the pair descended into drunkenness they could barely conceal. With last orders just ten minutes away they were all but alone, the warring students having kissed, made up and headed back to their campus dorms.

"So, how you feeling, mate?" asked Toby.

"Fuck me!" said Diamond. "We have been here almost two hours and now you finally ask how your terminally ill friend is doing! You selfish twat."

Toby dissolved into laughter, bending double as he howled. Diamond joined in, also howling until his eyes filled with tears.

"How good of you to ask. I am doing very well, thanks. Guess who cold-called me yesterday? A bloke selling life insurance. I let him deliver his little speech, then I pretended to burst into tears as I told him I'm dying. It was so funny.

"Yeah, I'm OK. I have been a little weepy over the past couple of weeks but Dr Marshall told me that it's only to be expected. He gave me the name of a counsellor he recommended but I don't think I'll bother as the last thing I need right now is someone telling me that death might not actually be as bad as it sounds. That reminds me of the time a mate of mine went to a dermatology clinic with his dodgy skin, to be met by a large poster which read, 'Psoriasis Can Be Fun,'" said Diamond.

As the barman gazed at them with an air of suspicion, probably presuming they were high on something illegal, both began rolling with laughter again.

Toby bought one last round, adding some fibre to their liquid-only diet by way of two bags of salted peanuts. "I have a plan," he said, his head beginning to sway gently from side to side. "I am going to break into Porton Down one night and steal things. I will start with the Wonder Weapon, *Die Glocke*. I will then go back in time to try and meet someone famous. The by-product will be leukaemia – so it will also be a form of very slow suicide. Good, eh?"

"Well, I can't actually recommend cancer, old boy. It is just one of those rare things in life that don't have a funny side. So, if suicide is your objective then I would suggest shooting yourself. I saw a documentary on suicide and it definitely put me off hanging and overdoses," said Diamond.

"Sorry, I wasn't being dismissive of your illness. I feel really bad n—"

"Oh, shut up. You will have to try harder than that to upset me. I have become impervious to unkind and sarcastic comments since being diagnosed. If you live to be ninety, life is too short to be bothered with trivial insults – so if you aren't going to see your thirty-fourth birthday... well... you know what I mean," said Diamond.

Bizarrely, after clearing the tables and making a half-hearted attempt at sweeping clean a floor covered by discarded crisp packets and shredded newspapers, the barman wandered over and asked if they'd like to stay behind for another drink, saying he was in charge for the night as the landlord was away in Torquay.

Being invited to a 'lock-in' always made Diamond feel special, so he thanked his host and ordered two more pints and two more brandies. The barman not only brought them over on a tray, he said, "On the house, lads."

Toby, a man who always believed that there had to be an ulterior motive behind any act of kindness from strangers, immediately suspected that the just-locked door was about to burst open and that he was going to be gang-raped by a troupe of gay clowns from a travelling circus.

No one burst in, so the giggling, well-drunk pair dived into their free glasses of alcohol, Toby continuing with his theme of what he would like to do if he could find the one courageous bone in his body.

"OK, Precious, if I was to give you *Die Glocke* for one day, where would you go and what would you do?" he asked.

"When I was little – and by that I mean nine or ten years old – I would watch *Doctor Who* from behind the settee and then spend the rest of the evening daydreaming," said Diamond. "Like all the kids who watched the show, I imagined that I was the good Doctor and that I could sneak into the TARDIS and fly through time at the push of a button.

"We used to play a game at our school on the Monday morning after the latest episode had been broadcast. We would sit in the playground and take it in turns to announce where we would go in the time machine if we had the choice.

"The suggestions were usually pretty standard – remember, we were young boys – chasing Red Indians on horseback, travelling to the moon, fighting Martians. Of course, the problem was, they weren't time-travel adventures, just boyish dreams; nine-year-olds can't suggest going back in time with any historical gravitas because they haven't lived long enough.

"I was always slightly different insomuch as I couldn't really see the point in having a free ride in the TARDIS unless I was going to do something truly worthwhile. I kept telling my mates that if I went back in time I would want to do something which would make the world a better place. It was all very altruistic and very, very naive.

"The first time I was asked where I would go, I actually said I would go back and stop the Romans crucifying Jesus Christ because he was the Son of God and it all seemed a bit unfair. They laughed at me. The only thing I ever came up with which met with their collective approval was going back to the day when Mr Payne, the bastard of a PE teacher, was born and levelling him with a plank of wood.

"Even now I cannot see the point in doing the apparently impossible, moving around within time and space, unless there is a genuine purpose. In my non-negotiable view, a mission without meaning, without a point, is a waste of effort. So, my answer is, I really don't know – but it would be something cool, something that would enrich our lives, something for the good of all."

At this point Toby slumped forward, and Diamond, a seasoned watcher of the inebriated, assumed he was going to throw up. He didn't, though; he regained his balance, pushed himself back in his seat and said, "Nope. Not good enough, my good man. You are being deliberately vague, which is something no drunken scientist would ever accept. I give you the keys to *Die Glocke* – where do you go?"

"This sounds like a debate we should be having when stone-cold sober," said Diamond. "It isn't easy because there are many things I would love to change, many things I would like to set right; I am spoiled for choice.

"OK. It will always come down to personal choice. I could choose to go back and eradicate cholera or the plague. I could land in Pudding Lane and prevent the Great Fire of London from taking hold. I could stop the assassination of Becket, or maybe the drowning of Shelley.

"But my hero is – and always will be – Oscar Wilde; a genius of unimaginable scope and scale. He is now regarded as a largely misunderstood giant amongst men, but the last few years of his life were so sad – so very, very sad. I remember when I first read of what befell Wilde in his latter years – I was in a state of total shock. I had no idea that a man who gave so much to the world ended up in such a horrible, awful mess. It hurt me, it genuinely hurt me.

"He went to prison in 1895, I think it was, having been set up and then stitched up by some of the rent boys of the day. He got two years, but for a man accustomed to life's finer things that must have seemed like a life sentence. His health declined really quickly and he burst an eardrum in a fall whilst in Wandsworth Prison. He received inadequate treatment, and ultimately what would be regarded as a minor problem today contributed to his early death.

"When he was released he went into self-imposed exile, moving around before settling in Paris; a great city for the affluent but not for a penniless, broken man who had lost the will to write.

"He died of cerebral meningitis – linked to the old ear problem – on November 30th, 1900, in a nasty, run-down hotel on the Left Bank. My God, if anyone deserved better it was him. Even worse, they buried him in a pauper's grave. It was another ten years before he was disinterred and moved to Père Lachaise, the final resting place of great men and women – Balzac, Sarah Bernhardt, Chopin, Bizet, Proust, Rossini... even Jim Morrison of The Doors," he added.

Toby, still giving the distinct impression that he was poised to slip into unconsciousness, smiled broadly at his friend. "Typically noble. Marvellous sentiment," he said. "Actually, hand on heart, I like the idea of saving Wilde. I have only ever read the books he wrote for his kids, but they were wonderful. How old was he when he died?"

"I think he was forty-six. I don't think he was even allowed to see his two children after he left prison. It wasn't even the sort of heroic death that used to feature in his epic poems. Having been abandoned by most of his friends, he just sort of faded away," said Diamond.

Whilst Toby was so drunk he would have remained in situ until dawn broke, Diamond was weary and in need of the medication he so often forgot to take. He lifted his friend to his feet and ushered him towards the door, the chances of another lock-in at The King's Arms receding quite dramatically as he shouted across at his host, "You may now go to your bed, my good man. You are dismissed for the night."

Diamond waved at the stony-faced barman and pushed Toby out onto a dark and deserted street. It took them longer than it should have done to retreat to Diamond's flat, and once inside, both collapsed – one on the bed, one on the settee.

Diamond woke earlier than he had anticipated, checked his friend was still breathing and headed to the kitchen to drink as much cold water as his stomach could take. He felt surprisingly good, even if there was still a slight drunken dizziness to his steps.

He couldn't remember whether Toby was supposed to be in work today. He decided he couldn't be as he usually stayed on site for several days at a time – plus he looked like someone who would shortly be dealing with a hangover of such severity that he would, within thirty minutes of waking, declare himself to be teetotal for the remainder of his life.

If Diamond had bet good money on that sentiment being the first to pass Toby's lips when he finally opened his eyes, he would have lost.

"Fuck me, what happened?" was Toby's opening line as he held up a hand to his face in an attempt to block out the sunlight.

"We drank rather too much in The King's Arms," said Diamond. "We were even invited to stay behind after hours by the convivial host."

"There weren't any gay clowns involved at any point, were there?" asked Toby.

"What?" said Diamond.

"That's it, I'm packing in drinking. I can't ever do that again," said Toby.

Diamond smiled all the way as he walked back into the kitchen to make two cups of coffee.

Toby seemed to find even talking difficult, so Diamond suggested he go home and feel sorry for himself in the privacy of more familiar surroundings.

Predictably, Toby spoke the words of a man unaccustomed to the debilitating effects of a hangover – "I think I'm dying" – before stepping unsteadily into the warmth of a day which was unlikely to help speed his return to sobriety.

Although he had concealed as much, Diamond also felt pretty rough, and he shuddered as he mentally reran the previous night's epic drinking session. "Brandy? What were we thinking of?" he said to no one.

As was always the case the day after the night before, memories of conversations and actions came back in fragments, his brain dusting down and then delivering information in jigsaw-sized chunks. Diamond knew it had been a night of many, many laughs, and some of the jokes and interchanges were still funny some eighteen hours on – so much so that he giggled intermittently as he fought back against his hangover with an endless supply of water and a small mountain of paracetamol.

He tried desperately hard not to fall asleep because the curse of the recovering drunk is the short nap, as it often seems to accomplish nothing more than rebooting the hangover. He did reasonably well until he opted to watch a late-afternoon quiz programme which was so stupefyingly easy its target audience simply had to be the ill-educated. The urge to sleep was overwhelming, and he slipped away with barely a struggle.

In those initial moments which lie between a man being awake and asleep – the hinterland of a dream state – Diamond resurrected his conversation with Toby about stealing *Die Glocke* and then travelling around in time for one's own amusement. He then dredged up his input into that debate – his wish that he could somehow make the world a better place by saving Oscar Wilde from a premature and unnecessary death in a squalid Parisienne hotel.

For the good of all. That was the phrase he had used – for the good of all. The recollections were coming back out of sync and cloaked in the sort of cartoon-like nonsense which afflicts all dreams. Even so, he remembered Toby saying he was so sick of his professional life that he would like to use *Die Glocke* as a method of ending his own life. He would travel in *Die Glocke*, have a measure of fun and then give himself up to the leukaemia which, ironically and tragically, had killed with such speed Eric David, the only person to ever use von Braun's machine.

Diamond awoke with a start, his mind and body jerking back into full life almost as if he had been attached to an electrical circuit board. His eyes darted around his living room and his breathing was laboured.

"My God," he said, jumping to his feet with such force that his right foot caught the underside of the table which stood between the settee and television set, sending a cold cup of coffee arcing onto the floor. "My God," he said again as he scrambled for his mobile. He rang Toby, suspecting, or rather knowing, that his friend would be in the very deepest of sleeps.

The call went straight to voicemail. Diamond waited for Toby's infuriatingly lengthy message to run its course before saying, "It's me. You need to call me as soon as you wake up. It's important. It's really important – so do it straight away. OK?"

Diamond stood beneath the shower, moved the dial from the red section to the blue, and pushed the button. The cascade of cold water was intended to revive his senses and organs which had been dulled by the previous night's alcohol intake. He managed to last around sixty seconds before the icy stream drove the air from his lungs, leaving him shaking and gasping for breath; but he was now fully awake and alert.

As he waited for Toby to ring, he became a slave to impatience – pacing up and down; picking up, then discarding magazines; channel-hopping across the news channels; making cups of coffee he didn't want. Twice he picked up his mobile and considered trying Toby again. He didn't because, even when ill, he knew Toby to be one of the most sensible men he had ever met. The very second he sensed the urgency in Diamond's voice on his answering machine, he would ring. He knew he would.

And he eventually did. It was just after 11pm when Diamond's mobile crackled into life.

"Hi. Sorry, I've been in bed sleeping and in the bathroom being ill," said Toby.

"Listen. I have a plan. Something came to me, something that will sound plain fucking mad but which does actually make a lot of sense," said Diamond.

"OK. I'm all ears – what is it?"

"No. I don't want to go through it now – just promise me you will hear me out tomorrow and that you will take me seriously."

"Bit difficult to do that when I don't have a clue what you're talking about."

"Trust me, this'll be great. You're not in work tomorrow, are you?"

"No, I'm off until Monday. Let's meet at 9am in that cafe."

"Aurora's? Great. See you in the morning," said Diamond.

The wonder was that Diamond slept at all. He felt like a kid on Christmas Eve; a nervous, excited, twitching mass of expectancy, as if he could burst at any moment.

He had always regarded himself as a pragmatist, a man who understood why dreams were often denied by a cocktail of lack of self-belief and common sense. He had a great sense of the romantic, but too often, he felt, he was willing to bury it in the face of someone else's cold logic – he felt he bowed to the somewhat-less-than-inevitable far too easily, far too readily.

This time, he was determined to stand his ground. This time he would be dominant and not submissive. This time he would prevail – if only because he wished to bookend his fading life with a genuine sense of achievement.

He awoke early and was tucked away at a table to the rear of the cafe a good thirty minutes before his agreed rendezvous with Toby. As his stomach had still not fully recovered from the battering it had taken in The King's Arms, he opted for nothing more adventurous than tea and toast, much to the surprise of Aurora, who looked almost upset by his selection.

Toby arrived just before 9am, pale-faced and unshaven.

"Do you want anything to eat?" asked Diamond.

"You must be joking. I haven't eaten a bloody thing since I left yours yesterday. I feel like death – and don't say it, yes, I know I also look like death," said Toby.

"It was an interesting night out – but one I suspect you won't wish to repeat in a hurry."

"Correct. I saw some kid drinking from a can of lager in the street yesterday evening and just the sight of someone taking alcohol was enough to make me feel ill. So what's so urgent that I have to drag my sick body out of bed and drive to this emporium of exotic culinary delights?"

"Do you remember, when we were about eighty per cent pissed the other night, telling me how you had decided to commit slow suicide by stealing *Die Glocke* and travelling back to meet someone of your choosing?" asked Diamond.

"Yeah, vaguely. I was going to become the second man to time-travel, contract cancer and die a noble death. Yes?"

"Yes, just about."

"Why does alcohol make even intelligent people talk complete and utter bollocks?"

"Maybe it wasn't bollocks… maybe it was your finest moment, your best ever suggestion."

"Explain?"

"OK, but don't shout me down, don't dismiss this out of hand, don't call me mental. Yes, your idea is bollocks – but it is only bollocks for you, not for me. If you did it, you would, presumably, come back with the death sentence of untreatable leukaemia so it isn't an option, sober or drunk. I couldn't contract leukaemia by using *Die Glocke* because I already have it, Toby."

"Oh no. Stop right there. You—"

"You promised to hear me out, so please do. Yes, this does on the surface sound a little crazy but, as ever, there's a certain logic to my madness. The fact is that only those who are terminally ill with leukaemia are fit to ride the machine – and I know how utterly perverse that sounds," said Diamond. "I could step in and out of *Die Glocke* without the potential for causing myself damage because you really cannot damage something which is already broken beyond repair. You have mankind's greatest ever invention gathering dust in a sealed room deep underground – all I am saying is that if I am willing to gamble, then maybe you or Dr Stockwell will also be up for it.

"Trust me, it's a really cute plan. No one would even know we had done it – but you and whoever else was involved would be living the ultimate dream of any scientist: you'd be breaking down barriers and, quite literally, rewriting history."

Toby sat in silent reflection, unmoving apart from the fingers of his right hand which drummed out a regular beat on the stained tabletop. "No, it's a mad idea. it's nuts; it's impossible. It would be dangerous, illegal, unethical and unworkable. Someone would end up in prison and you'd probably end up dead," he said.

"Mate, I'm already dead. I am a goner, I'm done for. As I sit here with you, drinking weak tea and eating cold toast, I do so on borrowed time. My heart is still pumping blood – infected blood – around my body but I died the very moment I was diagnosed with an illness which, for me, has no cure. I continue to exist only because I choose to do so. The simple way out would have been to swallow a hundred of my tablets or take a one-way trip to that Dignitas clinic in Switzerland. I chose not to take what I regarded as the easy way out because I wanted to enjoy the time I have left. If I had money I would gamble. If I was good-looking I would be out playing the field. If I was of a violent nature I would go out and hunt down soft targets every night and enjoy battering them senseless with a blunt instrument.

"I understand what you are saying, but how often do you scientists get a genuine offer from a genuine human guinea pig? Think about it, Toby... think about it for me and try to consider it from my perspective. I thought that, perhaps, my last great adventure was going to be a night in a pole-dancing club in Soho, but now I find, right at the very bottom of my bucket list, a card which says, 'You can go time-travelling if you want.'"

Toby again lapsed into a period of silence; one which, at times, seemed to border on prayer. "Look, I fully understand what you are saying, Diamond, honestly I do. And I am not going to say that it doesn't appeal to both the scientist and the romantic in me – because it does. It is so absolutely crazy that it has great appeal. Let me go through some basic points of logic here; some of the hurdles which currently stand between you – or us – as we study in detail a plan which boasts all the hallmarks of lunacy," he said.

"Firstly, I could give it my total and absolute support but that still wouldn't be even twenty-five per cent of what would be required. Remember, Dr Stockwell is a lot older than me and so, presumably, wiser and more cautious. I don't believe that he has ever 'done' reckless in his life. He once told me that he had driven through a red light in Battersea and he seemed to think that put him up there on a par with the likes of Robin Hood and Che Guevara. I would put the chances of him even giving it more than ten seconds of consideration at dramatically less than five per cent.

"Secondly, we would need the help – and subsequent silence – of maybe another three people to use the machine. It isn't a toy; it takes a lot of preparation and quite a bit of expertise to get it fully functional.

"Thirdly, we arrive back at the old problem of the obvious dangers not just to yourself, but to the human race as it currently is. It is the question of time-travel paradoxes – the old crushed-butterfly theory. You go back, you do something and there is then a quite seismic change in the order of things when you return. We can't risk that, really, can we?"

"I do fully understand all about the paradoxes – as you know, sci-fi, time travel etc. has been one of my obsessions since I was in junior school," said Diamond. "But when Eric David went back, he returned to an unchanged world. Admittedly, all he said he did was chat to a stranger and accept the gift of a newspaper, but the lesson there is that if you tread warily, a trip can be accomplished without detrimental effects.

"There are people who, given the opportunity, would move back in *Die Glocke* and do all manner of things which would result in the seismic changes you mentioned. We all know the sort of things – shoot Hitler dead when he was a boy, stop whoever was responsible for assassinating Kennedy, bump Stalin off before he reached junior school. I'm not dumb enough to either want to do or consider doing such a thing. My argument is that anyone who returns to the past with good intentions is not a danger to himself or to anyone else.

"In the unlikely event that Dr Stockwell is interested in my mad, crazy, lunatic plan, we will obviously have to sit down and work out the parameters with regard to what I can and can't do," he added.

"I am listening to you, although God only knows why," said Toby, with his first smile of the day.

"Tell me this," said Diamond. "What is going to happen to *Die Glocke*? I mean, is it going to end up being melted down and turned into commemorative ashtrays or toast racks? Where is it now, for example?"

"It's in the unit and, as you suggested, it is gathering dust in a locked room," said Toby. "That's one of the reasons Dr Stockwell and I are so despondent. As part of the financial and personnel cutbacks, we have been told that all work on *Die Glocke* must stop. In fact, I'm using the wrong tense because all work stopped about a month ago.

"Your joke about it being melted down may not prove to be too far removed from the truth, actually. Dr Stockwell spoke to his counterparts over at Area 51 in the States, told them the situation and said he would be arranging for von Braun's invention to be shipped back across the Atlantic. And y'know what? They said they didn't want it back under any circumstances; that, in their opinion, it would be safer for us all if it were dismantled, crushed or dropped into a very deep hole. So, right now, we are waiting for the government mandarins to decide what they would like us to do with it. The problem is that so few people actually know of its existence – so getting those who do know to assemble inside a room or take part in a conference call in search of a common consensus is proving rather tricky.

"Dr Stockwell initially railed against the decision, but after talking things through with those in the know – he calls them his 'magic circle' – he came to the conclusion that maybe, just maybe, those above him in the food chain are right. So we wait. The machine is idle, and those who know about its true capabilities – maybe a dozen people – are very unhappy and deeply frustrated."

Diamond picked at a piece of toast which had become lodged between his front teeth, and motioned for Aurora to bring over two cappuccinos. "Suppose that I can also understand why those in high authority don't want much to do with it. If you look at it from a purely financial perspective, *Die Glocke* is, and always has been, a total waste of taxpayers' money because no Prime Minister would ever go public with the news of its existence," he said. "I just assume that they would reverse-engineer it in the hope of finding some elements that are useful for building yet more weapons of mass destruction. I presume they have tried to do that?"

"Not really, because they don't have to. *Die Glocke* is the ultimate weapon of mass destruction if you think about it. If it was to fall into the hands of a group like, say, the Taliban, can you imagine what would happen? The military view is that you cannot improve on perfection – and that, in terms of war and warfare, *Die Glocke* is the most perfect machine ever to move from drawing board to reality," said Toby.

Aurora delivered two cups of a liquid which was as far removed from an authentic Italian cappuccino as was possible to imagine.

"Tell you what," said Diamond. "When next you sit with Stockwell, tell him of our conversation; tell him of my mad proposal and let's see what his reaction is. I know there's little or no chance of him doing anything other than laughing, but if I have learned anything over the past few months it is that a one per cent chance is better than no chance at all."

"OK, I will, but as I said, don't hold your breath. Dr Stockwell is a conservative with a small 'c' and is not, in my experience, prone to taking outrageous gambles, but I promise on my aching head that I will at least speak to him," said Toby.

"All I am saying is that if he wants to gamble, wants to experiment, then I am available. I know what I would love to do if allowed to – but that's for another day... perhaps a day which will never arrive," said Diamond.

Toby left with a promise that he would speak to Dr Stockwell inside the next forty-eight hours, and would then arrange to meet Diamond for a meal.

CHAPTER

FOURTEEN

Diamond returned home to find Noreen standing in a cloud of steam in the kitchen.

"Noreen Taylor, you're wearing an apron!" he shouted.

"I am indeed," she said. "I am pretending to be a contestant on *Master Chef* as I attempt to prepare you a dish of rare quality."

"Great – what is it?"

"It is Moroccan lamb with a couscous base and shallots."

"My God, real food – a meat-based product, but nonetheless it most definitely counts as real food. I had a friend at the college who was adamant that unless a meal came in a box with a film lid, and fitted snugly inside a microwave, it wasn't food at all. He was a real philistine who now, strangely, works in catering," said Diamond.

Despite his reservations about Dr Stockwell's ability to add at least one flourish of derring-do to his life of orthodoxy, Diamond's spirits had been lifted by his conversation with Toby, his logic being that, if you can't actually accomplish something monumental, then the next best thing is to at least try.

What he had been concealing from both Toby and Noreen was that he had been feeling increasingly unwell over the past fortnight; weak in the mornings and massively fatigued come late afternoon. He continued to take his medication but Dr Marshall had warned him that the uplift he gained in the hours after ingesting it would reduce as the weeks rolled by. Diamond's fears that his body had now reached saturation point in terms of the painkillers had been heightened two days earlier when he took his daily dose and felt precisely nothing in terms of a boost. He had immediately rung Dr Marshall's office and booked an appointment, although he had decided against telling Noreen because he believed that sometimes a problem shared isn't halved at all.

Their evening was a happy one. They watched a truly diabolical quiz show which served only to throw into question the efficiency of the British schooling system, and then ploughed their way through a most earnest subtitled Czech film which had been described by *The Guardian* as "dark and thought-provoking", but which reduced them to tears of laughter. A good night ended with unhurried kissing and lovemaking as they listened to one of their favourite albums: Joni Mitchell's *Blue*. As the strains of 'A Case of You' faded away, they were wrapped in each other's arms, Diamond doing what he had always done to hasten his partner's passage through to sleep: talking away inanely about anything which came into his head.

By the time he woke, Noreen had departed – long departed, according to the note she had scribbled at 6.30am and left for him on the kitchen table. It held kind and flattering words, so instead of tossing it into the bin he folded it neatly and placed it in the small section of his wallet which he reserved for messages of love, hope and inspiration. It tucked in neatly alongside a note she had written on a paper napkin at a motorway service station two months ago, which read, "Fight, you bastard, fight. I don't want you to leave me."

Diamond read both as he sat on the Tube heading for his hospital appointment. He tended to steer clear of over-sentimental mementos because all they did was remind him that he was being showered in love and affection because he was dying. He knew that assessment to be unduly harsh, but more and more as he travelled down the lonely road to his destiny he was putting up barrier after barrier to try and keep his emotions in check.

As he lay on the bed in a spartan consulting room, Diamond, always aware of his mortality when inside hospital walls, wondered if this might be the last time he saw Dr Marshall. He knew that a very sharp decline in his health could come at any time, and that, despite his best efforts to stay away from the edge of the cliff, he would, sooner rather than later, tumble and fall.

Dr Marshall breezed in as if he were inspecting sunbeds around a swimming pool, moving from bed to bed, carrying out a cursory inspection before ticking a box on his clipboard. Diamond's bed was his last port of call. He smiled and stretched out his right hand as he approached. "My dear old thing, how are you?" he asked.

"Hello, snake-oil man. I am doing reasonably well under the prevailing circumstances, thank you very much," said Diamond.

"So how are you really? I can only presume you have a problem, unless this is a social visit."

"I feel crap; have done for about two weeks. I know that there's not really anything that you can do, but when I have a turn for the worse my instinct is to seek an audience with the man who has been overseeing my well-being... and unfortunately from your perspective, that's you."

"So what are the new symptoms?"

"I feel very weak, so very tired, and I have the sort of permanent aches and pains I used to get when I had been kicked black and blue on a football pitch. I am still taking the medication but it is as you told me it would be: less effective than once it was."

"Yes, that's the problem. As your body weakens your defences go down and you tend to be vulnerable to almost every germ or infection that is doing the rounds. That's to say, things which wouldn't have tested your immune system in the past will now give you cause for concern."

"Nothing I can do, then?"

"No, not really, I'm afraid. All I can suggest is that you stay away from people who have things like the common cold, and do try to exercise a little – that will help. On top of that, eat healthily and don't drink alcohol," said Dr Marshall, smiling broadly.

"Yeah, right. So you'd seriously like me to remove one of my few remaining pleasures?"

"As your doctor, I have to say yes – as your friend, I would say, 'Drink heartily, for tomorrow we ride.' Just don't tell the matron that I gave you such unethical advice, please."

"So you still can't give me any form of timescale?"

"Even if I could, I wouldn't. You've done well and you are continuing to do well. Trust me, there are a few people in this building who are surprised that you are still with us. I think some had you marked down as one who might just give up and surrender to his fate."

"Do they run sweepstakes on that sort of thing?"

"It has been known – but only when the patient concerned is either rude to or dismissive of those who are lining up to try and help him."

"Bloody hell. What a cynical bunch you lot are."

"You're a journalist! Pot, kettle; kettle, pot."

"Fair point."

"Right, I must run, I have a busy day. Too many patients, not enough hours in the day."

"I hope to see you again, Doctor."

"I share that sentiment, Steve. Take care, and remember – never give up," said Dr Marshall before disappearing through the room's double doors, pursued by two nurses who struggled to match his military-style pace.

Some fifteen minutes later Diamond was woken up by a fair-haired young woman, and initially struggled to work out precisely where he was. She smiled beguilingly and said that they had to wake him as the bed was required for another of Dr Marshall's patients.

"Sorry. So sorry. I can't remember falling asleep," said Diamond, more than a little confused.

"It isn't a problem. Go get yourself a cup of tea before you go home. No rush," she added, with what Diamond had always referred to as the 'oncology face'; a smile which hinted at both concern and compassion.

Diamond prised himself up and away from the bed, waving to no one in particular as he exited and made for the cafe just down the corridor. He had largely steered clear of the place over the past year or so because it was crammed full of ill-looking patients with attached drips; concerned, often teary-eyed relatives; and a staff made up entirely of elderly volunteers who seemed to work out prices in the pre-decimal currency of a long-gone era.

He asked for a tea and a bottle of cold water – something which was all too confusing for the little lady behind the counter, who looked as if she had dressed for a meeting with royalty.

"Yes, dear, we have both – which one do you want?" she asked.

"I would like both, please," said Diamond, offering a smile of encouragement.

"So you would like both tea *and* a bottle of water?"

"Yes, please."

"I'll have to charge you for both, I'm afraid."

"That's fine, thanks."

He sat at a table as far away from other people as was possible, drinking his lukewarm tea first before almost draining his water in four large gulps. He had muted his mobile on arrival at the hospital, but as it sat in front of him it started to vibrate and flash.

"Hi, Toby," he said.

"You OK? It sounds like you are under water; where are you?"

"I'm at the hospital – just having a cup of tea and doing a spot of people-watching before I head home."

"Listen, I spoke to Dr Stockwell about twenty minutes ago on the phone. I was going to wait until I went back into work but I was so convinced he would be totally dismissive of your crazy scheme that I decided to get it out of the way as fast as I could."

"Well, thanks for that ringing endorsement, mate," said Diamond.

"No, listen – he didn't dismiss it totally. He listened and, whilst he admitted that, yes, it is totally nuts, he said he would like to meet up with you."

"You're joking?"

"Amazingly, no, I'm not."

"Bloody hell."

"There's something else, too – he told me that he has not only resigned, but also retired. It would seem he had a long conference call with his superiors yesterday and that it didn't go very well. He told me he disagreed with virtually everything that was said to him, so he told them to stuff it. It could be that I unwittingly picked just the right time to speak to him."

"So when does he want to get together, Toby?"

"Tomorrow, if you're free."

"Obviously I will have to check my diary and consult with my PA… Of course I'm free, you moron – what else do I have to do? The shopping? The washing-up? Opening the junk mail? Arrange it, do it now… right now, Toby," said Diamond.

"Yes, sorry. Right, let's say 1pm. It will have to be central, though, as he lives miles away. How about the Hard Rock Cafe in the City?"

"Is that in Old Park Lane?"

"That's it, yes."

"Right, I will see you there at 1pm. Anything else I should know before I meet him?"

"He likes Barry Manilow, is very quiet and he dresses like Mr Polly," said Toby.

"Fuck," said Diamond.

Toby's call gave Diamond the sort of lift in spirits which his drugs had previously provided. By the time he pushed his key into his front door he was whistling and mentally working on what he would say to the good doctor – he was preparing a PowerPoint presentation which would be delivered orally rather than visually.

Once inside he pulled a pen and notebook out of a drawer and began to jot down a series of bullet points. He wouldn't need to take the finished list with him the following day as the one part of his frail being which had survived the scourge of cancer was his memory. If anything, his ability to recall information and resurrect memories had grown stronger, almost in direct proportion to the weakening of his flesh and blood. He had read something about the phenomenon somewhere; how the body compensates for a weakness in one area by heightening the senses in another. An image of Stephen Hawking flashed across his mind.

It was gone 9pm before he realised that he hadn't had a drink; a situation swiftly rectified by the opening of a bottle of Merlot he found hidden away in a cupboard used mainly for the storing of those kitchen utensils which had been used once and then discarded – steak mallets, liquidisers and the like.

Diamond stopped writing and started drinking. He also began to mentally rehearse his answers to the more obvious questions which he was quietly confident Dr Stockwell would ask of him. He knew he had to sound enthusiastic but measured, adventurous but not mad, and, above all, level-headed and not manic. Simply because Toby would have informed Dr Stockwell of the parlous state of his health, Diamond wasn't expecting a grilling or a rough ride. After all, he reasoned, why would Dr Stockwell have asked for a meeting if he wasn't at least interested in listening to Diamond's seemingly bizarre proposal?

The wine didn't last long. Diamond refused to concede as much – either to himself or to Noreen – but his appetite for food was on the wane; he was beginning to lose weight, and feared that he was moving rather smartly down the road to the gaunt, almost translucent look which so characterises those who are damned by cancer.

He so wished he had another bottle to enjoy but the cupboard was bare, so he headed for bed and a radio station which prided itself on playing a non-stop selection of heavy and hard rock classics. As he drifted off to sleep his companions were Led Zeppelin, Stevie Ray Vaughan and The Sisters of Mercy.

He woke early to the strains of Deep Purple, his radio still defiantly delivering a barrage of noise. He wondered if his illness had begun to compromise his hearing.

He checked his mobile, hoping against hope that there was no text from Toby announcing a cancellation of his meeting with Dr Stockwell. There wasn't – just a short message from Noreen wishing him a good day.

Diamond had long hated the journey into Central London, believing that the phrase "Abandon all hope, ye who enter here" had been penned not for the *Divine Comedy* but for sorties into the capital.

It was always busy, people always pushed and shoved you, no one smiled, there was a complete absence of courtesy and chivalry, there was body odour, halitosis, broken wind – and usually no seats to sit on. It was as close to hell as he could imagine, so he did what everyone else seemed to do: closed his eyes and wished for swift deliverance.

Once free of the Tube and its foul stenches, Diamond's mood lifted several notches and he was able to appreciate the beauty of the sprawling metropolis upon whose outskirts he had lived for so long. As he strolled towards the meeting point he attempted to count up how many times he had travelled into the heart of London over the past two years; a handful, maybe, and always to see a show or gig, never to play tourist. That was usually the way wherever you lived. He had a friend who had lived in Liverpool for many years and admitted that he had never been on the ferry 'cross the Mersey, and another who lived in Brighton and had never been near the resort's famous pier. *We want what we can't have whilst dismissing what we do have*, thought Diamond as he spotted the Hard Rock Cafe in the distance.

CHAPTER

FIFTEEN

Diamond disliked the Hard Rock; always had, believing it to be elitist and little more than a fast-food outlet which got away with selling overpriced burgers and hot dogs because its customers were surrounded by a collection of rock-and-roll memorabilia. Given a choice between eating a cheap cheeseburger whilst staring at a Dalí print or an expensive one whilst looking at one of Prince's discarded shoes, he would opt for the former every time.

As he entered the restaurant – which was suitably dark and filled with the strains of a guitar solo by Joe Perry – he peered into the gloom but couldn't see Toby. He presumed that Toby would be meeting Dr Stockwell elsewhere as it seemed highly unlikely that he was a regular patron of the Hard Rock.

Diamond perched on a bar stool and ordered a mineral water, having decided the least he could do was to try and project a vision of sobriety. He was halfway down something which tasted as though it had been taken from a tap rather than a bottle when Toby and his boss wandered in, fending off menu-carrying waitresses as they pointed in Diamond's direction.

"Steve, this is Dr Stockwell," said Toby.

"Hi, I am very pleased to meet you. It is traditional that I say I have heard much about you, and on this occasion at least that is correct," said Diamond.

"Good to meet you too. I haven't heard that much about you – but I have heard enough to want to come and meet you. It may be that we are both wasting our time – and with Toby having explained your medical circumstances, I know that is something which must be very precious to you, so I am grateful that you made the effort," said Dr Stockwell.

"Toby usually pays when we go out, so, ill as I am, I was not going to turn down the offer of a free lunch," said Diamond, breaking into many pieces any remaining first-conversation ice.

They asked for a quiet table – difficult inside a room with non-stop rolling music – and were, mercifully, rewarded with one to the rear of the restaurant, away from the Japanese tourists with their ever-flashing cameras and the oversized Americans who seemed to order two of everything. Having indulged in pleasant small talk which didn't touch upon either football or women, they ordered – plain burgers for Diamond and Toby; a Caesar salad for the doctor. Diamond caught Toby's eye as if to say, *He comes to a bloody burger bar and eats salad.*

As they waited for their waitress – Moonbeam, according to her name tag – to bring their food, Dr Stockwell opened the conversation by launching into a totally unexpected and quite vitriolic assault on those for whom he had worked for so long. It represented a soul-baring exercise which Diamond actually thought would have been better delivered to his wife or partner if he had one.

The gist of it was, Dr Stockwell was totally and absolutely pissed off with his work and consequently his life, as you couldn't slide a cigarette paper between the two; they were almost indivisible. He fundamentally disagreed with the recent cutbacks, the redundancies, the streamlining, the stated objectives, the wage freeze, the abandoning of various projects, the dismissal of two men for what he described as "inconsequential" breaches of protocol, and he also berated his employers for the poor quality of the food in the staff canteen. Diamond half-expected him to go on and castigate Prince for allowing one of his shoes to be exhibited in a glass box.

As the doctor finally fell silent, Diamond looked up and said, "But apart from that, everything's OK, is it?"

Dr Stockwell, a man who most believed had had his funny bones removed at birth, burst out laughing. "Your timing is good, Steve... it's very good," he said.

"As I have said to many people over the past year or so, my body is falling to bits but my brain is still functioning as it should," said Diamond.

"Toby told me about your two conversations – the one conducted under the influence and the more coherent one the following day. If I hadn't decided to resign and retire I wouldn't be here, as it would be wholly unethical and, despite the fact that I have long detested the red tape which suffocates people in roles such as mine, I have always been what you might best describe as a 'company man,'" said Dr Stockwell.

"As I suspect you know, the powers that be – and I am talking about the Prime Minister and his immediate subordinates – have decided that *Die Glocke* is now a redundant piece of invented genius. Ironic, isn't it, that mankind strives constantly to move forwards, to advance in terms of technology, and yet we are now ready to dismantle the greatest find of all?

"Still, they know best – at least they think they do. At the moment the machine is under lock and key in a room at Porton Down – and I have the only key. There is always a security guard standing outside the room, but he could be guarding a complete set of *Pokémon* cards for all he knows; he has never been inside the room and he never will.

"We have carried out the same exhaustive tests on the machine as did the Americans. I have copies of all their reports and they match ours totally – they are mirror images. That's to say, we know all we can know about it unless we take the next step and actually switch it on and use it – the consequences of which we believe we know full well.

"I have never told anyone this – not even you, Toby – but six months ago when I feared patience amongst the bureaucrats was beginning to run low, I volunteered to pilot *Die Glocke* on a test run. They said no, as I suspected they would, predictably stating that the only person to have undertaken such a trip came home with a newspaper and cancer.

"I told them I would be willing to take a chance, to run that considerable risk, but they were having none of it. It was at that point that I realised my time was up with scientific research and I decided to retire gracefully. I was – indeed, still am – bitter. I believe that if a man is willing to put his own life on the line in the name of meaningful research then that should be respected.

"They showed me no respect at all. They didn't want to discuss my offer; they simply dismissed me as an idiot and my idea as ridiculous. That hurt me a great deal. Mark Twain once said, 'Never argue with stupid people, they will drag you down to their level and then beat you with experience', and that about sums it up for me. Don't get me wrong, I am not looking for a way to get even or to get my own back; I am simply a disenchanted man who is now staring at his career's end and who is willing to listen to suggestions he would previously have scoffed at and dismissed."

"I understand all that," said Diamond, choosing his words with undue care. "Toby is a very discreet man and never gives away too many of your dark secrets, but his professional unhappiness has been clear to me for quite a while now; he too is totally frustrated and beginning to wonder what the point is in continuing down a career road which is seemingly littered with tollbooths and barricades.

"You're right, the mad scheme he talked to you about did indeed come about after a night of far too much alcohol – but some of the world's great minds have produced their most memorable works whilst under the influence of either alcohol or drugs. It was all silly, throwaway stuff; two drunk men of a certain level of intellect ranting against their respective worlds and coming up with outlandish suggestions. And then, when I thought about it, they suddenly didn't seem quite so outlandish – bizarre, yes, but hidden away beneath the layers of craziness was the germ of what I saw to be a workable idea.

"You know what that idea is and what its basis is. The only person who travelled inside *Die Glocke* contracted leukaemia and died pretty quickly. The conclusion was drawn that everyone who travelled inside *Die Glocke* would suffer the same fate, and so the machine must be destroyed or abandoned or buried or something.

"They employed basic logic – so I did the same. I can't contract leukaemia by piloting *Die Glocke* as I already have it. Who knows – if they are right and time is a great healer, perhaps I will return home free of the disease? That's a joke at my expense, by the way, because I know that isn't going to happen! My point is that the only people who can use the machine without the fear of picking up a death sentence are people like me – those of us who already have the life expectancy of a house fly."

Dr Stockwell nodded in what Diamond took to be an approving manner before inspecting the salad which had just been set before him, carefully lifting a piece of lettuce with his knife, rather as a pathologist might a piece of skin on a cadaver. Before placing a crouton in his mouth, he passed it before his eyes as if to confirm it was edible. Diamond again sought out Toby with a look that said, *We could be eating this meal at midnight.*

Having spent ten minutes eating very little of what was a rather bland dish, Dr Stockwell placed his knife and fork inside his dish, pulled his glasses away from his face and said, "Supposing you were to use *Die Glocke*, Steve – what precisely did you have in mind? Let's be frank here; I can see very little point in moving back in time simply to confirm the thing works because we know it does, so there has to be more, something so worthy that I would seriously consider it.

"I feel certain that Toby has already made you fully aware of the enormous catalogue of reasons why man should never, ever seek to tamper with the space-time continuum. Apart from H. G. Wells, who was, in essence, a fantasy writer and would-be visionary, I can't actually think of anyone who would be declared sufficiently learned who would approve of such an action. Yes, there have been many who have said that they believe time travel to be a possibility – notably Hawking – but all were simply theorising; I don't believe any of them truly believed that it would one day be a reality. To them it was a tabletop exercise; they were asked if it was possible and they responded by using the laws of physics, mathematics and chemistry to insist that, technically, it was – and there they left it. No one who put forward a theory actually raised his or her hand to express an interest in actually seeking out one of science's Holy Grails.

"What von Braun managed to achieve so many years ago is so extraordinary, so utterly breathtaking, that it is off the scale. He was so far ahead of his time that we haven't yet caught up with him some seventy years after he first designed and built *Die Glocke*. So, using the logic which has been my constant companion since I entered university, I cannot find even one good reason why the machine should be switched on again. In fact, I have come to the conclusion – albeit with great reluctance – that the governments of the United Kingdom and the USA are correct in their joint belief that *Die Glocke* should be destroyed. It is the Frankenstein's monster of inventions and I think that, perhaps, it should suffer the same fate as Mary Shelley's antihero."

Diamond sensed that he was no longer pushing at an open door, which disappointed him as he had genuinely thought the doctor was showing distinct signs of being open to persuasion. Undeterred, he gathered his thoughts, took a large bite out of a burger which he had to concede was exceptionally good, and delivered a response which he knew would have to tick many boxes if he was to successfully change the mind of the man opposite, who was now fiddling with a tomato.

"It is very difficult to disagree with much of what you say, Doctor," he said. "I am neither a scientist nor a bureaucrat; I am just someone whose sense of adventure – and, yes, mischief – has been driven into overdrive by his prevailing circumstances; namely that I will not be here to share a meal with you in six months' time.

"All I am saying is that if you are of a mind to defy the establishment, the men in black, for maybe the first and last time, then I am your man. I could die next week and, in my final hours, reflect on a life which was largely enjoyable, but I would rather die in a few months' time knowing that I had been a part of something very special.

"I understand and fully agree with your assertion that to use *Die Glocke* simply because it is available to us is pointless. I don't have a problem with that argument at all because it is sound and it holds a great deal of water. You asked for my counterargument; you wanted to know, if I was to be permitted to use the machine, what would be my raison d'être?

"Toby and I have discussed the paradoxes of time travel on countless occasions over the past ten years or so. I wouldn't say it has been an obsession with me, but it is a concept which has mentally engaged me since I first read Ray Bradbury and Isaac Asimov. You know as well as I do that if you sit down and add reason and logic to any debate about time travel the end product is an argument which doesn't stand up – none of it makes any sense, it doesn't work… it cannot work. And yet now, because of the genius of von Braun and the bravery of Eric David, we know that it does work and that many of the paradoxes are themselves governed and manipulated by secondary paradoxes.

"I would never pretend to understand it all, but it would seem to my uneducated mind that the theory behind the reasons why we can't travel in time is shredded to a large degree by the actual physical act of doing it; that's to say, when you achieve the impossible there simply are no rules, and what you must do afterwards is see where the pieces fall and then attempt to draw a conclusion.

"I don't know how all this works and I suspect neither do you – and I say that hoping that you know I have an enormous amount of respect for both you and Toby. If you dip your toe into a lake you really don't know where the ripples will run to or where they will ultimately fade and die.

"So what would I do if you, the sole keyholder, opened the door and let me sit in *Die Glocke*'s pilot seat? I know that to go back and meddle with the true foundations of the world as it was would represent a grand and unthinkable folly. It is the usual argument – go back and kill Hitler and then get back home to find everyone is speaking German.

"I am fully aware of what I shouldn't do, trust me on that. So, what would I do? I would want to make minor, cosmetic changes to the world; changes which would not destroy its fabric or even alter the grand scheme of things, but which would make the world, then and now, a better place. I would like to do something which is for the good of all. I appreciate that that sounds hopelessly romantic and grandiose to a degree which verges on arrogance but I think it could be done, I honestly do."

Diamond was pleased with the force of his statement and waited for the doctor to respond, which he did after finally consuming the last traces of his watery salad.

"Very noble sentiments, Steve... very noble. The problem is, there is a difference between nobility and danger. I'd love to go back and save Joan of Arc because I regard her as a truly great woman who was badly wronged, but to do so would be to risk calamity.

"OK, let's boil this right down to basics. If you went back, what would you do? Give me, maybe, three examples," he said.

Diamond pushed his empty plate to the far end of the table, took a sip of water and said, "I would go back and save the life of Oscar Wilde. I would also save the life of Jim Morrison, and I would like to watch – but not interfere with in any way – the assassination of President Kennedy."

"Excuse my ignorance, but who is Jim Morrison?" asked Dr Stockwell.

"He was the lead singer and main songwriter with the American rock band The Doors. He died needlessly in Paris in 1971 – not too far away from where Wilde had died seventy years earlier. The French capital is a very popular place for my personal heroes to perish," said Diamond.

"I also love Wilde, so on purely artistic grounds I cannot find any fault with your mission," said Dr Stockwell. "But of course, we come back to the paradox situation. How can any of us be absolutely certain that by extending Wilde's life we won't open a Pandora's box of possible changes? I know what you will say – that it is extremely unlikely – and, yes, I agree. You said that you are only interested in acts which would be for the good of all, and I doubt anyone could argue against the notion that more works from the pen of Wilde would be a wonderful thing. Morrison I'm not so sure about as I have never heard of him – but clearly he was of some cultural significance."

"Morrison is actually buried reasonably close to Wilde in Père Lachaise Cemetery, so the French obviously believed him to be a worthy composer and poet. You will hate this, but his grave sees more visitors than does Chopin's," said Diamond with a smile.

"There will never be any accounting for taste, young man," said Dr Stockwell, clearly taken aback. "So, how would you mastermind the saving of these two men? I am totally ruling out the Kennedy assassination in Dallas – that's a global political event, most definitely not a cultural one."

"Well, Wilde died of cerebral meningitis brought on by a very simple ear injury and subsequent infection which he picked up during his time in prison. I have done a little internet research, and the problem, I am certain, could have been cleared up by very basic medical care. It was care he never received because at the end of his life he was poverty-stricken and had been abandoned by family and friends alike. Had he had access to basic antibiotics, I think he would have lived; I don't think there is any doubt about that. In the end he simply gave up because the burden of living in relative squalor as a figure of some ridicule was all too much for him. To my mind, the lonely and painful death of Oscar Wilde is one of the world's greatest ever tragedies.

"He didn't have any influence on the rise of the Nazis, the fall of communism or the massive socio-economic changes in the African belt, so I think we would be pretty safe. Same argument with Morrison, really – he was a popular rock star who was loved by a great many people but who, in the final count, didn't move the world on its axis or fundamentally change anything of real significance," said Diamond.

"How did Mr Morrison die?" asked Dr Stockwell.

"He allegedly drowned in his bath after a night out in a Left Bank nightclub. I say allegedly because, like virtually every other curious death involving a celebrity, there are countless conspiracy theories," said Diamond.

"Which are?"

"Oh, that he died in the club's toilet of a drug overdose and was smuggled out to avoid a scandal. That he was murdered either by a drug dealer or by the lover of one of the countless women he seduced whilst living in Paris. He was quite a lad, was Jim," said Diamond.

"He does sound a particularly unsavoury specimen," said Dr Stockwell.

Both Diamond and Toby laughed out loud, their spontaneity even bringing a smile to Dr Stockwell's face.

"Well, I need to think, and to do that I need to be somewhere peaceful, not sitting in a dark and noisy room such as this one. My head tells me to decline your offer, to shake your hand and walk away. We shall see," said Dr Stockwell.

"What does your heart tell you?" asked Toby.

"Ah, well, that's confidential, my boy," he replied, before rising, saying a courteous goodbye and leaving.

Toby and Diamond looked on, bemused, as the doctor marched up to the man behind the bar en route to the door to tell him that the music was being played at "a disgracefully high volume".

"Wow, he's pretty cool for a scientist," said Diamond. "How do you think we did?"

"I didn't do anything – but I thought you put your case forward really well. I know that man inside out and he doesn't sit and talk to idiots. If he had you marked down as a fool he would have left after ten minutes," said Toby.

"Do you think he's interested?"

"I do – but whether he has the balls to do anything, I'm not so sure. As he said, he has always been a company man – not a yes-man, but a man who doesn't enjoy rocking the boat. What I do know is that he will come to a decision quickly – he always does. I suspect that by the time he gets home he will have decided one way or the other," said Toby, fumbling in his wallet for a credit card.

They parted, with Toby promising he would contact Diamond the moment he heard anything – be it good or bad. Toby headed home, and Diamond opted to take advantage of a rather rare sortie into the capital's centre by looking for a new pair of jeans.

As he stood rifling through a rack of denims in Debenhams he was hit, and almost crushed, by a tidal wave of harsh reality. As his heart rate began to increase, as the sweat began to form across his brow, he asked himself why he was contemplating spending £60 on an item of clothing – unless, that was, he wished to be cremated in it.

For the two hours he had been with Toby and Dr Stockwell he had all but lost himself; all but slipped into an alternative reality where he was vibrant and healthy. It reminded him of the first time he attempted to quit smoking. All had gone well until he actually forgot that he had stopped, and he was halfway down a Marlboro Gold before he remembered.

Diamond returned the jeans to the rack and almost ran from the shop. He was on the verge of crying and needed to return to the sanctuary of his flat as soon as possible. Unable to face the Tube, he stuck his right arm in the air and hailed a hackney cab – it was going to be expensive but it would be quick, and it would be a journey made away from the prying eyes of those who wouldn't understand why a grown man was weeping uncontrollably in the mid-afternoon sunshine.

Once home, he showered, had a cup of coffee, and decided he would rest on his bed in an attempt to relax; he was upset, and as emotional as he had been for many weeks.

As he lay completely still with his eyes shut, Diamond decided that he was going to die tomorrow. The panic attack in the department store was, he believed, a warning that the final countdown had begun – it was a signal telling him that if there was anything left he wished to achieve in his life he should act very quickly because the curtains were beginning to close.

As he drifted in and out of sleep, he wondered what it would actually be like to die, from both a physical and a mental perspective. Would the lights just go out as if he had been unplugged? Would there be a last-second crescendo of light and sound? Would a golden staircase materialise before his very eyes? He felt it more likely that it would be a slow and relatively peaceful fading away; that, in a millisecond, something would become nothing.

When he heard the sound of his new ringtone – a catchy little tune composed by Bach – he was momentarily tempted to look for the golden staircase, but it wasn't the Almighty summoning him forth; it was a rather breathless Toby, who sounded as if he had contracted Tourette's en route from the Hard Rock to his home.

"Fuck me, bugger me," he said. "It's me. You won't bastard believe this, but I think he's going to do it."

"You're joking. What exactly did he say?"

"I had only just got in when he rang. He said that he didn't understand what was happening to him, but he was of a mind to give the matter serious consideration."

"Well, that doesn't mean it's a 'yes', does it?"

"You have to know him as I do to read between the lines. In my opinion, that means he is ninety per cent on board."

"My God, I just assumed he would say it was a lovely idea but that he didn't wish to be involved in criminal or unethical acts right at the end of his career. So what do we do now?"

"I will speak with him again later tonight. He asked me to ring after 10pm, which I thought was a little unusual – but then I decided that he's probably going to reach a final decision with a little help from the fine Irish whiskey he joins forces with from time to time. Can you just imagine if he agrees?"

"I fell asleep – what time is it now?"

"A little after 7pm. Are you going out or is Noreen there tonight?"

"I'm staying home alone. Noreen is at her mum's, she's unwell again, so I will be here awaiting your call to arms."

"Great. Speak later, mate," said Toby, hanging up.

Diamond felt he must do something to prevent him succumbing again to his now almost perpetual fatigue, so he went for a walk down by the canal to help clear a head which was struggling to separate fact from fiction in the wake of Toby's call.

In his youth, he always recalled canal banks as being idyllic and pretty places where families walked together with their dogs and where barges vied for position alongside countless welcoming pubs which were always bedecked in flowers and plants of loud colours. Not any more, sadly. As he walked slowly towards the first lock he had to tread warily to avoid dog faeces, discarded beer cans, fouled nappies and even used condoms. It was a mess and a disgrace; one he found so unsettling that he moved though 360 degrees to begin the march back home.

As he turned he halted with a start – standing in front of him, no more than six feet away, was the bedraggled figure of a man who looked as though he had just clambered off a Viking longboat. At least a foot taller than Diamond, the man had long, greasy hair and a beard which appeared to be matted with the contents of his last dozen meals.

Instinctively, Diamond asked, "Can I help you?", before mentally flaying himself for the stupidity of the question.

"Give me your money," said the man.

Convinced that the creature before him was probably called Ragnar and had a substantial axe concealed somewhere about his person, all Diamond could come up with in response was, "No chance, matey."

Ragnar seemed a little confused by Diamond's refusal to comply with his request, and began to move forwards, raising his right arm as he did. Diamond, a self-confessed lifelong coward, weighed up his limited options before drawing back his own right arm and hurling his balled fist forwards with every ounce of effort he could muster.

The first thing he felt was pain as his punch collided with Ragnar's face flush on his substantial nose. He was then overcome with surprise as the big man toppled backwards on his heels before falling heavily to the sodden turf which bordered the canal. His last emotion was joy as he started to run back to the main road, his would-be attacker still horizontal as he searched for his lost senses. Diamond didn't look back until he was a good hundred yards from the scene of combat. Astonishingly, although Ragnar had raised himself to his feet, he wasn't in hot pursuit; he was walking away in the opposite direction, holding his face.

Diamond ducked into the nearest pub, The Halfway House, and asked the barman for a large brandy with lemonade. He was shaking; in fact he was trembling so much that, having delivered his drink, the barman asked if he was OK.

"Yes, I'm fine, thanks. Someone just tried to mug me so I am a little shaken, but this will help," said Diamond as he drained his glass in one swift movement.

"Shall I call the police?" asked the barman.

"Nah, I'm cool now. I'd like the same again, though."

Another double brandy was delivered, the barman telling him it was on the house and insisting that, "It isn't normally like that round here."

Diamond thanked him for his concern and his reassurances, knocked back his free gift inside thirty seconds and said his goodbyes.

He didn't feel totally secure until he was back home behind a door which he double-locked just in case Ragnar had followed him home and lay in wait beneath the horse chestnut tree. As he sat back and exhaled deeply, his mobile rang; not Toby, but Noreen.

"Hi, sweetie, you OK?" she asked.

"Yeah. Just been attacked by a Viking but I put him down with one punch. How's your mum?"

"Yeah, you wish. She's doing OK now. It was a bit scary earlier, though, as her blood pressure went through the roof for no apparent reason. Anyway, she's stabilised and is asleep, so I feel better than I did."

"That's great; give her my love when she wakes up."

"You never send her your love… what's happened to you? Gone all mature on me, Diamond?"

"Just reassessing my attitude to life, my little temptress. It's nothing serious and it won't last for long."

"I will come over and stay tomorrow if that's OK?"

"Sure is. We'll go out for a meal."

"Look forward to it. Gotta run, hon. Love you."

"You too."

At last Diamond felt safe, having convinced himself that Ragnar had most definitely not followed him home, and that he was probably just an addict in need of a fix. No excuse for daylight robbery and threats, of course, but if anyone understood the consequences of withdrawing medication from a man who was wholly dependent upon it, it was Diamond. Forgiveness was easy when there was virtually no time left to waste on hatred.

Determined to stay awake so that he would be fully alert when – or if – Toby rang, Diamond dragged his ageing vacuum cleaner out of a cupboard and began a furious session of cleaning, clutching his mobile in his left hand so as not to miss any incoming call.

He had all but finished his war on dust when Toby rang. He switched off the vacuum, sat himself down in front of the television, muted the sound, mouthed the word "Please" and answered the call.

"He has asked the both of us to go to Porton Down on Sunday night in readiness for what he described as 'the operation' the following morning," said Toby.

"So it's on, then… is that what you're saying?" asked Diamond, almost holding his breath.

"I am assuming as much. Dr Stockwell can often talk in riddles but I think it is highly unlikely he would have us travel to the bunker unless he had made a decision."

"Never in my very wildest dreams did I think he would do this. When I made the suggestion I thought there was a five per cent chance, and then after talking to you that dropped down to about two per cent. I'm not sure what to say, mate. This could be epic."

"If it does happen it will be slightly more than epic, Diamond. What you mustn't do is tell anyone – Noreen, I mean."

"Do you think she'd believe me if I did? I told her earlier that I had been attacked by a mad Viking – did she believe me? No chance."

"Of course you were. I'm not being disrespectful to either you or Noreen but there's secret, top secret, above top secret, and then this. OK?"

"I was actually attacked by a…" Diamond abandoned the sentence, having realised it sounded about as plausible as someone claiming that they were going time-travelling early next week. "OK. Not a word shall pass my lips. So what's the script, Toby? Can you pick me up on Sunday afternoon and drive us there?"

"Yes, that'll be fine. I will call you over the weekend. If I hear again from Dr Stockwell I will let you know."

"Do you think he's likely to change his mind?"

"Unlikely. He's a man who has based much of his life on decision-making and logic. If he has decided that what you have proposed is logical – even though it may be wholly unethical and certainly illegal – then he will go with it. I have only known him to change his mind once in all the years we have worked together, and that was when he cancelled a ham omelette and opted for a pork chop in the staff canteen."

"Cool. Speak soon – and thanks, mate."

"Nothing to thank me for, Diamond. You were the one who came up with the crazy idea and then backed it up with a heroic speech. Be good," said Toby.

Diamond reinstated the audio on his television, sat back and wondered what a man who had just been given the green light to bend the laws of physics should do to fill the gap between the here and now and the event itself.

Feeling slightly woozy and a little bit inebriated from his post-fight brandies, he decided to raise a celebratory glass of wine to himself and to absent friends. The Shiraz was atrocious but the alcohol content was enticingly high, and within the hour Diamond had drained the bottle.

He looked on, appalled as mobile-phone footage of jihadist militants carrying out summary roadside executions far, far away filled his screen, before flicking through the channels and finding yet another rerun of *Airplane!*, a film which still made him laugh out loud some twenty years after he had first queued outside the Odeon to see it.

When he awoke, he was surprised by two things – that morning had broken, and that he was actually in bed, as he had absolutely no recollection of leaving his armchair the previous evening. As he speculated as to who had released a swarm of angry wasps inside his head, he struggled to remember what day it was.

Saturday, it was Saturday, which meant… which meant that Noreen was coming over, and that Toby was picking him up tomorrow in readiness for his journey into the Twilight Zone.

He couldn't remember what time Noreen had said she would be arriving but he assumed it would be later, giving him time to remove all the evidence of another night of excessive drinking. Not that she would condemn him because she had once admitted that, had she been diagnosed as had he, she would drink champagne every day and start smoking again.

CHAPTER

SIXTEEN

Quite often, Diamond became tearful when he thought about the effect his passing might have on those around him; particularly Noreen. When one person dies, his or her suffering may be ended but, regretfully, it is the signal for the suffering of others to intensify – something which Diamond regarded as, perhaps, the cruellest of ironies. He knew that the very moment his fight was over, hers would begin in earnest – and that saddened him more than anyone would ever fully appreciate.

He lay back in his bed and switched on the radio, an ever-present companion which often successfully moved him away from reality and into the sort of comfort zone which only familiar music could provide. He tunelessly sang along to Bob Marley's imperious 'No Woman, No Cry' before throwing to the floor a duvet which most definitely could do with a scrub. He stripped the bed, placed its entire contents in the washing machine and then stood naked whilst preparing his first coffee of the day. He would see Noreen later, Toby tomorrow, and *Die Glocke* on Monday morning. He felt a sense of contentment verging on fulfilment.

Noreen burst through the front door around 7pm, all smiles and positively radiant. They simply held each other tightly for almost a minute; words were not necessary.

"Right, dickhead, where are we going?" she asked eventually.

"I thought we might try that new Chinese down the main road; the one which has opened where the record shop used to be," said Diamond. "When I was a teenager dancing to the music of Duran Duran and Adam Ant, the whole world seemed to be crammed to the gills with record shops. These days you struggle to find one outside of the city-centre megastores; it's such a shame. They used to let you go in and listen to stuff you were considering buying on headphones.

"It's the new world of downloads that's killed the local guy who used to flog vinyl. That's why they have all but abandoned the Top Forty charts – there's no point in having them as no one goes out to buy music any more; they stay home and switch on their computers to get what they want.

"Remember a few years ago, some top band actually allowed people to download their latest album and then invited them to pay what they thought it was worth? It used to be that bands made money on album sales and then lost it on tours – the reverse is now true; they give away their music and then rake it in by playing in front of a hundred thousand people in some concrete dust bowl in the middle of nowhere. Radiohead; I think it was them who gave away their album online. Not a bad move actually, as they'd have to pay me to listen to any of their stuff, miserable bastards."

Noreen picked up Diamond's jacket and trainers, tossed them to him and said, "Let's go. I am so hungry I would even consider eating one of your corned-beef toasties – and may God forgive me for saying that."

They walked arm in arm to the restaurant; an almost deserted, lantern-filled room which featured a fish tank, appalling piped music and the sort of laminated menus which always seem to be covered in some sort of sauce. The fact that it was undisputedly tacky and that they were the last two people in the area to be made aware of this fact amused them greatly, and as the evening unfolded they found humour in practically everything from the service to the food to the toilets.

"Here I am, just weeks from my demise, sitting in one of the worst restaurants I have ever been in," said Diamond. "I should be spending my evenings in one of London's finest gentlemen's clubs, sucking on a pipe as I entertain and educate an audience made up of eminent lawyers and surgeons."

"Shut the fuck up and eat your sweet-and-sour chicken," said Noreen, trying to suppress a bolt of laughter for fear of upsetting a waiter who, she suspected, was fully aware that they would never return.

As they strolled back, hand in hand, they were both gloriously happy; Noreen because she knew her man – her doomed man – had enjoyed his evening, and Diamond because he knew that within forty-eight hours there was every chance that he would become a real-life Doctor Who.

Contentment often moves people to the very cusp of complete relaxation. Once back inside Diamond's flat they undressed and crawled into bed, happy simply to hold each other in the few moments which separated them from a deep sleep.

When Diamond woke, he was alone beneath his freshly laundered duvet. He could hear Noreen moving around in the kitchen, whistling what sounded like excerpts from *Joseph and the Amazing Technicolor Dreamcoat*; a curious choice for a woman who did not require an invitation to condemn any musical which came after *West Side Story*.

To the strains of 'Any Dream Will Do', Diamond dressed and pondered as to whether he should tell Noreen about his plans for the next couple of days. He decided that "Oh, by the way, honey, I am going away for a spot of time travel" wouldn't best please his beloved partner, so he would fall in line with Toby's request and keep quiet.

Noreen left around lunchtime, having prepared a fine breakfast which, she insisted, was low on calories and high on protein despite containing sausages, bacon and black pudding. Counting calories was not something which had featured at all on Diamond's list of post-diagnosis priorities; if it tasted good, he ate it.

He packed an overnight bag with the bare essentials, thought about including a half-bottle of vodka he found in his bedroom cupboard, but then regained his senses and opted for a litre of fresh orange juice.

He was nervous, and was actually prowling up and down his living room like a caged bear when Toby arrived.

"Time for a spot of adventure, old stick," said Toby. "Time to gamble, time to be bold, time to live a little."

"Onwards and upwards, let's go," said Diamond, as they headed off for Porton Down.

With the radio playing far too loud, there was initially no room for conversation as Greater London disappeared in the rear-view mirror.

As they moved from urban sprawl to the lush greenery of the English countryside, Toby suspected that his friend was on the verge of falling asleep, so struck up a conversation. "Did you bring any notes on Wilde and Morrison to show Dr Stockwell?" he asked.

"I pulled together as much information as I could – mostly relating to their deaths. I also got addresses, dates etc.; it isn't much but hopefully it will be more than I need. I suspect that it will be me asking most of the questions as I haven't a clue how *Die Glocke* works or what I am likely to experience. We have two separate parts of a shared equation here – I am doing this to save the lives of two men I regard as cultural icons, whereas Dr Stockwell is looking at this as an experiment, an event he can learn from. I am also acutely aware that this is his parting shot, his one and only opportunity to wave two fingers at the bureaucrats he so obviously – and understandably – blames not just for the impending destruction of *Die Glocke*, but for the premature end of his career. So, it's debatable as to who will get the most out of this: him or me," said Diamond.

"If he has sanctioned this then he is far, far more angry and pissed off than I realised. All I ask is that you agree with whatever he suggests, whatever he asks. He is not a man accustomed to hearing the word 'no', so park your rebellious side for a few days and let's see where it takes us," said Toby.

"I promise to behave, sir," said Diamond mockingly.

Toby gave up the fight to keep his friend talking and let him sleep, waking him only as they approached the base. "We're almost there," he said, jabbing Diamond on his right shoulder.

"Cool. I wasn't asleep; just collecting my thoughts and working out a plan of action for when your doctor friend catapults me back in time to confront men of great worth and import," said Diamond.

"When we go through the various security checks you are Dr Steven Diamond, OK? Dr Stockwell should have phoned through to let them know you are with me. I've worked there for years and years but the men with the tin hats and the rifles treat me as a total stranger each and every time they meet me. So straighten your back and make an attempt to look educated. Once we are inside and with Dr Stockwell it doesn't really matter who you are, as they work on the basis that if you are wandering around the labs and offices and not slaughtering the staff whilst screaming, 'God is great', then you're most welcome," Toby added.

"Do I actually look like a scientist?" asked Diamond, staring into the sun-visor mirror and attempting to push his hair back into something approaching an acceptable shape.

"Trust me, they come in all shapes and sizes. There's a small group in one of the basement sub-wings who are working on something to do with growing carrots inside a vacuum. If they wandered out onto a stage somewhere everyone would assume that they were a thrash-metal band. So don't worry," said Toby.

The security was just as Toby had said it would be – thorough, threatening and seemingly never-ending. It took more than fifteen minutes for them to negotiate the concentric rings of defence.

They finally entered the secret world of Porton Down through a small, shabby blue door, and waiting in a reception area – which shimmered, such was the combination of neon and glass – was Dr Stockwell.

"Good to see you again, Dr Diamond," he said, offering his hand. "And you, Toby. I hope you are both well. If you will follow me, I have some coffee waiting for us."

Although they passed few people on their rather long journey down into the bowels of a complex which was every bit as impressive as Toby had led him to believe, Diamond played along, keeping in character by knotting his hands behind his back – something he had seen genuine scientists do in countless American TV shows.

They finally arrived at a box of an office; a characterless, windowless, plant-less room with four chairs and one table, upon which were three cups and a jug which was belching out steam.

"Well," said Dr Stockwell. "Here we all are again, then. Sadly, I am unable to offer you the sort of fare you both enjoyed last time in that dreadful burger bar, but I'm sure that later you will find something to your liking in the canteen.

"I have arranged for you to share one of the family rooms, so shall we say we will get together for a long chat later – around 8pm in the quieter section of the canteen? I have had a word with our resident chef and he will make sure that we are guaranteed some privacy as we talk. I will see you both later."

Diamond and Toby were led to their room by a rather attractive woman in her mid forties. She bristled with authority, but the tight uniform she wore clung enticingly to her body and both men were happy to walk in her wake, smirking at each other like teenagers.

Diamond was still unconvinced that Dr Stockwell would find the courage to make the sort of quantum leap which would be required if *Die Glocke* was to fly again. Even though the eleventh hour had arrived and was ticking down, he expected the man with the golden key to undergo a change of heart and dismiss as unworkable the idea of meddling with the past.

It was nearly 8.30pm when Dr Stockwell strolled into the canteen to take his place opposite Toby and Diamond. The canteen was all but deserted, and as the chef shuffled forwards to take their order he surprised two-thirds of those present by planting down on the table three bottles of beer and a carafe of red wine.

"I thought we needed to be relaxed and at our most open and honest," said Dr Stockwell, picking up a beer and drinking from the bottle.

Toby's perception of his mentor was changing on an almost hourly basis, and all he could think to do was follow suit by lifting a bottle to his lips. Diamond did precisely the same, and in so doing mentally reassessed the allegedly uncool doctor as extremely cool indeed.

"I have done a great deal of soul-searching and amateur self-analysis since last we met, and my conclusion is that I now find myself in a most curious place," said Dr Stockwell. "My belief is that we all have demons and angels fighting for space inside our minds, and at the moment these two disparate forces are engaged in what I can only describe as a battle royal. The angelic side of my nature, the side which has largely governed my life since childhood, is telling me that with age has come a certain foolishness which it neither recognises nor accepts. It reminds me, constantly, that I have been a lifelong advocate of toeing the line, and that my most rebellious act was sneaking into a cinema when I was just seventeen to watch *The Exorcist*. Now, that is hardly a recipe for the prompting of unbridled anarchy at a point in my life when I should be trawling through eBay or Amazon looking for comfy slippers and a second-hand train set.

"Whilst I do suspect that both angels and demons enjoy the gift of precognition, the former, I am absolutely certain, look at any future event from the perspective of what might be lost as opposed to what might be gained. The reverse is, of course, true of the latter, who insist that throwing caution to the prevailing wind will not only prove to be productive, but is to be admired.

"As I sat on the train home after our meeting the other day, I did what I have always done when faced with a dilemma which does not easily throw up a solution: I mentally listed the pros and cons and employed the sort of dull logic which has always seen me marked down as a desperately uninteresting man who cries like a small child when he inadvertently sets foot off the straight and narrow.

"Working out why I should never allow anyone to set foot in *Die Glocke* again was so very simple because the usual answers came to me time and time again – danger, treachery, crass stupidity, unprofessional etc.

"Listing the plus points was an altogether more difficult affair as, in truth, there aren't any above and beyond an understandable desire for more knowledge. You wish to extend the lives of two people; one I admire greatly, one I had never even heard of until a few days ago. That is a most laudable objective, and yet, in my opinion, hardly sufficient grounds to see a loyal and honest servant of the Crown transformed into a deceitful rogue who may quite possibly see his reputation shredded and his pension stopped, all for one act of bravado," he said, before refilling his wine glass and taking a sip.

"Right," said Toby. "So we can take it that, after weighing things up, you have decided against it?"

"Look, we understand and it's probably right that I apologise to you for putting you in such a difficult situation. All I wanted to—" began Diamond, before being interrupted by Dr Stockwell.

"Quiet, gentlemen," he said. "I am a fool – but at least I am a relatively old fool. I think we should do it. If we do not, if I turn you down, I will spend every minute of every waking hour until I die wondering… well, just wondering what might have happened. I will also be filled with the two emotions I despise the most: bitterness and regret."

"So we are on?" said Diamond disbelievingly.

"If you insist upon using street parlance then, yes, we are on. In fact we are very much on," said Dr Stockwell. "It is getting late, so I will leave you two to finish the wine. Let's meet here for breakfast around 9am. We will then make some plans and take some decisions. Remember, whilst *Die Glocke* is the most advanced piece of hardware ever invented and constructed, its operation is very simple – that's to say, there is little in the way of preparatory work to undertake. The machine is ready; now we must ensure that we too are ready."

Dr Stockwell stood, waved a goodbye to the chef and disappeared into the corridor, leaving Diamond and Toby staring, speechless, at each other, their bottom lips dangling in cartoonish fashion.

"Fuck me," said Diamond. "He gives us a totally negative speech and then turns everything on its head by announcing he is going to ignore all his inner voices and do it."

"I think he was telling us that he had listened to the inner demon he mentioned – it obviously shouted louder than did the angel," said Toby. "But you're spot on; I also assumed he had decided against it halfway through his monologue. He loves a good speech, does Dr Stockwell; he loves to play to an attentive audience."

Diamond split the remainder of the wine between their glasses before raising his towards his friend. "Cheers, and the very best of luck, Darth Vader," he said.

"Cheers, and the very best of luck to you too, Doctor Who," replied Toby.

The pair slept only fitfully, the temptation to discuss what lay in wait constantly getting the better of them. Diamond asked about the processes involved in the operation of *Die Glocke*; Toby said he only knew what he had read in the documents which both had seen. Toby asked if his friend was at all apprehensive about using an apparatus which hadn't been used or tested for many years and which, as far as he could work out, did not boast even one safety feature.

"I am excited, but not at all scared," said Diamond. "I think I lost my sense of fear at the very moment I accepted my diagnosis and decided to try and enjoy what remains of my life. After all, what's the very worst thing that can happen? I could die, right? Big deal. We all have a finite number of days to live – it just so happens that mine can be counted in dozens rather than thousands.

"If *Die Glocke* does manage to move me backwards from the present and something then goes wrong, I will simply be a man with leukaemia in 1900 or 1971 rather than here and now. If I am stuck in 1900 I will become Wilde's new best friend, most definitely. Can you imagine it – spending time drinking up and down the Left Bank with a man like that? Reading with him, maybe writing with him, sleeping with him?"

"What? Sleeping with him? I know you're a big fan but that's just not right," said Toby.

"I was joking. I just wanted to see your reaction. He's not my type, actually – he wore far too much fur for my liking, and what about those socks?; a total fashion disaster," said Diamond.

They filed into the canteen the next morning to be told by the man behind the counter that Dr Stockwell was waiting for them in Meeting Room 74. They found it in a rather quieter section of the base, far from the madding crowd.

"Because this place is rather like that maze in the movie version of *The Shining* I can't be one hundred per cent certain, but I think the room where they used to keep *Die Glocke* is around here somewhere. It would be nuts to say it looks familiar because whoever designed Porton Down had a one-track vision with regard to corridors and rooms," said Toby.

The door to Meeting Room 74 was ajar. Dr Stockwell, in jeans and a T-shirt, was sitting behind a table well stocked with food and drink. "Morning. I took the liberty of changing our venue because over the past few years I have learned that walls do quite often have ears in this place. The one thing I can guarantee is that this particular room is not bugged in any way. Many here are, and I have in my desk a list of the ones which are wired for sound," he said.

"Right, let's get to the point. I have obviously taken leave of my senses, but I want to do this. Let's move on from the countless moral dilemmas and the rights and wrongs. I am not quite sure just how much Toby has told you about how *Die Glocke* works, Steve, but it is quite simple. It has the capacity to move back in time to a set year and set location but not a set date – that's to say, you will arrive on the same date you left. Today is July 1st, so if you go back to a year of your choosing right now, you will still be on July 1st, but in a different year. We have no way to modify the machine so we are stuck with what we have. It is difficult to be critical of creative perfection. Now, Steve, tell me what it is you wish to do."

Despite being somewhat taken aback by the brevity of Dr Stockwell's statement, Diamond swallowed a mouthful of coffee before attempting to swiftly compile a suitably succinct response. "As I said, I want to go back and save the lives of two men I believe to be worthy of salvation: Oscar Wilde and Jim Morrison. Perhaps significantly – and certainly usefully – they both shared the same adopted city: Paris," he said. "I shall put this in the most basic of terms: Wilde needs what today is regarded as simple medication, and Morrison needs someone sober and with a clear head to point out who the bad guys are. The really significant thing – the almost spooky thing – is that Morrison died forty-three years ago on July 3rd, the day after tomorrow, so our timing is ridiculously spot on," he said.

"What about Wilde, when did he die?" asked Dr Stockwell.

"He died on November 30th, 1900. The thing we need to think about is that the two deaths were totally different. Morrison died a very unpleasant death totally out of the blue, whereas Wilde's demise was drawn out, protracted. The point is that Wilde could have been saved had he received proper medical attention in the months leading up to his death – he didn't because he was impoverished, almost totally destitute.

By the time the true nature of his illness was correctly diagnosed it was far too late," said Diamond.

"So we do Morrison first and then Wilde on any second trip?" asked Dr Stockwell.

"Yes. Because we cannot select anything other than a year and a location we'll have to do Morrison ahead of Wilde – in fact, we'll have to move quickly before the window of opportunity closes," said Diamond.

"From what you say, we don't have to wait until Wilde is on his deathbed… we could go back much earlier and deliver the medication which will reverse his decline?" said Dr Stockwell.

"That's correct. If we can provide the antibiotics to cure his inner-ear problem it is unlikely that he will go on to develop the meningitis which ultimately killed him. Wilde died for two reasons – he didn't receive even rudimentary care and he actually gave up wanting to live. He was probably one of the ten smartest men ever to grace our planet, but once he had been stripped of the love and adoration which had sustained him for so many years he could see very little point in carrying on," said Diamond.

"Are you convinced that by treating what sounds like a very simple ear infection we can save him?" asked Dr Stockwell.

"Yes. I have read as many accounts of his death as I could find – and there are several. The general consensus is that he simply lost the will to live as he had been really unwell for several months. I honestly believe that had he been stronger, had he been feeling fitter, he would have fought his way through the depression which had gripped him and then attempted to rebuild both his reputation and career," said Diamond.

"That's fine. I bow to your superior knowledge, Steve. Wilde is for another day, so tell me about the other man, this pop singer," said Dr Stockwell.

"In many ways Morrison was your archetypal rebellious rock star: a gifted songwriter and poet who quickly tired of fame – or, in his case, infamy – and who tried to slip away from the limelight," said Diamond. "He moved to Paris, with his girlfriend, Pamela Courson, as he had become disillusioned with a life in music.

"The problem was that, by the time he relocated to France, he had become a world figure, so there was never really any chance of the anonymity he claimed he craved. All he managed to do was move from one mad circus to another – he was as recognisable on the streets of Paris as he was back in Los Angeles or New York.

"Drugs were an accepted part of the bohemian lifestyle back then, so, from what I can gather, he made little attempt to change his ways; that's to say, he didn't go there to clean up his act. He did in Paris what he had done back home in the States – he lived happily off life's excesses.

"He was a smart man, and after his death those closest to him insisted that he was the victim of either a simple, fatal mistake, or the sort of impromptu violence which will always stalk those whose staple diet is alcohol and illegal substances. There are quite contrasting versions of his death – it depends whether you choose to go with the official police report or the more elaborate version put forward by his friends. The official version states that he drowned in his bath after a riotous night out; a story rubbished by his friends, who insist he was either murdered or died of an accidental overdose in a club.

"Having read widely on the subject, I think the likeliest scenario is that, on July 3rd, 1971, Morrison visited the Rock 'n' Roll Circus nightclub in Rue Mazarine on the Left Bank, Saint-Germain-des-Prés. It was the place to be at the time, and a sort of magnet for rock stars, artists, groupies and drug dealers. The club does still stand, although it is now a totally respectable venue called Jane.

"A high percentage of those who have looked into his death have reached the same conclusion: he took both cocaine and alcohol on that night and was, according to various sources, 'on good form'. Morrison had a deserved reputation for being both brusque and moody, but on the night of his death he seemed to be in full-on party mood.

"I believe that, at a point when he was probably past caring what it was he was snorting or swallowing, he was offered yet another line of what he believed to be cocaine. He went to the toilets, locked himself inside a cubicle and inhaled the substance – the problem being, it was heroin and not cocaine.

"I'm no chemist but I suspect he would have died pretty quickly; certainly before he was in a position to leave the cubicle and appeal for help. He was found slumped on the floor after a staff member had kicked in the door.

"The dilemma for the club management was very simple – they had a world-famous celebrity dead on their premises, the victim of an overdose. If they left him in situ and called the police the subsequent publicity would force the hand of the local licensing authority, who would have had little option but to take a meaningful stand against drug abuse by closing down the club.

"Many, many people now believe that Morrison's body was smuggled out of the back door, placed in a car and driven back to his apartment in Rue Beautreillis, which is in the Marais district on the Right Bank. Once there, the body was taken upstairs, the bath was run, and he was stripped and placed inside it. When he was eventually found everything pointed to an accidental overdose at home. In fact, so convinced were the authorities that there wasn't even a hint of foul play that they didn't even bother to order a post-mortem."

Dr Stockwell buttered a piece of cold toast and poured himself another coffee. "Evidently, you know a great deal more about Morrison than I do. I will take your word for it when you say he is worth saving. So what's your plan? Let's assume we can get *Die Glocke* to work and you land back in Paris on the day he died in 1971."

"I suppose the only thing I can do is somehow get into the club and then try and ensure that he does not disappear into the toilets with what he believes to be cocaine," said Diamond. "It isn't going to be easy because I suppose he will be surrounded by friends-cum-minders, the place will be very busy, and the man himself is likely to be drunk and stoned – and not in the mood to discuss his own well-being.

"All I can do is try. If it doesn't work, it doesn't work and Morrison will be right on time for his appointment with his own death. If you were to push me I would have to concede that I honestly do not know what I will do. I suspect that my actions will be shaped by the circumstances; I may have a chance to change history, I may not."

"So what we need to do is try and get you back to somewhere quiet and secluded in Paris which isn't too far away from the club in question? The location is absolutely crucial, as is the timing, because I don't want you there for a moment longer than is necessary," said Dr Stockwell.

"I agree with you one hundred per cent. I like to think that, if we can pick the right time, I can be all done inside thirty minutes. If I can get into the club, I can do something – obviously, if I cannot get beyond the doormen, I will be back inside *Die Glocke* within minutes," said Diamond.

Both Dr Stockwell and Diamond fell silent as they mentally attempted to move from basic plan to fine detail.

"Do we know what time he is supposed to have died, or perhaps what time he was spotted inside this nightclub?" asked Dr Stockwell.

"No, all I can find is that his body was found in his apartment in the early hours. I am guessing, but I would say he was probably in the club between, say, 11pm and 1am, so I aim to be there during those hours," said Diamond.

"So if he died in the early hours of July 3rd, you'll have to travel tomorrow, won't you?"

"That's right. I was a bit fearful of pointing that out in case you said it wasn't possible, that you would need more time."

"I have spent two days looking into the practicalities of the whole exercise. I had planned to invite a couple of my colleagues to assist us, but I decided against it for two reasons – we don't really need them, and the fewer people who know about all this the better."

"You're in charge, Doctor," said Diamond. "So are you saying that we can try for tomorrow night?"

"If we are to save the man I know so little about, yes, that is correct," said Dr Stockwell. "From your point of view there is very little left for you to do, Steve. Toby and I will ready *Die Glocke*, starting this afternoon and continuing into tomorrow. At our initial meeting you told me that you have been a regular visitor to Paris over the past few years, so all I ask is that you study the various maps of the city which I will have delivered to your room and try to pinpoint a place we can aim for; a landing site. Once we have a location we can work out the coordinates, and then it will simply be a matter of when we push the button to move you back to 1971. I sound quite matter-of-fact but, trust me, I am as perplexed and excited by this as you are," he added.

As Toby and Dr Stockwell disappeared around the bend of a long corridor, Diamond returned to his shared room. He was glad of the silence and the solitude as his bouts of ill health were becoming more frequent and more debilitating.

He was searching for his Tupperware box of tablets when there was an almost apologetic knock on the door. A young girl, probably no more than twenty-five years old, smiled and said simply, "For you" as she handed over a pile of maps; some old, some new.

He spread them out on his bed; all maps of central Paris dating from 1959 through to 2014. It was an impressive collection, and his first thought was that the library of hard-copy material at Porton Down must be extraordinarily extensive.

The maps confirmed what Diamond had suspected: that, be it Left Bank or Right Bank, central Paris had changed very little since Haussmann completed his brilliant seventeen-year programme of reshaping, remodelling and boulevard construction in the late nineteenth century. The street map for 1971 was to all intents and purposes the same as the one printed in 2013, the only discernible change being that the latter recorded slightly more industrial development.

Diamond's problem was that there was nowhere in the immediate vicinity of the Rock 'n' Roll Circus club which he felt would offer sufficient cover for a large metal bell. He consoled himself with the fact that, even though it was the height of summer, his arrival would at least be under the cover of darkness. The obvious thing to do, he decided, was to try and find somewhere which would likely be deserted between the hours of 11pm and 1am. The index finger of his right hand moved down onto the most recent of the street maps, Diamond uttering just one word.

"There."

CHAPTER

SEVENTEEN

The beautiful Church of Saint-Germain-des-Prés was a Gothic gem; one which Diamond had visited on several occasions. He estimated that it would take him between fifteen and twenty minutes to cover the ground between church and club.

The only problem was that the target area, a patch of ancient trees to the left of the main building as you looked at the entrance, was relatively small. Any slight miscalculation could see *Die Glocke* materialise in open ground – deserted open ground, but open ground nonetheless.

He had raised the subject of a miscalculation with Toby, but had been told not to worry as Porton Down had access to the most sophisticated satellite technology, and that Dr Stockwell could find the coordinates for a discarded Coke bottle anywhere on the planet if he so wished.

Diamond rang Noreen and, having told her he was spending the weekend on a drinking binge with Toby, felt slightly guilty as he waited for her to answer. They spoke only briefly, Diamond confirming that the beer was flowing and that he loved her very much.

He was curled up in the classic foetal position and snoring loudly when Toby returned to the room. He attempted to tiptoe around his friend, but Diamond slept fitfully and lightly and was awake within seconds.

"Hi. Must have fallen asleep on the job again," said Diamond.

"No problem. I don't blame you, actually – there isn't much to do here, really. When I first arrived I suggested they fill one of the rooms with video-game consoles but they said they deal in reality and not fantasy; something which, having just spent a few hours standing toe to toe with *Die Glocke*, I can confirm to be utter bollocks," said Toby.

"You did? What's it like – I mean, did you get to go inside it?"

"I did, yes. It's smaller than I thought it would be; definitely a one-person craft. It looks like what it is – a rudimentary construction whose secrets are hidden within its base. It reminds me so much of a prop from a '50s or '60s sci-fi movie; you know, those really bad films which had bug-eyed monsters from Mars conquering the earth. It is difficult to look at it and touch it without feeling an absolute sense of awe. I felt so privileged that I had tears in my eyes for the first few minutes. Childish, I know, but it was such a special moment," Toby said.

"Is it ready – is everything OK?"

"Yes, it's all set," said Toby. "We worked our way through Dr Stockwell's 'must-do' list and he was right: there really wasn't that much to fine-tune. We have checked everything, and it is, as our American cousins might say, good to go."

"I have found somewhere we can aim for in Paris," Diamond offered. "Unfortunately, there's nowhere suitable within a few hundred yards of the club, so I had to look a little further afield, but if we can land where I have chosen, I think we will be fine. It will mean me having to walk a fair distance but that isn't a problem just so long as the machine is hidden from view."

"Show me," said Toby.

Diamond unfolded the 2013 street map of Paris and pointed to the green-shaded area which stood just to the side of Saint-Germain. He then pointed out the nightclub, telling Toby that he believed the two locations were perhaps a mile apart.

"Where did Morrison live?" asked Toby.

"Oh, miles away over here," replied Diamond, pointing to an area on the other side of the River Seine. "I am hoping that the accounts given by his friends and family are right; that he did visit the club on the night of his death. If he didn't, if he stayed at home as per the official police reports, then we will be wasting our time because I won't risk travelling all the way to the Marais."

Toby talked Diamond through the basics of what would happen the following night – setting the date and location, the ignition process, what he might experience, what might go wrong, the return journey. "Have you told Noreen?" he asked.

"No. I admit I was tempted, but in the end I opted to follow your advice and keep quiet. I know what you are going to say now – you're going to ask what you should say to her if I somehow end up stranded in 1971, right?" said Diamond.

"Right," said Toby.

"But if I do get stuck there, won't I simply become another paradox? The very second I find I am unable to return I will never have existed in your life or in hers, so you won't be required to say anything. Right?"

"Probably. It's all too complicated for me, I'm afraid. As I said the other day, the paradoxes and the possible implications are complex and many – that's probably why we shouldn't be doing this. I asked Dr Stockwell about them yesterday and his belief is that there are no set rules or paradoxes," said Toby. "What he will do before we try and make the machine work is talk you through everything, including the obvious and not-so-obvious risks. He said we are to enjoy our night here – but not drink or eat too much – and to meet him in the canteen at 8pm tomorrow for what he described as a 'last supper'. An interesting choice of phrase, I think."

"Has he taken into account that France is on Central European Summer Time and is one hour ahead of us? That will mean me leaving around 10pm rather than 11pm," asked Diamond.

"Actually, France wasn't on Central European Summer Time back in 1971. Dr Stockwell checks – and double checks – absolutely everything; he has a mind like a very powerful PC," said Toby. "So, what do you want to do now, if anything? It's 9pm. A quick bite to eat and then sleep?"

"Sounds good to me. Don't tell the good doctor but I'm nervous; I've always hated flying," said Diamond.

Toby laughed. "It's not really flying, though, is it? You will simply be in one place when you blink your eyes and another when you repeat the process a second or two later. There won't be a tedious check-in procedure or a safety drill from a pretty air hostess. This is *Star Trek* stuff – one push of a button and there you are; Gay Paree in the warmth of a midsummer evening. It sounds so good I wish I was going with you."

They ate and drank little as they indulged in what was nothing more than an exercise in killing time. By 11pm they were both in bed, Toby reading a book by Michel Faber and Diamond struggling to enjoy the latest album by Arcade Fire on his iPod.

When Toby awoke at 8am his book lay open on the floor and he could still hear the strains of music drifting from his friend's earphones. As he headed for the bathroom, Diamond woke up with a start, pulling the earphones away from his head.

"There must be some battery inside that thing – it's been running all night long, I think," said Toby.

"Fuck, I'm always doing that; falling asleep with it switched on. Is it any wonder I get so many headaches?" said Diamond, lying back and closing his eyes.

The day passed swiftly for Toby as he worked alongside Dr Stockwell, but agonisingly for Diamond, who felt as if he were a young child counting down the minutes to Father Christmas's departure from the North Pole. He had decided against ringing Noreen, fearing that any pent-up emotion would likely manifest itself in tears and a gushing soliloquy. He was desperate to keep any emotion in check until after his return, when he could replace the fluid of any shed tears with several celebratory cold beers.

When Toby entered their room at 7.30pm, Diamond was halfway through *Under the Skin*, the Faber book which his friend had almost finished.

"This is really good," said Diamond, waving the paperback in the air.

"Sure is, he's a really cool writer," said Toby. "Actually, that's not his best. I'll buy you a collection of his books for Christmas."

"If I'm still with you, you mean! I could be dead, or I could be living it up with the last dregs of the hippy population down by Notre Dame Cathedral," said Diamond.

"Right, let's go. You wearing what you've got on now?" asked Toby.

"No one can argue with a T-shirt, jeans and deck shoes, can they?"

"I guess not. Standard issue back in the '70s. You've always been a retro man. Come on, he's waiting."

Toby led the way down three corridors, across a landing which actually featured a potted plant, and finally through two sets of doors. Their destination lay behind a very heavy-looking door which was protected – or guarded, dependent upon your viewpoint – by a uniformed man who appeared to have been hewn out of solid granite. He didn't carry a firearm because he probably didn't need one. As the pair approached the door, Toby waved two passes in the big man's general direction. He stepped backwards and pulled back a flap on the wall to reveal a green button, which he pushed.

The metallic door in front of Toby and Diamond parted in the centre, the two halves sliding away in almost total silence. The immediate interior of the room was dark, lit only by inlaid roof spotlights which were clearly designed to simply mark a route forwards rather than genuinely illuminate. Twenty or so yards in, the room was suddenly flooded with light. Dr Stockwell was wearing a white lab coat and clutching a clipboard – but Diamond wasn't looking at him; he was transfixed by the object which dominated the room from floor to ceiling.

There it was: *Die Glocke*, the Wonder Weapon; the impossible made possible.

"Fuck me," said Diamond instinctively, before turning to Dr Stockwell and apologising for his language.

"Not a problem, Steve," said Dr Stockwell. "If you can't use that expression now, when can you use it?"

"It doesn't look like I thought it would. I thought it would be… well, I'm not sure what I thought it would look like, really. It looks really old. It looks like something which should be lowered into the sea – a diving bell. Wow, I'm amazed," said Diamond. "Can I have a look inside? Would that be OK?"

"Of course you can. That's why I wanted you here early: so you can familiarise yourself with everything. As I have said, its operation is surprisingly simple, but you need a basic understanding of what all the buttons and switches are for. Go on, get inside and sit down," said Dr Stockwell.

Diamond moved forwards and ran his hands over the outside of *Die Glocke*, touching the rivets which ran, equidistant, down the six main exterior seams. He reached the machine's open door and stepped inside, lowering his head as he took his place in the pilot's seat. "It's so small," he said. "And it looks older inside than it does outside. The control panel looks like something taken off one of those very early computers – the ones which were forty feet long and which could only do simple calculations. It's the sort of thing you'd see at a sci-fi convention and dismiss as an art-school project gone badly wrong."

It took Dr Stockwell no more than an hour to describe in detail the function of everything inside *Die Glocke*. Diamond had always had the ability to absorb information quickly but, aware that his senses had been dulled by a long period of medication, he asked the doctor to go over everything a second time, which he happily did.

When they had finished, the doctor handed Diamond an A3-size photograph of the control panel, labelled with small boxed sentences, linked to the component parts by arrows, explaining the various functions. He also handed over a sheet of A4 paper which contained the start-up instructions.

Diamond felt just as he had before he took his driving test – he had known how to drive, how to reverse, how to park, how to accomplish a three-point turn, and yet he'd been almost frozen by panic as the moment approached for him to deliver the proof to a complete stranger. Now, he didn't fear moving through time, landing in a Paris churchyard or meeting Jim Morrison; he was afraid only of making a basic mistake which might leave others disappointed. It was altruism gone mad, he thought as he sat back with a black coffee and studied the photograph.

It was almost 8pm before Dr Stockwell spoke to him again. He motioned for Diamond to join him in a small side room which housed a huge monitor screen and a bank of electronic equipment. The machines hummed in unison, giving the impression that the room was actually vibrating.

"This will give us the precise coordinates of your chosen destination in Paris," said Dr Stockwell. "Toby said that you had picked your spot?"

"Yes, I have," said Diamond, removing from his pocket the 2013 street map and spreading it out on the table, behind which the doctor sat polishing his glasses. Pointing to the Saint-Germain Church, he said, "That's it there: in the churchyard. It should be deserted at that time of night, and it isn't too far from the club where I hope to find Morrison."

"How far is 'not too far'?"

"I think about a mile; no more than that."

"Are you comfortable with that – walking that far, I mean?"

"Yeah, that won't be a problem – although it might be if I have to run back to *Die Glocke* whilst being chased by an angry mob," added Diamond.

Dr Stockwell punched some words into his keyboard and sat back. On the screen, what appeared to be a more intricate and much faster version of Google Earth began to pinpoint the church. Within seconds the view was crystal clear, almost high definition.

"Is that satellite technology?" asked Diamond.

"Yes. We claim it to be the best in the world, but the Americans, who always like a game of one-upmanship, insist they have a better one," said Dr Stockwell. He zoomed in and then moved the 'x' of the cursor onto a patch of scrub grass set inside a small circle of tall and leafy trees. "How about there?"

"Looks perfect to me. It will be dark, and unless a couple sneak into the grounds for some late-night alfresco fun that should be fine," said Diamond.

Dr Stockwell demanded more of the machine and it duly delivered, printing out the exact coordinates of the site which Diamond had selected.

"OK, we are all set. All we need to do now is wait for the appropriate hour," said Dr Stockwell.

"What about the guard outside? And how do we keep this quiet?" asked Toby.

"I have told security that I will be working inside this room all night, so removing the need for the big man outside. The irony is, he hasn't a clue what's on our side of the door. I did once ask him if he was at all interested in what it was he was being asked to protect, and he said, 'It could be the Pope, it could be a dead squirrel – it's all the same to me.' It was the single most confusing statement I have ever heard," said Dr Stockwell.

"What you have to remember, Toby, is that what we are doing is straightforward. It is noisy, but those who work here in this bunker are so accustomed to loud bangs and crashes that I doubt they would flinch were we to be struck by an thermonuclear bomb. I also doubt anyone will be sufficiently interested in what we are doing to come calling – and even if they do, by the time they arrive it'll be all over," he added.

They agreed to reassemble at 10.45pm, Dr Stockwell showing uncharacteristic emotion by grabbing hold of Diamond's shoulders, pulling him close and saying, "Relax – you'll be great."

Back in their room, Toby and Diamond sat on their beds and just stared at each other, reflecting on the indisputable danger of what they were about to do.

"Are we likely to see a last-minute change of heart, dear boy?" asked Toby.

"No chance. I suppose if I was fit, healthy, and had, say, another thirty years of hedonistic living to look forward to, I might be silently questioning why I volunteered for this madcap idea. But that's just not the way it is. I am living on borrowed time, so I am gambling with very little. If I roll the dice and lose, so be it," Diamond said.

"Everything will be fine. In a few hours' time you'll be back in this room, so excited that you won't be able to sleep. Trust me, you're in very good hands," said Toby.

By 10.45pm all three men were gathered in front of *Die Glocke*, almost as if they wished to silently underscore their admiration for von Braun's invention.

"This is how it will work, Steve – and I know we have been through this enough times for you to be able to repeat my speech in your sleep," said Dr Stockwell. "Once inside, just strap yourself in and try to get a feel for the machine. Stay focused and alert whilst attempting to relax.

"The flap which covers the red button down to the right of your seat has been removed to give you the easiest of access. It is absolutely vital that, the very second you hear *Die Glocke* slow down and then cease running, you depress it, because, as you know, that is in effect the pause button which will allow you stay put until it is pushed again. You may have to unfasten your seat belt to reach it.

"From Dr Eric David's detailed report into his flight, the most unsettling thing was the noise which he said enveloped the machine as it was brought to life – so be ready for that. I thought about providing you with earplugs but discounted the idea because I want you alert – and if being alert also means being a little frightened then you'll have to live with it.

"Once you have depressed the button you will be free to leave *Die Glocke* and head for the nightclub. I wouldn't bother making any attempt to conceal the machine – it's too big for that. What I have done – and this is so un-tech that you won't believe it – is fit a bog-standard lock and clasp to the door. Just put the padlock in place and lock it as you would a shed door."

With that, and much to the amusement of Diamond and Toby, the doctor handed over a lock and key.

"It is hardly a truly efficient last line of defence, but it will hopefully deter anyone who may chance across *Die Glocke*," said Dr Stockwell. "Apart from that, I can't think of much to add except be quick, be efficient, and do not hang around looking for souvenirs. You are not on a mission from God – in this instance you are actually playing God, so act the part and do your job."

"Can I ask about the paradoxes, Doctor?" asked Diamond.

"You can, but I doubt I will have any satisfactory answers."

"If I do somehow manage to save Jim Morrison's life, then when I get back that will have been fact since July 3rd, 1971 – so you two will have grown up with that as nothing other than the true history of the man. That right?"

"Sounds right, but as I have no interest at all in him or his music, his name will still mean nothing to me," said Dr Stockwell.

"I don't like him either, so it will mean sod all to me as well," chipped in Toby.

"OK. I'm ready. I promise not to shoot any politicians, and that I will return as soon as possible – that's to say, I won't be hanging around irrespective of whether I am successful or not. Unless, that is, a very pretty blonde in the club takes a fancy to me. In that case I may have no option but to invite her back to my space rocket for a private chat," said Diamond.

Even the doctor was smiling as Diamond made his way towards *Die Glocke*. He checked his watch – it was 10.57pm. Time to go.

Diamond stuffed his hand-drawn route map into his pocket along with the padlock key, placed the lock itself on the floor of the machine, and fastened himself into the pilot's seat. He glanced down to his right and could clearly see the red button. Extending his arm and stretching out his fingers, he was pleased to note that he could reach it without unfastening the seat belt, which was fashioned from crude leather and reminded him of a harness.

The doctor leaned inside and punched into the control panel the relevant details – the year, and the map coordinates for the sanctuary of the shaded area inside the grounds of a famous old Parisienne church. "Any last questions?" he asked.

"Nope. Let's do it," said Diamond.

Toby appeared briefly at the hatch, leant forwards, whispered, "Good luck" in Diamond's right ear, and kissed his friend gently on the cheek. As the hatch was slammed shut by Dr Stockwell, Diamond was still smiling at Toby's act of male bonding. It was one of the most beautiful moments of his life.

Toby and Dr Stockwell retreated behind the glass partition. They exchanged a brief glance; one which was taken by both men as tacit approval to go ahead. Dr Stockwell placed his finger above the button which would flood *Die Glocke* with power, and with one purposeful stab he set the process in motion.

It took a few seconds for the first sounds to leak out of *Die Glocke*; an initial low groan which quickly began to grow, first to a rumble and then to a wall of sound. Toby, sensing that the air around *Die Glocke* was, in some way, swirling and crashing like waves against a sea wall, moved out from behind the partition he had promised not to leave to get a better view.

"The air is turning blue, Doctor," he said.

"Yes, I can see. It's fascinating," said Dr Stockwell.

Inside *Die Glocke*, Diamond felt as though he was being executed in the electric chair. The charged air was humming, particles of dust and dirt were rising from the floor, and the lights on the control panel almost seemed to have been sequenced as they burned bright, then fell away into darkness. As the doctor had warned, it was the noise that made him strain against the straps which kept him bound tight to his chair. Within fifteen seconds, what started out as a dull thudding became a deafening roar, and from where Diamond was sitting it did sound as though *Die Glocke* had decided to move into self-destruct mode.

He moved his head to the right and stared at the tiny window. The small square – which had previously been filled with neon light – was, he was certain, bathed in a blue hue. Just as he had always done when forced onto a roller coaster he did not really wish to ride, Diamond took the sensible decision to close his eyes and wish for a speedy end to his scary discomfort.

He didn't have long to wait. Ten seconds after closing his eyes, he reopened them, prompted by a winding-down sound which he believed signalled the end of *Die Glocke*'s brief journey. He immediately reached down to his right, found the red button and pushed it firmly. It clicked and locked into place.

He sat and listened, hearing exactly what he wanted to hear – nothing. He glanced across at the window and saw the branch of a tree brushing against the glass as it moved and bent in the wind. He unfastened the seat belt, checked his watch and pushed the lever to release the door hatch.

As the door opened, *Die Glocke* was flooded with warm air which carried the scent of freshly mown grass.

Diamond spoke out loud. "Toto, I've a feeling we're not in Kansas anymore."

Placing his hands on either side of the hatch, he pulled himself forwards and stepped down and out of the machine. He closed the hatch door and checked he still had the small key in his pocket before inserting the padlock into the latch and squeezing it shut.

With *Die Glocke* secured, Diamond moved forwards to the periphery of the ring of trees and, through the gloom, could just make out the expanse of the church rising above him. It was most definitely the Église de Saint-Germain-des-Prés; a place revered by lovers, and one which he would visit on several occasions many years from now.

Diamond had no proof that he was, indeed, back in 1971, although he was most definitely in the French capital. He left the churchyard and quickly found the Boulevard Saint-Germain; a road which, thirty years from now, would house some of the most exclusive shops Paris had to offer. It was reasonably quiet, although there appeared to be a small jazz band performing in a nearby bar. His sense of paranoia had been heightened to such a degree that he assumed everyone who walked by had picked him out as a visitor from another world – but to them he was just another broke tourist out looking for a cheap burger joint.

Without feeling the need to consult his hand-drawn route map, Diamond moved swiftly down the boulevard before branching left onto Rue de Buci. He passed very few people, but when he did he instinctively lowered his head, as might a convict who had just escaped from a local prison.

Ten minutes later he again veered left onto Rue Mazarine, believing and hoping that the famed Rock 'n' Roll Circus club was now within striking distance.

He heard the club before he saw it; a raucous ball of distorted sound cutting a swathe through the otherwise still and peaceful night. The club was on his left as he approached, and was, from the outside at least, a good deal less grand than he had been anticipating. The entrance was narrow and banked on either side by enormous exterior doors. There was just one doorman, who stood with his arms crossed and pulled tight to his chest as he spoke to a group of maybe ten people, mostly young women.

It certainly looked like the '70s. Hair was long and adorned with flowers, jeans and trousers were high-waisted and flared, and there was a noticeable smell of both patchouli oil and cannabis.

As Diamond approached the club he picked up one of the countless advertising flyers which had been accepted by club-bound punters, only to be immediately discarded.

Live at the Olympia Theatre, Paris, August 24th, 1971
– The Kinks.

Tangible proof; not quite a copy of *Le Monde*, but more than enough to convince Diamond that he was now officially the world's second time traveller. Despite being warned against collecting souvenirs, he carefully folded the small poster and tucked it inside his back pocket.

He approached the club's front door slowly, taking in the surroundings and avoiding eye contact with the doorman, a predictably large man with a shaved head and a tattoo of a tiger which ran down the right side of his neck.

Diamond began to mount the steps, smiling at the big man as he did. An arm the size of a tree trunk immediately halted his progress.

"*Nous sommes complet,*" the doorman growled.

"Sorry? *Parlez-vous Anglais?*" asked Diamond.

"*Foutre, garçon Américain,*" came the reply.

A small group of teenagers to Diamond's left laughed out loud, leaving him to draw the conclusion that he had been told, rather impolitely, to go forth and prosper.

As he took a step back and considered his options, Diamond found himself staring blankly into the first hole to appear in Dr Stockwell's master plan – he had arrived in Paris without a single franc to his name.

"Can I come in, please? I have come a long way," he said, with more than a hint of desperation.

"*Quel est la valeur que vous montre-bracelet?*" said the doorman.

Nonplussed, Diamond smiled and shrugged his shoulders to indicate that he didn't understand the question.

"He asked how much your watch is worth," said a thin voice coming from his left. It was a girl in a bright yellow knitted hat and a kaftan.

"Oh, right. Thanks... I mean *merci*. Can you tell him it's a new model I bought in London just last week?" said Diamond, inaccurately describing the watch he had bought in a local Wembley market for £12.50 two years earlier.

The girl shuffled towards the doorman and whispered into his ear.

"He says he would like to have a close look at it," she said.

Diamond removed the watch and handed it to the man. He looked at both back and front before placing it in the inside pocket of his jacket.

"*Vous allez dans,*" he said, pointing at the club's open front door.

"He says you can go in," said the girl.

"Thanks, I'm so grateful for your help," said Diamond, hurrying inside before the man-mountain changed his mind.

Diamond's first impression of the Rock 'n' Roll Circus was that this must have been what all nightclubs looked like before the days of Health and Safety checks. The corridor he was walking down was poorly lit and the carpet so sodden that his shoes were actually sticking to the floor.

At the end of the corridor was a spiral staircase leading down into the main body of the club; a black hole of an area which resembled a sauna filled with the smoke of a thousand cigarettes and joints. He had expected the place to be overflowing but it wasn't – it was probably full in the technical sense of the word, but there was at least room to move about. To his left was a dance floor of polished wood which was separated from a cluster of tables and chairs by a latticework partition covered in fake vines and shrubbery.

'Tacky' was the word which came readily to Diamond's mind as he moved from the foot of the staircase to the bar. As he walked by a table, two couples stood and made their way towards the exit, leaving behind several half-finished drinks. Diamond, who had honed beer mine-sweeping into something akin to an art form during his student days, stealthily gathered up two pint glasses, poured the contents of one into the other, and sat on a bar stool.

The beer tasted good and the music was also to his liking – a blend of the very best of British and American rock. He went to check his watch, forgetting that he had been forced to surrender it to gain admission to what he had seen described on the internet as "the place to be, back in the '70s". It was cute in a trashy sort of a way, but he found it hard to believe that a city with as diverse a cultural and racial make-up as Paris didn't have more attractive and vibrant venues to offer both residents and visitors.

As Diamond sipped his beer and lost himself in the music – a lot of Hendrix and Rolling Stones – he began to wonder just how long he should wait before deciding that Morrison had not, after all, visited the club in the hours before his death. He considered asking one of the gyrating barmaids if The Doors frontman was a regular visitor but, conscious that his command of the French language was decidedly poor, he opted to remain silent.

He had been inside the club for around an hour when there was a noticeable rise in the noise level. It wasn't the music which had been turned up; it was the sound of voices coming from above the staircase. There was a little shouting, a short burst of applause, and then someone could quite clearly be heard saying, "The Lizard King."

Diamond placed his glass down on the bar and felt his heart rate begin to rise. Morrison had been known as 'the Lizard King' since using the moniker in a poem which was printed on the sleeve of one of his band's early albums.

A group began to descend the staircase; first two blonde-haired girls in miniskirts, then a beefy man with an open shirt and far too much chest hair – and then, lastly, Jim Morrison, lead singer of one of America's finest ever rock acts and, unbeknownst to him, enjoying his last night on planet earth.

Diamond could hardly breathe. There, standing no more than twenty feet away, was one of his first musical heroes. Since moving to Paris and into semi-retirement, Morrison had put on quite a bit of weight. The boyish good looks which had driven so many young women to the point of frenzy during his mythical live shows had faded and, with his face covered by a fulsome beard, he looked a good deal older than his twenty-seven years.

As Diamond had never actually believed that he would share floor space with Morrison, he found himself incapable of doing anything other than staring. The idea of travelling back in time to save a man from his own demons was, he still believed, a good one – but how was he to achieve it? If the conspiracy theorists were correct and Morrison did take an overdose in this nightclub on this very night, how was he to intervene and stop it?

These were questions he should have sought answers to before he stepped inside *Die Glocke*. This represented yet another sizeable hole in the master plan.

One thing was clear: Morrison was surrounded by his mini entourage at all times, so following him around like a besotted fan was out of the question. Diamond could wait until Morrison went to the toilet and then follow him, but knocking on a locked cubicle door and shouting, "Don't do it, Jim – I've come from the future to save you!" would probably reduce the singer to laughter rather than persuade him to flush away the fatal dose of heroin.

In any case, Morrison seemed to have a bladder the size of a basketball. He drank four large beers inside forty-five minutes without having to take a toilet break. Diamond was running low on patience, time and beer, the barmaid twice asking him if he wanted another drink. He either had to do something or accept failure and head back to the churchyard, so he stood up and walked directly over to Morrison.

Morrison was trying to have a conversation with one of the blondes, but as he was pitted against Creedence Clearwater Revival's 'Bad Moon Rising' it was all but a lost cause. Diamond stood motionless at Morrison's side, waiting for the song's final chord.

When his opportunity arrived he took it, leaning forwards to say, "Mr Morrison, do you believe in fate?"

"What's that, man?" said Morrison, his words slightly slurred.

"Tonight, in this club, you will be offered what you believe to be cocaine. It won't be, it will be heroin, and if you take it you will die."

"What the fuck you talking about, man?"

"Do not take the cocaine, Jim. I am no guardian angel, I am no madman – but I am here to pass on this message. I know you to be a spiritual man who has always embraced mysticism. Trust me, I have come a very long way to try and save you."

Before Morrison could answer, his companion with the open shirt intervened, grabbing Diamond by the throat and pushing him to the ground whilst shouting something in French.

Diamond expected to be pounced upon and promptly beaten to a pulp by a group of club staff, but no one arrived. Instead, as he lay on the floor, the crowd parted and he was free to get back to his feet. His lip was cut and he could feel blood running down into his mouth as he tried to regain both his balance and his senses.

"Are you OK, friend?" asked Morrison, with a look of genuine concern. "What's that you were saying about heroin?"

As Diamond launched himself forwards he shouted, "Forgive me, Jim", before landing on the bridge of Morrison's nose the sort of dream punch which had once laid low a Viking.

As Diamond and Morrison fell to the ground locked together, all hell broke loose inside the Rock 'n' Roll Circus club. As the rock star and his would-be saviour grappled on the filthy floor, blows and kicks rained down on Diamond's prone body. As he attempted to stand he caught sight of Morrison's bloodied and distorted face, his nose clearly broken by the impact of the blow and his eyes rolling back in their sockets.

Without warning, Diamond found himself moved from the upright to the horizontal as four suited men picked him up as if he was a rolled-up carpet and began to move him, at some speed, towards the back of the club. He feared they were preparing to force him into a back room where he would, presumably, be battered to within an inch of his life; but, mercifully, he was proved wrong. As his head prepared to make contact with a closed door, one of his captors lashed out with his right leg and kicked it open. Diamond's next experience was one of free fall as he was thrown, quite literally, out of the building and onto cobbled ground. Two of the men took the opportunity to shout loudly in his direction; it didn't sound like an invitation to return as their guests at any time in the near future.

Diamond stood up and ran towards a gap in the wall which surrounded the yard into which he had been thrown. Despite a stabbing pain which possibly indicated at least one fractured rib, he moved smartly into a back alley and then crept slowly towards the main road.

Glancing to his left, he could see a gathering of many people. As voices were raised to a crescendo, a car screeched to a halt outside the club and seconds later Jim Morrison, shirt covered in his own blood and hand clasped to his nose, was ushered into the back seat as flashbulbs illuminated the scene. Morrison was either on his way to hospital or to his home across the river – the one thing he wouldn't be doing was falling prey to a drug pusher who had failed to properly label his wares.

Diamond turned and started to walk back down Rue Mazarine towards the church. As he did so he checked his pocket to make sure that he hadn't lost the padlock key during his scuffle with rock-and-roll royalty. It was safe, and he was already starting to feel rather smug at preventing the unnecessary death of a talented man. The world, he felt, owed him a favour. Morrison would recover quickly from his injuries and the incident would just add to his reputation as a man who acted as a magnet for controversy – so Diamond felt Morrison owed him a favour too.

It took him almost twenty minutes to get back to the churchyard, his progress hindered by a cut just above his right knee. He leant against the perimeter wall, as much to catch his breath as to check that he was alone. Hearing nothing but the hooting of an owl somewhere in the distance, he moved through the bushes and trees towards *Die Glocke*. Momentarily he thought the machine had vanished, that he was stranded in 1971, but he had simply miscalculated and was looking in the wrong place. He tiptoed fifty yards to his right and crept forwards, constantly moving his head through 180 degrees to ensure he was the only living soul in the resting place of so many. There it was – *Die Glocke*, still there, still locked up, still his ride back home.

"Thank fuck for that," he said out loud as he removed the lock and sat himself down in the pilot's seat.

He strapped himself in and sucked air into lungs which ached after the kicking he had received in the nightclub. He closed the hatch, double-checked that it was firmly in place, and moved his right arm down to the side of his chair to feel for the red button.

Whilst never a man to place his trust in a divine force, Diamond found himself uttering what amounted to a short and very personal prayer as he closed his eyes and placed his index finger on the button. He pushed down firmly, the button dropping half an inch before clicking back upwards. Immediately the machine was engulfed by the noise of droning engines; a different sound to the one he remembered from the lab, almost as if *Die Glocke* was resuming its work mid-cycle.

He felt a quite distinct upwards motion, almost as if the machine was attempting to physically lift itself free of the ground on which it stood. He could smell some form of electrical charge, and as he looked towards the window the air seemed to have thickened, almost curdled. Outside, where just seconds ago there had been the waving branch of a tree, was just a light blue patch, flecked with royal-blue streaks which moved, left to right, like ribbons in the wind.

The rattling, the banging, the crashing continued for perhaps thirty seconds as the noise inside *Die Glocke* built to a crescendo which Diamond feared might end in an almighty explosion.

His hands were down by his sides and gripping the seat so tightly that his fingers were crying out for relief – and then everything stopped; not quite immediately because the sounds from the machine's base continued to drop in intensity and volume until there was almost perfect silence.

One blue light on the control panel in front of him flashed on and off just once. Diamond wasn't sure where he was – either in terms of time or location – but he was sufficiently relieved to utter the words "You may now smoke" before unfastening the ties which bound him to a seat that was soaked in sweat.

Dr Stockwell had told him that upon his return he should remain in situ; simply sit and wait for his heart and breathing rates to return to normal before even attempting to make an exit.

He leaned forwards to get a better view out of the window and, whilst he could clearly see a bright light, the glass was marked, scuffed and dirty. The truth was, he was actually scared to open the hatch for fear of finding himself somewhere he didn't wish to be. Ridiculously, his biggest fear was that he had landed in the very centre of Rome's Colosseum on a day when mad Caligula was feeding anyone and everyone to an assortment of savage animals.

His eyes were closed when he heard a tapping coming from his right. He sat up, opened them and turned his head.

It was Toby, giving a thumbs-up in Caligula style. Diamond smiled and reached forwards to release the hatch. The colder air of the lab poured into *Die Glocke*, raising the hairs on his arms.

"Steve– you OK?" asked Toby.

"You will refer to me as Sir Steve from now on, as surely I must be in line for a knighthood for services to science and physics," said Diamond, his face creased with laughter.

Dr Stockwell's face appeared next to Toby's. "How did it go, Steve? Did you make it?" he asked.

"I made it, it went well, I got beaten up, I've got the cuts and bruises to prove it – but I did it... or rather, *we* did it," Diamond replied.

"What do you mean, you got beaten up – by whom? Jim Morrison?" asked Toby.

Before Diamond could deliver an answer, Dr Stockwell stepped in to pour common sense over the situation, suggesting that he be allowed to get out of the machine and rest for a while.

Diamond, not without discomfort, forced himself into an upright position and then levered himself out through the hatch into the glaring lights of 2014. "Can you turn the lights down just a little, please?" he asked.

Once seated in a semi-dark room, he drank a bottle of mineral water in one gulp and asked Toby to fetch him a cappuccino from the canteen.

As Toby scurried away, Dr Stockwell knelt down in front of Diamond, patted him on the knee and said, "Well done. I am so proud of you. Actually, if I am being honest, I am proud and envious. You have blazed a trail today – something I will never get to do."

"Thanks," said Diamond. "At the moment it doesn't feel at all real – I feel as though I have just been dragged out of a comforting dream. I should be running around screaming and shouting as I have just completed the adventure of a lifetime, but I just feel a bit numb. I also feel exhausted, which is odd as it isn't as if I have been away for a number of days."

"You said you were hurt?" asked Dr Stockwell.

"Nothing too serious. I was punched and kicked a few times, that's all."

"How come?"

"The only way I could stop Morrison taking the drugs which would have killed him was to get him out of the club – and the only way I could think of to do that was to punch him in the face – hard. I think I may have broken his nose but it worked; the last thing I saw before I headed back to the churchyard was Morrison being helped into the back of a waiting car," Diamond said.

"Wow, so mission accomplished, then?"

"I think so, yes."

"I think we should get you down to the first-aid post so they can give you a quick examination. I will tell them that you are a doctor friend of Toby's and that you were mugged on the streets of London last night. OK?"

"Sure," said Diamond.

Having drunk his coffee, Diamond was escorted to the first-aid room by Toby and introduced to a surprisingly young-looking doctor called Bobby.

"What you been up to, then?" he asked, with an accent which pointed to an upbringing either in, or close to, Liverpool.

"I went back in time and was attacked by a group of men in ill-fitting suits and cheap sunglasses," Diamond said, smiling.

"Ah, right – and I'm Mary Poppins," Bobby replied, before asking him to remove his shirt and jeans. "Wow, looks like one of your attackers was Mike Tyson," he remarked, dabbing

Diamond's cut leg with some form of antiseptic. "Does it hurt much?"

"The leg doesn't, but I have some pain in my ribs here," said Diamond, touching the left-hand side of his ribcage.

Bobby touched and poked and kneaded. "There's nothing broken, so it will just turn a delightful shade of red, then purple, then black, then yellow," he said. As he got to his feet he added, "Next time you go back in time, go to Formby in 2003 and make sure that I don't talk to the woman in the Crescendo Bar who went on to become my wife, will you?"

"I promise," said Diamond, leaving.

CHAPTER

EIGHTEEN

Diamond returned to the lab to find Dr Stockwell and Toby lost in an animated conversation. As he entered the room, both began to applaud enthusiastically.

"OK, hero, tell us what happened," said Toby.

"Give us the edited highlights," said Dr Stockwell. "You look absolutely shot, totally exhausted."

"I am; I feel as though I haven't slept for several days – and I ache all over after my barroom brawl," said Diamond.

"It all went exactly as we planned. The journey backwards was a bit on the scary side, more because of the noise levels. When I go again I would like to wear earplugs. The map coordinates were spot on; *Die Glocke* landed precisely where we wanted it to, in the middle of that clump of trees.

"The walk to the club went without incident. Disappointingly, because it was pitch black, I wasn't able to see how Paris looked all those years ago. The only problems I had came after I arrived at the club. I will tell you about that later. Once inside I sat and waited… and waited… and waited. If I am honest, I was probably fifteen minutes away from admitting defeat and going back to the churchyard when Morrison and his friends arrived.

"For me, a big fan of his, it was obviously a quite startling moment. He was there, standing right in front of me; Jim Morrison. The short version is that the only way I could think of to get him out of the club was to attack him – which I did.

"I got a bit roughed up after my one lucky punch had flattened Morrison, but all they did was throw me outside into the backyard. I passed virtually no one on the walk back to *Die Glocke*, and the return journey was almost identical to the outward one; that's to say, a little bumpy."

"Wonderful," said Dr Stockwell. "From our point of view it went just as it did for those who observed Eric David's flight all those years ago – the noise, the air distortion, the flashes of radiant blue. You went and then you returned. We all sound so blasé about it now, and yet history was not only made in this small room today; it was revisited."

Diamond said that he needed to go back to his room, take his medication, ring Noreen and then sleep. Toby had already moved his stuff into an adjoining single room to give his friend time, space and quiet in which to rest his weary body and mind.

When he opened the door to his room, Diamond found the table which stood between the beds covered with various treats – sandwiches, biscuits, fruit of many types, two cans of lager and a bottle of Australian Shiraz.

He lay on the bed and called Noreen, forgetting that it was the early hours of the morning.

"Shit, what's wrong? What's happened?" she asked.

"Nothing, why? I just wanted to say hello."

"At two in the morning?"

"Fuck. Is it? Sorry. I must have fallen asleep and woken up thinking it was morning. I will call later, when you're up. OK?"

"You sure everything is OK, Steve?"

"I am absolutely positive. Night."

"Night, hon," said Noreen.

Diamond smiled, realised he would have to buy a new watch, and lay back on his bed wondering if he actually had the energy to open the wine. As he weighed up the pros and cons of starting to drink in the early hours he fell asleep, and did not wake for just short of twenty hours.

When his eyes did finally open he felt as though he was emerging from a general anaesthetic and didn't have a clue where he was. It was only when he saw the heavily laden table that the words 'Porton Down' formed inside his mind. He looked around for Toby, but he was alone in the room.

With no means of telling the time and no window allowing him to gauge if it was day or night, he struggled to his feet and headed for the bathroom. The man looking back at him from the mirror was a pitiful sight: crumpled clothes, messy hair, deep-sunken eyes and two rising bruises on his left cheek.

He couldn't be certain if Toby had moved into the room to his left or his right, so he knocked on both doors at the same time. The sound of shuffling feet told Diamond that he had definitely disturbed someone.

Toby's face peered through a small gap in the door before he pushed it wide open and ushered his friend into his room. "Well hello, Sleeping Beauty," he said.

"Sorry, mate. I knew I was tired, but not that tired. What time is it?" asked Diamond.

"It is 10pm – yes, ten at night; you've been asleep forever."

"So I've been asleep all day?"

"Yes, you have. I crept in and checked on you a couple of times but, unusually for you, you didn't even stir or bother to get undressed – and you didn't touch the little feast I prepared for you."

"I remember lying down and thinking about opening the wine – the next thing I knew I was waking up. I don't think I have ever felt so tired. I remember that Eric David had the same problem when he used *Die Glocke*... that right?"

"Yes, he also went home exhausted and slept for a very long time; it must be a curious side effect."

"How's the doctor doing? Still bursting with excitement?"

"He's like a kid who has just been given a free, lifelong pass to Disneyland. He is assessing data and stats and dull stuff like that. He's just happy that you got back in one piece. He said he wasn't sure it was an experience you would care to repeat."

"Really? He's wrong. I can't wait to go again. I was excited by the prospect of meeting Jim Morrison – but Oscar Wilde? Well, that moves the whole concept of meeting your heroes onto a different level."

"Go get that wine," said Toby.

They drank it sitting cross-legged on the floor, like students in a university dorm. Diamond went through every detail of his journey back to 1971, and so utterly wondrous was his story that he never once felt the need for embellishment or elaboration. Toby sat in silence, lapping up every last detail and feeling (whilst he never conceded as much) jealous to his very core.

When the moment came to call it a night, Diamond asked, "When do you think he will let us do it again?"

"Not sure, really. I know he's concerned about the injuries you picked up. If I had to hazard a guess, I'd say he wants the second trip doing pretty quickly so he can end the deceit and remove the sense of guilt he feels. He's asked that we join him for a late breakfast, around 10am," said Toby.

"That's cool. See you in the morning," said Diamond.

He returned to his room, showered and climbed into bed. He then reached for his iPhone and did what logic had told him to do the second he stepped out of *Die Glocke*, but which he had been afraid to do. He logged on to the internet, called up Google and typed in the name "Jim Morrison".

There were more than two million results; the first, as usual, being Morrison's Wikipedia page. Diamond clicked and opened it, his eyes immediately drawn to what amounted to an executive summary of Morrison's life at the top right-hand corner.

Born: December 8th, 1943. Died: September 25th, 1972.

"Jesus Christ," said Diamond, sitting up and throwing back the duvet. He read on.

Diamond was late for his breakfast meeting, having spent the hour between his waking and his leaving to meet Toby and Dr Stockwell listening online to the final album Morrison had recorded with The Doors in the fifteen months of extra life granted to him by one well-timed punch on the nose.

"Sorry I'm late," he said. "Just very, very tired."

"It isn't a problem," said Dr Stockwell. "You can rest as much as you like. You have been on a quite extraordinary journey – an almost unique journey – and your health and general well-being are all that matter to me."

"Thanks for that. Apart from the cuts and bruises I feel just fine. I didn't sleep too well last night as I kept rerunning my ninety minutes in 1971. I am still finding it difficult to believe that I met Jim Morrison – stupidly, I find that more amazing than the fact that I had to time-travel to do it. I suppose I will always be more of a rock-music fan than a scientist," said Diamond.

Dr Stockwell laughed out loud, shaking his head in a paternal way, as would a father chastising a son for his naivety.

"As I had never heard of him, I am not in the least bit jealous," he said. "But if you do get to go back a second time and meet up with Oscar Wilde, I will most definitely be jealous – as jealous as hell."

"Talking about Wilde," said Diamond, "have you any views on when we can try for him?"

"I did mention to Toby that I felt there was a chance that your first experience would serve to put you off attempting a second. That's not the case, I take it?" asked Dr Stockwell.

"Not a chance. I'd like to go as soon as possible, and this time I promise not to take a beating," said Diamond.

"I think you'll be safer in the company of Wilde than you were with Morrison. As we both know, Oscar was a staunch advocate of pacifism – a man who inflicted damage on his enemies with his words rather than his fists."

"I can't imagine Wilde raising his hands in anger, really," Diamond mused. "Though whether he will take kindly to a strangely dressed man offering him medication to cure a problem he doesn't even know he has is another matter. Then again, if I had to pick one man from the past who may just be prepared to listen to sensible advice – however ridiculous that advice might sound – it would be Wilde.

"I was thinking about this last night. Wilde was such a visionary, such a forward-thinking man, that if I tell him I've come from a far-distant future to save him, he may actually sit, listen and accept. I doubt I will opt for that particular route if I can find him, but I will be relying on the fact that he was a quite unique man who always enjoyed the company and support of other people of similar intellect."

"They are very good points, Steve," said Dr Stockwell. "I think you're right; I think Wilde will be fascinated by the prospect that he is in the same room as someone from the future. I think he'll be utterly intrigued."

"So when do you think you might be ready to fire up *Die Glocke* again?" asked Diamond.

"You need to rest and recover from your injuries. We then need to do as we did with Morrison: work out a location and a suitable time. Maybe another forty-eight or seventy-two hours? Or would you like longer? It's your call," said Dr Stockwell.

"Forty-eight sounds good to me," said Diamond. "The interesting thing – the spooky thing – is that Wilde will be very close to where we found Morrison. Different era, obviously, but in geographic terms they were almost neighbours."

As Toby and the doctor busied themselves with the sort of technical chit-chat which bored him to death, Diamond retreated to his room and checked his voicemail. There was just one message, from Noreen. She wasn't happy, and sounded on the verge of outright panic as she repeatedly asked if he was OK and why he hadn't kept his promise and rung her back. He dialled her number with some trepidation, propping himself up on his pillow in readiness for a bollocking.

"Hi, it's me," he said. "Don't shout! Sorry I didn't get back to you."

"Are you OK? I have been waiting twenty-four hours for you to ring; I just get into a bit of a state when I can't get hold of you," she said.

"My fault – no excuses. I'm not at home, I'm at Porton Down with Toby; he invited me up to take a look around."

"What is there to look at? I thought it was all test tubes and laptops."

"No, it's actually really interesting, although I think the bits they won't let me see would be even more interesting. It's a weird place but they serve good food and they provide free wine for visitors, so it's a bit like being at a spa resort."

"I need a pedicure; I'll get my coat and hat."

"I wish. I have missed you a lot, soppy, romantic bastard that I am."

"I miss you too. I was beginning to wonder if you'd found yourself another woman; maybe a nurse."

"I wish."

"I have to run. Ring me later?"

"Will do. Love you."

"Love you, too," she said.

Diamond felt he had escaped lightly, cursed himself for telling yet more lies, and then went back to studying the last days of Oscar Wilde – as they currently stood.

Wilde died in 1900, on November 30th, but Diamond and Dr Stockwell had agreed that there would be absolutely no point in waiting the best part of five months to travel back on or around the actual date of a death which was the result of a lengthy and slow decline. The root cause of Wilde's death from meningitis was a burst eardrum he sustained after a fall during his incarceration between 1895 and 1897; a problem which had received only the most rudimentary of treatments by a somewhat less than sympathetic prison regime.

By the time Wilde fled abroad, first to Italy and then to Paris, he was, in essence, a dead man walking. Having moved into Paris's run-down Hôtel d'Alsace in the Saint-Germain district, he was already suffering from the illness which would kill him. On October 12th he sent a telegram to one of his young lovers, Robbie Ross, which read, pitifully, "Terribly weak, please come." Six weeks later the greatest wit of any generation was dead.

Diamond believed that his plan to rescue Wilde from his fate was far more straightforward than the one behind what had proved to be only the brief delaying of Morrison's death. It was simple: go back to Paris in July 1900, track Wilde down, convince him that the medicine he was being offered would be of enormous benefit, embrace him and head back home on the next time machine.

The main problem would again be the concealment of *Die Glocke*, although Diamond was almost certain that, even if the machine were to be discovered, it was highly unlikely that those living in an age of limited technological advancement would dare go near it, let alone attempt to gain entry. He again scanned the maps of Paris, seeking out Rue des Beaux-Arts where the hotel stood, and was astonished by what he discovered – Wilde died less than a mile from where Diamond had assaulted Morrison seventy-one years later. Diamond clapped his hands together in joy – he could return to his previous parking spot inside the grounds of the Saint-Germain Church.

His excitement was such that he almost sprinted back to the lab where Toby and Dr Stockwell were still locked in their debriefing session. "I have wonderful news," said Diamond. "The hotel where Wilde died is no more than a mile from the club where I met Morrison, which means we can take *Die Glocke* back to the exact same spot next to the church. What are the chances of that, eh? A huge, huge city like Paris and the two people I want to go back and help are just yards apart – years apart, but yards apart. They trod the same ground and probably shared the same bars and restaurants."

"That does make things a whole lot easier," said Dr Stockwell. "I must admit I was worrying about finding a second secluded site to set down *Die Glocke*. Yes, that is quite an amazing coincidence."

"Sure is," said Diamond. "So when can we go? Now that I know I will have no problems finding my destination I am pumped up and ready. Don't even think about my cuts and bruises – I have sustained far worse playing Sunday League football."

"You seem to be in quite a rush," said Dr Stockwell.

"Time is always of the essence for me these days, whether I am watching it dribble away or whether I am moving backwards through it."

"I'm sorry, that was really insensitive of me, Steve."

"No it wasn't – it was actually very refreshing because you are doing exactly what I want: you are treating me as a normal, healthy person. Don't worry, sometimes even I forget that I have a major health issue, and that's the way I like it. Anyway, there's no time for sentiment or regrets when we are on a mission from God!" added Diamond.

"I wouldn't go quite that far," said Dr Stockwell. "We are on a mission devised by two young fools and set in motion by a previously sensible man who should know better."

Dr Stockwell agreed to let them know by early afternoon when Diamond could use *Die Glocke* for a second time.

"Apart from the TARDIS, is there anything else interesting to see around here?" asked Diamond.

"There must be a thousand and one things which would astound or interest us both, but Porton Down is like a huge box full of very small boxes, each one locked and barred to all but a handful of people. I sometimes wish everyone who works here could get together in the main lecture theatre and take it in turns to go up on stage and shout out what great secret they are currently working on," said Toby.

"There must be rumours, though?"

"Plenty, yes. If I chose to believe all the whispers I have heard, then we are reverse-engineering alien spaceships; trying to resurrect the dinosaurs, *Jurassic Park*-style; working on the surgical technology which will lead to head transplants; and closing in on cures for cancer, Alzheimer's and Parkinson's."

"No Loch Ness monster, then?"

"Sadly, no – but I am sure we are still looking. We do have a large swimming pool here they could use if they ever find her," added Toby.

The pair decided to head to the in-house cinema to see what was available and if the rather grumpy Glaswegian who ran it was in the mood to play projectionist. When they arrived the Scotsman was nowhere to be found, and the lad seated in the control box reading a music magazine looked barely above school-leaving age.

"Good morning," said Toby.

"Hi," said the youth, putting down the magazine and sitting upright in case he was in the presence of important people.

"Where's that miserable bastard who normally runs the show?"

"He's on holiday, which, from what I can gather, involves crawling around the pubs of Easterhouse with his old mates."

"That's good; I'd hate to think he wasn't doing something productive. This is Dr Steve Diamond and we were wondering if you have anything which might put on hold our growing sense of boredom for the next couple of hours?"

"Right, let's see. I have a few new ones in – but I can't give you a recommendation as I haven't seen any of them. We have *Under the Skin*, *The Raid*, *Philomena*, *The Wolf of Wall Street*, *Pompeii* and *Blue Ruin*."

"So you don't have *Lesbian Sex Workers Storm Mars*, then?" asked Toby, straight-faced.

"No, maybe next week."

"I was joking. So what do you fancy, Dr Diamond?" Toby asked his friend.

"*Under the Skin*. I've read the book and it was extremely weird – it's about a female alien who arrives on earth and sort of collects men."

"Sounds perfect," said Toby, moving through into an auditorium which held just thirty-two seats.

They sat and watched the film, speaking only as the final credits rolled.

"You were right, that was very weird. Good, though. In fact, in parts it was very good," said Toby.

"True to the book, too, from what I can remember. It was one of those films which receive great reviews but which no one bothers to go and see. The critic in *The Guardian*, I think it was, described it as a modern-day masterpiece," said Diamond, as they headed back to the lab to see if Dr Stockwell had made a decision.

"Where've you two been?" asked Dr Stockwell.

"To the cinema – *Under the Skin*; an odd but very good film," said Toby.

"From the book by Michel Faber? I haven't seen the movie but I have read the book, which I thought was exceptional."

"I thought I was the only man alive who read Faber's stuff," said Diamond. "Apparently he lives in the Outer Hebrides or somewhere equally remote. After I had finished reading all his books I sent him a letter to tell him how gifted he was. He didn't reply."

"So how are you feeling, Steve?" asked Dr Stockwell.

"I feel really good. The aches and pains have all but gone, my head is clear, and for once I don't feel overcome by fatigue."

"That's good to hear. How about you make your second journey later today, then?"

"Really? Yes, that would be great. What time were you thinking of?"

"I think it would be sensible to again go under the cover of darkness – and after the church has been locked up for the day – so I was thinking maybe 9pm. Of course, by that time

Wilde, if he is well enough, may have headed out for a meal or a drink, so you will either have to wait at the hotel or venture out to try and find him."

"That sounds perfect to me. Have you decided what medication I should take with me?"

"Yes, amoxycillin will probably be the most effective. We use it today for the treatment of inner-ear infections, which is what I suspect Wilde ended up with after perforating his eardrum. If he takes the whole prescribed course, the problem should clear up very quickly, but as you said yesterday, getting him to accept tablets from a complete stranger may prove to be more difficult than we think. I will remove all packaging to avoid any awkward questions about ingredients," said Dr Stockwell.

"I can be quite persuasive when I set my mind to it, and we must hope that when Wilde's contemporaries described him as not only a great orator but also a good listener, they were correct," said Diamond.

Despite his claims to the contrary, Diamond was still exhausted and returned to his room to rest, asking Toby to hammer on his door if he hadn't heard or seen him before 7.30pm. One of Diamond's favourite pastimes whilst at college had been trying to emulate the legendary one-liners of Oscar Wilde, the Irishman quite often referred to as the most quoted man in history. Before going to bed, Diamond spent twenty minutes jotting down the handful of his own efforts which he could remember – all were Wildean in their construction, even if a couple were perhaps too risqué to be handed over to a man who had been jailed for acts of gross indecency.

Diamond swallowed two days' worth of tablets, having forgotten to take any in the previous twenty-four hours, and slept happily until he was awoken by the shouts of, "Wake up, dickhead" coming from the other side of the door. Clearly, it wasn't Dr Stockwell, he thought as he yawned and rose to shower.

As a T-shirt and deck shoes clearly wouldn't be appropriate for Wilde's era, Diamond put on a more formal shirt, a waistcoat, a pair of dark trousers, and borrowed a pair of standard brown office-style shoes from his fellow Size 10, Toby.

NINETEEN

By 8.30pm the three men were again gathered in the lab, all of them staring at *Die Glocke* with a mixture of awe and admiration.

"You're a lucky man, Steve," said Toby.

"Apart from the terminal cancer, you mean?" said Diamond, gently punching his friend on the shoulder.

They both smiled as Dr Stockwell went through his checklist of non-negotiable instructions for the second time in three days.

"In and out as quickly as possible. Don't forget to lock *Die Glocke* up when you get there. Don't hunt for souvenirs, don't get into any fights. Here are the tablets – there's two months' supply," he said, handing Diamond a small white box.

Diamond pushed the box into his trouser pocket, which also contained another hand-drawn map, the scribbled notes he had made earlier, the padlock and its key, and, unbeknownst to anyone, his tiny replica of the TARDIS.

"I think we should wait another forty-five minutes to ensure it is dark when you arrive," said Dr Stockwell. "The good thing is that there should be even fewer people around than there were when you went back to 1971. I would imagine that most self-respecting Parisiennes will be tucked up in bed by the time you get there. You may, however, encounter prostitutes and their clients – it isn't the most salubrious part of town.

"Saint-Germain then will not be as it is now. Today it is very, very plush and upmarket, but in 1900 it was one of the poorer arrondissements, full of cheap hotels, brothels and seedy bars, so be careful who you talk to. Oh, and bearing in mind the problem you had when you went back to 1971, we have found some francs from the era for you," he added, handing over a small wad of well-thumbed notes.

"Hey, I can go out on the town with Oscar Wilde – two dandies out looking for a bit of late-night action," said Diamond.

"Be careful what you wish for," said Toby.

The minutes crawled by as Diamond nibbled on an apple and Toby and his boss checked plugs, wiring and light bulbs.

"Have you ever come to any conclusions about how the thing works?" Diamond shouted across to the men in white coats.

"We have indeed," said Dr Stockwell. "The unanimous conclusion is that we haven't a clue."

It was 9.23pm when the doctor announced that he had completed his battery of tests and successfully inputted both the map coordinates and the year 1900.

Toby walked with Diamond towards *Die Glocke*'s hatch and gave him a hug, saying, "Bon voyage, matey."

Dr Stockwell mouthed the words "Take care" as Diamond wrestled himself into the pilot's seat and strapped himself in. For no good reason, he checked that the red button was still in situ down to the right of his chair before giving the thumbs-up and closing the hatch.

"This is the bit I don't like," he said out loud to himself as he closed his eyes, held tight to the chair and waited for the ignition blast. As the first roar began to rise from the churning, rotating engines beneath his feet, he again spoke out loud. "Fuck!" he shouted, having realised that he had forgotten to ask the doctor for some earplugs.

Much as he did when at the dentist, Diamond kept his eyes closed and tried desperately hard not to interpret any of the sounds which filled his ears. He was partially successful insomuch as his journey this time seemed somehow shorter and less traumatic, and almost before he knew it *Die Glocke*'s engines were winding down and one final shudder of the big machine signalled that he had arrived… somewhere.

Having reached down and pushed the button to place *Die Glocke* in neutral, he glanced towards the hatch, hoping to see the reassuring sight of a tree branch slapping gently against the window. He saw nothing.

Almost immediately he recognised the first flaw in this, his second foray into the past – the trees inside the Saint-Germain churchyard would be seventy-one years younger than they had been during his last visit, which meant *Die Glocke* might not, after all, be shrouded in green, but out in the open. The good thing was, it was dark outside; in fact it was very dark. He opened the hatch and, despite it being early July, the craft was immediately filled with a blast of very cold air. This time there was no discernible smell of grass, cut or otherwise, but mercifully there was also no sound apart from the distant clanging of a bell.

He squeezed himself out of the machine and looked around, but with no sign of any street lights in any direction all he could see was the church rising above him, silhouetted against a clear, almost full moon. Whilst the trees were nowhere near as fulsome as they would be by 1971, *Die Glocke* had come to rest inside a small cluster of oaks which stood perhaps fifteen metres tall; it wasn't perfect, but it would do.

Diamond locked the machine with the padlock and moved out of the churchyard, turning right onto Boulevard Saint-Germain. He then turned right again onto Rue Bonaparte before stopping and spotting in the distance a bar-cum-restaurant which had the traditional line of tables and chairs out on the pavement. It was the famed Les Deux Magots, where the legendary writers, poets and artists of successive generations gathered to discuss philosophy. He remembered visiting the bar on his first trip to Paris when he was seventeen years old simply because the guidebook he'd bought at Heathrow had listed those who had been regular patrons down the years – Ernest Hemingway, Jean-Paul Sartre, Pablo Picasso, James Joyce, Albert Camus and, of course, Wilde.

The thought came to Diamond that perhaps Wilde was inside right now, using alcohol – absinthe, most likely – to ease his pain and soothe his depression. It was plausible, so it was certainly possible. Diamond moved slowly across the road, aware that his clothing would likely be totally out of keeping with those who sat inside the bar.

It was full and smoky inside, with no women at all; just men of varying sizes and ages swigging wine and beer whilst sucking on untipped cigarettes. There were several smaller rooms located off the main bar, but Diamond didn't feel inclined to undertake a thorough search even though his heart was racing at the prospect of being just feet away from the one man to have attained true hero status in his short life.

He retreated to the front door, casting one final, lingering glance around the bar in the hope of spotting Wilde. Then he turned and continued up Rue Bonaparte until he reached the École Nationale Supérieure des Beaux-Arts.

Rue des Beaux-Arts was off to the right – and a hundred yards or so down, Diamond found the Hôtel d'Alsace, its faded veneer of peeling paint and cracked window frames emphasising just how dramatic Wilde's descent into anonymity and poverty had been. It was not the sort of place any decent man would choose to stay for one night, never mind live out his final days. Even before he entered the building Diamond's senses were assailed by a thick, musty smell which hinted at blocked drains and boiled cabbage.

The lobby, which held a tiny reception desk, was dark and unwelcoming; the carpet which ran up a spiral staircase in front of Diamond was threadbare and dirty – everything seemed soiled and unkempt. Diamond could find nobody, so he returned to the reception desk and picked up and rang the bronze bell which he assumed was designed to wake up the hotel staff.

Two minutes passed before a tired-looking elderly man appeared from behind a heavy curtain to say, "Oui?"

"Parlez-vous Anglais, monsieur?" asked Diamond.

"I do, sir – not perfect but enough. I spent some time in England a few years ago with a lady friend who is now no longer living. Do you wish for a room?"

"No, I am looking for someone – Oscar Wilde."

"Ah, Monsieur Wilde, the Irishman who will not pay any of his bills. He is staying with us since the Hôtel Marsollier threw him out onto the street like a dog no one wants anymore."

"Is he here now?"

"I think not, sir. He has been sick but he has started to take the air at night – and also a little bit of the red wine."

"What sort of a man is he?"

"He tells me that he writes books and poems. He amuses me with his stories. He tells me many things to make me laugh – and he tells me that he misses his children. You wear the strange clothes, sir. Where are you from?"

"I am from England, a place near London. We dress somewhat differently over there. Do you know where I might find Mr Wilde now? Will he be in Les Deux Magots?"

"No, no. He was told to not go back there because he had not paid for his wine. There is a bar further down the street here, try there."

"I am very grateful to you. Thank you, monsieur," said Diamond.

He was more than happy to leave the hotel and inhale the cool night air. Turning to his right, he carried on down the street. In the distance, perhaps a hundred yards away, he could see the glow of lights and hear a piano playing. Always fearful that he would return to the bad habit of his youth and lose something of importance, Diamond checked his pocket – everything was still there.

The bar had no name and few customers and, like Les Deux Magots in this age long, long before the dangers of smoking had been revealed, it was thick with smoke. Diamond made his way to the bar, fully aware that most of his fellow patrons were staring at him.

The barman, who sported a moustache to die for, sauntered across and said, "*Bonsoir, monsieur.*"

"*Bonsoir,*" replied Diamond. "*Un petit verre de biere, s'il vous plaît.*"

As he silently congratulated himself on his pidgin French, the barman poured him his beer before returning to his stool to continue reading.

Mercifully, most of the other customers had now lost interest in Diamond, so he moved deeper into the building, seeking out the rear of the bar. As in many Paris bars of that era, there were several side rooms or snugs. Diamond wandered around for a few minutes before becoming so self-conscious that he sat down at an empty table to reassess his limited options. The man at the hotel had been friendly and helpful, so he knew he could return there without fear of being labelled a nuisance. His problem was that Wilde may well have drifted further afield; Paris was a huge city with many bars and restaurants more than willing to cater for those down on their luck.

Diamond was in the process of finishing his drink, the glass raised to his lips and at an angle, when he saw someone wander past him in the direction of the toilets. Through the bottom of his glass and the last dregs of foam and beer, he saw a man with shaggy, collar-length hair, wearing a heavy coat, slide by with either an unusual gait or a pronounced limp. He pulled the glass away from his mouth but he was too late; whoever it was had disappeared down a dark corridor. His heart was beating like a piston as he waited to see if the man would return, because it was possible that he had already left by a back door.

It was several minutes before the man emerged from the cloying darkness; a tall man with angular features carrying a cane and a newspaper. As he moved ever closer, Diamond feared that he would be unable to speak – he also feared that he might faint.

The man was moving towards the front door when Diamond finally found his voice, coughing loudly to clear his throat before saying, "Mr Wilde?"

The man stopped, turned through 180 degrees, spread his arms wide in a welcoming pose and replied, "Indeed, and you, sir, must be the guardian angel I have long awaited in this land of artistic barbarism and unusually strong alcohol."

"You are Oscar Wilde?" asked Diamond, still struggling to come to terms with the fact that he was actually standing toe to toe with the great man.

"As I previously confirmed, that is both my pleasure and my downfall. Yes, I am Oscar Wilde – writer, poet, playwright, lover and convicted felon. And who, may I ask, are you, sir?"

"I am an admirer, Mr Wilde, of some years' standing. Can I buy you a drink?"

"There are offers I decline, offers I choose not to hear, offers which are utterly deceitful – and then there is the offer of a drink. Thank you, I would very much like to enjoy a cognac with you," said Wilde.

Wilde headed into a small room off the bar as Diamond ordered two large cognacs. Only when seated opposite Wilde was he able to study him properly. Compared to the better-known photographs of him taken during his years of success and pomp, he had lost a considerable amount of weight. His eyes were as precise and piercing as ever, but his skin was pale, almost translucent. His hair was still unfashionably long, but it had lost its lustre and seemed matted in places. Wilde sat with his hands atop his cane, leaned forwards and stared into Diamond's face – a moment which would remain with the boy from Wembley for the remainder of his life.

"So tell me, young man, what moved you to seek out a modern-day pariah, an individual so reviled that even former lovers dare not speak his name?" asked Wilde.

"I am a fan," said Diamond.

"A fan? What do you mean, you are a fan? Women and the Greek lovers of fair Florence carry fans."

"Sorry, I meant that I am a great lover of your work, all of it."

"That is a most kind and a most welcome sentiment. It has been some considerable time since last I was bathed in anything approaching praise. Indeed, I had forgotten how good it feels. It was once an everyday occurrence but, alas, of late it has been reserved for those few occasions when I pay my bills," said Wilde, laughing.

"I called in at your hotel looking for you," said Diamond.

"You poor soul. It is a place fit only for creatures of four legs; a disgusting cesspit where I am fearful to lay my head of an evening lest I wake to discover it has been stolen away by the various demons of the night who, I suspect, are not berated as am I for failing to pay their rent. The thought that it may come to represent my final resting place fills me with dread. I am grateful only for the fact that Vyvyan and Cyril, my two beloved children, are not aware of where their father currently resides. I pray that they believe me to be living in palatial splendour in some far-flung corner of the Empire."

"May I ask your view of modern-day medicine, Mr Wilde?" said Diamond.

"Quacks, dear boy. Medicine is largely a profession awash with charlatans and con men who have acquired the art of speaking with an authoritative flourish. They have become elevated to the level of gods; they speak and people believe – it is an admirable skill. Why do you ask?" said Wilde.

"Because I suspect that you are ill – probably more ill than you realise," said Diamond.

"And how would you have come by this knowledge?"

"Now that is rather difficult to explain."

"Do try. What is your name?"

"Steven."

"Pray, carry on, Steven."

"I believe it is correct to suggest that whilst in jail back in England you suffered a bad fall which left you with a damaged eardrum?"

"Yes, that is correct."

"It won't heal properly without care and the correct medication – and I doubt that you have access to either."

"That is a matter of conjecture, Steven. The current state of my health is known only to a few – and you are not one of those few. Enlighten me if you will – where have you gathered such knowledge of a man you have never met?"

"Let's just say that I was made aware of your predicament and that I have sought you out to offer a solution. I ask nothing for this favour, if that is what you regard it as. As I said, I am simply an admirer of your work and someone who believes that you have been harshly treated by those who orchestrated your downfall."

"Carefully chosen words, Steven. It is true that I have been in ill health for some considerable time now, and that I have neither the means nor the inclination to seek a suitable remedy for the problems which afflict me," said Wilde.

"I am totally at a loss to explain your arrival here. Certainly you are educated and well intentioned, but you bring with you more than kind sentiments and sympathy. You do not seem to be of this place at all – of another realm, perhaps. Your clothes are unfamiliar to me, the manner in which you wear your hair is more worthy of discussion than is mine, and whilst you speak the Queen's English well, there is a touch of the unknown to it.

"I suspect that you would retain your secrets even under the most sustained of questioning, so I shall press you no further on the subject save to say I will listen to what you have to impart and accept whatever it is you may wish to give me. A little knowledge can be a dangerous thing, but on this occasion I shall cast caution to the winds."

Wilde drained his glass in a manner which suggested he would not decline a refill. Diamond obliged, returning from the bar with two large brandies and a bottle of house red.

"Your largesse knows no bounds, dear boy," said Wilde, opening the wine. "So tell me, how do you propose to restore me to fulsome health?"

"This is going to sound ridiculously simple, but all you have to do is take these," said Diamond, pushing the box of amoxycillin across the table.

Wilde picked up one box, read the label carefully and then removed the bubble-wrapped tablets from within. "I have never seen such a typeface before – nor have I seen pills delivered to a patient in such a form. It is all very intriguing," he said.

"You take three every day, that's one every four hours. It is important that you complete the whole course because if you don't I am told that you may not get the full benefit," said Diamond.

"What are they composed of?" asked Wilde, scouring the box for more information.

"They are antibiotics; used to fight against infections. They work," said Diamond.

"That is what they are... what are they composed of?"

"I haven't a clue, Mr Wilde; various chemicals, I suppose."

"And you would have me ingest something which is a mystery to both of us? You must have great faith in either the pills or the doctor who prescribed them."

"I have taken them myself in the past – on many occasions."

"Why is it, then, that I have never heard of them, never seen them before, never had them recommended to me previously? The mystery deepens, does it not?"

"Yes, I suppose it does."

"I suspect I shouldn't ask you for further details as there is nothing quite so annoying as a question which is batted back across the net. You intrigue me, Steven."

"Not as much as you intrigue me, Mr Wilde."

"Please, call me Oscar; it helps me feel younger."

"Of course, Oscar. Are you still writing?"

"Fitfully. The words which would normally have already been preserved on paper remain inside my head. I fear that society's appetite for my works has been fully sated, and that I have faded away even from the minds of those who once coveted me, who rejoiced in sharing my company."

"But you must write, Oscar, it is your gift to the world – and trust me when I say it is a grateful world."

"Is it really? Why, then, have I been cast aside in such a cruel and heartless manner? Your assertion is correct; my work was for the world. I sought only to entertain and to inform – and, perhaps, to educate to a degree. And now? Now I find myself banished to the pitiful, dark side of a fine city. I am friendless, penniless and without even the means to sustain the most basic of lifestyles," said Wilde. "You have come from wherever and, it would seem, presented me with the means to extend my life – but why would I wish to do so? When a man is in intolerable pain, he wishes it to end. My love of life was lost long ago.

"We all look at our small and usually insignificant worlds and believe that we matter when, in fact, we do not. What I write today will be forgotten tomorrow. My spirit has been weakened to such a degree that, as I sit here now, the prospect of writing holds all the allure of a full lavatory. All our lives invariably peak at some point and thereafter there is nothing but a slow and unedifying decline into an abyss of self-recrimination."

"You must live because there will be a renaissance and a redemption," said Diamond, using what he wished for as a bridge between them. "The sweetest victories are those won against the greatest of enemies. Imagine the pain your detractors would feel if you fought your way back into the hearts of the British public."

"That, I fear, is rather unlikely. The crimes of which I was convicted are not crimes at all. How can any act of love be so described? Buggery is not a crime if it is done well," said Wilde, laughing and, Diamond suspected, mentally filing away the quip.

Diamond also laughed, fully appreciating that the man opposite could conjure up, on an almost minute-by-minute basis, a line which would endure for hundreds of years. He had to help him live; he simply had to.

Wilde fiddled with one of the tablets inside its wrapping before pushing it out and onto the table between himself and Diamond. He picked it up, threw it to the back of his throat and swallowed it down with a gulp of the cheap wine. "It is done, Steven; I am all but cured," he said.

"Just the sight of you doing that makes me very, very happy," said Diamond. "I am hardly in a position to chide you like a child in the hope that you will take all the remaining pills, but I hope you will. If you do, I promise you that you will escape that dreadful hotel and that awful wallpaper in your room."

"How do you know my wallpaper is awful, sir? It is – but the fact that you have knowledge of the interior of Chez Oscar is confusing and a little worrying. Still, no mind; I have enjoyed your company and you will leave me an intrigued man.

"I do not know where you have come from, young Steven, nor do I know who sent you, but perhaps you are, indeed, my guardian angel sent from heaven to shine a light on a path forwards for me. If that is the case then you have my thanks and my blessing," said Wilde.

Diamond had tears in his eyes as he stood to bid farewell to Wilde. The pair moved out into the corridor where they had first met, Diamond offering his right hand.

Wilde moved forwards and embraced him, kissing him gently on his left cheek before saying, "If this is nothing but a dream, I have enjoyed it immensely. Go now. I wish you good luck always – the luck of the Irish."

Diamond stepped back, smiled and bowed slightly before turning and walking out into the cool night air.

It took him no more than fifteen minutes to return to the churchyard where *Die Glocke* stood, still locked and seemingly undiscovered.

Diamond climbed in and secured the hatch before closing his eyes and mouthing the words, "I don't believe it. I don't believe it. Oscar Wilde just kissed me."

With that he fastened the seat belt and then reached down and released the red button, moving himself back into the eye of the machine's storm.

So all-consuming was his desire to try and store away every last detail of his conversation with Wilde that, before he knew it, Diamond was listening to the final sounds of *Die Glocke*'s flight cycle. Even after the machine's violent shaking had totally subsided and the familiar smell of burning rubber had drifted away, he remained stationary, eyes closed, lost in his own world of wonderment.

CHAPTER

TWENTY

It wasn't until he heard someone banging frantically on the window that he released his seat belt and pushed the hatch's release switch.

"Are you OK? We thought maybe there was a problem," said Toby.

"There is no problem, other than the platonic love one man can feel for another," replied Diamond, climbing through the opening and out into the lab.

Dr Stockwell moved forwards and shook his hand to welcome him back. Toby stood awaiting a bullet-point account of his journey.

"You see that?" said Diamond, pointing to his left cheek. "Oscar Wilde planted a kiss on that just a few minutes ago. Well, 114 years ago, to be precise, but you know what I mean."

"Good Lord," said Dr Stockwell. "You met him? You gave him the tablets?"

"Yes and yes. Now tell me, Doctor, when did Oscar Wilde die?" asked Diamond.

"It was around 1916, I think. I can't remember exactly," Dr Stockwell said.

"Bingo!" cried Diamond. "One of the great time-travel paradoxes has just come into play."

"Which one?" asked a confused-looking Toby.

"When I left here a few minutes ago, Wilde was destined to die in the year 1900. I went back and changed that by giving him a shedload of antibiotics – but to you, Wilde had always lived until 1916 or whenever. Which of his works do you like the best, Doctor?" said Diamond.

"Tricky question as I am a fan of them all. Probably the *Parisienne Trio*," Dr Stockwell said.

"I don't know those too well; can you describe them for me?" asked Diamond.

"He wrote a trilogy, three novellas, whilst in Paris – *The Bringer of Darkness*, *The Bringer of Light* and *The Redemption*. They represent a sort of rise-and-fall history of what he described as the most difficult period of his life. The final part covers his return to England and to favour; the forgiveness of a nation."

"Right now I am two things," said Diamond. "I am the happiest man in the world, and I am also the sleepiest man in the world. We have done a truly wonderful thing today. Thank you so much."

Toby accompanied Diamond back to his room, all the while complaining that he was somewhat confused.

"You need to think about the paradox situation. I changed something, but because I effected that change before you were born you grew up accepting what I had altered as given fact. To you – and to everyone else – Wilde didn't die until 1916. Before I set off in *Die Glocke* a short while ago, he died in 1900. Let's chat over a beer tomorrow. I am so very tired," said Diamond.

"Yes, sorry, you must be exhausted. I'm so pleased you're OK, and that whatever you did worked," said Toby.

When Diamond awoke any joy he had felt had gone, to be replaced by a feeling of complete and utter helplessness. His body, seemingly every square inch of it, was covered in cold sweat; every limb ached, and his head was not so much banging as exploding.

It felt like the midpoint of a dose of flu, but try as he might he could not stop wondering if his time inside *Die Glocke* had in some way served to accelerate his cancer by several degrees. Although he deemed that highly unlikely, he had never before felt such weakness, and it took him a considerable amount of effort to find and then use his mobile to call Toby.

Toby almost sprinted through the door, half-expecting to find his friend lying in bed surrounded by photographs of Wilde and Morrison. Diamond was actually in the bathroom, throwing up in between bouts of sustained, guttural coughing.

"You OK?" asked Toby.

"That has to be a rhetorical question," replied Diamond, spitting into the sink and searching for a clean towel.

"Shall I ask Dr Stockwell to take a look at you?"

"He's a scientist not a GP, Toby! I think I probably need some of those antibiotics I so kindly handed over to Mr Wilde 114 years ago. Can you nip down to the first-aid room and see what Bobby can do for me?"

"Sure. Wait here, I'll be back in ten minutes," said Toby.

Diamond sat on his bed and wondered if he was actually going to die that very day. He thought not, but rang Noreen just in case. "Hi, hon," he said. "How's your life?"

"You OK? What's happened to your voice? You sound like Kermit the Frog," she said.

"Woke up feeling really crappy – headache, cough, stomach pains; must be a virus or something. Anyway, I will be home later today, I think."

"I would imagine that the last place you want to catch a virus is inside Porton Down; it might be from Mars."

"Now there's a thought. I will call you when I am on the way back with Toby, OK?"

"OK. Take good care of yourself," she added.

Diamond lay back on his bed and closed his eyes. If he did die now it would at least be with a clear conscience.

Toby returned with Bobby, who was laden down with all manner of medications.

The first thing Diamond saw was a syringe the size of a drainpipe. "No, no, no," he said. "I have had enough injections to last me two lifetimes. Give me something orally, as the actress said to the bishop."

"A few basic tests first, I think," said Bobby. "Toby tells me that you have leukaemia?"

"Yes. I was thinking of getting a T-shirt printed announcing the fact to an inquisitive world."

"How advanced is it?"

"Very."

Bobby, who swiftly managed to adopt an oncology smile, took Diamond's blood pressure and temperature, and checked his heart rate.

"Clinically dead?" asked Diamond.

"Not quite. Your temperature is high, as is your BP. What medication are you currently taking?" Bobby asked.

"It would be simpler to list the medicines I am *not* taking. The stuff I take is in that suitably large shoulder bag over there on that chair."

Bobby studied the contents of Diamond's bag before telling him that he had almost certainly picked up a virus as a direct consequence of his failing immune system offering the resistance of tissue paper rather than a suit of armour. "When you get back home, make an appointment with your specialist and then go to bed for as long as it takes for your temperature to return to normal – which is around 37 degrees. Do you have a thermometer?" he asked.

"No, I'm a single man," said Diamond.

"Here, take this one with you," said Bobby, producing one out of his jacket pocket.

"Thanks. Sorry to have bothered you."

"It's my pleasure. I like sick people," Bobby said, before leaving.

"Would you like to go straight home?" asked Toby.

"Yes, I think I would. Let's go see Dr Stockwell so that I can have an emotional send-off," said Diamond.

The three men met in the reception area and seemed to be almost lost for words. It was Dr Stockwell who finally took on the role of the grown-up of the group.

"It's actually quite difficult to know what to say, Steve," he said. "What has happened to the three of us – and in particular what has happened to you – over the past few days has been so extraordinary that it is off the scale. You have achieved something which you should be so very proud of.

"You are a very brave man and it has been my privilege to have met you and to have worked with you. Although I myself didn't travel inside *Die Glocke* I now have sufficient information and data to keep me occupied for the next six months. They can do what they like with the machine now; I have moved on from it with my printouts and my readings.

"I am envious of you in so many ways – you have moved through time, you met with the great Oscar Wilde – but it is your spirit I so admire and envy. It was an adventure which precious few would have undertaken in full, blossoming health, but you chose to do so whilst very ill – and that says more about your inner strength than ever I could.

"Please, please keep in touch with me. You may remember things which may prove useful to me, or you may just wish to talk – I will always be available to you. All I can do now is wish you a happy and long life, Steve. For the last time, thank you."

"Wow," said Diamond, trying desperately hard to stop his eyes filling up. "I was going to say a few things but I will wait; I will write when I am back home and not quite as emotional and knackered as I am right now. All I'll say for now is thank you for the greatest experience of my life."

With that, Diamond moved forwards and embraced Dr Stockwell; a gesture which was reciprocated. Tearful and rather sad, he turned and walked out of Porton Down's front door followed by his bag-carrier, Toby.

Diamond slept most of the way home, dreaming about the 1960 film version of Wells' *The Time Machine*, the subtle difference being that the lead role was taken not by B-movie star Rod Taylor, but by one Steve Diamond.

TWENTY-ONE

As he sat at home, Diamond's mind began to wander to altogether more mundane matters – like when he would die. The run-up to Christmas had begun and he was rather fond of the twee, commercial nonsense which surrounded the festive season.

The drugs he took could not halt the march of the cancer in his blood, but they did lessen the pain and lift his mood, much as had the antidepressants he'd been prescribed after his mother had died.

Because he was a terminal patient, he was given an appointment to see Dr Marshall in the morning; the ability to queue-jump was probably the only benefit of having cancer. Diamond tried to find safe passage through the fog inside his head so that he might remember the last time he saw him. Three months ago? Maybe four? Not that it mattered particularly.

On the day he'd decided to quit the chemotherapy, Dr Marshall had said he might live for nine months – the caveat which rendered that forecast absolutely useless being that it could be longer or it could be shorter. Diamond thought that that was eleven months ago now, although he couldn't be certain. The one thing he had learned very early on was not to count the days, because doing so seemed to make them fly past at a quite extraordinary rate.

He could feel his body slowing down on an almost weekly basis. The simple tasks he had accomplished without discomfort two months ago were not totally beyond him now, but completing them was an effort – and often he just couldn't raise sufficient energy or willpower to even attempt them.

To a great degree he relied upon Noreen and Toby to bring him the things he needed to survive – food and alcohol, mostly. One of the very first things he'd done after being diagnosed was check online as to whether or not he could carry on drinking. Virtually every single source he read said it wasn't recommended but that it was unlikely to prove detrimental. That was good enough for him.

Some nights, as he sat at home reading or writing, Diamond seriously considered taking up everything the nanny-state experts had declared to be bad for the human body. He decided to overload his failing body with junk food – burgers, pizzas and the like. That was fun for about a fortnight, until he was driven back onto the path of righteous eating not by the threat of additional calories, but by the sheer boredom of consuming food which tasted as though it had already passed through someone else's system.

He considered sneaking off to The King's Arms to try and get his hands on some cannabis or speed – but the thought of having to deal with some smart-arsed, scarf-wearing student with pimples was enough to cut short that little dream.

So, in the end, he was left with his dear, reliable friend, alcohol. He had stopped drinking beer a while back as he seemed to spend almost every night dragging himself to the bathroom every ninety minutes or so. He meant to ask Dr Marshall if the weakening of a person's bladder was an as-yet-unacknowledged side effect of leukaemia.

He had moved on, full time, to red wine, aided by Toby's financial backing and his gift for selecting something with taste and bollocks – usually an Australian or a South African. Diamond was drinking a little too much, he knew that, but he could see little point in reining himself in as his liver was, presumably, already damaged beyond repair.

His occasional downfall was brandy; a drink his father had always loved and one Diamond had first tasted one Christmas when he was about fifteen, sneaking the bottle out of the sideboard cupboard whilst his parents exchanged season's greetings and cigarettes with neighbours they didn't actually like over the garden fence.

People – family and friends – often rang to say they would be calling, and almost inevitably ended the conversation with the question, "Is there anything you need, Steve?"

His answer was always the same: "Need? No. Would like? Yes... brandy."

The caller always laughed, presumably before putting down the phone and cursing Diamond's gall. And so, his flat was often awash with brandy, from the cheap own-brand stuff which all supermarkets now sell, to the classy stuff: Rémy Martin and, his personal favourite, Courvoisier.

His father had always told him that brandy should be 'taken' at the end of the day, should not be rushed, should be savoured and should be appreciated. It was sound advice from a man whose next-best effort was, "Don't use the withdrawal method with ladies, son – it doesn't work and you are the living proof."

Diamond always tried to follow his father's advice with regard to brandy, usually managing to delay a first glass until after he had downed a bottle of red. It wasn't a perfect system or a precise science but it certainly ensured that he slept well on most nights.

The bad dreams still plagued him from time to time, and when they came, not even the brandy could prevent them burrowing their way into his subconscious mind. He had made mention of them to Dr Marshall because their intensity and clarity were such that he often awoke in a start, frightened and utterly convinced that the swirling figures who laid claim to him after his eyes had shut were just a little bit more real than perhaps they should be.

It was as if he was seeing, night after night, a perverse and skewed video playback of his own life. He had dreamt of friends who had died, of family members long since gone, and of the small things which had so frightened him as a young boy. Like all dreams, they faded fast once he was sat bolt upright in bed, but always when he was calm enough to return his head to the pillow it was soaking wet with sweat.

He constantly dreamed of happy relationships, bad relationships and lost loves. The most prominent amongst this roll call of fine women was the one who got away, the one who broke his heart and for whom he had always reserved a small space in his excuse for a soul.

Joanne was her name; a beautiful, combative flower of the Emerald Isle, from a pretty little town called Trim some thirty miles north of Dublin. She was the only woman he had ever asked to marry him. She'd made him the happiest man in the world by saying yes, only to change her mind without any hint of a warning six months later, thereby reducing him to rubble. He had given her everything he had, everything she asked for, everything she craved; except, perhaps, the one thing she truly wanted: a child.

Sometimes in life there is a light which never goes out. As Diamond's light began to fade and die, he thought of Joanne often. In so many ways she had totally ruined his life, but he would carry a torch for her for the rest of his days.

Although he hadn't confirmed as much to either Toby or Dr Stockwell, he had decided that he definitely wouldn't be making any more trips in *Die Glocke*. It wasn't that he didn't find the experience truly exhilarating, because he did. It wasn't that he no longer wished to help his friend understand the complexities of the machine von Braun had created – it was simply that, on both occasions he had moved backwards in time, he had returned withered and exhausted. He hadn't told either of them just how truly draining – physically and mentally – he had found it. They weren't in any way blasé about his medical condition, but Diamond felt that they both suspected that he would seek to carry on travelling, as time's tide would shortly swallow him whole.

When he had finished drinking for the night, Diamond quite often talked to himself. It was a self-defence mechanism, because he knew the alternative was to pick up the phone and subject someone to a 'woe-is-me' type of speech. Sadly, that was precisely what he had done on several occasions over the past few months, only stopping when he received a call-back from the Samaritans asking if he was feeling any more stable than he had the previous night, when he had rung them in some distress around midnight. He couldn't remember making that call, so it was a straight choice – either stop drinking or stop picking up the phone. No contest, really.

On the rare occasions he didn't actually feel like drinking, Diamond went to bed early and tried to read whilst watching his small portable television set over the top of the page.

After convincing Toby and Dr Stockwell that he should be allowed to travel inside *Die Glocke*, he had seriously considered doing what Dr David had done all those years ago – record his thoughts and his actions in a diary.

Toby, suspecting that the journalist still lurked within his friend, had asked him not to commit anything to page, print or email, his argument being that, if there was a paper trail, someone, somewhere at some point would chance upon it and reveal all.

Diamond had respected that view and stood down his pen and notebook. That left him with only his thoughts and his memories of what he had undertaken and achieved.

Twice he had travelled back in time, and on both occasions he had achieved his aim without making any fundamental changes to the world he returned to. Oscar Wilde had lived another sixteen years, regaining his health and his stature before penning several quite wonderful books, plays and poems; and whilst Diamond had managed to extend Jim Morrison's life by only a year or so, it had been long enough for him to deliver one final album with The Doors. That Morrison then succumbed to his love of drugs and alcohol was, perhaps, inevitable. Diamond often reminded himself that sometimes you simply cannot help those who will not help themselves. He took comfort from the fact that Wilde had died peacefully in his sleep of heart failure.

All those fears about paradoxes, squashed butterflies and changed worlds had proved to be groundless; everything was as it should be and the world he had returned to was a better one than the one he had briefly left behind – which was precisely what he had set out to achieve after successfully convincing Messrs Callaghan and Stockwell that gift horses should be lovingly embraced and not simply stared at.

As he was due at the hospital very early the next morning, Diamond went to bed early, managing only ten pages of Patrick Süskind's *Perfume* before slipping into an uneasy sleep.

Before falling ill, he had always struggled to wake and rise early, but these days, almost as if his body now regarded sleep as wasted time, he was usually up, dressed and drinking coffee by 7am.

He left early for the hospital because his walking pace had slowed quite considerably in recent weeks, and that, coupled with the unreliability of the Tube, pointed to the very real possibility of a late arrival – and Dr Marshall was a man who was very keen on punctuality.

As it was, Diamond's body moved smoothly and smartly and the train was on time, so he arrived a good thirty minutes before his appointment. He was summoned into the ward – same one, same awful paint job – by an over-talkative nurse with the fixed smile of someone who deals regularly with oncology patients.

After giving a blood sample, he closed his eyes and was almost asleep when he heard Dr Marshall enter the room.

"Diamond, young sir. How the devil are you?" he enquired.

"I am cured, Doctor. I am going to live for a hundred years," replied Diamond, adopting the slapstick, pantomime dialogue which had for so long been a key feature of their meetings.

"Absolutely splendid. Do tell – how did you chance upon the cure for leukaemia? Share it with the world so that others might benefit."

"I travelled to the farthest, darkest corner of Indonesia and befriended a shaman who took pity on me and allowed me to stay with his family in their beguiling two-up-two-down hut. He spent twenty-four hours smearing me with ox dung and chanting ancient rhymes and, hey presto, I was cured," said Diamond.

"Marvellous," responded Dr Marshall. "To think we here in the West have wasted so many years and so many billions of pounds searching for a cure, and there it was all the time, lying in a field.

"So, how are you really, Steve?"

Diamond wanted to tell his doctor that he was now a member of the world's most elite club – just him and one Dr Eric David. He so wanted to tell Dr Marshall that he had turned all logic on its head and, even in the twilight of his young life, achieved something staggering. He couldn't, of course – not that the doctor would have believed a word if he had.

"I am still fucked, I suppose," said Diamond. "I tire very easily; I get anxious and depressed even easier. I drink too much. I feel sorry for myself a lot. I have become insular and withdrawn. I hate the world and everyone in it."

"Good. So, perfectly normal, then," said Dr Marshall, with an almost paternal smile. "You have done well and you continue to do well. Don't think for one second that I am not full of admiration for how you have held yourself together – and don't believe for one second that, just because I have spent twenty-five years dealing with people in your position, I truly understand what you are going through.

"Everyone reacts differently to the news that old age will not be coming their way. Thirteen of my patients were dead within a month of being told; lacking as they did the spirit to carry on, they committed suicide. One is in a persistent vegetative state in a different wing of this very hospital, having tried to end it all by throwing himself out of his living-room window. If you ever decide to go for that option, make sure you don't live on the first floor.

"The irony sometimes is that patients with a restricted lifespan – that's diplomatic speak for terminal patients – do actually look better and healthier after they have stopped the chemotherapy. You are a classic example. You have lost some weight and the spring in your step is now more of a low bounce – but you look pretty good under the circumstances."

"I know what you mean," said Diamond. "I do feel reasonably good on most days. I struggle at night because I can't sleep – and when I do I am still having those vivid dreams. Sometimes they're good; sometimes they aren't. It is a bit like living in the Twilight Zone between normality and my very own stairway to heaven. I don't feel it is worth actually starting anything, undertaking anything, apart from the thousand-piece jigsaw my auntie gave me two weeks ago. Do you know what she said to me? 'I hope you get to finish it.' Nice, eh? A woman who simply oozes compassion and pity," he added, with a smile.

Dr Marshall laughed out loud, his outburst causing several nurses to turn and stare at him. "People have different ways of showing they care," he said. "Anyway, you will get to finish it – although, to be honest, I have never really understood the concept of jigsaws. You spend days, sometimes weeks, doing them, and then when you have finally finished the damned thing you just take it apart and put the pieces back in a box. I can think of far better ways to entertain myself in pursuit of a sense of accomplishment.

"We will have the results of your blood tests in about an hour but I don't expect them to tell us anything we don't already know, so you can get bored here or you can wait for us to email you."

"I'll sod off, then, I think. Are we meeting again? Sounds a bit crazy to book an appointment for three or six months' time when I may not be available, for the obvious reasons."

"We will include your next appointment date in the email. Stay strong, and remember that life – however long – is there to be embraced and enjoyed. That may sound a little patronising but I think you know me better than that by now," said Dr Marshall.

"Of course I don't think you're being patronising. I couldn't have been in better or more sympathetic hands. If I win the lottery before I finally head skywards, I will leave you a hefty slice," said Diamond.

Once home, he rang and left a message for Toby before again entering into a debate with himself about the rights and wrongs of committing his exploits to paper. For perhaps the tenth time he abandoned the idea, but this time not so much out of loyalty or respect for his friend but because he accepted it was probably beyond him.

He hadn't said as much to Dr Marshall, but he was struggling now. His entire body ached, and he felt weak and in need of rest most of the time, as opposed to just some of the time. He felt as though his body clock was finally running down and he had no way of rewinding it.

He suspected that his decision to turn his back on *Die Glocke* was partially to blame, because once he had mentally ruled out a third trip in what Toby always referred to as the "infernal machine" it was as if his reason for hanging on had gone – he had no target left to aim for and his entire being seemed to sink in readiness to accept his fate.

Still, there was always the comfort afforded by good company and strong alcohol – he was grateful for both.

He knew that if he sat down and switched on the television he would be asleep in double-quick time, probably five minutes. He also knew that a body and mind that craved recuperative rest would sleep for at least two hours. As it was only 1pm he wasn't yet ready to abandon the day, so he forced himself to leave home again. This time he wasn't going to offload blood, but the sun was shining and he felt almost obliged to head for a pub with a beer garden.

Unable to face the rubbish bins of The King's Arms, he headed instead to a pub he rarely visited, The Swan Hotel, as it always reminded him of the Irishwoman he still loved but who had driven a ten-ton truck through his hopes and dreams. It was a little upmarket for him – it had proper carpets and clean toilets – but the tables outside overlooked the canal, and the 'no riff-raff' rule meant it was largely a student-free zone.

Diamond sat in the early afternoon sunshine, drank his chilled lager and felt happy to be alive. It was a fleeting joy but he was, briefly at least, content. He had long subscribed to the theory that those terminally ill individuals who gave themselves up to their fate died first. At that moment, a beer in his hand and the sun cascading down onto a face which had known its fair share of tears in recent months, Diamond resolved to stay alive for just as long as his cancer permitted.

He knew he was fighting a losing battle but he promised himself that he would attempt to go down smiling – he felt he owed that much to those who had stood by him after ill health had become a death sentence. Some had deserted him as he journeyed from diagnosis to departure lounge, but he had never for one second felt the need to silently condemn them. There are many who cannot face the prospect of death – even when it is someone else who has been handed the role of victim.

Being a confirmed atheist, Diamond couldn't even find salvation in the prospect of arriving at a fine set of Pearly Gates and demanding entry on the grounds that he was kind to small animals and always gave a few pounds on Children in Need night. But he was at ease with his lack of belief, and fully prepared to fight his corner should the Lord of Darkness appear before him in the seconds after his body finally gave out.

His peaceful daydreaming was cut short by the shrieking blare of his mobile's ringtone – still too loud and still very antisocial.

"Hello, Tobias Callaghan," he said.

"Very formal – are you drunk, old boy?" asked Toby.

"Nah, but I am sitting in the sun rediscovering the joy of cold beer. I have decided that if we are afforded a choice of heavens after leaving behind our earthy remains then this is what I will go for – an eternity of warm sunshine and lager. If I am given the chance to choose a drinking partner I'll go for Wilde, and then he can formally thank me for extending his life."

"All sounds very sensible. Where are you? I can't hear the squawking of adolescents so it can't be The King's Arms. But I can hear voices so it can't be The Laughing Cavalier."

"Your powers of deduction never cease to amaze me, Watson. I am in The Swan Hotel. Yes, it holds rather crappy memories for me but the garden is lovely and, anyway, there's nothing wrong with a little bit of self-pity. I don't need a machine to stagger around in my own past – all I have to do is close my eyes and rewind," Diamond said.

"Isn't that where she dumped you?" asked Toby.

"No, it's where she accepted my proposal of marriage. She dragged me halfway across Ireland and found a pub which sold a thousand different brands of whiskey to tell me I was surplus to her requirements. What you up to?"

"I am cleaning the flat as it's a total mess. You?"

"I went down the hospital first thing to be told absolutely nothing in particular, and then I resisted the temptation to go back to bed – just – and came here. You want to drive over for an hour? Hand on heart, it is really pleasant here."

"Sure. Give me twenty minutes, mate," said Toby, already starting to pack away his Hoover.

Diamond's glass was empty but he didn't feel the need for an instant refill, so he stretched out his legs, tipped his head back and began the swift decline into a very light sleep – the sort of sleep where you are perfectly relaxed and content but can still hear things going on around you.

His peace was shattered when Toby slammed two pints of beer down on the table, followed by a pile of magazines and his two mobile phones.

"I have never asked, but why do you always have two mobiles with you? What's the point?" asked Diamond.

"Well, one is for work and the other is for personal calls," said Toby.

"But neither of them ever rings. I can comfortably count on the fingers of one hand the number of times you have taken a call whilst with me – your mother, your weird mate from the electrical store, that slapper who religiously stole something from your bedroom every time she stayed over... that's about it."

"Always be ready for the unexpected – that's my motto."

"No it isn't. Your motto is 'Fuck the consequences and the possible dangers; I will send my best friend back in time to place the entire world in jeopardy.'"

"Wrong – that's my mission statement; there's a difference."

"Have you read any of the 'new' Wilde stuff? I feel guilty as I haven't. I went to the library and looked but he didn't dedicate anything to the mystery man who turned up one night clutching the medication which would save his life... bit mean, that."

"No, I haven't, but I did buy The Doors' last album even though I have always loathed them. It sounds like all the rest of their stuff – basic rock with Morrison shouting his pseudo-poetry over the best guitar breaks. It's really not for me," said Toby.

"So, you're telling me I wasted my time, then – going back to make minor alterations to humanity's fabric?"

"No... you know what I mean. Maybe you should have gone back and marched into a young Hitler's bedroom and hit him with a large spade."

"Yeah, right, and come back to find that the world was even worse without him? I suspect that if it hadn't been him it would have been someone else wanting to play dress-up in baggy trousers and ill-fitting tunics. Hey, it could even have been Goering. At least he would have been something of a role model for the larger gentlemen of the day," said Diamond.

He had decided that it was only fair that he tell Toby that his days as a modern-day Doctor Who were now at an end. He was only halfway through the speech he had composed whilst dozing when Toby interrupted.

"I know – well, I suspected. I was talking about it with Dr Stockwell yesterday. We aren't stupid and we know what a toll it has taken on you. In fact, we were both surprised that you volunteered to go for a second trip; we didn't think you would," he said.

"So I needn't have had all these guilty feelings over the past few days, then? Bastards. I just didn't want to feel as though I was letting the pair of you down. If I was fit and healthy you wouldn't be able to stop me leaping about in time."

"If you were fit and healthy, you wouldn't be able to leap around in time, Diamond," said Toby pointedly.

"Yeah, that's true," said Diamond. "So, is all well with the world? You haven't discovered a Nazi enclave in the Far East as a consequence of my trips back?"

"No, but if you think about it, any change that occurred as a result of your actions wouldn't be a surprise to us, would it? It would be totally natural insomuch as we would have grown up with it. The permutations in terms of paradoxes and possibilities are endless – which is why they always told us at university that time travel would never prove to be possible," said Toby.

They drank two pints each before Toby announced that he was leaving as he had a date with one of the bar staff from The Rubicon.

"Does she have a mate with a soft spot for the nearly dead?" asked Diamond.

"You've got Noreen, my friend – and you should be eternally grateful that you have, as no one else would put up with you, healthy or sick. Right, I'll ring you tomorrow. I brought these magazines for you. They were designed to help kill the hours leading up to your nightly head-to-head with alcohol, but clearly you have started early today," said Toby.

Diamond wandered home, his legs and arms aching and with the growing suspicion of another bad headache on the way. Once home, he thought about eating, thought about television – before opting for bed.

He placed Toby's stash of magazines on his bedside table, more or less assuming that they would be Sunday supplements from several weeks back. He was pleasantly surprised – Toby, it seemed, had apparently visited a proper newsagent and paid out good money. There were two music magazines (Q and the NME), something about men's heath, and, curiously, a copy of *Tatler*, which Diamond had always believed was about minor royals, ponies and expensive wine.

His love of music had carried him through many a crisis in his life, particularly after he had been fired from the *Islington*

Gazette and was of a mind to resign from the human race to become a bisexual beachcomber in Kent. His tastes were varied – many said eclectic – and before having to sell up to avoid bankruptcy five years ago he'd possessed a collection of more than five hundred CDs. These days he had just five – two by Hendrix and one each by Stevie Ray Vaughan, Joni Mitchell and Mott the Hoople.

Unsure as to whether he would bother getting up again after his nap, Diamond locked up, turned off the lights and did the washing-up prior to climbing beneath a duvet which he conceded was most definitely in need of bleaching, never mind washing.

He picked up *Q* first because the front page carried the sort of teaser which all music fans love – "We list the greatest 100 albums of all time." Diamond always loved features of that nature, firstly because he liked to check how many of them he actually owned (or had owned at some point), and secondly because it gave him the perfect opportunity to rail against the choices of the muppets who compiled the list.

Diamond suddenly felt very, very old – five of the albums in the bottom twenty he had never even heard of, never mind owned. "Turin Brakes? What the fuck are they doing in here?" he asked out loud.

Things did improve a little as he made his way upwards from number seventy to number forty. He had owned twelve of the albums, and approved, just about, of another dozen or so. He realised that the rather large gap in his musical education and knowledge centred around hip-hop and rap, as he had never been near works by the Notorious B.I.G., Tupac Shakur or the Wu-Tang Clan.

Before even turning the page to read the countdown from ten to one, he was one hundred per cent certain that he would disagree so vehemently that he would be required to rise from his sickbed and pour himself a large nightcap. He knew he had some cheap brandy in the kitchen, so he turned and read on.

He had no real issue with Hendrix's *Electric Ladyland* at ten, Van Morrison's *Astral Weeks* at nine and The Clash's *London Calling* at eight, but he could barely contain himself when he saw Radiohead's *OK Computer* at number seven. He loathed the prissy art-school scene which had given rise to Radiohead and their fellow miserabilists, Coldplay. He was annoyed, but read on. Number six was Bowie's *Station to Station*. Neil Young's *After the Gold Rush* was next, followed by Dylan's *The Freewheelin' Bob Dylan*.

The top three were, Diamond had to admit, rather predictable in a populist magazine like Q – The Sex Pistols' *Never Mind the Bollocks*, The Smiths' *The Queen is Dead*, and finally Nirvana's *Nevermind*. He had always quite liked Nirvana, but often wondered if their star would have faded quickly had Kurt Cobain not applied a large bullet to his forehead when at the peak of his powers – there's nothing quite like death to extend a career in showbiz.

Diamond wasn't too upset by the list but still decided that a late-night drink was in order. He had read multiple articles online which suggested that as a cancer sufferer's general health began to slip away, so too did his desire for many of life's accepted pleasures, notably sex, good food, cigarettes and alcohol. Working on the childish basis that it was only right and proper that he indulge in something approaching a feast before the famine enveloped him, he left his bedroom and half-filled his Popeye glass with brandy.

Noreen was due back tomorrow, having spent the past week at her ailing mother's bedside. Diamond was looking forward to seeing her; she had become his muse, his touchstone, and, in his own sad little way, he loved her very, very much.

As the brandy warmed his throat and lifted his spirits, Diamond settled down to watch the news; a broadcast which featured a litany of gross violations of the basic codes of civilised behaviour. Even though he had more than enough to contend with, he continued to be astonished by mankind's propensity for self-destruction.

He drained his glass, but decided against draining the bottle. He moved back to his bedroom, scanned *Tatler* for five minutes and then switched off his bedside lamp. He was asleep within minutes.

Again he awoke early, fumbling to find his portable radio which had seemingly disappeared beneath his bed. He leaned down and pulled out all manner of items before finally locating the radio; a basic unit which Noreen had always described as something of a museum piece.

As he listened to the 7am news bulletin, something which had been stamping its feet on the periphery of his conscious mind finally gained sufficient impetus to prompt a stream of sensible and ordered questions.

It was that *Q* list. Whilst Diamond had forgiven them for not including anything by The Kinks – the world's most overlooked band – where the fuck were The Beatles?

As the gap between the Swinging '60s and the present day grew ever wider it was, predictably if not understandably, 'cool' for modern-day critics weaned on indie bands to belittle pop's greatest ever exponents – but to ignore them totally was not just crass but well-nigh unforgivable.

Diamond reopened the magazine and checked the list again. No *Sgt. Pepper's*, no *Abbey Road*, no *Rubber Soul*, no *Revolver*, no White Album – no bloody anything by the acknowledged band of all bands. He ran though the list again – no, he was right; The Beatles were no longer considered worthy of even a lowly slot in the Top 100 albums.

He wondered how Turin Brakes, however good, could be better than The Beatles. Everything was a matter of choice and perspective, but how could the editor of a respected magazine with a healthy circulation possibly allow the publication of such a list without calling together his staff and asking, "What the fuck is going on here, boys and girls?"

Diamond was so disgusted that he almost rang Noreen to complain, but she had grown increasingly irritated by his rants and these days she rarely lasted thirty seconds before hanging up. To make himself feel at least a little better, Diamond sent Toby a text: "Thanks for that Q magazine. Top 100 albums of all time and no sight of The Beatles… wankers. See you soon."

In readiness for the return of the admirable Noreen, Diamond decided to make an effort to transform his tip of a flat into a show home. That involved washing the bedclothes, cleaning the kitchen and bathroom, and hoovering some of the carpets. It took him almost two hours, but for the first time in weeks he felt a genuine sense of achievement.

She arrived just after 7pm, looking drawn and tired. Her mum had been diagnosed with emphysema and wasn't responding at all well to the prescribed medication. In fact, after changing tablets she had come out in an all-over rash which resembled measles.

Diamond held her tight for five minutes, consoling her and revelling in the fact that she was back. Pleasingly, Noreen spotted that her normally lazy boyfriend had spent some time cleaning up, and was not false in her praise. Diamond felt suitably smug as he pointed out that even the bedclothes had been washed.

As Noreen prepared a meal of pasta and something which had the distinct smell of pickled herrings, Diamond received a text from Toby.

Sorry. Really busy with a new project – dull but has to be done. Sorry about Q; I always thought it was a cool magazine. Obviously not. We all have our own ideas about who should be in a list like that. Never heard of your lot but I'm sure they're great... really bad name, though. See you soon. Say hi to Noreen for me.

Noreen's meal was predictably tasty and filling. Diamond was fully aware that as his health deteriorated she was increasing the size of his portions to help maintain his energy levels. He never mentioned it, and always attempted to clear his plate without comment or complaint.

They made love that night. It was quick and it was fun – and it was beneath a clean duvet which gave off the aroma of jasmine as they rolled around like love-struck teenagers.

Afterwards, as he struggled for breath and she attempted to find a decent station on his radio, she asked how Toby was doing down in the coal mine, as she was prone to calling Porton Down.

"He's good; I saw him yesterday and he sends his very fondest regards. He's going out with that girl from The Rubicon," said Diamond.

"What, the one with the huge breasts and the very small brain? God, he can do better than that. What on earth does he see in her?" asked Noreen.

"Huge breasts," replied Diamond.

"Right," said Noreen, instinctively doing that uniquely female thing and casting a quick glance down at her own chest.

"Pass me that Q magazine, hon," she said, spotting it lying on the floor beneath her discarded bra.

"I wouldn't bother – the people who write it are obviously about eighteen years old, have never moved outside of London, and don't believe any song is worthy unless it references 'bitches and pimps'. There's a poll in there, the hundred greatest albums of all time, and guess which band doesn't even get one entry?"

"Dunno. Duran Duran? Grand Funk Railroad? One Direction?"

"Be serious. The Beatles, that's who. For those of us who have more than one working part in our brain it's just insulting and it makes a mockery of the entire exercise – and it's spread across eight fucking pages. I'm not old, but I am respectful of the great older bands."

"So old I've never heard of them," said Noreen, before abandoning her reading and snuggling up between Diamond's left arm and his chest.

"Yeah, right," said Diamond, pulling tight his arms and closing his eyes.

That night there were no dreams of note to disturb his sleep, and by the time he woke up – late by his standards, at 9am – Noreen had already left for work.

He attempted to read *Tatler* again but gave up when he came across a feature on polo horses. He climbed out of bed, realised that he felt pretty good in relative terms, and then mentally berated himself for not writing down his to-do list before sleeping; he had promised himself that he would do something this morning, but for the moment that task, fun or otherwise, proved to be elusive.

As he attempted to throw together a basic breakfast of toast and coffee, he spotted one of Noreen's infamous scrawled notes. He had always believed that her handwriting was sufficiently bad that it would guarantee her entry into the medical profession without the requirement for those pesky qualifications.

Hi, I didn't disturb you because you looked so cute lying there, snoring like a pig. Last night was good – I've missed you. You'll have to tell me more about The Beetles – I am always willing to learn at the feet of a master. Love ya. xxx

Diamond shook his head in a dismissive manner before saying to himself, "I'm dying and she still thinks she can take the piss. Women…"

And then it came to him, the mini task he had set for himself late last night – buy the album by The Doors that he had heard just the once. Rather pleased with himself, Diamond decided to browse world events from his armchair before formally placing the day on its rails and pushing it forwards.

It was the previous week that he'd realised that, if he wasn't standing up, he was always halfway to falling asleep. He could no longer sit for endless hours watching vacuous television programmes about antiques and holiday destinations without gently slipping away into various states and depths of slumber. As Sky News reported live from one of the Middle East's trouble spots, Diamond closed his eyes and let his head fall backwards onto a large cushion which bore an image of Peppa Pig. He hadn't a clue when or how it had come into his life, but every child under the age of ten who had ever entered his flat had wanted to take it home with them.

As the television droned and next door's dog began its daily assault on the local paperboy, Diamond's thoughts turned to The Beatles. He decided that they should have at least four, maybe five, of their albums in anyone's Top 100, and wondered if, perhaps, the poll had only included albums from 1970 onwards. It was a theory he quickly dismissed when he remembered the elevated position of one of Dylan's better albums from the '60s.

As sleep beckoned and Diamond's mind began to jump illogically from topic to topic, the wording of Toby's text came back to him. What had he said when told there were no Beatles albums in that chart? "Never heard of them"? Was that what he said? And what was it Noreen had written in her note? "Tell me more about The Beetles"?

"What sorcery is this?" Diamond said out loud, as he dragged himself up from the settee and into the kitchen for yet another cup of tasteless coffee.

For no good reason, he suddenly had the most desperate craving for a cigarette. He had given up three years ago when the price became prohibitive and the government, cheerful souls that they are, placed warnings on every packet stating that smoking can cause cancer. *Seemingly, so can not smoking,* thought Diamond as he checked his small change and headed out of the front door.

The nearest shop was the purveyor of bad wine, but all he wanted was ten Marlboro Lights and a newspaper. Irrespective of the hour, it was always the same man behind the counter: an Indian called Salim who, despite being robbed on six separate occasions in the previous eighteen months, smiled engagingly at everyone – even those who carried a ten-pound lump hammer, it would seem.

Diamond made his purchase and was heading for the door when he turned and said to Salim, "What's your favourite Beatles song, mate?"

With the rather haunted look of a man who would rather be mugged than asked questions about English music, Salim shrugged his shoulders and said, "'I Can't Getta Me No Satisfactions.'"

"Thanks – very helpful," said Diamond, as he left, shaking his head.

He headed for the nearby park – a positive magnet for incontinent dogs large and small – and sat on a bench in order to fully savour his first nicotine in years. He lit, inhaled and, predictably, coughed and coughed and coughed. His head was swimming and his eyes watering, but he pushed on in a manly fashion, drawing heavily until the deed was done. "Well, that was absolutely fucking awful," he said to himself, before laughing loudly.

He checked his mobile but no one had called; no one had sent him a text or an email. Of late, he had taken to deciding in mid afternoon precisely how he would fill his evening. Tonight he quite fancied watching a DVD featuring an alien serial killer which he had borrowed from Toby, having sex with Noreen again, and writing to the editor of *Q* to express his disgust at the glaring omissions from the poll. If his email was printed he would receive £100 which, he had already calculated, would buy him thirteen bottles of reasonably good wine. However, to be published an email had to be craftily constructed, it had to be entertaining and it had to promote further debate amongst the magazine's readership.

Having walked back home at a pace which would have shamed a snail, Diamond made the mandatory cup of coffee before sitting down at his laptop to berate – in an entertaining manner – *Q*'s editor. His believed his points to be well made and his argument strong. He was forceful, but never overtly insulting. He was passionate about the subject, but never overly biased. He read and reread his email until he was happy with its content.

As he stood over the toilet checking that his urine wasn't flecked with traces of blood – Dr Marshall's suggestion – he tried to come up with a fitting, almost triumphant denouement. He needed a good, solid one-liner to ensure his correspondence ended with a real flourish.

"Got it," he said out loud.

He returned to his laptop and, at the bottom of his prose, typed, "It's as if they never even existed."

In much the same way as love can grab you by the balls and embrace you almost in an instant – an instant you never saw coming – fear can spread throughout a human body in as little time as it takes to say, "Fuck."

Diamond leaned back in his chair and closed his eyes. As a shudder the like of which he had not known since he received confirmation of his cancer's severity surged through his entire frame, his fingers began to tingle and shake. Almost instantly, he was cold, very cold.

The thought which had occurred to him, the one prompted by the adding of the final line to his email, was writ large inside his head, yet still he tried to deny it was worth seriously pursuing.

Twice he had done his thing with *Die Glocke*, and on both occasions nothing had changed, in a negative sense, when he returned. Only good had come from his two visits to Paris in earlier eras – Wilde had been saved from a totally needless death, as had Morrison.

Diamond knew that the confirmation of his fears lay at his fingertips. All he had to do was open up Google and type in, "The Beatles". It wasn't just the logical solution, it was arguably the only one – but Diamond had always been more frightened of damning lies than incontrovertible truths. To him being proved right had often been far, far worse than discovering he was wrong.

He picked up his laptop and logged on to Google. The box with the flashing cursor almost seemed to be smiling at him, inviting him to roll the dice and ask the big question.

Not yet, he thought, picking up his mobile and ringing Toby.

"Hi, mate, it's only me," he said.

"What's up? Something wrong?" asked Toby with genuine concern.

"No, I'm fine, just a little bored."

"Good – I thought you were going to say that you'd collapsed and were haemorrhaging blood."

"Not a bad idea bearing in mind the state my blood is in. I was just writing an email to the editor of *Q* informing him of my displeasure."

"Ah, the poll you mentioned. Who was top, by the way?"

"It was Nirvana; not the *In Utero* album, the other one – the good one. I don't have a problem with that; it's the complete absence of Beatles albums that's pissing me off," said Diamond, almost wincing as he awaited Toby's response.

"Sorry, remind me – what did they do?"

"Toby, are you seriously telling me that you have never heard of The Beatles?"

"Can't say I have. It's a dumb name, though. Where are they from, the States?"

"Fuck. I need to see you, Toby."

"OK. What about tomorrow, I—"

"No, Toby, right now. Immediately. It is so urgent you wouldn't believe it."

Diamond wanted to crawl into the first available hole, curl up and die. Could it be possible that he, one totally insignificant man, had so changed the order of things that he had denied the world the genius of Lennon and McCartney? He was puzzled, asking himself over and over again, *How could this have happened?*

He mentally reran his two trips in *Die Glocke* back to 1900 and 1971. He couldn't find anything untoward in either his deeds or his actions. He had moved swiftly and precisely once outside of the machine. He had not interacted or conversed at undue length with anyone – not even Wilde or Morrison.

Toby, who was taking off a week of accrued days owing, had said he would drive over straight away; he'd sounded as worried as Diamond felt.

Diamond was almost asleep when his friend arrived. Toby made two cups of coffee, sat opposite him and asked him what was wrong.

"I have a horrible feeling that I changed things – or, rather, *we* have changed things," said Diamond.

"In what way? Everything seems as it was to me – no jackbooted warriors marching up and down Peckham High Street," said Toby, trying to drain the tension out of the conversation by adding a dash of humour.

"Look, Toby, before I set foot in *Die Glocke*, The Beatles were the biggest band in the history of popular music. They came from Liverpool, they were known as the Fab Four, they were universally loved, they sold trillions of records and they were simply the benchmark for everything which came afterwards."

"OK. When are we talking about here?" asked Toby.

"Sixties – from about '63 up until '69. You just would not believe how huge they were, Toby. John, Paul, George and Ringo – does that mean anything to you?"

"Ringo? That was a popular name in Liverpool back then, was it? No, I haven't heard of them. Fuck me. What do we do?"

"Do? We can't do anything, can we? It isn't as if I can slip back in time and change things because I wouldn't know what I was looking to change. Sweet Jesus, what a mess."

"Yes, but remember, it is only a mess for you, Steve. No one else is lamenting the absence of this band in their lives because to me and everyone else they were never in our lives in the first place."

"True. But what I don't understand is this. If they never existed, then how come I know loads of their songs and the basic outline of their career? That doesn't seem right to me. Surely my memory of them should have been wiped along with everyone else's?" asked Diamond.

"That's a great point. Remember when we spoke about the many so-called paradoxes of time travel? How it doesn't really make any sense at all, and every scenario could be unpicked by logic and common sense? What I'm saying is that you have seemingly presented us with another strange paradox – the man doing the time-travelling is unique in that his world remains largely the same even after he has deliberately distorted or realigned past events. And before you ask, no, I can't explain what I mean because it truly doesn't make any sense at all," said Toby.

The two sat in silence for several minutes before Diamond picked up his laptop, opened Google and typed in, "The Beatles".

The response was exactly as he had feared. "Not known. Did you mean 'Beetles'?"

"Fuck," said Diamond.

"Fuck," said Toby.

"The obvious question is, if I managed to airbrush The Beatles from the world's history, what else might I have done? My dad always told me never to mess with things I didn't understand. He was a total arse most of the time but maybe he had a point," said Diamond.

"And my dear old mum always used to say to me that I shouldn't worry about things I couldn't change," countered Toby.

"That is also a reasonable point, I guess. I need some time to think about this. If I too had surrendered all knowledge of The Beatles then, self-evidently, this wouldn't be a problem, but as it is, I am the only person on the planet who can sing their songs. I feel guilty, as though I have robbed the world of something really precious," said Diamond.

Toby left with a promise that he would call Diamond first thing in the morning unless he heard from him first.

CHAPTER

TWENTY-TWO

Diamond returned to Google, typing in the names of The Beatles' members individually. It was to no avail – according to the search engine, John Lennon, Paul McCartney, George Harrison and Ringo Starr had done absolutely nothing of any note with their lives. They had managed to negotiate safe passage from birth to either old age or death without troubling anyone.

Diamond didn't require much of an excuse to drink to excess, so the fact that he had somehow managed to disband Liverpool's finest before they had even struck up a harmony together was akin to a godsend.

He felt that he should go out and wander around the various pubs which had played a pivotal role in his adolescence, but he knew that he was becoming more and more insular with every passing week. So he checked his kitchen cupboards to ensure he had sufficient alcohol to fully meet his requirements, and promptly took up the challenge of getting as inebriated as possible.

He did a fine job. By midnight he was roaring and rolling drunk, berating the world for its cruelty and its unfairness.

After his bottle had run dry he contented himself with singing Beatles songs – 'Penny Lane', 'Paperback Writer' and 'A Day in the Life' featuring prominently as he sat and laughed and cried.

As he lay in his bed an hour later, scanning the Q poll to ensure that Elvis Presley had not fallen victim to his revisionist trips back to Paris, the vaguest and most illogical of plans began to gather momentum inside a brain which even he conceded had been made cloudy by coarse red wine and even coarser brandy.

He needed to know – he needed to know what had happened to The Beatles. He needed to know why his journeys in *Die Glocke* had prevented the formation and rise to stardom of the greatest pop group of them all.

Diamond had grown to trust his basic instincts since his diagnosis. He knew he had no time to regret or repent at his leisure, and that once he had dismissed an option it was just that: dismissed forever. It wasn't delayed or postponed or put on hold; it was dead in the water, Jim Morrison-style. Diamond was now a man for whom second chances just didn't exist.

He resolved to find out what had become of McCartney and Co. If that meant a trip up north to Liverpool for a few days, then so be it.

He awoke with the sort of hangover which inevitably prompts a man to reassess his relationship with alcohol. He felt as though he was wearing a mask which had been pulled tight by drawstrings at the back of his head. His eyes wouldn't open fully, his eyelids stubbornly moving in the wrong direction to block out the early morning sunshine which poured through the open curtains.

All hangovers promote a feeling of helplessness and self-pity, and Diamond's natural instinct was to pull the duvet over his pounding temples and hide away. But, like all seasoned drinkers, he knew that self-inflicted wounds were best dealt with swiftly and by way of traditional methods.

Thirty minutes later he had thrown up, showered, drunk two litres of cold tap water, taken four painkillers and, of course, vowed never to get hammered again. He then scrambled three eggs, buttered two slices of toast, filled his largest mug with coffee and planted himself in front of the television.

It was 9.34am when he formally wrote off the day and decided that he would spend the rest of it drinking yet more water whilst in bed. Noreen was staying that night and the very last thing he needed was a lecture on the evils of the old demon alcohol from the one person he simply could not afford to fall out with.

When he awoke it was early evening. He moved his head slowly from side to side to gauge the severity of any lingering pain. He felt what recovering drunks would call dull and woolly but the pain had, mercifully, subsided.

He headed for the shower in the hope that by the time Noreen arrived he would be able to present a picture of healthy normality – a dying leukaemia sufferer, but one with a smile on his face. He tidied up as best he could, moving the evidence of the previous night's teenage rampage to an outside bin; one which seemed, more and more, to resemble a bottle bank.

By the time his lady arrived, all was well. They embraced and chatted, they sat and ate, they drank coffee and watched television. He even managed to win a measure of praise by declining the offer of a short trip to the pub, insisting that he believed he might have been drinking a little too much of late, and that he didn't wish to be regarded by those who knew him by sight or reputation as some sad old drunk with serious health issues.

Noreen was duly impressed and suggested that they should, perhaps, swap one form of pleasure for another and go to bed at an outrageously early hour to share a bout of intimacy. Diamond, working on the basis that his next bang may well prove to be his last one, smiled and agreed. They ran like kids to the bedroom, shrieking as they raced to be first beneath the covers.

Despite the masses of medication he swallowed daily to help prolong his life, Diamond's libido did still match, if not surpass, Noreen's. They played happily in his bed for two hours before coming up for air and settling down to drink coffee and read.

"What's your plan for the next few days?" asked Diamond.

"I am going to see my mum again. Her emphysema is getting worse and her doctor has asked me to visit him to discuss the possibility of providing her with one of those face masks, so she may end up having to push a trolley with a tank of oxygen inside when – or if – she goes outside the house. I will probably stay a couple of nights as my brother is away on business, which means she is starved of company if I can't call in."

"OK. Say hello to her from me. I think I might go away too," Diamond said, preparing to issue a stream of lies to his nearest and dearest.

"Where? South of France? Miami?"

"Hardly. No, Liverpool. Remember that friend I had who went to college up there – Heather? Heather Ibbotson? Well, after she got her degree she stayed on Merseyside. She rang me the other day, out of the blue, to see how I am. I told her the grim news and she told me to pack a bag and head up there pronto."

"Didn't you once tell me that she was the one you adored, loved and wanted to live with?" asked Noreen.

"Yes," said Diamond. "On the day I was going to ask her to move in with me, she announced that she had found herself a new bloke. So me and her never really happened but, yes, I do still love her very much."

"Awwww, you old romantic, you. How you getting there, and when you going?"

"Train, I think. I may go tomorrow. I haven't checked the timetable yet but I will do first thing. It'll be good to see her. I think she married a local bloke and had several kids," said Diamond, relieved that his illness had in no way diminished his ability to spin a good yarn.

"Great. Well, as you may get to Liverpool, meet one of the city's seductive beauties, fall in love and never return to downtown Wembley, maybe we should have one last, lingering kiss before you go," said a beaming Noreen.

They made love for a third time and promptly sank into the sort of contented and happy sleep which only sex can provide.

Diamond had already checked out and booked his train tickets. The cheapest – or, as most people saw it, the least expensive – way to get to Liverpool and back was to travel to London's Euston. He wasn't quite sure what he would do when he arrived at Liverpool's Lime Street Station because he wasn't sure what it was he was looking for.

He settled on heading to the main library or the offices of the *Liverpool Echo* newspaper in the hope of tracing and then maybe even tracking down the men who would have long quit the city with full pockets but for his unplanned interference.

He armed himself with a notebook, a pen, his camera and a bottle of mineral water, deciding against taking his laptop; his body ached enough without having to drag his unfashionably bulky computer up and down the streets of a city he was only vaguely familiar with.

His journey into London was without incident, save feeling obliged to hand over 50p to a man on the Tube who seemed to believe that he had a gift for impersonating famous figures of the day. Confirmation that he himself was rather unsure about the quality of his work came before every impression when he casually announced who it was going to be. Diamond didn't have the heart to tell this funny-for-all-the-wrong-reasons entertainer that his Tony Blair sounded exactly the same as his George Bush, which sounded exactly the same as his Sean Connery.

Euston is always a nightmare for anyone who craves peace and quiet. A seething mass of humanity – no one appears to speak but, even so, the cavernous vault of a main hall is always filled with noise.

Diamond's last visit to Liverpool had been more than five years earlier when he travelled with a mate to see an eighty-year-old Andy Williams perform at the city's legendary Empire Theatre; a venue whose boards had been trodden by anyone who was anyone, from Laurel and Hardy to AC/DC. Diamond had always loved the music of Williams; his mother had sung 'Moon River' and 'Can't Get Used To Losing You' to him when he was a small child. He was glad he'd made the effort to see him live, as the great American crooner died a few years later.

When Diamond had last alighted at Lime Street Station, Liverpool had been midway through a period of long-overdue renaissance and resurrection – the evidence silhouetted against the late-afternoon sky in the shape of countless huge cranes tearing down the old in readiness for the new.

Diamond had always defended Liverpool against the usual accusations levelled by those who have never travelled to Merseyside – "Self-Pity City", a town awash with hard-line militants, a place where everyone is happy to live in the past, glorying in a long-gone reputation as one of the world's great ports. He loved the place from day one, falling for its beautiful buildings, its inbred sense of pride and its people's warmth and humour. Today would be his eighth visit, and he was keen to see if the town planners' vision of a city fit for a new millennium had been fully realised.

He had been told by an old journalist colleague, who now worked on the *Liverpool Echo*, that the city had been dragged back from the brink and was now moving effortlessly towards parity with Manchester, the age-old rival from just down the East Lancs Road.

Diamond had debated whether he should ring his friend, Tom, who lived just outside the city in a leafy suburb called Formby, but decided against it, instead booking two nights in the Malmaison Hotel, a new-build which stood on the very banks of the River Mersey.

He had a plan. He would be in his hotel room by 2pm, he would unpack and then head straight out to the main library, which he knew to be centrally located. Once there, he would sweet-talk whoever was on the front desk, presuming it was a she and not a he, and he would then play the investigative reporter and track down the four members of The Beatles.

It was, he knew full well, a difficult task; a ridiculous task. He was smart enough to place the odds on him succeeding in finding even one member of the band at less than twenty per cent. But if it was to be a failure it would be an enjoyable failure, as he knew Liverpool to be a place of excellent and varied restaurants, and bars which boasted both tradition and unique characters. On his last visit he had called into a pub just a stone's throw from the station to find that the man standing next to him at the bar had on his shoulder a small monkey which he fed peanuts as he drank his beer; not the sort of thing you see in North London.

The journey north was pleasant enough, with just three stops – Stafford, Crewe and Runcorn – before Liverpool's two cathedrals came into view. It had always amused Diamond that, in the moments before a train reached its destination, a high percentage of those on board would leap to their feet and start scrambling for cases and briefcases. They would then jostle for position at the doors, all grimly determined to be the first to disembark, almost as if they believed that someone on the platform was ready to hand out prizes.

Although a large city, Liverpool has a relatively compact centre, making it easy for those new arrivals who are not heading off to the suburbs to actually walk to their hotel or place of business. Diamond suspected that his hotel was probably a fifteen-minute stroll away, but decided to use a black cab because time was short in more ways than one.

The Malmaison proved to be splendid – a glitzy yet Gothic sort of a place decorated in blacks and purples and featuring an improbable number of mirrors. The girl on the reception desk was as Scouse as they come, with an accent so thick she could almost have been a caricature. As Diamond filled out forms which he had always believed were tossed into a bin the moment the customer turned his back, she delighted in telling him that many celebrities, both local and national, stayed at the hotel regularly.

"I could have given you the room Katie Price stayed in last week, but someone took it a few minutes ago," she said, looking genuinely upset.

"Never mind, eh?" said Diamond, neatly concealing the fact that he had about as much interest in the rather disproportionately chesty model as she probably had in the works of Percy Shelley.

His room was like the main reception area – dark and serene in a very attractive sort of a way. The view was of the city rather than the river, but he wasn't here to sight-see.

Diamond dumped his bags, asked for directions to the library and set off on foot. It took him just twenty minutes to find it; a magnificent, recently refurbished building opposite the Empire Theatre and adjacent to the equally stunning St George's Hall. He considered ringing Heather but knew that he wouldn't; the pain of romantic failure had cursed him down the years.

As he walked in, he was reminded of advice given to him before his first ever visit to the city many years ago – when walking around Liverpool, always look up, not down, because the buildings are almost without equal in the United Kingdom.

Although he wasn't on a sight-seeing trip, he spent thirty minutes just drinking in the sumptuous interior of the building before approaching a young woman behind the main reception desk – a young woman who looked like an identikit version of everyone's vision of a library assistant: tall, slim, black hair swept back into a ponytail, and dark-rimmed glasses which served to add a veneer of mystique.

"Good morning," said Diamond.

"Well, it probably is a good morning in New York right now – but here in Liverpool it's mid afternoon," she replied, with a flashing smile.

"Sorry, yes. I'm a bit tired. It's jet lag – I've just come up from London."

"A southerner lost in Liverpool, eh? How can I help you?"

"This will probably sound odd but I have the names of four people who were definitely born here and I want to try and either track them down or find out what happened to them."

"OK. Do you know if they are dead or alive?"

"No."

"OK. Do you have their dates of birth?"

"No."

"Right. So all you have is four names?"

"Yes – and a vague idea of when they were born; around the early to mid 1940s."

"Is this a family tree sort of thing? Distant relatives?"

"No, nothing like that. I could attempt to explain but, trust me, long before I reach the end of that explanation you'll call for a van to drag me away to that hospital where they keep Ian Brady stashed away. That's in Liverpool, isn't it?"

"It's in Maghull, which is about eight miles away. I presume that you have already tried an internet search?"

"Yes, I gave that a go but found nothing at all – hence my decision to travel up here."

"It must be quite important for you to find them to have come all this way, what with the price of petrol."

"I got the train, but that cost me a small fortune. Yes, I need answers to some questions. There's nothing shady or underhand or anything like that. I am just an inquisitive Londoner seeking information about four men from Liverpool whom I have never met," said Diamond.

"Well, you could probably spend forever and a day rooting through what we have here – as you can see there's quite a lot – so I think your best bet would be to head for the Births, Deaths and Marriages Office to see if they can help you," she said.

"Fine. Don't tell me – it's the other side of town?"

"You're in luck – it's fifty yards away inside St George's Hall, literally just over the road."

"Great, I'll give that a go. Thanks, you've been really helpful."

"It's the way we are in this part of the world. Bye," she said, closing the conversation.

It was raining; in fact, it was pouring. As he hurried across the cobblestoned street towards St George's Hall, Diamond glanced to his left to take in the massive frontage of the Empire Theatre. Up in lights this week was *Evita*, starring Madalena Alberto and Marti Pellow; the latter, if Diamond remembered correctly, being the former frontman with Wet Wet Wet, a superior pop band of the '80s and '90s with sweet harmonies and winning smiles.

Once inside St George's Hall, Diamond shuffled around taking in its majesty for several minutes before seeking out the information desk. His wit and charm were unlikely to prove quite so persuasive as they had in the library, as the man behind the counter looked as though he had just completed a night shift as a doorman at a venue of dubious reputation. 'Large' wasn't the word – he looked like two people of normal build somehow stitched together.

"How can I help you, son?" he said, placing the largest set of hands Diamond had ever seen on the desk in front of him. The knuckles of both bore the traditional tattoos, 'Mam' and 'Dad' – probably provided by an equally ham-fisted mate after a night of beer and womanising.

"I am looking for some help," said Diamond, noticing that when the man smiled he seemed to have an awful lot of gum and tongue but very little in the way of teeth. "I am trying to find out what happened to four people who were born in Liverpool back in the '40s. I have their names but, sadly, no other information."

"They owe you money?" asked the toothless man.

"No, no – it's nothing like that at all. There's nothing mysterious about this; I would just like to locate them if that's possible."

"It probably is possible, but this is council territory, which means two things – cost and delay; we specialise in both. You could fill out a few forms, hand over a few quid and leave it to one of our young bucks to turn a seemingly straightforward task into a complex affair. That's what most people do. I wouldn't do that, of course, because I know most of the idiots who work here and I wouldn't trust any of 'em to find their own arse with two hands."

"So what would you do, then?" asked Diamond, waiting for another stream of invective.

"Me? I'd go to the *Echo* and ask them nicely if they could run the names through one of their big computers – see if anything comes out of the other end. Do you know where the *Echo* building is? Old Hall Street," said the toothless man.

"That's great. You've been really helpful. Thanks a lot," said Diamond, turning to leave.

"Where you from, mate?" asked the toothless man.

"Just outside London," said Diamond.

"Poor bugger," said the toothless man with a half-smile.

Diamond beat a hasty retreat, returning to the rain and the wind as he looked for a passing taxi. He could have walked, but he had the feeling his fact-finding mission wasn't destined to run quite as smoothly as he had envisaged as he sat on the train a few hours earlier. Whilst no one was being obstructive or defeatist, Diamond was only now realising just how strange was the request he was making of people he had never met before. Only by mentally moving himself to the other side of the conversations did he fully appreciate how curious it must be to be faced with a man from London trying to track down four men from Liverpool whom he had never met.

As he stood and waited to see the glowing yellow 'vacant' light of a hackney cab, Diamond started to feel like a journalist again; a man on a mission, a man against the world. The thought made him smile, and for no good reason it also caused him to remember that he needed to ring Noreen, definitely, and Toby, possibly.

He had learned early on in his illness that those who are damned to an unfortunate early death do tend to become a little selfish, insomuch as they too often leave those people who genuinely care for their well-being in the dark. Noreen had quite rightly said on many occasions that as long as she knew he was all right, then she was also all right. He accepted that communication was the key, so as he waited for the elusive taxi he rang his woman to inform her that he was both alive and soaking wet.

He then phoned his mate Tom – which, he now conceded, he should have done yesterday when his plan was still very much in its formative stage.

"Bloody hell, which stone have you crawled from beneath, Steve?" asked Tom.

"A very wet one just outside St George's Hall as it happens, mate," said Diamond.

"Our St George's Hall – in Liverpool?"

"The very one, sir. I got here a couple of hours ago on the proverbial mission from God. The problem is, with the mission having already hit the rocks, I thought to myself, *Who could lend a helping hand?*"

"And the answer was me, right? No problem. You looking for a bed for the night?"

"No, that bit is sorted. I'm booked into the Malmaison for two nights."

"Very swish. I've only been there once and it was so dark I couldn't see the very expensive and small steak on the very large plate in front of me. What you doing up here?"

"Long story. Are you in work? Because I think – or rather, I hope – you will be able to help me."

"I'm off today but in tomorrow at 9am. Shall I come down tonight for a drink or two? It's only twenty minutes on the train into the centre from where I live."

"That would be great – 8pm at the hotel?"

"Look forward to it. See you later. Bye," said Tom.

At the precise moment Tom cleared the line, a black cab pulled up offering a lift back to the riverfront and sanctuary from the increasingly foul weather.

By London standards the prices in the hotel bar were fairly reasonable, but Diamond could understand fully why – staff apart – he didn't hear even one local accent as he sat clutching his glass of Merlot. Tom was late, but tardiness had always been his trademark.

Diamond was halfway down his second glass when Tom finally bowled through the doors, his hair in absolute disarray, another victim of an unpredictable riverfront breeze which could lay waste to the most prepared and pampered of flamboyantly dressed hen parties. As he began to proffer his traditional excuses, Diamond cut him short by raising his right arm and pointing to the bar in a universally acknowledged gesture which meant, *Get the drinks in*. He did just that, returning with a bottle of Cabernet Sauvignon, one glass and a bar menu.

"So, my long-lost friend, how are you?" asked Tom.

"Funny you should ask that because I'm not as well as I might be – in fact, I'm dying; I have cancer," said Diamond.

"Fuck off," said Tom, with the look of a man who had suddenly seen the curtain drop on what he had anticipated would be a grand reunion awash with alcohol and bouts of mirthful reminiscence.

"Sadly, it's true, but I am – so I am repeatedly told – bearing my illness and my fate stoically and with great bravery.

That's bollocks because I'm pissed off and more than a little bit frightened. Trust me, there is no dignity in despair."

"Fuck. I don't really know what to say, mate. Obviously, I didn't know. What sort of cancer is it?"

"Leukaemia."

"Is it treatable? I mean, I was going to say that you look good having…"

"Lost a bit of weight?"

"Yeah. Sorry."

"Don't be," said Diamond. "As Forrest Gump reminded us, shit happens. I would love to say that I have come to terms with it, but I don't believe anyone who makes that claim is being truly honest. You can live with it, you can accept it – but I don't believe you can come to terms with it because, ironically, the biggest thing to ever happen in your life is the thing which will take that life.

"All I have done is start to appreciate that there's absolutely nothing I can do about it. I have seen the best doctors, had the chemotherapy, swallowed the pills – nothing has worked. So, I realised that I had a stark choice – either fade away in an ocean of self-pity, or try to spend the time I have left doing the things I enjoy. I like alcohol and sex so, bizarrely, I have been having quite a good time since I was diagnosed.

"One of my favourite bands, It's Immaterial, called their first album *Life's Hard and Then You Die*, which just about sums it all up. I'm like everyone else – I think I'm indestructible, that I will never have to face up to the end. We all seem to do that, even though, all the time, people around us are dying. It is a protective shield we throw over ourselves. The only time we actually think about death – and its consequences – is when it's right in our face, when someone who matters to us does the unthinkable, the unforgivable, and dies. We largely live in a make-believe utopian world where everyone is happy and no one gets ill; I mean *really* ill.

"I have always struggled with the fact that the true reality of life is, ultimately, death. I go to funerals, I stare at the coffin, I console the bereaved, I mourn in my own private way – but I still deny that it has any place in my life. What we don't like, the things which truly hurt and disturb us, we hide away from. That, I believe, is human nature. I accept it is wholly wrong, and yet I cannot condemn those who seek refuge in false hopes and dreams when the alternative is abject grief and misery. Is it any wonder that mankind invented God? People are scared; they don't wish to believe that threescore and ten is all they're going to get – they need something to believe in, to hang on to... so they invented the prospect of a loving, protective super-guardian who will grant them eternal life.

"Jesus, Tom. I'm dying, but that's all it is; in the grand scheme of things it is no more significant than the death of a housefly in a spider's web. It is life; it is fate. I am no martyr. What I am is fucking unlucky.

"I bear no grudges. I don't sit around feeling that life has been grossly unfair, and that my fate should instead have befallen him, or him, or him. I wish it hadn't happened to me but it has, and slowly – ever so slowly – I have accepted it. As I said, I will never really come to terms with it, but we all have an undetermined lifespan and mine just happens to be a good deal shorter than I thought it would be. *C'est la vie et le mort.*

"Death is not serene and is rarely noble as the poets and the scholars would have us believe. There is nothing but finality, and the route towards that endless blackness is only rarely without pain and regret. There is, clearly, an art to dying, but it is one we cannot rehearse, only fear."

Tom sat back in his chair, puffed out his cheeks and exhaled loudly. He then raised his glass to his old friend and smiled.

"Strong stuff – you're obviously still in love with Oscar Wilde, Steve. You two would have got on well, I think," he said.

"We did," said Diamond.

"Right, that's the emotional stuff out of the way. What are you doing up here in the frozen north?" asked Tom.

"This is going to sound very odd, and I cannot fill you in on all the details because if I do you'll assume it's my mind and not my blood which has been poisoned," said Diamond. "I am seeking information on four men who were all born in Liverpool in the 1940s – well, I think they were. All I have are names."

"OK. Am I allowed to ask why?" said Tom.

"Nah, leave it. It's a mad thing, but something I want to do before… well, before I can't do it. I went to the Central Library and the St George's Hall, but they suggested the *Echo* might actually be the best bet as you will have all the births, deaths and marriages logged away on some hard drive somewhere. What do you reckon?"

"We quite possibly have – it will just be a question of trying to find them. I wouldn't know where to start, but I will speak to our head of IT now if I can. He's a mate, and he can be very efficient when he's in the mood," said Tom, disappearing out of the hotel's front door in search of a stronger signal.

He returned five minutes later with the thumb of his right hand in the air, Emperor-style. "No problem; he says he will help you all he can. If you come to the office first thing in the morning he will sit you down in front of a screen and show you which buttons to press. He can't guarantee that you will find what you are looking for but he agrees that our records are your best bet by a mile," he said.

"That's great. I think this is going to take a little longer than I thought, so I may hang around for a few days – and before you ask, no, I'm fine; I will simply extend my stay here. Compared to London prices, the cost of staying here is staggeringly cheap. On top of that, I have realised I quite like this place. I judge hotels by one thing and one thing alone – the comfort of the bed and the one in my room looks and feels just fine.

"Shall we go out for a short wander? I don't want to be too late going to bed and I do tire very easily at the moment, so my days as an all-night drinker and chaser of dodgy women are definitely well behind me," said Diamond.

After he had booked an additional night's stay, they left and walked a short distance to a bar which had loud music and countless members of staff, but virtually no customers.

"Liverpool has changed a lot in recent years. Most people now realise they don't have to head out early; that they can come out late and stay out late. You have always been able to drink around the clock in this city – quite literally – but the trendier places, such as this one, don't tend to fill up until after 10pm," said Tom. "It is easy to understand why Liverpool is now the number-one destination for students – and why so many of them remain in the area after completing their studies. It's a cool place, and getting cooler by the month."

They sat and talked for an hour. The old stories were embroidered and trotted out, to be met by gales of laughter. When Diamond finally got back to the Malmaison and closed his bedroom door, he realised that he felt glad to be alive. He went to bed, cried a little and then fell into a deep and untroubled sleep.

Diamond arrived at the *Echo* office at precisely 9am and asked to see Tom. Ten minutes later he was shaking hands with the head of IT – Nathan, a large man with a kindly face – and was then ushered into a side room and sat in front of an old-style column PC.

Nathan explained the rudimentary aspects of searching for information and told Diamond he mustn't hesitate to shout out if he needed help or advice. Tom stayed for a coffee before heading off to the Crown Court to cover what he anticipated would be the final day of a lengthy trial involving one of the city's more nefarious villains, who had graduated from shoplifting to drug-pushing to murder.

On his journey north, Diamond had written down everything he could remember about the four members of The Beatles. It didn't amount to much but it did at least provide him with a starting point.

Complex by nature, yet singularly incisive when gifted a platform upon which to unfurl what he called his love of anti-logic, Diamond began his search by looking for arguably the least feted of The Beatles, Ringo Starr. All he could remember about him was that his real name was Richard Starkey, that he hailed from a part of the city called The Dingle, and that he had played drums with many local bands during the 1950s and early '60s.

He typed in "Ringo Starr" but the search yielded no hits – so at least Diamond knew that without The Beatles he never got to adopt his famous stage name. Next he typed "Richard Starkey, drummer" and, wonder of wonders, a variety of small but relevant entries appeared on his screen.

The first was a mention of a band called Eddie Clayton and the Clayton Squares. It was a review of a show in somewhere called Seaforth, and made mention of the fact that "drummer Richard Starkey hammered out a quite compelling rhythm all night long". The next listing was again a very short review of a show in Bootle; Starkey playing drums for Alex Caldwell's Texans. There were then several mentions of him as a member of Rory Storm and the Hurricanes; a band which, according to the cuttings, was constantly tipped for great things without ever actually moving from local to national prominence.

The last cutting was dated 1963 – but thereafter, nothing at all. So Diamond accepted that either something had happened to Starkey or he had simply become disillusioned with chasing the big break which never came and abandoned his fledgling career in music.

In the 1963 cutting Starkey was listed as twenty-three years old – which prompted Diamond to start searching the listings for births in 1940. Nathan had told him that, whilst the practice of parents announcing the arrival of their children via the pages of the *Echo* had dropped off dramatically over the past twenty years or so, it was once regarded as absolutely essential.

Diamond scrolled and typed and repeated the tedious process until his eyes ached and his throat was crying out for a cool beer. He was preparing to give Tom a call to see if Mr Big had been dispatched to prison for life when he found it. There it was, in faded black and white: "Richard and Elsie Starkey are proud to announce the birth of a son, Richard, on July 7, 1940 at their home, 9 Madryn Street, Dingle. God bless him."

A positive lead at last. Diamond scribbled down the details and, hope renewed, typed in the name George Harrison – the Beatle whose early life he knew the least about. He scanned and searched for an hour but came up with nothing at all, and without a date of birth his hunt was at a premature and frustrating end.

He could feel his energy levels gradually subsiding, so he told Nathan he would be back in ninety minutes, went outside and rang Tom's mobile. He had just left the court, and agreed to meet Diamond in a nearby coffee shop.

"How are you getting on?" asked Tom, dropping his notebook, pen and mini recorder to the floor as he sugared his cappuccino.

"Not too bad – found one, lost one. Will try the remaining two when I get back to your office. What happened to the murdering drug dealer?"

"He is, indeed, now officially a murderer. He was given a minimum of twenty-two years and – thankfully for me and the other press lads – he hurled abuse at the judge as he was carted off to the cells. They all tend to do that, but I have a mate who works at Walton Prison and he tells me the bravado wears off pretty quickly when they are banged up for their first night of a life sentence. So what do you intend doing with the one you have found? Is he still alive?" said Tom.

"I haven't a clue whether he's still with us. The last mention of him was back in the early '60s, so God only knows where he is now. I have an address, so I may go visit. It is a long shot but it would be crass of me to come all this way and then give up halfway through," said Diamond.

"OK, well, give me a call later on and let me know how you got on. I'm out at a dinner tonight but will be around tomorrow," said Tom.

Diamond returned to the *Echo* office, checked in with Nathan and then went back to the PC. He typed in the name Paul McCartney and sat back in his seat, barely able to look at the screen in front of him. Nothing. The revelation made him laugh out loud, with such force that a passing member of the *Echo* staff put her head around the door to see who was having such a good time.

Diamond reckoned that, had he typed McCartney's name into any search engine before he had accidentally erased from history the man's monumental contribution to the world of music, he would have been met with simply millions of found items. But now, following his brief time inside *Die Glocke*, the man who had been destined to become the most successful writer of popular music ever had seemingly never strummed a guitar or depressed a piano key in anger. Not for the first time, Diamond was overcome by a sense of great loss – combined with all-consuming guilt for the part he had played in the realigning of both the past and the present. His life would end soon and, whilst few would know it, his legacy would be the removal of a soundtrack from the lives of so many people, young and old.

Diamond sat back, wondering if there was another angle he might use to sharpen his search for McCartney. The name of the street in which he was raised had once come up in a pub quiz, but Diamond didn't know the answer then and couldn't remember it now.

He headed for the coffee machine and took a stroll around the busy newsroom. In no way did it resemble the crumbling, archaic offices of the *Islington Gazette* – but the buzz was a familiar one.

As he looked on in silence, a tall, ginger-haired man of about twenty-five wandered towards him and proffered his outstretched hand. "You're Tom's mate from London, aren't you?" he said, with a quite pronounced local accent.

"Yes, I am. Just doing a bit of research. I haven't been to Liverpool for years – it's changed quite a lot since I was last here; for the better, too," said Diamond.

"We call it the Great Renaissance. I wasn't around in the '70s and '80s but people tell me it was pretty grim in the days when the militant Labour council here was at war with Maggie Thatcher and her wrecking-ball ministers. The change has taken a long time but it has been worth it – Liverpool is now one of the most visited cities in Europe. God, I sound like a spokesman for the tourist board, don't I?!" said the clearly proud Scouser. "Anyway, it was good to meet you and I hope your research goes well. It should do, as the library and the records here are exceptional. I don't know what we would do without them."

"Thanks, I appreciate that. What's your name, by the way?" said Diamond.

"James. James O'Brien," the man replied, before retreating behind a desk liberally strewn with discarded coffee cups and old newspapers.

Diamond went back to his little room, sat down, closed his eyes – and then felt, coursing through his body, the very special tingle which always accompanies a moment of inspiration.

He sat up and mouthed, "James O'Brien." That was it. McCartney's first name wasn't Paul at all – it was James. He had been christened James Paul McCartney after his father.

Diamond shuffled closer to the screen and typed in the three names. There were four entries – all from the births column; one from the '50s and two from the '40s. As soon as he saw the address he knew he had it – 20 Forthlin Road in Allerton, Liverpool, the address he remembered from the pub quiz.

In a different world, the world he had unwittingly changed with his crushed-butterfly moment, whatever that had been, Diamond remembered that the house where McCartney was raised had been bought by someone – the National Trust, maybe – restored to how it looked back in the 1940s and opened as a tourist attraction for the many thousands of Beatles fans who made the pilgrimage to Merseyside.

He was impressed with himself; very briefly, he actually felt like a proper journalist.

John Lennon was the Beatle with whom Diamond was most familiar, not just because his post-band solo material was very much to his liking, but because of the manner of his death in the pre-altered world; shot dead by an American loser in New York in late 1980.

He knew that Lennon's middle name was Winston – after the wartime leader, Churchill – and that he had spent most of his formative years living with his Aunt Mimi in a house called Mendips.

He typed in "John Winston Lennon" and waited patiently for the screen to crackle into life.

As far as the *Liverpool Echo* archives were concerned there had only ever been one man born with that name in the paper's catchment area – on October 9th, 1940 to parents called Alfred and Julia. That was him; that was *the* John Lennon.

But that was it; as with McCartney, it was a sole entry. Of course, that didn't mean that Lennon had not experienced any noteworthy events in his life – or indeed that he was still alive – it just meant that any such events had not been officially recorded by the newspaper.

Diamond sat back to ponder the implications of that reasoning. The logic behind it suggested that thousands upon thousands of people from the city would live, prosper and die without ever troubling the *Echo* typesetters. Lennon could have got up to all sorts – and probably did, bearing in mind the anarchic streak which was evident throughout his 'other' life – but his antics wouldn't have found their way into the pages of his local newspaper. Even if he was now dead, his passing would almost certainly have gone unreported unless someone in his family was generous enough to pay for an entry in the deaths column. So he was either still alive or his relatives were tight-fisted.

Diamond searched for the word 'Mendips' and found it in a small news piece relating to a fundraising event staged in the property's rear garden back in 1976. He now had the address – 251 Menlove Avenue, Woolton.

Despite drawing an infuriating blank with Harrison, Diamond still felt inclined to declare the day a success. He had three addresses to visit, and whilst he thought it highly unlikely he would turn up anything of great significance, his mission was still alive and breathing – in the intensive care unit, but alive.

Diamond returned to his hotel and was asked by the girl behind the reception desk, Norma, if he would like to move rooms – a river-view suite had become available and he could upgrade if he wished following his decision to stay an additional night.

"Is it worth the effort?" he asked.

"Oh, yes," said Norma. "The views are really lovely, particularly as the sun begins to go down over the Wirral – and if we have a thunderstorm you are in for a real treat."

"OK, I will trust you and swap. Thanks," said Diamond.

Twenty minutes later, he was glad that he had had his arm gently twisted. Norma was right; the sweeping panoramic view was magnificent. One of the world's great rivers snaked out towards the Irish Sea, the setting sun bathing the peninsula opposite in a warm orange glow which was almost surreal in its intensity. He wanted to sleep, but couldn't take his eyes off the Turneresque vision in front of him. Instead of slipping out of his clothes and into bed, he opened the minibar and poured himself a glass of Shiraz.

He awoke probably an hour later with a stiff neck, an empty glass and darkness before him, night having swallowed up the day's glorious finale as he dreamed of childhood holidays with his mum and dad on Clacton Beach. As he made his way to the shower he wondered if the age-old claim was, perhaps, right: maybe your life did start to pass before your eyes as it neared its end.

Diamond showered and then fell asleep again, waking only when his mobile burst into life. Momentarily uncertain as to precisely where he was, he looked around, spotted that it wasn't his own bedroom, and then remembered he was quite a long way from home.

"Hello," he said, at the same time as clearing his dry throat.

"Hi, tiger – you OK?" asked Noreen.

"Oh, hiya… sorry, you woke me up. I keep falling asleep, which is a bloody nuisance if I'm honest."

"That's your body telling you it needs rest and that you should probably slow down a little. So how's it going up there? What you been up to?"

"It's going fine. I met with that mate of mine and we've had a few laughs about life as it is now and as it was then – it always seems to be easier to laugh when you are looking back. I am going to stay an extra night so I will be travelling back the day after tomorrow."

"An extra day, eh? You found yourself a nice woman, Diamond?"

"Yes; you. I'm just enjoying being out of the flat. The hotel here is great and they moved me into a far better room – with a wonderful view – at no extra cost. It must be that famous northern hospitality."

"Not missing me, then?"

"I am actually, but I wasn't going to raise that subject unless you did. When time starts to run out I suppose you get things into perspective far quicker and appreciate what you have. So, yes, I am missing you."

"That's really sweet, thanks. OK, I have to run. I'm going out with one of the girls from work. She is two-timing her husband of just nine months and seems very anxious to tell me all about it. I just hope she isn't expecting sensible or saintly advice because that's not exactly my speciality. Take care, and make sure you ring me tomorrow. I love you, sick boy," said Noreen.

"And I love you, healthy girl," said Diamond.

He decided against going out; in fact, he decided that he didn't even wish to leave his room that night. He ordered a steak sandwich with chips from room service, along with a bottle of the house red.

As he ate he watched a documentary about the plight of Syrian children caught in the midst of the cruellest and most unnecessary of civil wars. He wished he could help them, but was acutely aware that hope and salvation are little more than a pipe dream for so many people.

Again he slept well, waking only when the telephone on his bedside table rang. He glanced at his watch before picking up the handset – it was 8am.

"You still in bed, you lazy bastard?" asked Tom.

"Actually, yes I am. I spent a very happy night in with a very pleasant bottle of wine and then took half a sleeping tablet," said Diamond.

"I have spare time today. I have a meeting about Everton's proposed new stadium at 2pm, but I'm largely free until then if you wanted a lift anywhere?"

"Great. Can you pick me up here in, say, an hour?"

"Sure. See you at 9am," said Tom.

Tom arrived on time, and Diamond felt it necessary to finally make a point about his lousy timekeeping by asking Norma behind the reception desk if there was a photographer on hand to record for posterity a momentous occasion.

"Cruel but true," said Tom. "Where are we going, oh great one?"

"We are going to 9 Madryn Street in a place called The Dingle," replied Diamond.

"Did you ever watch that comedy series called *Bread* back in the '80s? It was set in Dingle. It was written by that

Liverpool woman who spends her time saving cats... can't remember her name."

"Carla Something-or-Other, wasn't it?"

"Lane. Carla Lane, that's it, yes. It was watched by millions but was fucking awful. It did this city no favours at all, portraying almost everyone as dole scroungers," added Tom.

It took no more than fifteen minutes for Tom to find the address, enjoying a clear run down the waterfront after he had worked his way through the late rush-hour traffic down by the Pier Head.

"Here we are," he said, parking fifty or so yards away from a small-looking terraced house which was indistinguishable from the dozens of others in the street.

"You stay here. I will go knock on the door... maybe a couple of doors. That OK?" asked Diamond, his heart beginning to race as the chase hotted up.

"Sure thing. I am but a lowly taxi driver," replied Tom, opening up a copy of the *Daily Mirror*.

Diamond approached the house. His cursory inspection didn't take too long as there was so little to see. Neat and tidy front with a potted plant beside a dirt-free front step. The curtains in the living room were open; dark, heavy affairs which reminded him of the ones which used to hang in his grandma's house. The upstairs window had old-style venetian blinds in place, closed against the morning sunshine which made the house's red brickwork look three shades lighter than it actually was.

"Let's do it," Diamond said under his breath as he lifted the heavy imitation-brass knocker and tapped twice. He waited around thirty seconds before knocking again – three times this time.

He was readying himself to step back to see if he could see anyone through the living-room window when the door opened. Through a gap of no more than four inches, a female voice drenched in the local accent asked who he was.

"Sorry to bother you. I wonder if you could help me. I am trying to track down someone who I think used to live here quite a while back," said Diamond.

"Does he owe you money?" she asked.

Remembering what the toothless man in St George's Hall had said to him the previous day, Diamond wondered if everyone in the city was obsessed with money and debt. "No, no… nothing at all like that," he said.

The door opened slowly to reveal a woman who must have been in her late seventies, maybe even her eighties. She wore an apron and slippers, and looked like the sort of careworn person who probably only ventured out twice a week – and then only as far as the corner shop to buy milk and bread for herself and cheap food for the cat Diamond could hear meowing away in the background.

"I won't know him, but who are youse looking for, son?" she said.

"His name is Richard Starkey and I believe he lived here for a few years after his birth in 1940. He then went to live in Admiral Grove, which I don't know but you may do."

"Starkey, you say? I know that name; everyone around here knew that name. Back then we lived in each other's pockets. No need to lock doors and be frightened to walk the streets in those days. None of us had much, but what we had we shared. If I had something one week, I probably wouldn't have it the next, but someone else might. We got through by trusting each other.

"The Starkeys were good people; reliable folk who would do you a good turn without asking for one in return. I liked them, and so did everyone else," she added, with a look which told Diamond that her mind was spinning back to hard times which she would undoubtedly label 'the good old days'.

"Do you remember their son, Richard? He was quite ill as a kid, I think. He always wanted to be a musician, a drummer," said Diamond.

"Sweet Jesus, the ugly little kid with the tin drum and the big nose? Yes, I remember him – bloody nuisance, he was, always walking up and down these streets banging on dustbin lids and drainpipes. What's he done?" she said, half-leaving her home and staring at Diamond for the first time.

"Nothing, nothing at all as far as I'm aware. Any idea what happened to him?"

"He was around here for years doing bits and pieces. He was actually a nice lad, and I liked him after he packed in all that noisy stuff. He used to drink in The Empress, which is just up the road. Everyone knew him in there. Go and ask there. Sid, the landlord, has been there since God was a boy so he may be able to help you," she said, before moving backwards as if on castors and closing the door.

Diamond returned to the car, planted himself in the passenger seat and asked Tom to drive up the road in search of a pub called The Empress.

The journey was somewhat less than ninety seconds. The Empress was set at the end of the terraced street and looked as if it had been there since alcohol was first invented. Diamond left the car and stared at a building which was a good deal higher than it was wide. He knew this place – he'd seen it before somewhere. He stared for so long that Tom shouted across to make sure he was OK. Again Diamond found himself speaking words only he could hear.

"Fucking hell, it's the album cover," he said, as he walked towards the pub's open door.

Diamond had never owned anything released by Ringo Starr as a solo artist, but he had once seen a list of the Top 100 greatest album covers of all time – ironically, in Q magazine –

and a picture of this very pub, The Empress, was in it. It was, he believed, Starr's first solo album after The Beatles had split up.

Diamond didn't really understand why the pub was open at 9.45am, but he stepped inside to be greeted by a smell which suggested the cigarette police were not actively enforcing the smoking ban in this part of Liverpool. The place was deserted, so Diamond headed for the bar, peering over the top and down towards the floor, where many a landlord was often to be found emptying spillage trays and fiddling with the tubes which carried beer from cellar to pump. He was leaning and gazing at the optics rack when a voice cut through the musty air.

"Can I help you?" said a large man with skin so aged and cracked that he looked like a lizard standing on its hind legs.

"Hi. Sorry to bother you – I wasn't sure if you were open or not. I saw the door open so I came in," said Diamond.

"We don't open for an hour or so but I like to fill the place with clean, fresh air in the mornings. What can I do for you, son?"

"It's a long story which I won't bore you with, but I am trying to track someone down and a lady down the road suggested I ask you for help. Well, that's if you're Sid."

"Yep, that's me. Sid by name, cynical bastard by nature," the landlord said.

Diamond didn't understand his last statement at all, but took it to mean that Sid was a man of few words who didn't like anyone, never mind total strangers, wasting his time.

"Richard Starkey – that's who I am enquiring about. Was born down the road and, according to the lady I spoke to, was quite well known around here."

"Richard Starkey," said Sid, the ghost of a smile moving across his face at lightning speed. "My God, there's a name I haven't heard for a while. Yes, I know him… in fact I've known him for a very long time. I haven't seen him for a long time, mind – but I have known him for donkey's years."

"OK, great," said Diamond. "Is he still alive?"

"As far as I know he is, yes. He stopped drinking here about seven or eight years ago after a bit of a set-to with another of the locals. It was a dispute over what songs to play on the jukebox we used to have, would you believe.

"Last I heard he had taken his custom to The Albert in Lark Lane, about a mile-and-a-half from here. It's near Sefton Park, which is where he moved to when his wife left him," added Sid.

"What does he do for a living?" asked Diamond.

"Nothing now – he must be in his seventies. He used to work for the Royal Mail, I think," said Sid.

"Didn't he used to play drums in a few local bands?" asked Diamond.

"Yeah, but he dumped that when he was quite young. He once told me that, apart from the groupies, it was a total waste of time and that he'd never earn enough money to raise a family hitting drums with a stick."

"OK. Thanks very much. I'm grateful," said Diamond, reaching forwards to shake Sid by the hand before leaving.

Diamond returned to Tom's car and to the sound of raucous rap music pouring out of several speakers. "That's not Andy Williams, is it?" he said.

"I am doing the music reviews this week as the guy who normally does them is away in Cuba. It's some American band I've never heard of – it'll be getting one star out of five in Friday's arts section. What a fucking racket," said Tom.

"Do you know The Albert pub in Lark Lane?" asked Diamond.

"Yes. I lived nearby when I first moved here. Back then that part of Liverpool was known as the 'Echo Ghetto' as most of the reporting staff seemed to live there. The area likes to think of itself as a sort of bohemian quarter but it's just a street full of bars and restaurants close to what is, I admit, a really lovely area of parkland," said Tom, shifting through the gears and driving away far too fast to guarantee the safety of those residents who had emerged, blinking, into the warm sunshine.

Sid was spot on; The Albert wasn't too far away at all – the problem was, it was closed. Tom reiterated that he had time on his hands and that he was happy to play chauffeur for at least another couple of hours, so they parked up and headed to a small cafe sandwiched between a hairdressers and some sort of health-food shop which had large posters in its front window urging people to "Eat Healthy – Eat the Rich."

Having already consumed a tasty breakfast in the Malmaison, Diamond wanted nothing more than a pot of tea. Teapots were obviously hard to come by in this fashionable locale – he received a cup of hot, milky water with a teabag bobbing up and down just beneath the surface.

Tom, who had always claimed he never ate breakfast as his body was a temple, ordered the full English, which was a meat-based feast covered in a thin layer of bubbling lard. "So you aren't going to tell me what you're up to, then?" he asked, between mouthfuls of what appeared to be purified egg.

"No. It's just another of my madcap schemes – and, bearing in mind the rather parlous state of my health, probably the last one I will undertake. What time will The Albert open?" said Diamond.

"Should be open very shortly; problem being, the chances of this man you are looking for being first through the door are, I fear, a little on the low side."

"Yeah, I know. But first I want to see if he's still alive, and if he is I will just leave a message for him. If no one has heard of him, maybe we can head to one of the other addresses I have."

"Sure – where are they?"

"One is in Woolton and the other in Allerton. Are they miles away?"

"No, not really – and they are quite close together, actually," said Tom.

"Right, you wait here, I'm going to the pub. I don't think I will be too long," said Diamond.

He made his way back up a street which almost had a Parisienne feel to it, with delis standing alongside twee craft shops and eateries of various nationalities. The Albert's front door was flung wide open. He entered and, just as he had in The Empress, found himself a lone figure on the public side of an impressively long and spotlessly clean bar.

"What can I get you?" asked a male voice from the shadows.

"Morning. I am hoping that you can help me rather than serve me," said Diamond.

"Beer is expensive but information is free," said the man, from behind a luxurious ginger beard.

"I am trying to track down one of your customers – and before you ask, no, he doesn't owe me any money," said Diamond. "His name is Richard Starkey. He is probably seventy-plus now, and used to live in Dingle."

"Postman Pat, you mean? That's what they call him in here. He worked for the Royal Mail for many years, and after he's had a little too much to drink – which is most nights – he wanders around telling anyone who will listen that pushing the post through letter boxes isn't what it used to be," said the bearded man.

"That sounds like him. So he comes in most nights, then?"

"Every night without fail, and always within two or three minutes of 9.30pm. God knows where he gets his money from."

"If I scribble out a short note, could you give it to him later – or will your shift have finished before he arrives?"

"I run the place so my shift never finishes. Sure, not a problem," said the bearded man.

Diamond pulled out his notebook and wrote:

Dear Mr Starkey,

You don't know me but I would very much like to talk to you. I am up from London researching a book on the Liverpool music scene of the late '50s and early '60s, and I have been told you were involved with various bands during that period.

I am staying at the Malmaison Hotel down on the waterfront. If you would like to come down for a few drinks that would be great. My mobile number is 07786 144213.

Thanks.

Steve Diamond.

He handed over the note, shook the beardy man's hand and walked back to the cafe, calling into a newsagents en route to buy a copy of *The Guardian*.

"Sorted," he said to Tom. "Drive on, my good man."

"Where to?" asked Tom.

"251 Menlove Avenue in Woolton, please – and don't spare the horses," said Diamond.

"Did you find who you were looking for?"

"Sort of. He's still alive and he does drink in there, so I left him a note. I'll just have to hope that he's tempted by the prospect of a few free beers," said Diamond, as Tom drove with typical recklessness around the perimeter of a huge park.

Menlove Avenue was a very impressive sight; a sweeping boulevard lined by trees and boasting houses of considerable size which Tom said were amongst the most highly priced and coveted in the city. Number 251 was fronted by an immaculately groomed garden mixing lawn and borders full of flowers of many colours.

Diamond rang the doorbell and waited. There was no reply. He tried again – still no reply. He scribbled out another short note asking if the occupier would be kind enough to give him a call later that day, then headed back to the car, somewhat less than hopeful.

"Failed!" he said, as they set off for Allerton and the final address.

In a purely geographic sense, 20 Forthlin Street wasn't too far from Aunt Mimi's house in Woolton, but it might have been the proverbial world away. A neat and tidy 1920s build, it stood in a largely working-class part of the city and was unremarkable in both design and adornment.

Diamond, his levels of optimism dramatically lowered by his failure to get a response at Lennon's old home, knocked on the door and was almost turning on his heel when it was thrown wide open by a man of indeterminable age.

"Yes?" he said with a wheeze which suggested he had enjoyed tobacco for most of his life.

"Hello. Sorry to bother you. I am trying to trace a man who I believe used to live here. James McCartney is his name," said Diamond.

"Paul, you mean. He never really liked the name James so he switched them around," said the man.

"Oh, you know him?"

"I should do; he's my brother."

"Wow. Does he still live here?"

"No. God, he's been gone from here for so many years now – must have been around 1970 when he left. He emigrated to Canada; said he was heading off for a better life."

"Did he find one – a better life, I mean?"

"No, he was back inside five years, divorced, broke and a much wiser man. He met some woman out there and, basically, she stitched him up – took him for all he was worth, which wasn't much."

"Where is he now?"

"He'll be at home, I suppose. What time is it – 1pm… yeah, at home."

"Where's home these days?"

"St Michael's in the Hamlet. Do you know it?"

"No, I'm from London."

"What you doing up here chasing my brother?"

"Long story, but it's nothing to do with either money or women."

"St Michael's is down on the quiet side of Aigburth Road. Nice place, lots of trees and not too many noisy kids. He lives at 6 Springbourne Road. He isn't in trouble again, is he?"

"Again?"

"Oh, he fell in with a couple of bad 'uns about ten years ago. They were involved with some scam involving credit cards. Our Paul had nothing to do with it but got pulled in with them just because they drank in the same pub. They went to jail but he was innocent so he was fine. It scared him a bit, though."

"He's retired now?"

"Just about. He has an auto shop just off the Dock Road. He has run it for years and years but he only tends to go in for a few hours a week now."

"That's great. I am very grateful for your help… sorry, what was your name?"

"Mike. Mike McCartney."

"Thanks, Mike."

With Tom now due at his meeting, they headed back to the Malmaison, this time at a conservative speed which did at least give the pedestrians some hope of survival.

"You're going home tomorrow?" asked Tom.

"That's the plan, but it's fluid. If I get a call from any of the men I've been looking for I suppose I will end up staying. That wouldn't be a burden as I have really enjoyed being here – either that or I have enjoyed being away from London. I will ring you in the morning if that's OK. I will try and get out to that house in St Michael's as early as I can," said Diamond.

"That's fine. Have a good night. I'd come down for a drink and a curry but my woman is going to start to get suspicious. She's from the Wirral so it's her nature," said Tom.

CHAPTER
TWENTY-THREE

Diamond waved heartily at Norma the receptionist as he walked through the Malmaison's front lounge. He got back to his room, undressed and climbed into a freshly made bed which smelled of rose petals. It was not yet mid afternoon, but he was exhausted.

He awoke with a start and, again, momentarily didn't have a clue where he was. As his eyes tried to focus on the unfamiliar surroundings he called out for Noreen – only then remembering where he was.

He felt as though he was climbing out of a coma; his head pounding and his eyes initially refusing to stay fully open. He needed something to keep him awake and focused, so he picked up his mobile and rang Noreen.

She answered swiftly, always fearing the worst and hoping for the best. "Hi, hon. You OK?" she said.

"Yeah. Fell asleep and woke up with monsters in the room," he replied.

"Nasty ones or Disney-style nice ones?"

"Both – but the nice ones said some magic words and

made the bad ones disappear in a puff of smoke."

"How lovely. What you been up to? Is it going well?"

"Yes, things are fine. At the moment I will be coming home tomorrow, but that might change if I get a phone call or two. Not sure yet, but when I know for definite I will text you."

"Good man. How's your mate doing – is he looking after you?"

"He's been great. I was with him all morning and I may see him again tomorrow."

"You going out tonight?"

"No, too tired. I will get something from room service and watch TV, I think. OK, look – I will call you tomorrow. I do miss you."

"Awwwwww… what a sweetie. Love you too. Night, hon."

Diamond ran through the room-service menu and settled on chicken korma with rice and the obligatory bottle of red wine.

Like so many others, he had always found crass, brash reality television shows strangely beguiling and almost impossible to switch off once he had identified a twenty-two-carat hate figure. The one filling his small screen was about a group of invariably drunk Geordies who seemed to spend every waking hour indulging in sex, looking for sex or talking about sex. Well, apart from one of the dumb-beyond-belief girls locked inside the house who had seemingly taken – quite contentedly – to wetting herself at regular intervals. It reminded Diamond of staring in amusement at the inhabitants of the monkey house at London Zoo; animals of lower intelligence entertaining onlookers simply by doing what came naturally. They too were prone to urinating where and when they so chose.

He was mopping his plate of the last vestiges of what had been a pretty good meal when his mobile rang. He presumed it would be either Noreen or Toby, so he was surprised to see the always-worrying "Unknown Caller" message flash up on the screen.

"Hello, Steve here," he said.

"Hi. My name is Richard Starkey. You're looking for me, mate?" came the nasally growl of a reply.

Diamond sat bolt upright in his chair, momentarily lost for words. One of the four men he had denied wealth and stardom was actually on the phone.

"Hi, yes, thanks very much for calling. As my note said, I am doing research on the music scenes in various cities – Liverpool, London, Belfast – for a book on life in the late '50s and '60s. I was told that you were involved in the scene back then, and thought maybe you could help me," said Diamond.

"I was, yes – obviously it didn't work out for me but some of my mates from that time did good," said Starkey.

"Can you come down here for a few beers and a chat? I'm in the Malmaison down by the Liver Building."

"Problem is, I don't drive and I am in South Liverpool."

"Get a cab – I will meet you outside the hotel's entrance and pay. I will also pay for your return journey. I'd probably only need thirty minutes of your time."

"You sure? OK. I will be there about 8pm. I have to be back up at The Albert by 9.30 as I am in the darts team and we have a local derby against The Ingle Nook tonight," added Starkey.

"Great – see you at 8pm," said Diamond.

Hanging up, he stared out across the Mersey at the balletic rise and fall of a flock of seabirds before uttering a predictable, "Fuck me – a Beatle is coming to see me."

He decided against meeting Mr Starkey stark bollock naked, and showered before throwing on a T-shirt and jeans. It was only 7pm but he was dizzy with excitement. He found his notebook and pen in order that he might play along with the small, white lie that he was preparing to write a book, and poured himself another glass of wine.

At 7.45pm he locked up and headed down to reception, where the ever-present figure of young Norma was standing behind the desk. Diamond wondered if she had a twin sister who also worked at the hotel. He positioned himself on one of three disturbingly deep sofas; the one closest to the main door, which gave him a perfect view of arriving and departing hackney and private-hire cabs.

The first two cabs delivered only giggling girls in short skirts, with outrageously prominent eyelashes and what appeared, at both first and second glance, to be orange skin. Diamond thought that they were, perhaps, attending some sort of cosmetics convention.

By 8.10pm, he had convinced himself that Mr Starkey had decided against trekking into the heart of his city to meet a complete stranger. At 8.15 he was proved wrong when a man stepped out of a black cab and looked around for someone to pay his fare. Diamond moved as fast as he had done for months and shook the passenger by the hand before leaning inside the vehicle to pay the driver.

The cab drove off, leaving Diamond standing on the pavement face to face with the man who would have become one of the most famous musicians in the history of world music.

He was trying to remember the last time he had seen a photograph of Ringo Starr. A world-renowned figure he may have been but, having announced that he wished to spend his remaining years in almost splendid isolation, he wasn't deemed to be newsworthy by a modern media which fed off instant celebrity.

Even so, Diamond had a mental image of Starr, the almost reclusive former musician – greying hair, reasonably slim and with dark glasses. The man before him was the same man, but minus forty-five years of pampering, high-class food and stress. Starkey wore his hair very short, a grey crew cut serving to accentuate his more outstanding features – his larger-than-average ears and his famous Roman nose. There were no glasses at all to cover eyes which looked tired and almost hollow. His clothes were shabby, but most definitely not in a chic or fashionable way. His feet were covered by the sort of cheap deck shoes which can be picked up for £4 in any branch of Primark.

"Let's have a drink," said Diamond, ushering Starkey into the hotel with a wave of his right hand.

"Nice place. Bit dark, though – it reminds me of some of the hellhole clubs I used to perform in way, way back," said Starkey.

"What would you like to drink?"

"A pint of lager please, mate… Carlsberg if they've got it."

Diamond ordered a pint and a large glass of red wine, sat down, opened his notebook and simply stared at the man opposite him. "So, tell me about the Liverpool music scene back in what everyone tends to refer to as 'the good old days'," he said.

"Trust me, they weren't so good at all. It was a grind, it was hard work, it was badly paid and it was time-consuming. The people who promoted and managed us had us over a barrel because they knew we were all chasing the dream; we all wanted that one big opening," said Starkey. "Looking back is pretty easy when you have put on a pair of rose-tinted glasses. You tend to just remember the good times – and don't get me wrong, there were plenty of them. I think I was pretty good at what I did. I was known as one of the best drummers in the city. I was never spectacular, but I was really steady and could keep any beat in any musical format," he added.

In between swallowing his pint at a quite furious pace, Starkey eruditely outlined the life of a musician in the late '50s. Diamond, of course, wasn't remotely interested in his general recollections, but had to play the role of the intrigued journalist until such a time as he could steer his subject onto more specific matters.

Thirty minutes and another downed pint later, Diamond sensed his moment had come and asked Starkey about his time with what was to be his final band, Rory Storm and the Hurricanes.

"We were good. I really thought we would make the breakthrough from local to national level. We were huge on Merseyside and in North Wales but we just couldn't seem to catch the eye of the major movers and shakers, who were mostly based in London," said Starkey. "If we had got the right deal at that time – around 1962 – I think we could have gone on to be as big as The Searchers or Gerry and the Pacemakers. Hand on heart, I thought we were better than both of them. I did, honestly."

"Did you ever have the chance to leave Rory's band and join another?" asked Diamond.

"There were rumours that a couple of acts who had signed record deals were interested, but I never got a direct offer from anyone. I hung on for as long as I could, but in the end I realised I was never going to make any money out of music, so I packed it in. I actually sold my drum kit just two days after I told Rory I'd had enough. I haven't played properly since," Starkey replied.

"I have spoken to quite a few other musicians from that time," lied Diamond. "Did you ever come across people like John Lennon, Paul McCartney or George Harrison?"

"No, never heard of them, sorry. Which bands did they play in?" Starkey said.

Diamond was acutely aware that he was doing nothing more than staring at Starkey, and struggled to compose a response. "Not sure, actually," he said. "Their names just came up a couple of times when I was chatting with other people."

Starkey's admission that he had never heard of the other

three Beatles all but ended Diamond's interest in him. As he drained his third pint, the former drummer moved into a rant against the modern practices employed by the Royal Mail, and became almost lost in the mists of his own argument.

"Right, I have taken up more than enough of your time, Richard," said Diamond. "You have been really helpful and I'm glad we met. I'm sure you are right – if you'd just had that one break you would have gone on to be a top star."

He walked Starkey to a line of waiting taxis outside the front door, pressed a £10 note into his hand and wished him well. As the taxi disappeared into the distance, Diamond sat down on the hotel's front step and spent five minutes mentally castigating himself for unwittingly destroying the dreams of one of the four men who would have shaken the world.

Unable to sleep, he again raided the minibar in his room. He was seeking a short, sharp cure for insomnia and not a lazy, pleasurable drink, so he opted for the two miniature bottles of brandy, pouring both into one glass. He threw half the glass back in one gulp, the liquid burning its way down his throat and leaving him almost gasping for breath through puckered lips. He sat on the edge of the bed and considered ringing Noreen, but all he could see, whether his eyes were open or shut, was the haunted look on Starkey's face; a man who, at one point, had been so utterly confident in his own abilities that he knew he could have been a contender.

Diamond undressed, crawled into bed, turned on the television and sipped the remainder of his brandy beneath the warm sanctuary of the heavy sheets. He had accomplished much, but what was initially regret had now turned into genuine sadness.

"Don't worry about things you cannot change," he said out loud as he flicked through the channels in search of Sky News.

Diamond was awakened by the sound of hammering on his door. He glanced at his watch – 8.30am; a little early for a chambermaid to resort to such tactics.

He crawled out of bed, grabbed a towel to preserve at least some of his modesty, and opened the door a couple of inches to gaze out.

"You lazy bastard," said Tom, with the enthusiasm of someone who had clearly been up and about for at least two hours.

"Oh, hi. Did you say you were picking me up?" said Diamond.

"To be fair, no, I didn't. I have to be at the Town Hall at 11am for some dull council committee meeting, so I thought I'd call and see if you wanted to head out to that other address. Did that bloke ring you?"

"Starkey? Yes, he did – and he came down here for an hour," said Diamond.

"Did you get what you wanted?"

"Yes… yes, I did. Sadly, he didn't."

"What do you mean?"

"Nothing. Sorry, just rambling. I think I had a drop too much to drink last night."

"Get dressed. I'll wait downstairs in reception," said Tom, heading for the lift.

Twenty minutes later the pair were in Tom's car and heading – at a predictably ferocious speed – for St Michael's in the Hamlet.

Whilst not quite as grand as its name might have suggested, St Michael's was a leafy enclave crammed with a curious mixture of traditional, old-style streets and huge detached buildings.

Springbourne Road was, like so much of Liverpool, two rows of neat and well-maintained terraced houses, many with potted plants on the doorstep to add a touch of colour and individuality. Number 6 was at the junction end of a cul-de-sac, almost crimson in colour and with pale venetian blinds hanging inside every visible window.

Diamond knocked on the door and waited. He was nervous; far more nervous than he had been with Starkey. If the door opened he may well find himself face to face with a man who should have become an idol to millions.

There was no reply, so he tried again. The very second he delivered his last knock, a door swung open – not Number 6, but Number 4.

"He ain't in, babe," said a woman of about fifty in a tatty pink dressing gown and equally unattractive slippers.

"Paul?" said Diamond.

"Yeah. He always leaves dead early; God only knows why."

"Any idea where I can find him?"

"Not at this time of the day, no. He disappears to weird places like New Brighton and Rhyl. He is usually back at his workshop by about 3pm, though. Then he will get back here about 10pm after calling in for a drink somewhere in town."

"Do you know where his workshop is? What is it – a garage?"

"It's a body shop. He fixes up cars that have been in smashes. It's down off the Dock Road; either Cotton Street or Dickson Street, can't remember which but it's got a sign above the door," she added.

"OK, thanks a lot," said Diamond.

He returned to the car and asked Tom if he knew where the two streets mentioned by McCartney's neighbour were. Tom removed his A to Z from the glove compartment, thumbed through the index and said, "You're in luck; they are just down the road from where you're staying – about half a mile, I would estimate."

"Really? That's great; I can go down there after 3pm when that lady said he'd probably be back. Apparently he tends to go off wandering in the mornings before getting down to work in the afternoon – he fixes cars," said Diamond, mentally picturing one of the world's greatest ever musical talents covered in grease and clutching a spanner.

Tom returned Diamond to the Malmaison and they said their goodbyes.

"So you're going home this evening?" asked Tom.

"That's the plan. If I don't my friends and lovers down south will start to assume I have forsaken them for a life up north. It has been really great to see you again – and thanks for all your help with the chauffeuring."

"My pleasure. Take care, and please keep in touch. Oh, and good luck with you-know-what," added Tom, the latest in a long line of people unable or unwilling to use the word 'cancer'.

Diamond checked the train times back to London at the reception desk and arranged a late checkout before retreating to his room and climbing into bed. His energy levels were on the wane and he knew it. He set his bedside alarm for 3pm and fell headlong into another deep sleep.

Despite having been staying on the banks of the River Mersey for several days, Diamond didn't have a clue where he was when the alarm cut a swathe through his dream about library books with legs. It took him almost a minute to regain his mental compass, and a further thirty seconds to remember why he had set the alarm in the first place.

If McCartney's neighbour was to be believed, then he should be back at his workshop by now, ferreting around beneath a four-times-owned car with more than a hundred thousand miles on the clock.

Diamond showered, dressed, placed his pen and notebook in his shoulder bag along with a bottle of water from the minibar, and headed for the lift. He walked away from the city centre along one of Liverpool's rejuvenated docksides in search of either Dickson Street or Cotton Street. To his left was a massive old warehouse which had been transformed into luxury apartments; to his right a Costco wholesale outlet and the ubiquitous Toys 'R' Us store.

He had walked no more than half a mile when he came across Cotton Street; a narrow thoroughfare which divided enormous buildings that hinted at the city's famous past as one of the world's great seaports. Several of the ground-floor spaces had been converted into car-repair shops but none bore the name McCartney. He turned left at the top and then left again into Dickson Street.

He was midway down the road when he saw the blue flash of an acetylene torch beneath an ageing BMW which was suspended above a traditional mechanic's pit. The two front doors of the premises – like stable doors – had been flung open to allow the smoke to pour out and the fresher air to flood in. The woodwork was damaged and the paintwork faded, but across the top of the door to his left Diamond could quite clearly see the name "McCartney's Autos".

He stood completely still for several minutes, staring at the sign and listening to the man in the pit singing along to his radio. The song was 'Pictures of Matchstick Men' by Status Quo.

Diamond approached the pit and was just feet away when a voice came from beneath him.

"All right, mate. Won't be a minute. What is it and what's the problem?" said the man, with a pronounced Scouse accent.

"Hi. Sorry – what's what?" said Diamond.

"What make is she and what's wrong with her? I can fix

just about anything but I don't do clocking, so if that's what you want I'm not your man."

"I don't have a car with me – and what's clocking?"

"Clocking, you know – winding back the clock so it looks as though the car hasn't done as many miles as it has. It's a common practice, totally illegal but very widespread. I'll come up from here now. Hang on," said the mechanic.

Diamond stood back and watched as the man shuffled to the far end of the pit, where there was a short ladder which rose to ground level. He climbed up, clambering out with some difficulty at the bonnet end of the BMW. He emerged from the darkness, walking slowly forwards as he attempted to wipe oil and lubricant off his hands with a dirty cloth. He wore a badly stained, dark blue boiler suit, and heavy shoes with exposed steel caps at the toe. He was heavier than Diamond had expected, and his hair was steely grey. He wore old fashioned, heavy-rimmed glasses – but he was most definitely Paul McCartney.

"Hi," said McCartney, jutting out his right hand for Diamond to shake, which he did without uttering a response.

Diamond had been mesmerised when he'd met Ringo Starr, but this was Paul McCartney – *Sir* Paul McCartney – the man who used to be in the *Guinness Book of Records* as the most successful songwriter in the history of world music. But he wasn't any more; he was a slightly overweight, elderly mechanic working in a Liverpool backstreet to help make ends meet.

McCartney took off his glasses to wipe his eyes; the famous puppy-dog eyes which, but for Diamond's intervention, would have captivated literally millions of women across all continents and across several generations. "Right, that's better," he said. "If you don't have a car you must be the bearer of bad news. Do I owe someone money, lad?"

"Do I look like a debt collector?" asked Diamond, smiling.

"Someone once told me I looked like an undertaker – but never a debt collector."

"No, don't suppose you do, actually – too young, too pretty. So what can I do for you?"

"My name is Steve Diamond and I'm in Liverpool doing some research for a book I'm writing about the Merseyside music scene of the late '50s and early '60s. A couple of the people I have met suggested that I talk to you. You were involved in the scene back then?"

"I was to a degree, but I am amazed that anyone mentioned my name. I was on the edge of things, but that was all. At one point, really early on, I did think that maybe I had a chance of turning music into something more than a hobby but it just didn't pan out for me. Could've been my fault, I suppose; maybe I didn't give it enough time – or maybe I just got diverted by the prospect of a steady job, a regular income and a good woman waiting for me at home."

"Are you willing to sit with me for fifteen minutes and just chat?"

"Sure, that's not a problem. I like talking but I do not like fixing the gearboxes on BMWs. Let's go inside and see if I can find a clean cup for you," said McCartney, with the grace and humour he had displayed throughout the life Diamond had unwittingly stolen from him.

McCartney made two cups of strong tea, handed one to Diamond and sat facing him across a table which bore the remains of a takeaway lunch.

"You'll have to excuse the mess. Every bloody day I promise myself that I will have a major tidy-up but I always find something better to do. Right, fire away," he said.

"So, you wanted to be a pop star?" asked Diamond.

"Jesus, back in those days they weren't called that – they were crooners or skiffle kings or balladeers. I knew from an early age that I had something of a gift for music. I was one of those lucky kids who could pick up an instrument and learn to play it pretty quickly – in the same way that some people can learn languages. My dad bought me a bloody trumpet but I never really took to it, so I traded it in for an acoustic guitar. He also wanted me to take piano lessons but I was far more comfortable just finding my own way around a keyboard," said McCartney.

"So did you form bands and perform?" asked Diamond.

"Sort of, yes. The first time I performed in public was in a talent show at Butlin's – I sang Little Richard's 'Long Tall Sally'. I think I was about fourteen. It felt good; it gave me a real buzz.

"Back then, in the late '50s, skiffle was the thing. All you needed were a couple of cheap guitars, a washboard and someone who could half-hold a tune and you were away. I was only about fifteen when I started playing as part of a group – and even then it was usually in someone's back room, or at the local church hall if you were really lucky. It was good fun but that's all it was; fun," McCartney said.

"Did you write your own songs?"

"All the time; loads of them. I came across plenty of musicians who were technically better songwriters than I was, but they all told me I had a gift for harmony and that I could write catchy tunes. Some of them were pretty good – well, I thought they were."

"So did you ever get close to making it big; to being in a group which had real potential?"

"I suppose it's impossible to answer that question, because if I had ever felt that I had a future in music I suppose I would have stuck with it instead of drifting away into a 'safe' profession, as ninety-nine per cent of us did. There were a couple of times when I auditioned for groups who had managers and a residency somewhere, but it just didn't happen."

"Which groups were they – can you remember?"

"I nearly joined Faron's Flamingos – bad name, eh? – but they chose someone else to play bass at the last minute."

"What year would that have been?"

"Probably around 1961, maybe '62."

"Have you ever heard of George Harrison?"

"No."

"Richard Starkey?"

"Yes… didn't he play drums with Rory Storm and the Hurricanes? He had a really good reputation but I don't think I ever met him."

The landline rang out in the small, partitioned-off section of his kingdom which McCartney called his office.

"Hang on. I'd better answer it. Car mechanics are ten a penny in this city so if they don't speak to me they'll move on pretty damn quickly," he said.

Diamond watched McCartney disappear into the darkness of what was really nothing more than a vast, windowless room. He took solace from the fact that McCartney seemed happy and didn't appear to harbour any bitterness towards those who could have helped him transform ambition into stardom all those years ago.

McCartney returned, smiling. "Sorry about that. Another job booked in for tomorrow, which is handy as I am hoping to get away the weekend after next," he said.

"Where are you planning on going?" asked Diamond.

"My mate has a caravan in Talacre on the North Wales coast. It's cheap and cheerful there – more Scousers than Welsh during the summer."

"OK, I am so grateful for your time. One last question. I was told that you almost joined a group called The Quarrymen in the late '50s; that true?"

"God, that was a long, long time ago," said McCartney. "It

was a strange and sad thing, really. I think it was 1957; it was a long, hot summer if I remember correctly. I had been playing guitar with various groups which had been formed by mates at school.

"The Quarrymen were one step ahead of most of us because they had been playing together for about a year and had performed at parties, school dances, cinemas and amateur skiffle competitions. I knew one of them – Colin Hanton – and he had told the rest of the group that I was pretty useful on both guitar and piano. At that point they were keen to go more mainstream. Skiffle was great but there were just too many groups on Merseyside playing the same songs in the same style.

"I was invited to play with them at a gig and the impression I got was that if all went well I would definitely be asked to join them on a permanent basis. I was convinced that it was a goer – so much so that I even told the lads at school that I would be joining a group full time. They were dead jealous.

"Anyway, it was set – they were booked in to play at a church fete in Woolton. It was July 6th; I will always remember the date because it was the birthday of one of my best friends at school, and he had asked me to go to the cinema with him on that day. But it never happened… it never happened."

"Why didn't it happen – why didn't you get to play with The Quarrymen on that day?" asked Diamond.

"As I said, it was all very sad," said McCartney. "One of the band died a few days before the show, so, obviously, they had to cancel."

"What happened?"

"He was hit by a car as he crossed the road. All my schoolmates knew and were passing around the story – the suggestion was that he'd had a few drinks. Anyway, he was killed instantly; I think he was only sixteen years old," said McCartney.

"Can you remember his name, Paul?"

"John, I think. Yes, John. Can't remember his last name."

"Lennon?"

"Yes, yes. John Lennon, that was it. Poor bastard."

"Whereabouts in Liverpool was he killed?"

"Oh, it wasn't in Liverpool – he was in Dublin when he died," said McCartney.

In the seconds which followed McCartney saying the word 'Dublin', Diamond felt as though his world had been reduced to half-speed. Everything slowed as he stared at the man in front of him.

Eventually, after clearing his throat, he asked, "Dublin? What was he doing over there?"

"I only know what came to me as half rumour, half fact as I never met John – but he was a huge admirer of Oscar Wilde, who obviously was born there. He had gone over on the ferry from Holyhead in Anglesey for one night as there was a big celebration on – well, I say celebration, it was actually more of a commemoration," said McCartney.

"Can you remember what they were commemorating?" asked Diamond.

"Yes, it was the fortieth anniversary of Wilde's death," said McCartney.

"Right... I see..." said Diamond, as McCartney's office phone began to ring again.

"More work! Won't be a minute," said McCartney.

McCartney was unaware but Diamond had started to shake, placing his hands securely between his knees to try and conceal the evidence. Lennon had died because he went to mark, forty years on, the anniversary of Wilde's death in a Dublin hospital on July 3rd, 1916 – sixteen years after he should have been claimed by meningitis in a tawdry Paris hotel.

Lennon had died because he happened to be in Dublin in the wrong street at the wrong time in the path of the wrong car. He'd died purely and simply because Wilde's life had been extended by a fellow admirer who was presented with the means to go back in time and save him.

Lennon had died because people who should have known better ignored all the old warnings about paradoxes and the butterfly effect.

Lennon had died because Wilde had lived beyond his allotted time and, as a direct and quite awful consequence, the world had been denied the genius of The Beatles.

By the time McCartney returned, Diamond was almost in tears and was staring at an ant which was working its way up the leg of his jeans.

"It was my next-door neighbour telling me a young man was looking for me," said McCartney. "That'll be you, I presume?"

"Yes, yes, it was me. Look, I have to run now; I have to get to Lime Street to catch a train back to London," said Diamond.

"I'll give you a lift. I've had enough of this place for one day," said McCartney, pointing to his car, a battered Renault Clio which had different-coloured doors.

The journey should have taken no more than ten minutes, but as they reached a dual carriageway which carried the locals to and from the Birkenhead Tunnel, they found themselves trapped in an ugly traffic snarl-up.

"Must have been an accident down by the tunnel entrance," said McCartney. "It happens all the time as drivers try to change lanes at the very last minute."

"It's not a problem; my train doesn't leave for twenty five minutes ," said Diamond.

When they were finally free of the congestion, McCartney

looked across at Diamond and smiled. As he did so, he looked to his right and into the wing mirror, and started to whistle. Diamond's eyes were shut – fast shut – but as he tried to remember whether his rail ticket was in his shoulder bag or his wallet, he began to pick up on the melodic refrain which was pouring out from McCartney's puckered lips. He knew the tune, it was familiar – in fact it was more than familiar. As McCartney continued to whistle, Diamond, ever so quietly, began to sing along under his breath.

He sat up, turned to face McCartney and asked, "What's that song, Paul?"

"Oh, it's one I wrote a very long time ago. I wrote loads but that's one which seems to have stayed with me. Believe it or not, that one actually came to me in my sleep one night. It still sounds pretty good to me," McCartney said.

"Does it have a title?" asked Diamond.

"No, it doesn't even have words; it was just a pretty little tune which came into my head all those years ago," said McCartney.

"You would have called it 'Yesterday', Paul. I think it would have been rather popular." said Diamond.

"You asked me earlier if I regretted not making it in the music business and I said it didn't really bother me. I've been thinking about it and, actually, it does bother me a bit because I think I could have made a go of it. Still, a bit late for regrets now, isn't it?!" he added, turning the car into the dropping-off zone at Lime Street Station. "There y'go, mate." said McCartney.

Diamond shook McCartney by the hand and then, as he leaned across and kissed him on the forehead, he said, "Forgive me." With that he climbed out of the car and walked quickly towards the station, never once looking back.

EPILOGUE

Diamond died four weeks later, fading away much as he had imagined he would: surrounded by a couple of those who had really mattered to him during his brief life.

He had often discussed with Dr Marshall whether it was possible for a person to determine the timing of his or her own death, and their shared opinion was that, if there wasn't to be a suicidal element, it was most definitely not possible. However, Dr Marshall was adamant that patients with a terminal illness knew when it was time to go, time to give up fighting. And that is what Diamond did; he gave up fighting just six days before his death in his own bed, in his own home.

He had talked things through with a weepy Noreen and, whilst she was petrified of losing him, she eventually said that she fully understood and backed his decision.

He called Dr Marshall and told him that he had decided it was the right moment to start releasing his frantic grip on life. The doctor agreed, told him he was as brave as they come, and then moved on to his next patient.

Diamond changed nothing in physical terms as he began his peaceful countdown to the end. He continued to take his medication, to eat as well as he could, to drink when the opportunity arose, and to make love to his woman.

It was his mental outlook which changed, and as he pulled down the barriers which he had set in place to help him cope with the growing pain and the all-consuming depression, his body and his resolve weakened markedly and swiftly. It was as if he had sought out individual audiences with his major organs to thank them for their service down the years and inform them that their work was done.

Day by day, the hours he was awake reduced and the hours he slept rose, until, twenty-four hours before his heart finally stopped beating, he fought his way out of a comatose state only rarely, and then only for a few minutes at a time.

Sixty minutes before he finally succumbed, he opened his eyes for one last time to see Noreen and Toby seated beside his bed. He tried to speak but couldn't force the words out of his mouth.

"I love you, Diamond," said Noreen.

"So do I," said Toby.

The very last thing Diamond saw before his eyes closed, never to reopen, was the plastic TARDIS which stood on his bedside cabinet.

ACKNOWLEDGEMENTS

Before I underwent major heart surgery in 2015, my surgeon, the prodigiously gifted Andrew Muir, warned me that a degree of memory loss was possible during my recuperation period.

He was right.

As a result of post-op complications, I spent rather longer in Liverpool's Broadgreen Hospital than I had expected - three weeks in a coma on life-support in and five weeks in the Intensive Care Unit.

Some time after returning home I decided to clear out my ageing laptop in readiness for the purchase of a new model.

That is when I came across " For The Good Of All ". I simply could not remember writing it; strange but true.

Unbeknownst to the man with the repaired heart, he had written the entire piece - all 120,000 words of it - in a seven week period just months before entering hospital. Surprised? Just a bit.

I am grateful to those who helped me bring this story to the market and to those who have always supported me in the darker days we all endure.

Thanks to : Jennifer and Barrie, Eric and Roz, Noreen Taylor, June Macdonald, Kathryn Cherry, Bill Kenwright, David Harrison, Dr Phil Cumberlidge, Megan, Sue, TT, everyone at Troubador and The Book Guild and, of course, my much-missed Mum and Dad.

Special thanks to my fellow journalist Lynda Roughley who acted as proof-reader, advisor and encourager with remarkable enthusiasm.

Ian J Ross

ABOUT THE AUTHOR

Ian J Ross is a journalist of some forty-five years standing. Born and raised in Leeds, he has lived in Liverpool for more than forty years. Although he has had three non-fiction books published – all sport-related - this is his first novel. Ian has worked for the *Southport Visiter*, the *Liverpool Daily Post* and *Echo*, *The Times*, *The Daily Telegraph*, *The Guardian* and he spent a decade as the Director of Communications at Everton Football Club.

You can contact Ian on ianjrosswriter@aol.com